HAYLEE
and the
Last Traveler

Lisa Redfern

LITLE MOUNTAIN
PUBLISHING

FONTS
Haylee - Megan Greene, megangreenedesign.com
Nymphette - Lauren Thompson
Prociono – Barry Schwartz
Cinzel – Natanael Gama

Copyright © 2018 Lisa Redfern

All rights reserved.

ISBN-10: 0-9655998-9-2
ISBN-13: 978-0-9655998-9-4

Version 1.1

Library of Congress Control Number: 2017914782

Printed by CreateSpace, a DBA of On-Demand Publishing, LLC in
the United States of America

CONTENTS

CAST OF CHARACTERS

Northern California - 1980s

Haylee Garrett:
With a dead mom and a checked-out dad, Haylee is an outsider.
She's a kind-hearted girl who communicates with animals. She describes it as thought pictures instead of spoken words.
On her eighteenth birthday, Haylee transforms from a growth-stunted kid in hiding to a curvaceous beauty.
Almost as soon as Haylee learns to appreciate her new body and social status, she discovers that she's compelled to attack people, draining their personalities, to ward off the extreme pain.
Haylee has moved away from home and avoids the family for fear of hurting them.
She travels through time, led by the crystal in a family heirloom, to find Emis Laurent.

Eugene (Gene) Garrett:
Haylee's dad and a walnut farmer. Since his wife died, he avoids life and his daughter.
When Haylee passes out from heavy bleeding, he rushes her to the emergency room. At the brink of losing his daughter, Gene realizes the terrible cost of his grief.
Eugene spends close to a year caring for Glori.

Glori:
'No-nonsense', redheaded nurse who's given up on relationships and motherhood. Taking Eugene and Haylee in hand, her feelings of connection with them are a surprise.
Glori and Eugene fall in love and marry.
Glori is Haylee's first family victim. Glori's condition is like a walking coma.

Josh:
A sexy, persistent, and intelligent teaching assistant in Haylee's Psychology class at CSU, Berkeley. His attraction to Haylee increases as she tries to keep walls between them. Josh follows when Haylee goes hunting. Sickened by her behavior, he backs off. But soon his curiosity wins, and he returns to help figure out the mystery.
Josh becomes Haylee's second close-relationship victim.

Spencer:
Josh's handsome, athletic, wise-cracking younger brother.

Norah:
Travelers leap-frog through time. Norah has arrived from one-hundred-and-fifty-years in the future to find Haylee and Josh. She knows Josh as Dr. Herkowitz the father of Traveler Studies.

San Francisco - 1849-1851

Reece Keener:
Dark, broody, Irish businessman. He came to California to try mining, but returns to the family business, selling goods and supplies. He thinks he's lost it when he is drawn to the new store clerk his brother hired.
Emis manipulates Reece into adopting her daughter.
Reece and Haylee are about to have a child.

Edward Keener:
Reece's younger brother and a twin. He moved out west to help his brother expand their business. Edward is chatty and friendly. He hires Haylee (disguised as a man) to deliver goods and catch-up on the paperwork that Reece never gets too.

Emis Laurent:
Emis was an elegant soothsayer at the French Court. She lost her husband in the Napoleonic war. Political changes ejected her from influential circles. She came to California to work as a prostitute. She is also a Traveler and realizes that she will die once her child reaches seven.

Polly Laurent:
Six-year-old daughter of Emis. She knows things about people when she touches them. Her mother has kept their family history of Travelers and Crystal Carriers secret.

Song Zaho:
A Chinese friend to Reece and Edward. He's told them about missing his wife and daughters in China. Reece gets Song a job at the Bella Union to help protect Polly from the men her mother entertains.

Part One

UNSTICKING

❧1❧
FIRE!

1850

EDWARD HAD HIS FIRST spoonful of stew halfway to his mouth when they heard the church bells. The discordant cacophony, brash and vulgar, communicated a desperation that raised the hair on the back of their necks.

"What's that all about?" Reece said, pushing back his chair. Striding to the window, he pulled aside the curtains.

Frantic shouts of, "Fire! Fire!" drifted up from the street.

For a fraction of a second, everyone around the table stared wide-eyed at one another. Haylee's throat suddenly felt dry and tight.

Reece had always known that this day would come. People from all over the world arrived in San Francesco daily, as Gold Fever spread. He'd watched haphazard construction blanket the surrounding hills.

Demand for lumber exceeded supply. Craftsman and carpenters looked anywhere and everywhere for materials. Down by the docks, industrious men stayed busy, hammering, sawing, and dismantling abandoned sailing ships. From sunup to sundown, sounds of their toil was constant.

Reece had been relentless in his efforts to keep his family safe. He'd made them memorize escape routes, practice fire drills, and keep water buckets by the doors.

In private, Haylee had argued with him about this. "These methods are antiquated. A bucket brigade can't deliver water fast enough to do anything."

Frustrated he glared at her. "I *know*, it's different where you come from." Reece's refusal to relax his diligence was absolute, "It's the best we have, so that's what we are going to do."

When he learned that Haylee was pregnant, the drills became even more frequent.

Reece pulled Haylee to her feet, pressing both of her hands between his. In turn, he met the fearful gazes of Polly, their adopted daughter, his brother Edward, and Song, their right-hand-man. "It's going to be alright" he reassured them, "We know what to do."

Then they all moved at once.

"Wait!" Song urged. "Polly, take your apron. Fill the pockets with biscuits. Everyone take some...it might be a long time before we see another meal."

Polly ran to the front porch, leaving the door open, she shouted back to the others. "It's got to Dupont and California!" Reece, Edward, and Song raced to move the most important inventory items, shelved for efficient access, into a brick storage room. Haylee ran to the office. Into a basket stored near the door, she gathered the accounts receivable records, cash on hand, gold dust, nuggets, the Keener family bible, and their few photographs. She took everything to the underground fire safe that Reece had built.

Next, the men loaded all the explosives that the mercantile possessed into wheelbarrows that they rolled out to the street. Haylee hurried to gather additional personal items.

They met at the store entrance, prepared to go separate ways. Edward grabbed the sack that Haylee handed to him. Like a relay racer, he dashed to the stables to save their animals.

While Song sprinted back into the building, Reece took a moment to look inside. He knew that within hours, everything they'd work to build might be reduced to ash.

He turned to the girls, kneeling in front of Polly. Holding her firmly by the shoulders, he said, "I need you to be brave. Listen to Haylee. Do what she says." He pulled her into his arms, giving her a quick hug.

"I will, Papa Reece," she replied. Tears had gathered in her eyes, her chin trembled.

When he stood, he reached for Haylee. Bringing her in close, he looked deeply into her eyes before kissing her. With this intimate expression, he said everything that he could not voice. "Take good care of the wee ones." He reached down to caress her baby bump. "I'll see you at our meeting spot."

"Papa Reece!" Polly yelled, "The fire is only two buildings away!"

Haylee nodded, her feet felt like blocks of ice, her limbs were as heavy as stone. Placing her hands on either side of Reece's face, she pulled him down for a kiss. Through touch and tears, she transferred the love, devotion, and trust that she felt for this man into the expression. Wishing, with every fiber of her being, that she could prolong this moment, she trembled, worried that it would be their last.

Firmly, Reece pushed her away. With a tortured gaze, he scanned her face. He looked as if he were trying to memorize every nuance.

Haylee raised her voice above the deafening roar. "Stay safe. Remember how much I love you!"

"Our plan is good," he yelled in return, "It's going to work! Go!" He gave her a nudge to get her moving.

Grabbing Polly's hand, Haylee and the little girl took off.

Reece raised the speaking trumpet Song handed him. He rallied men to move explosives. They would set them off, creating fire breaks.

Thunderous, roaring flames licked and devoured tinder ripened for a feast. Shrieking, howling currents of scaling wind gyrated in a frenzied dance. The two forces, working together, like a giant beast, rattled the bars and chains at the gates of hell. Acrid, stinging smoke, the by-product of deconstruction, billowed in every direction.

Haylee braced against the searing assault. Coughing, she made futile attempts to protect eyes that felt like they were poaching in their sockets. She stopped, gathering up her skirt to cover her mouth and nose, getting Polly to do likewise. *We should have included the use of wet blankets in our emergency plan,* Haylee thought.

The ground rumbled, threatening to lay them flat. Another cloud of dust and flames reached for the heavens as a brick building collapsed nearby. Grasping Polly, Haylee screamed, "We have to get out of here!"

Timbers crashed, sparks and splinters sprayed out in burning waves. People with clothes, hair, and skin smoking and boiling screamed, running in senseless patterns, desperately trying to escape.

Animals of all sorts, dogs, cows, horses, pigs, cats, and chickens scattered in every direction. Confused and disoriented by the smoke, terror, and mayhem, Haylee lost track of which direction they needed to go.

Another sound, big and bold, like massive breakers crashing on rocks, boomed. Kearny Street filled with a hoard of escapees; the fire bore down upon them from the opposite direction. In the fray, Haylee lost her hold on the little girl. "Polly!" She screeched, searching frantically.

Haylee spotted a corner of Polly's apron near the ground; she lunged for it. Struggling and elbowing through tussling bodies, Haylee lifted the little girl back onto her feet before she could be trampled.

Crying, Polly clung to Haylee like a lifeline, soot and tear tracks marred her face. Barely able to maintain their position without being swept along, Haylee hauled Polly toward a pile of rubble. Scrambling over loose boards and stones, she gained height to get her bearings. Haylee registered loud cracks and groans but she focused on finding her escape route. She thought she could make out Reece's voice rasping out instructions through his speaking trumpet.

"Reece! Reece!" Haylee screamed.

Just then, a collective cry went up from the crowd surrounding them. Haylee turned in the direction they pointed. Over her shoulder was a towering wall of flames. The building swayed precariously, its footings weakened and rapidly disintegrating, its descent, right on top of where they were standing, moved as if in slow motion.

Haylee pulled Polly into her arms. Tightly pressing the little girl's face into her chest, she shouted in Polly's ear, "Hold tight, I've got you!" Haylee closed her eyes, bracing for impact.

A rain of fire pelted over her back, embers melted her hair and charbroiled pinpoints into her scalp. Haylee shrieked.

A voice, Reece's voice, reverberated through her brain, drowning out all else. It said, "The Traveler Returns."

❧2❧

GENE'S TESTIMONY

GARRETT, EUGENE - Entry #1

November 23, 1985, at approximately 9:45 p.m.,
Haylee disappeared.

Background:

MY HOUSE HAD BEEN full of energy and commotion.
My new wife Glori spent days getting ready for Haylee's
return from school. We were planning to celebrate her 19th
birthday and the holidays.

Haylee surprised us by showing up with an
unexpected guest. No phone call, no warning, just this tall,
gangly kid with glasses climbing out of the passenger seat
of her little blue VW Bug.

Glori, who'd been standing right next to me must have
felt me tense because she took my hand and quietly
whispered, "Oh Gene, Haylee's brought a friend. Isn't that
wonderful?"

One of the things I love about Glori is that she makes
me pause before I react as I usually would. I suppose if she
hadn't been there, things would have gone differently.

You were forthright and direct. I'll give you that. Though I must have been scowling, you didn't let that stop you. You came directly to me, shaking my hand, and introduced yourself. "Hello Mr. Garrett, I'm Josh Herkowitz. I'm a teaching assistant in one of your daughter's classes," you said.

It didn't take long for you to win me over. I liked you as soon as you told me that your family was in farming too. Citrus isn't that different from walnuts.

We'd had a few days to get to know each other. I could tell that Glori was charmed by you. She mentioned that she didn't understand why Haylee brought you home but didn't seem to be interested in you—in a romantic way.

I could see that you had moony eyes on my daughter. You and Haylee seemed comfortable together, but there were walls between you that I couldn't figure out.

On the day that it happened, I had equipment maintenance to do in the back fields. You and Haylee were planning to work on a research project. Glori had gone grocery shopping. I didn't finish troubleshooting the water pump till after dark.

When I got home, things were quiet— unnaturally so.

"Where is everyone?" I called, walking inside, fumbling for the light switch.

I heard Haylee's high, raspy voice coming out of the blackness.

"Daddy, I'm so, so sorry! I'm sorry!"

"Haylee? What's wrong!?" I shouted back, turning on the light.

She was curled in one of the stuffed chairs. Her eyes were bloodshot. I could see that she'd been crying. The lack of color in her face was alarming. She had a death grip on her backpack with one hand while the other, clamped into a tight, white fist, trembled, and pressed against her forehead. Haylee rocked back and forth in a way that looked crazed.

I thought she was sick again. We'd had a bad spell with her health about a year ago. Alarmed, I crossed to her.

"No! Don't come near me!" she croaked. Haylee held up an open hand. What I saw there, stopped me in mid-stride, nearly making me faint. Between her fingers was a fine, see-through webbing. It's hard to describe, especially since I only saw it that once. The webs didn't look thick, like a goose or an otter's foot, but they were delicate—like dragonfly wings. Small red veins were visible, they thrummed, moving fluid around.

"Haylee!" I yelled. No matter how well prepared you are as a parent, when something is suddenly very wrong with your kid, you go into GI Joe mode.

She pulled something from her pocket then dropped it as if it burned. "Ahhh!" Haylee screamed looking down into her lap. She jumped in her seat, wiping at her legs.

To hell with staying away! I thought, moving to her.

With a blinding flash, Haylee disappeared.

After slamming into the empty chair. I pulled back, calling her name. I ran my hands all over where she should have been. *Damn it! Where'd she go?*

When it dawned on me that my daughter was gone, I started screaming for Glori. She's always calm headed in emergencies. "Glori! I need you!" I yelled at the top of my lungs. "I need help!"

All the cars were in the driveway. I couldn't understand where you or Glori could be.

The door banged hard against the wall when I stormed into Haylee's room. My heart did a turn-over. Someone was in bed. "Haylee?" I called.

I stood there looking down at you. You were entirely clothed under the covers, lying there with eyes closed like you were taking a nap. I reached down to shake you, "Josh, wake up! Haylee's missing."

You didn't stir. I patted your cheek, "Josh!" I repeated, running my hands over you, making sure you weren't bleeding or broken. "Josh, son.... wake up. What's the matter?" You were breathing freely; your color was right.

Alarmed now, I ran to my room, intending to phone for help. When I crossed the threshold, I froze. *Oh God, not Glori too! Please don't do this to me, Lord.*

Everything after that is a blur. I must have carried you both to the truck and drove you to the hospital. I remember trying to communicate every scrap of information to Dr. Lester, hoping that she could clear up this mess.

The skeptical look on her face made me realize how I sounded.

"You say that you watched your daughter— disappear?" she asked.

I recalled the first time I'd met this woman. I brought Haylee in; she'd been bleeding. It wasn't a small amount of blood; it was like what you'd see when dressing down a deer.

At that time, Glori told me that Dr. Lester is the best there is this side of the Mississippi. I also remembered that the not-so-helpful Dr. Lester had not been able to give us a definitive answer about what was wrong with my daughter. I wasn't sure I wanted that woman having anything to do with Glori—even if she was her boss.

About that time is when Susan Sheridan joined the party. Sue is a nurse at the hospital and one of Glori's dearest friends. With her help— she ran interference between the Dr. and me—they did every conceivable test.

Sue helped me calm down. She offered to have her husband Randy, a deputy Sheriff, talk to me about Haylee's disappearance. By then, I realized that Glori needed me to be the voice that she no longer had. If I was going to be any help to her, I had better stop behaving like an insane person.

Unfortunately, Dr. Lester came back with the same diagnosis for Glori that she had for Haylee. 'Unexplained.'

Your parents came to collect you. Your mother all but accused me of dabbling in drugs. I cursed, asking if she thought that my *wife*, a nurse at this very hospital, was also taking drugs?

Sadly, your diagnosis was the same. Your father, Jason, took my number so that we could compare notes.

We stayed at the hospital for a week. Glori could move when prompted, chew and swallow when food was put in her mouth, and eliminate when taken to the bathroom...but nothing more. She had no expressions, no responses to physical, auditory, or emotional stimuli.

Rumors travel quickly through the hospital. Dr. Thomas came to visit. He was a tall, lanky black fellow. Soft-spoken, a keen observer, his eyes didn't miss a thing. He had a patient with similar symptoms, a local nineteen-year-old boy who didn't quite make it to his graduation last spring.

I went to the window, not wanting him to read the emotions on my face. I asked if there had been any change in his condition? Thomas's answer frightened the hell out of me— 'not one.

Dr. Thomas was looking for connections. I don't think that I let on, that I had one— a beautiful young woman who disappeared right in front of me.

Sue helped arrange for caregivers to come to my home.... our home.

I've always given the farm my best work. After my first wife, Doris, died, loneliness and missing her consumed me. The farm kept me going. It didn't cry or complain; it didn't need comfort or other things I didn't have to give. It let me know when it needed something and responded by providing life and abundance. In a way, it healed me when nothing else could.

With Glori it was different. I missed her—that sassy mouth of hers, her crooked smile. But part of her was still with me. I think if I had her there to look at, talk to...and touch, I had hope. Sometimes I'd beg her to wake up. "Can't some part of you do...something...anything to let me know that you hear me?"

Glori had a team of helpers. They watched her during the day, fed her, bathed her, took her for walks, and to physical therapy appointments. They had dinner waiting for me when I got home.

In the evenings, I read to her; I got so damn tired of hearing my voice! We went on long drives. I tried taking Glori to movies in town a couple of times, but the funny looks we got pissed me off.

Time went on that way—a great deal of it. The days ran together. There was a routine to the farm and a method to caring for Glori. I thought about Haylee and what happened to her during the days. I'd convinced myself that my mind had to have been playing tricks. What I thought I saw wasn't possible.

Rarely did I consider Dr. Thomas, or his patient.

Though I liked you, I rarely thought of you either. Periodic phone calls from your dad would change that, temporarily. Our shared sorrow brought us together. He asked about Haylee every time he called. My answer was the truth; I didn't know where she was. I think that he had the impression that she'd run away.

July 29, 1986, at approximately 7:30 p.m.

I was tired as all-get-out, filthy from the field, and not caring that my boots were leaving dirt clods on the carpet, I stared at the glowing TV box in an otherwise dark room. James Garner, as Rockford, was lamenting about the criminal mind.

I smelled smoke a few seconds before a black mass appeared in the center of the room. At first, I couldn't understand what I was seeing. Small flames burned around the edges of it. "What the...?"

Then it moved, coughed, and wheezed. I jumped up. Through the soot-caked all over her face, I could see that it was, "Haylee!"

Long forgotten training kicked into autopilot. When I was a younger man, sweltering in a humid jungle, I was a field medic for my platoon. I got burn experience when my squad was firebombed.

Grabbing a blanket off the couch, I threw it over Haylee, smothering the flames. Blanket and all, I picked her up, running to the bathroom. Turning the shower on gentle, at room temperature, I stepped in, letting the water do the rest.

----Testimony End----

❧3❧
HAYLEE'S HOME

GAGGING AND STRAINING TO breathe, Haylee fought. Eugene did his best to keep her subdued, speaking firmly in reassuring tones. He didn't know how badly she was hurt, every movement she made could be taking off skin.

He should have floated her in the bathtub, but there wasn't enough time to fill it. Most immediately, the residual heat from the burns needed to be cooled.

"Where's Polly? I have to find Polly!" Haylee rasped.

Haylee bucked and thrashed, making Gene struggle to keep from dropping her. Whipping her head violently, she shifted the material covering her face away from it. Taking a giant inward breath, she opened her mouth, screaming, "Polly! Where are you?" Her voice, gravelly and hoarse, sounded like a smoker who was about to be put on oxygen for the rest of their life.

"Haylee, you're home." Eugene set her on her feet. Keeping a steadying arm wrapped around the back of her shoulders, he peeled the wet blankets further back. "Hold onto me, so you don't slip." He shook his head to clear the water out of his eyes.

"Polly! Where is she? His daughters, desperate, claw-like hands clutched at the front of his shirt. "Mister! You have to help me; I lost a little girl!"

Relief flooded through him, making Gene feel lightheaded when he saw that the skin on her face, neck, and arms was alright. The hair inside her nose was still there— a sign that her lungs were okay. Thoroughly drenched, Eugene laughed. "Thank God for that!"

Haylee's eyes began to clear. She stopped fighting. As she steadied, Eugene loosened up his hold. Shaking off the heavy blanket, it dropped to the floor with a weighty plop. Wiping water and hair out of her eyes, Haylee looked like she recognized her father. "Dad?"

"Yes, that's right." Gene smiled. He turned off the water, then reached out to stroke her cheek. "I thought I'd never see you again." He pulled her into an embrace.

Clutching him, Haylee began to tremble. Great sobs consumed her.

When Eugene pulled away, Haylee didn't see his eyes widen when he looked down at her midsection. He backed up, stepping over the side of the bathtub. Gently, guiding his daughter, he urged her to join him.

The mass of her skirts, along with her weeping, hampered her movements. When Eugene bent forward to clutch a handful of the waterlogged material, he was surprised at its weight.

Leading Haylee to the toilet, he sat her down, handing her a dry towel. She took it. For a moment, her crying stopped, Gene was hopeful that she'd regained control. He watched her look at the cloth strangely, petting it like she would her cat, then the skin on her forehead bunched up. Taking a hitching breath, she let loose a wail, "It's so so-oft!" Her cries muffled as she pushed her face into the absorbent terry cloth.

Inhaling a steadying breath of his own, Gene stepped behind her. He noticed that parts of her hair, frizzy and stiff, were melted. With a light touch, he moved the surrounding mane so he could assess her scalp. The burns there were minor.

Turning his attention to her back, he jerked his hands away in surprise. Rows of tiny buttons lay in his way. "What the hell are you wearing?" he muttered.

His comment sent a fresh wave of lament into the towel. "I don't have time to mess around with this!" he said more to himself than to Haylee. Gene struggled to remove the pocket knife from his jeans. With a few efficient cuts and rips, he pulled carefully at the loosened material. Most of the fabric came away easily. Relief, once again, saturated his veins. One spot, near the outside of her left shoulder, was a problem. He sliced the material in a circle around it.

Finally understanding the extent of her injuries, Eugene focused on how he would treat them.

Starting at the waistband of her dress, he sliced through it in one clean motion. Gripping both sides of the material, he pulled in opposite directions, a flat ripping sound followed.

Noticing the yards of cotton underwear, she had on underneath, he experienced another moment of unreality. What the hell?

With a fresh towel, he carefully dabbed the skin around each wound. Grabbing a pair of tweezers, he slowly pulled tiny fragments of material away from the lesion.

Eugene was worried that he was hurting her. Haylee's crying remained constant. On the smaller injuries in her hair and on her back, he dabbed aloe gel. For the shoulder wound, he surrounded it with the gel but didn't touch anything to the raw, wet sore. He dressed it with gauze, leaving plenty of room for air to circulate.

His next concern was treatment for shock. He needed to get her out of the wet clothes. When he began pushing the material away, Haylee's cries halted. Lifting her head, she crossed her arms tightly over her front, resisting his efforts.

"Haylee, you were in a fire. You're out of it now. Do you understand?" he asked.

Squeezing her eyes closed, she nodded. Fresh tears mingled with water that dripped from her hair.

Snatching his bathrobe from a hook behind the door, he pushed it into her hands. "We have to get you warm and dry."

He helped her step out of the sopping material, "Luckily that dress is thick, most of the burns didn't reach the skin." He stopped talking when Haylee started shaking.

"Cold," she said through chattering teeth.

Hurrying to get her into his robe, he did his best to avoid seeing anything. "I wish Glori were here to help," he muttered.

Haylee's head snapped up. "Glori? Where is she?"

"She's here— but she's not in any shape to do anything."

⋘⋙

Tucked into bed with the heating blanket set to three, Haylee's emotions and shuddering subsided. A body can only take so much stress. Sooner or later, it runs low on energy; there's nothing left to do but surrender to the recuperative powers of sleep.

Eugene's hair and clothes were nearly dry by the time he left his daughter's bedside. The TV was still on in the living room, white noise and static had long since replaced his regularly scheduled programming. Turning it off, he plodded back to the bathroom noticing that his boots were making squishy sounds.

The smell of stale smoke assailed him. He tossed his socks, jeans, and shirt in an unorganized pile. Eugene walked to the shower to start the hot water. While he waited, testing its temperature, his gaze returned to the mound of wet cloth Haylee had been wearing.

Eugene approached the garments like they were alive. Bending over, he sorted drawers, pantaloons, petticoats? Next, he lifted the chemise; satin ribbons crisscrossed over the front, lace adorned the neckline.

There were long stockings and leather lace-up shoes. The outer wool dress, still hefty, was the most perplexing. "Where have you been? How did you arrive, out of nowhere, in the living room— pregnant?"

Rolling the clothing into a bundle, he carried it, leaving a trail of water, out to the clothesline, where he unceremoniously draped everything over a plastic-coated wire.

Steam, having filled the bathroom, billowed out when Eugene returned. Barely turning down the temperature on the tap, he stepped under the spray, letting the hot water turn his skin cherry red.

In the humid privacy of the tiny cubicle, Eugene unclasped the pressure valve holding his reactions tightly in check.

Dry and clean, Eugene slid beneath the covers next to his wife. She was warm when he reached for her, but Glori lay there like a wilted carrot. Nuzzling her ear, he inhaled the fresh smell of Prell.

Gene insisted that her home health workers continue buying the same shampoo brand that Glori had chosen— when she still could make choices. "Haylee's home, Glo," his voice sounded tired. "My girl's come back."

❧4❧
GLORI'S LAST DAY

WHEN SHE FIRST WOKE up, Haylee reached across the bed expecting to feel heat, skin and rough hair under her fingers. Calling softly, "Reece?" She was confused when she discovered that his pillow was empty and cold.

Awareness of where she was settled in. Stabbing pains pierced her heart. Haylee's arms cradled the mound of flesh in her middle. Tears gathered in her eyes.

When the upsurge of fresh grief passed, Haylee thought about the mornings she and Reece cuddled, gently pushing and prodding her belly, getting the baby to move. Haylee frowned, realizing that her usually active offspring had not stirred since before the fire.

Haylee felt lost and adrift. Her bedroom was familiar, but it wasn't home. Despite her turmoil, she noticed things that made life more comfortable here. Light and electricity at the touch of a finger, central heat and air, closets full of inexpensive ready-made clothes.

Did she have anything that would fit? Pushing the blankets away, Haylee swung her legs over the side of the bed. She groaned. Everything hurt, joints, muscles, and skin. *This must be what it feels like to be eighty.*

Looking down, she saw that she'd slept in her dad's robe. Clinging to the fabric, the faint aroma of his shaving cream was mildly comforting. Untying the sash, she let the soft material fall away. In another life, she would have been mortified to think that her father had seen her without clothes. Now, she didn't care. Haylee ran her hands over the roundness that concealed her and Reece's little girl. *Is she alright?*

Sorrow carried Haylee away, tumbling her in tempestuous tides. When it played out, it left her drained, gasping on arid shores.

Back on dry land, the business of life continued. Haylee found a pair of sweats in her dresser. A nightshirt that had been a tent on her before barely had room to spare. Her feet were the same size. Thankfully, she slipped into a pair of well-worn house slippers, welcoming them like old familiar friends. A forgiving sweater completed her day's ensemble.

Her dad knocked on the door. Coming in to check on Haylee, he seemed tongue-tied. She hadn't noticed, before, that his eyes spoke a language of compassion and understanding.

He reapplied aloe gel, changed her bandages, and told her when Glori's caregivers were scheduled to arrive. Haylee cried again after he left. Even in her grief-stricken state, she was glad to see him again.

Before braving the world beyond her door, Haylee went to the window, seeking familiar sights. The clothesline, where her clothes from yesterday hung, limp and empty, swayed in the breeze. She realized, suddenly, that she was missing something, something important!

Trotting through the house, she pushed on the screen door. A tiny, but mighty, kick jabbed her sharply. "Hey! That hurt!" Haylee stopped in mid-stride. Smiling, she blinked with relief. She looked down saying, "Good job in there, keep it up."

Haylee reclined in an Adirondack chair facing into the warm morning light. She adjusted her position, so she could lean on her back without irritating the burns. The fragrant, earthy smells of grass and flowers, the bees buzzing, hurrying passed on their way to their next destination, and the musical rhythms of birdsong unwound the knot of stress she carried.

Oscar, her Siamese cat, detected her in his territory. He crouched low in the tall weeds, making cautious, stealthy movements in her direction.

Haylee noticed his activities and sent loving thoughts into his mind. *Oscar! I am so happy to see you! Come over here, big fuzzy boy, so I can say hello.*

Giving up his stalk, he trotted over, leaping onto her lap. After landing, he encountered the unexpected obstacle. Oscar looked perplexed. Sitting on his haunches, regarding it, his tail swished in wide arcs like a soldier doing jumping jacks in basic training.

Haylee sat quietly; waiting. Until this moment, Oscar had been her one-and-only baby.

Haylee ran a hand over his head, ears, and back. His tail movements turned from abrupt to languid and snake-like. Purring, closing his eyes, Oscar gave himself over to the happy moments of reunification.

When they were done greeting each other, he perched on the wide arm of the chair sharing his images of Glori; walking woodenly around the property with strangers who came and went, her dad helping Glori into his truck, buckling the seat belt around her. *She not she...she like tree.*

"I know Oscar," Haylee sighed, gliding another caress down his back. She lifted her hands, spreading her fingers, "See, I got rid of the webs. I won't be doing that anymore."

Haylee resumed petting him. Oscar vibrated his response. Haylee's free hand rested on her belly. "I need to ask a favor. If this little one is still with us, after I bring Glori back, then I need you to sit with me until I wake up." Scratching under his chin, the way she knew he liked, Haylee asked, "Would you do that?"

⁓⁓⁓

After Oscar left to begin his rounds, Haylee pulled her feet up under her. She talked to her child, "Most of the time I was with your dad, I wished to get back here so that I could undo what I did to Glori, Josh, and the others. He wanted us to stay with him. He said that I should forget my former life and be happy there."

"You and I should have died in the fire. Instead, here we are. I think that's a sign that I am supposed to do what I came back to do. You're going to be alright in there, aren't you? You've made it through so much already, baby; you have to hang in there."

"Haylee?" Gene called as he came into view. "Is there someone here?" he asked.

Lowering her feet to the ground, she groaned, pushing her bulk up from the chair. "No, I was just talking to myself."

"When I couldn't find you, I thought—"

Resting a hand on the base of her aching back, Haylee waddled in his direction. "That I'd disappeared again? I'm still here. I don't think I'll be going anywhere again."

Frowning, "Sweetheart, I didn't mean—"

"I know, I'm sorry for being crabby. I just spent the night in a very comfortable bed, but I still woke up on the wrong side of it."

"Is there anything I can do?"

Haylee shook her head.

"Glori's aid is here and her friend, Sue, came by for a visit. She's a nurse too; I asked her if she'd look at your burns."

Haylee nodded, taking his arm and walking with him back toward the house.

Gene held the door open for her.

Haylee paused at the threshold, looking inside, "Oh— Glori's up." She noticed two other women she didn't know.

Glori was sitting at the kitchen table, her hands were folded on her lap. A cup of water with a straw sat in front of her. Haylee's breath caught in her throat. It was difficult to see Glori looking so— blank. Glori's short red hair had grown out, it was neatly combed. She wore a yellow blouse, a jean skirt, and slip on shoes. Haylee nodded, realizing that her dad had dressed her.

Eugene introduced Haylee to Sue and Mrs. Hanston, Glori's day minder.

"I was about to start breakfast," said Mrs. Hanston, "Is there anything that you'd like?"

Haylee wasn't hungry, but replied, "Thank you, anything's fine." The women staring at her made her nervous. Haylee glanced at her dad. *I have missed him. I've missed them both!* She brought her arm around his back, squeezing him. He returned the gesture.

"Haylee, I was at the hospital the night that Glori got sick. Your dad was so worried about you. Where have you been all this time?" Sue inquired.

Haylee's eyes grew round. Stepping away from her dad, she brought a hand up to her mouth, "Excuse me! I think I'm going to be sick!"

❦❦❦

After she got cleaned up, and Eugene had Sue look at Haylee's wounds, Haylee could tell that he was in a hurry to usher the woman out of the house. Haylee could hear their conversation in the hallway.

"You're joking? She shows up out of nowhere, pregnant, and you haven't grilled her about it? I'll tell you what happened; she took off with her boyfriend. When something between them went wrong, she came back. Randy filed a missing person's report! You need to tell him she's turned up so they can call off the search," Sue sounded indignant, "and, she probably hasn't seen an OB, Glori would be the first one to tell you how important that is."

"I know, Sue," her father's voice was soft, it grew faint with distance. "I can't thank you enough for all that you and Randy have done for us."

⁕⁕⁕

Mrs. Hanston cleaned up the breakfast dishes. She approached Eugene. "I'll grab a sweater for Mrs. Garrett, then we'll be off on our daily walk."

After they'd gone, Haylee and her dad regarded each other. Eugene poured himself a cup of coffee, taking it to the table where Haylee joined him.

Haylee started talking. "The father of my baby is Reece Keener. He's from San Francesco. Reece and his brother own a store. He's strong, adventurous, and kind— his family is Irish," Haylee beamed. "He is going to be a great father." She stopped, abruptly, squeezing her eyes shut. Wiping at tears, she looked away, amending quietly, "He would have made..."

Haylee checked her dad's reaction. Slouched in his seat, Gene crossed his arms. Frowning, he stared at his boots. She knew she had his undivided attention.

"All this time... I thought you disappeared," he said, deadly calm, "you've been living with some guy in San Francesco?"

"It's not like that!" Her voice was hard, defensive. *I don't know if I can do this,* she thought. *How can I tell him, so he'll understand...and believe me?* "I'm pretty sure that mom knew something about all the weirdness that happened."

Eugene's head snapped up, he looked like he was about to yell. "Your mother? How did we get from this Reece guy...?" He looked at her stomach pointedly, "to your mother?"

"She was part of the chain, part of the lineage I belong too. Only some of them do what I did to Glori and to Josh. The rest are carriers. Mom was a carrier and I am a Traveler. I was directed to another Traveler. When I met her, I learned what to do to bring Glori back."

Gene's eyes widened, his skin turned pale. A strange expression that Haylee didn't understand appeared on his face.

"Dad, are you OK?"

He nodded, not saying anything. He waved a hand indicating that she should continue.

"I need you to hear the rest of this before we help Glori."

Gene moved close to the table, leaning his elbows on it, giving her an intense stare. "Tell me what you did."

"I'm planning to," she snapped, "but you have to let me tell it in my way." Haylee moved to the opposite side of the kitchen. She rummaged in the cupboards.

Filling a kettle and putting it on the burner, she continued, "Mom told me a few things when I was little that made me think that she knew something." Haylee dropped a teabag inside a mug. She poured hot water over it. "Mom said that all of the women in our family have something that most people don't understand."

Haylee watched her dad cup his mug between his palms, staring into it like answers might appear in the reflection. "You saw some of my headaches.... but not all of them. Then there was that day that you took me to the emergency room. You saw the webs right before I...."

"Disappeared," he supplied.

Haylee nodded, then continued, "I'd had them for some time. They were easy to hide. I didn't understand why they were there until I started having convulsive fits. Once I...attacked someone, they'd stop for a while. Then the cycle started over."

"And you never said a word about it. Didn't you think I'd want to know? Maybe I could have helped?"

"What could you have done?"

"We could have gone to see doctors..."

"Yeah—like that worked out so well."

"Haylee..."

"Josh thought he could help find answers. After what I did at school... I thought there'd be a recovery period. I thought you'd be safe. I wouldn't have come if I ...but it got out of hand."

"You're not making sense."

"I know.... just let me get the rest of it out. That day I disappeared, I woke up in an open field. It was quiet...really, really, quiet. There was no traffic or planes." Haylee paused, facing her father. "This had something to do with it." She pulled out her pendant.

Haylee could tell that he recognized it. "This and another crystal that I was sent to find...took me to 1849, Dad. I was in San Francesco, but 137 years ago. Reece is still there—" Haylee closed her eyes. "Reece and the rest of the family, Edward, Polly, and Song."

Haylee clamped the lid on the emotional wave that was building inside. Digging in her pocket, she brought out the large crystal. Holding it up, she said, "This is what I was sent to find." Setting it on the table between them. "That's what's going to bring Glori back."

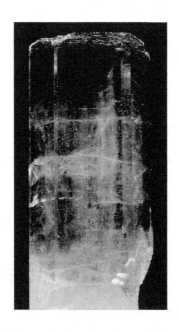

❧5❧
GLORI'S RETURN

THEY STOOD AT THE edge of the bed where Glori lay as the late afternoon light faded into tones of muted orange, pink, and gold. Dust particles hung suspended in the beams, swirling slowly like gravity had no power over them. Haylee held a shoe box. Inside were several items; a two-inch-long blue crystal and a decorative jewelry box.

Gene glanced at the contents. "That little case was your mom's."

Haylee drew her eyes away from Glori, turning to her father. Then she glanced into the box. "Josh and I found it with her things in the attic."

Gene nodded. He raised a hand as if he were going to touch it, but Haylee twisted away, extending her arms. "These are dangerous, Dad! DON'T TOUCH IT!"

"Haylee...." he looked confused, "I've handled it before."

"Not when it's with the crystal!" Exasperation stamped itself on her face. She stepped away, going to stare out the window. "The first time I touched the crystal, it shot me across the room. When Reece touched it, the blast nearly cracked his skull open. Something happened...back there.... that made it so that I can hold it. I don't want to take chances to see what it might do to someone else."

"This is what I'll use to bring Glori back," she continued. "When I'm done, I'm going to go down fast, as in pass out. I'll need you to do a few things. Catch me before I hit the ground. Take me to bed to let me sleep it off; it might take a few days. Hide this box in my room. There's a good place at the back of my closet. And make sure that neither you nor Glori goes near this thing."

"I don't understand," Gene stated.

"Neither do I."

"Will it hurt you—or the baby?"

This was the first time her dad had spoken of the child.

"It'll be alright. I've done this twice already. There's one more thing...I want you, and Glori, to watch how this goes. I'll need your help when it's time to do the same for Josh. Are you ready?" Haylee asked.

Gene's mouth compressed. He nodded, "Tell me what to do."

Haylee moved into place near Glori's head, "Stand close but don't touch me until you hear the crystal fall into the box."

"OK," Gene stepped behind her, spreading his feet wide, holding his arms out.

She put the box on the nightstand, carefully removing the crystal.

Gene watched a light grow in its center, pulsing like a heartbeat.

Haylee turned her head to the side, "and Dad..."

"Yeah?"

"When Glori wakes up. Tell her that I don't need to go the hospital."

In terse tones, Gene replied, "I'll tell her."

Haylee stood with the crystal pressed tightly between her palms. It vibrated slightly, then stopped. Focusing on Glori's forehead, she began to hum. As she did, the crystal grew increasingly warm. She closed her eyes, letting her mind go back to the first time she'd done this.

1849

It was morning aboard the Dicey. The ship rocked gently, on Yerba Buena Cove's incoming tide. She'd spent the night before, utterly engaged within Reece's arms. Warm, tender, kisses and passionate embraces, unfolded, for the first time, the motions and meaning of love. It dispelled the fear, pain, and horrific memories from the ceremony she'd been forced to endure.

After dressing slowly, they went to Edward's room. Reece stood across from where his brother lay. Holding a set of handwritten notes, he shuffled through them.

"What does it say?" she asked.

"It says you have to hold the crystal near your heart and sing or hum. This activates it."

"Is this going to hurt?" Haylee wondered out loud.

Looking up with a worried expression, he replied, "It doesn't say—"

⁓⌇⁓

Hearing Reece's deep voice, with his rolling r's and long O's, in her mind, Haylee remembered the instructions he'd read.

She continued to hum until the crystal had grown quite warm. Slowly, she raised her hands, cupping the crystal between them like a prayer. Touching the knuckles of her thumbs to her forehead, then to her chin, and finally, to her heart, Haylee intoned, "I honor the spirit that lives within you."

Tipping her hands forward, extending her arms so that the ends of her fingers pointed to Glori's forehead, Haylee opened her palms.

The crystal radiated bright blue light. It began to flicker. After half a dozen pulses, Gene saw Haylee stiffen.

A dim ball of light winked into existence, in the air, suspended above the crystal. A second appeared, then a third. With each arrival, Haylee whimpered, as if it hurt when the glowing spheres came out.

Gene watched the lights start circling slowly around each other. Suddenly one shot straight up to hover at the ceiling. The other two, looking like they did not want to be left behind, darted up to join it. Gene tilted his head so that he could follow their path.

The three lights floated together, touching one another, but separate, like balls on a Newton's Cradle. Faster than a finger snap, they sped toward Gene, halting six inches above his face. They twirled, hopped, and rotated around each other. Their antics made him smile.

As Haylee shifted her body weight toward Glori, the lights zipped over to resume hovering above the crystal.

Trembling slightly, Haylee's voice sounded strained, "I Haylee Louise request Upholder's Redemption for Glori Jean."

The lights grew brighter, huddled together, their edges merged until they became one.

Filling her lungs, Haylee blew at the glowing ball. It settled firmly onto Glori's forehead. With each successive puff, the ball sunk further into her skull. On Haylee's last big blow, it disappeared.

Haylee trembled, but she remained standing.

Eugene heard the crystal drop. He braced himself.

Haylee swayed, she slumped, her full weight dropped into Eugene's arms.

Gene shifted his burden. Sweeping his arms under her legs, he bent his knees, accepting the full load. Grunting, he pushed up; gravity defied his efforts.

Glancing down at his wife, Gene's heart leaped. Her nose was twitching! Her eyes were fluttering, the pattern of her breathing shifted, deepening.

Hope rose within him, an artesian well, opening his heart, straining to well up like a geyser.

He trundled down the hall, taking care to not drop the next generation of his family, or to bump Haylee's head on the door jamb. True to her description, she collapsed and appeared to be deeply asleep. Setting her down on her bed, he unfolded a light blanket, placing it over her. He rested a hand on her forehead, then lifted her arm to press his fingers against her wrist. Leaning over, he kissed her. He tucked the arm under the blanket.

Gene wondered what he'd witnessed. A rustling sound from his bedroom sent him bounding in that direction.

He grabbed a footstool that usually resided at the end of the bed, moving it near where Glori rested. He watched her slowly open her eyes. She stared at the ceiling, blinking. Reaching out, he lightly touched the knuckle of his forefinger against her temple. "Glori, Honey?"

Her blinking continued, a tiny frown line formed between her brows. Gene drew in a deep breath; *She's coming out of it!*

"Sweetheart?" He breathed urgently.

Glori turned toward the sound. He sat up straighter as her vivid blue and purple eyes focused on him. A hesitant smile lifted the corners of his mouth.

"G..." she tried to speak. A rough, grating sound came out.

"Would you like some water?"

She nodded.

He brought over a glass with a straw, "Do you want to sit up?"

"Uh..." she nodded.

Gene moved to help her change positions. His hands were shaking as he fluffed the pillow behind her.

After taking a few sips, Glori pressed her fingertips to the base of her neck. She cleared her throat. "My voice," she whisper-squeaked, "sounds funny."

Eugene's emotions felt as if they had reached an inflation threshold. Like a balloon, they were ready to burst. "It's the most wonderful thing I've ever heard!" Gene moved back to the footstool. He sat there grinning.

Glori looked at him quizzically, a soft smile played about her mouth. Gene lifted one of her hands, bringing it to his lips, kissing it," I've missed you, woman."

Her smile deepened then her small frown reappeared. She leaned toward him so that she could trace along the lines that radiated out from the edges of his eyes, "You have more of those than I remember."

Gene took a moment to savor her touch and the two-way communication between them. He turned his face into the palm of her hand, pressing another kiss there.

Glori ran her fingers through his hair, "You have more gray. How did this happen without my noticing?"

A short laugh escaped him. "You are back, aren't you?"

"Back?" she frowned, "I didn't go anywhere."

Overjoyed with the sound of her voice, Gene wanted to kiss the hell out of her, drag her into his arms, sink himself deeply into her and shout to the heavens.

Instead, he looked deeply into those oh-so-beautiful eyes and said, "Welcome home Mrs. Garrett—I've missed you."

❧6❧
PARADE

AS GLORI WENT THROUGH the motions of her day, she opened and closed her hands, exercising the muscles that had grown stiff. She vigorously rubbed her wrists and upper arms, flexed her ankles, and lunged as far as her strength would allow.

Weeks after emerging from her catatonic state, she was still struggling with the idea that months of her life had been wiped away—with no memory.

She'd seen the paraphernalia involved with her care, and she met Mrs. Hanston, who wept openly at their first, real, meeting.

Wracking her mind, Glori couldn't remember anything beyond unloading groceries from her car on the day that it happened. She'd grilled Eugene. He said he'd found her like that. With pain in his eyes, he admitted that Haylee claimed to be responsible.

When Glori let her thoughts linger on that, she grew anxious; her stomach tightened, nausea and headaches followed. At those times, Glori sat at Haylee's bedside, enduring the scrutiny of her feline sentry, as she wondered, what the girl could have done to induce her stupor?

Minus the milky-white complexion and heavy makeup, Haylee looked like Sleeping Beauty. Eugene called it a 'temporary sickness,' assuring her that Haylee would snap out of it— eventually.

When Glori went into Haylee's room to check vitals, look under bandages, or feel the baby, Oscar's unblinking stare, his low, barely audible, rumble, when she approached, unnerved her.

The cat stayed, ever steadfast and persistent, at the girl's side. It wasn't only Haylee and Oscar who had Glori fretting. Eugene's acceptance of the circumstances worried her too. He'd told her that Josh had a similar condition. All those things were alarming; however, what bothered Glori most was Haylee's pregnancy.

The sight of that distended belly, the baby within, responding to the pressure of her touch, woke longings within Glori that she'd thought she'd dealt with, putting them away, like the words written in an adolescent diary.

At one time, Glori had wanted to be a mother, the nurturing qualities of her spirit sought to express themselves in caring for another, tiny, innocent, human being. But Glori had snuffed out that possibility before she understood what she had done.

Haylee's pregnancy rekindled Glori's desires. Her stepdaughter's state felt like a cruel, hard, slap in the face.

⁂

Glori was cranky and foul-tempered, made more so by her husband's smiles and encouragement. When she couldn't stand him or herself any longer, she exploded, "Eugene! You've been normalizing things that you shouldn't! Can't you see that you're making it worse?"

Sighing heavily, his shoulders drooped, "What do you want me to do, Sweetheart?"

"Tell me what you know about Haylee and her 'condition.'"

"Something's not right, Glori," he'd started out choosing his words one-by-one. "That night that we met you, then Haylee running away, was only one episode in a long string of events."

Eugene knelt in front of Glori, pressing both her hands between his, looking like he'd entered a confessional. "Haylee's not bad, or malicious," he entreated, "she's helped hundreds of families around here with animal issues. She doesn't have a mean bone in her, Glo."

Glori leaned back, regarding her husband. She felt, intuitively, that he was speaking the truth, as far as he knew it. But could she trust him? Was his judgment impaired? "And, yet, you're telling me that she attacked me, your *wife*. Not just me, but Josh too, that nice young man. What must his parents be going through, Eugene?"

"Don't you think I've been wondering the same things? Whatever was going on, it was a mistake. She would never have harmed you, or that boy if she'd been able to control it. Wherever she went to, she found a way to reverse it. Bringing you back is what put her in that deep sleep."

Glori leaned forward, squinting, assessing. "Eugene, were you, ever, afraid for yourself?"

The thought must have shaken him. He recoiled, "No..." He blinked, his skin lost color, "I never considered that."

"Do you think that she'll 'lose control' again?"

Swinging his head from side-to-side his voice was adamant, "No. That's over."

When Glori questioned him further, he refused to continue.

❧❧❧

The scope of Glori's situation didn't hit her, entirely, until Gene had taken her to Dr. Lester for a check-up. Dr. Lester had been Glori's supervising physician and friend. Her office was at the hospital where, up until Glori's illness, she had worked for over a decade.

A cheer went up as Glori came through the sliding doors. Staffers lined the hallway clapping and offering congratulations. Through the parade of well-wishers, Glori felt like an ostentatious float moving, haltingly, one hand tucked in Gene's elbow, the other counterbalancing a cane, down the central boulevard.

Glori shook her head, trying to appear gracious, unable to prevent or wipe away her tears. She remembered when she'd been the one gathering co-workers to publicly encourage patients, who'd spent many months in recovery, on their final walk through the corridors, reclaiming their place in life.

The hospital had been the hub of Glori's world for a long time. Each face she passed had memories associated with them. The smells, antiseptic, laundry soap, and hand cleaner, although familiar, no longer created feelings of homecoming.

Instead of feeling encouraged, Glori was ashamed. She hated looking fragile, hated, even more, feeling weak. She didn't like being on the receiving end of the attention.

⸙

After going through a battery of tests, Carlie smiled a rare smile. "Glori, I don't often get to say this, but everything checks out fine."

Gene breathed a sigh of relief, placing a warm hand on top of hers, giving it a gentle squeeze.

"I recommend another month of physical therapy..."

When Glori made a pinched face, the Dr. changed her statement. "Think of it as personal training Glo—if you feel up to it after the month is up, I'll sign off on your coming back to work."

Glori nodded, looking at Gene who smiled back.

"The tests did show one thing that we need to discuss...." The Dr. shuffled papers on her desk. Not looking up she delivered her news, "Glori is three months pregnant."

Confused, Glori frowned, "But I...."

Dr. Lester looked directly at Gene. Glori twisted in her chair to regard her husband. Her expression was surprised and confused.

Gene, flushed a deep shade of crimson, ".... pregnant you say?"

৯7৯
VOICES

GLORI STOPPED AT THE threshold of Haylee's room, tapping a painted fingernail on the door jamb. Her mouth compressed when her gaze locked with the flashing green-eyed stare of the cat. Oscar perched in the crook of Haylee's arm. He looked as stiff and unmovable as a fence post hardening in cement.

Since Gene would be at a growers' meeting all day, Glori planned to have Carlie stop by to examine her step-daughter.

Glori went over her notes. Haylee's blood pressure had remained within reasonable limits as had her respiration. Her pupils continued to suggest that she was in a deep dream state.

Haylee spoke in her sleep at times. Most patient ramblings, induced by high fevers or medications, were incoherent, disjointed. Haylee's utterances were not. Glori had written some of them down.

"Haylee's turned hot! I am taking her out to the trestle to do her up good."

"Every overly self-confident hero is an idiot."

"When I did it, the little shit squealed like a suckling pig."

"Pickins are easy and the hangman's noose is loose in these parts."

"Traveler's work in pairs. My daughter won't be a Traveler."

Glori shook her head. Would those statements be of interest to Carlie? Now that Glori had the opportunity to have Dr. Lester look Haylee over, Glori had concerns that the girls' ever-present, fur covered guardian would thwart her plans.

⁓⁓⁓⁓⁓

A low rumble, like a car idling, intruded upon the floating kaleidoscope of images in Haylee's dreams. A picture sentence popped hazy bubbles, replacing them with moments of clarity.

Warm, salty blood flooded her mouth as sharp teeth crunched through light-weight bones and fur. Loose soil, shifting under padded feet would make the perfect sized hole.

Haylee rocked her head from side to side, rejecting the noise and images.

"Purrr...."

"Purrr......"

"Purrr...."

Voices—female voices—intruded.

"I can't get that cat out of here—he hisses whenever I approach."

"Have you been monitoring her vitals?"

"For weeks, do you want to review them?"

The voices receded. Haylee, gratefully, sunk back into her comfortable oblivion.

Wetness around her legs was warm, strangely comforting, and slightly confusing.

"Purrr...."

"Purrr..."

"Purrr..."

Pictures of herself appeared in Haylee's mind—but from a perspective below her chin. She could see tail swishes in her peripheral vision. Haylee realized that she was laying on her bed. "Oscar?"

"Purrr..."

"Purrr..."

"Purrr..."

Her fingers sought out his furry silkiness. She cracked open an eye, "It is you." She smiled.

Oscar stood, rubbing against her. Haylee's free hand went to feel the side of her bulbous abdomen. The skin was tight. The entire surface and inner muscles contracted painfully.

"Arg!" Haylee came fully awake.

When the pain subsided, it gave her a chance to catch her breath. Haylee took stock of her surroundings. She remembered that she was home, her husband was dead, and that Glori was back.

Another wave of agony seized her in greedy clutches, clamping down in a vise that wouldn't release. "Owww...ahhhh!" Haylee blurted.

Her bedroom door burst open. Glori and her dad stood there looking surprised. "Haylee, you're awake," Glori stated.

She tried to smile, but it turned into a grimace.

"The baby's coming!" Haylee heard Glori say. "Gene, go get fresh towels and my medical bag."

❧

For fourteen hours, Haylee labored. In between contractions, she napped. Glori and Eugene sat on the floor, next to Haylee's bed, frazzled, fatigued and ill at ease.

"This is taking too long," Glori commented. "I'm not experienced enough to handle complications, Eugene. We have to get her to the hospital or at least call Carlie to see if she will come."

"No," Gene glanced over at his daughter, noting her sweat soaked hair, plastered in dark, root-like formations, framing her pale face and neck "I've helped in plenty of births, she's still got enough strength in her to keep going."

Glori reached out to press a hand along his thigh, "But, Darling, you can't compare a livestock birth to a human birth. We need monitors to see how that baby is faring. It could be in distress."

He looked worried, but still shook his head, 'no.'

"What are you so afraid of, Eugene?"

With eyebrows steepling near the bridge of his nose, he gazed at her, still shaking his head. "Loss of freedom, bureaucrats poking into our business, investigations— maybe it's underlying feelings of loyalty to Doris." He shrugged, then continued, "Haylee said that she's planning to fix Josh next. If we get stuck in something that holds us back, we might not get the chance to help the boy."

Haylee groaned. It grew in force and volume. Her face, splotchy and bunched, wrinkled and creased like a California raisin.

Glori and Eugene rose, hurrying back to their support positions. Glori checked the baby's position. Making eye contact with her husband, who was bracing his daughter's shoulders, Glori spoke up, "We need some hard pushing now." Gene nodded, solemn. He leaned close to Haylee's ear encouraging, "Come on Hay, Hay, it's time to get that little sucker out of there."

Haylee opened her eyes, rolling them toward her father. "Oi, it's skilamalink that I'm up to dick," she replied breathless, with a thick, accent; panting.

Eugene's head snapped in Glori's direction. He frowned. Glori signaled that she didn't know what that was about. With Haylee's next exclamation, Glori refocused her attention to the baby's portal; tissue strained and resisted the sizable obstruction.

"The bog-jumper who put this thing in me is as black as the ace of spades, Da." Haylee said in her next breath. "I wish he was here, so I could rip out his hairy balls!" She doubled up, letting out a primal scream.

Their ears were still ringing when, with a pop and a gush, Eugene's granddaughter slipped into Glori's waiting hands. "Haylee, you did it!" Glori laughed, "We all did it! We have a little girl."

A tiny cry backed by powerful lungs filled the room. Cutting and clamping the umbilical cord, Glori gently wiped blood away; she was careful to leave the vernix in place. Securely wrapping the baby, she handed the bundle off to Eugene. As she listened to father and daughter cooing over the newest bud on the family tree, Glori smiled. She quietly and efficiently delivering the placenta, then tidied up.

When it was all over, and there was nothing left for her to do, Glori let her emotions loose. Standing witness at the powerful, life-affirming event, had moved her. Tears streamed down her face. Pressing a hand over her, slightly rounded abdomen, she imagined going through this to deliver her child.

Holding her daughter, noting features resembling each parent, Haylee wished that Reece was here. *Bittersweet,* Haylee thought, *my heart is overflowing with love for this little person and breaking for missing her father!*

❧8❧
BELIEF

THREE WEEKS AFTER SERENA was born, Haylee and
Glori sat next to each other on the living room couch. Glori
cradled Serena's head, supporting her body along the tops
of her thighs. They both regarded the little girl.

"Thank you for being there for me, Glori." Haylee
leaned on her step-mother's shoulder, rubbing the side of
her arm. "—Especially after everything—"

Glori stilled, looking over at Haylee. "I meant to ask
you about that."

Haylee nodded. She reached out, brushing a finger
over the baby's delicate dark hair. Distracted, she
commented," Serena looks so much like her father. He
named her after his grandmother."

"Your dad said that you traveled back in time...and
that's where the baby's father is?" Glori sounded doubtful.

Haylee's eyes had grown glassy. She leaned over,
lifting the babe into her arms. "It happened. And, yes, that
is where Serena's father is." Haylee stood up, holding
Serena against her, patting the small back. "I miss him!"
Her voice was hoarse, "I still can't believe that I won't ever
see him again."

Glori leaned her elbows on her knees, resting her chin in her hands. Her eyes followed Haylee's path as she paced. "I'd like to try to understand."

Haylee paused, checking to see if Serena was asleep. Going into the other room to put her in the bassinet, Haylee kissed the girl's forehead. "I love you," she whispered.

Glori followed. She smiled saying quietly, "She is a darling."

Both women returned to the living room. "Where do you want me to start?" Haylee asked.

"How about with the last thing I remember—your and Josh's visit."

"Ok. Do you remember surprising me in my room?"

Glori's brow furrowed. She shook her head, "No. I remember coming home from the grocery store.... but nothing after that."

Haylee inhaled, "Well, thank goodness for that!" She sounded relieved.

"What do you mean?"

"Glori, this is hard! .... I had a problem...A big problem at school. I tried to keep you, dad, and Josh safe—but I couldn't."

"Tell me about the problem."

Before Dad and I met you, I was getting sick a lot. Then I was eating everything I could. That night I took off from the hospital was because I couldn't get enough to eat without people becoming suspicious."

"You scared your dad half to death when we couldn't find you."

Nodding, "I know," Haylee said. "That was the night that something weird happened with my hands. "Do you promise not to look at me funny when I tell you?"

"I'll try..."

"Webbing.... I had webbing between my fingers. But it could come and go."

"Show me."

"I can't'; they aren't there now. When I had the webs, I used them to steal; souls. That's what I did to you, Glori."

Glori stood up abruptly. Walking in tight circles, she reached up to massage her neck. "Let's say, for argument, that these webs were there— "

"They were! Dad saw them. Ask him."

"I will! But let's stick to the topic. When you had the webs, how did you use them to....do what you did?"

"Well..." Haylee hesitated, "by the time the webs came out, I was more animal than human. Hungry; with a need to attack."

Goosebumps pulled the skin tight across Glori's arms. She took a step away.

Haylee followed, gritting her teeth as she spit out the next words. "I'd jump on them, take them down." Her voice was hard, clipped. "I was powerful, invincible. I held them down. It was effortless, as easy as pressing a sharp pin through a squirming bug."

Glori continued moving away until the back of her legs met furniture. Her eyes were wide; sweat varnished her upper lip.

Stopping within inches of Glori, Haylee flipped a hand back, stretching her fingers wide. She swung her arm toward Glori's face, stopping millimeters from her nose. Haylee froze, breathing hard.

They blinked at one another, both surprised, troubled, and unsettled.

Glori did not have direct memories of this, but her body responded as if it did. Freezing adrenaline flooded through her, the hair on her arms stood at attention. Her heart felt like a caged bird, crazed for freedom.

"Back off!" Glori shouted, pushing Haylee away.

Haylee stumbled. "I'm sorry, Glori! I didn't mean to do that!" She looked stricken.

Shaken, Glori responded, "You keep saying that."

"You're right..." Haylee sounded sarcastic. She stepped farther away, shoving her hands into her pockets.

As if to clear jumbled thoughts, Glori stomped around the room. She paused to stare directly at Haylee before biting out, "Finish."

"Finish what?"

"Finish what you were saying." Glori's tone was grim. She pointed at Haylee, warning, "But you stay on that side of the room."

Haylee nodded. She continued quietly, "The webs cover the mouth and nose. On contact, they attach, all breath is cut off. Then something happens—I don't know what— energy pours into me. I feel it coming in; it fills me, makes me stronger...and then, I..." she stammered, "I know what they are thinking...."

Glori felt glued to the floor. Her spine elongated; she stood up to her full height, "Thought transference?"

Haylee met Glori's gaze. She opened her mouth, as if she were about to respond, then turned toward her room. "I hear Serena. I need to go."

Alone, Glori resumed pacing. She mumbled under her breath. "This makes no sense. I've studied biology and physiology. It doesn't jive."

Haylee returned with Serena bundled in her arms. The sight of that innocent little girl melted Glori's agitation.

"You don't believe me," Haylee stated.

"It's not that...."

"Yes, it is." Haylee continued, "I *know* how it sounds Glori. Believe me, living it is worse than describing it. I can prove it."

"How can you...?"

A silent, heavy pause filled the space between them.

"If I concentrate, I can remember when your thoughts were mine. I'll go find something about you that no one knows...if you want me to."

Glori was confident that what Haylee said was impossible, but a small part of her was curious. She pushed her hands through her hair as she considered it. Resolutely Glori turned, "It's the only way to know for sure."

"OK. Can you take Serena?"

The baby changed hands. Haylee walked over to the couch to sit. "I usually work hard to keep these away.... the thoughts that don't belong to me. It will take a few minutes to sort out which ones are yours."

Those words crawled down Glori's spine with icy feet. She held Serena a little closer while she waited. Glori jumped when Haylee, finally, cleared her throat. The misery in the girl's expression communicated the severity of what she was about to say.

"Glori—?"

"It's the only way."

Haylee nodded, "You didn't tell the truth when you gave me the talk about the birds and the bees." Haylee's swallow was audible. "*Before* you met the boyfriend, Stephan..."

Glori's eyebrows shot up.

Haylee continued, "You were upset about your brother's death. You started hanging out with jocks—taking drugs and partying. You found out that you were pregnant and that you had chlamydia on the same day."

Blinking rapidly, Glori gave a short nod.

"You had an abortion, paying for it yourself. You never told anyone."

Glori turned to stare out the window. Her face didn't register emotion, but her tears flowed freely. Her hold on the baby tightened, causing Serena to squawk. Jiggling her and relaxing, Glori soothed the little one.

Haylee finished, "You've never forgiven yourself. You figured that not being able to get pregnant again was your punishment for aborting that other baby."

Haylee rose quietly. She went to Glori, gently taking Serena, she used her free hand to wipe away Glori's tears. "I'm so sorry, Glori."

The red-head nodded, scrubbing her face.

"You know that's stupid, don't you?"

Laughing through her tears, Glori remarked, "When you say it like that, it sounds stupid."

"So, this baby is a real surprise—huh?" Haylee asked.

Glori's hands reached down to where her miracle lived. She nodded. Glori looked back at Haylee, "I believe you."

Haylee nodded.

❧9❧
JOSH'S FATHER

Two and a half months later.

THERE WAS A GLOOMY, tired, silence in the cramped VW Bug when Eugene parked in an open spot at Denny's restaurant. Checking his watch, "We're about forty minutes early. Do you want to go inside and get a table, or stretch our legs?"

Glori sighed, scratching her scalp, "I have an immediate need to visit the little girl's room." She glanced in the back, "Serena's still asleep? Do you want to come with me, Haylee?"

"I'm OK; I want to talk to Dad for a few minutes."

"Thanks for driving that last stretch, Hon, that was a long one." Glori leaned over, lips puckered.

"No problem," Eugene responded, shifting toward her, making contact.

"I've got to stand for a while," Haylee said. "If we roll down the windows and stay near, Serena will be alright."

Leaning on the hood of the Bug, Haylee noticed her dad's look of concern, "What are you thinking?"

"I'm thinking Jason is going to have a lot of questions."

"....and?" Haylee prompted.

"Unless we satisfy his curiosity, he's not going to let us get anywhere near Josh."

"But we have Glori. You said that he saw her in the hospital. That the two of you talked and shared notes about her and Josh."

"That's right."

"So, how could he refuse?"

"I don't know Hay... It's just a worry." Crossing his arms, he shifted into a wide stance. Gene looked down at the pavement. "I'm going to tell Jason that unless he agrees to leave us completely alone with Josh—we're going to go home."

"What?" Haylee squawked. "I'm not going anywhere unless Josh is back to how he is supposed to be!"

Gene held up his hands. "I agree, we won't. I've thought about this. As soon as you've finished with the crystal, we must get you out of there without being seen. I've booked us a hotel room where we will stay until you can make the trip home."

"Oh...I've been so focused on getting to Josh, that I haven't put any thought into that."

Glori approached, "I told them that we'd need a table. Shall we go inside? You two can fill me in on your plan on the way."

⸞⸞⸞⸞

Gene stood when he saw the tall man wearing glasses come through the door.

Haylee turned to catch her first glimpse of Josh's father. He wore a light blue polo shirt and white slacks. Taller than his son, he had a paunch around his middle, salt, and pepper hair with bare scalp peeking through.

"Eugene!" Jason Herkowitz exclaimed, "You can't imagine how overjoyed I was to hear your news!"

Pumping hands vigorously, Gene patted him on the back. "It's good to see you again, Jason. How've you been?"

Jason's smile faded, "Nothing's changed." Melancholy filled the spaces between his words, the corners of his mouth drooped. "Right now, I want to see your lovely wife."

Jason turned his attention to Glori, "Mrs. Garrett, I must say that to behold you sitting there so bright, healthy, and beautiful is a wonder!"

Glori leaned over the table, extending a hand. "You are a charmer Mr. Herkowitz, I can't think of a single thing to say in response," she said, blushing.

"Please call me Jason."

"Only if you will return the favor by calling me, Glori."

"I'd be honored." Jason inclined his head.

Resting a hand on the other man's shoulder, Gene jumped in, "Jason, I'd like to introduce my daughter, Haylee, and my granddaughter, Serena."

Looking confused, the other man turned back to Gene, "Your daughter....? But I thought that she....?"

Haylee scooched off the bench seat to stand.

All the color drained from Jason's face. He stumbled back, his mouth, opening, and closing, like a fish attempting to breathe air.

Eugene reached out to steady him, "Hey! Hey! Pal, are you alright?"

Glori quickly got up, "Jason! Can you breathe?"

The man, nodded in the affirmative, all the while his eyes remained glued on the baby.

"Are you having pain in your jaw or arms?" Glori queried. At Jason's shake of his head, she continued, "I want you to focus on breathing normally. Take deep breaths with me...:" Glori pulled her shoulders up as she inhaled, "And then let it out..."

A waitress hurried over. "Is everything alright? Do I need to call 911?"

Gene looked to Glori with the question. She shook her head.

"I think he's having a stress reaction," she said in low tones.

"How about some coffee and water?" Gene asked the girl.

Following Glori in the breathing exercises, color returned to Jason's face.

"Shall we sit?" Gene asked. As Glori got Jason seated, Eugene turned around to make eye contact with the worried customers who'd been staring. 'He's alright,' Gene mouthed, nodding to them.

Water arrived at the table as they settled in their seats. With an unsteady hand, Jason reached for his water glass. Taking several gulps, he looked directly at Haylee, saying, "My apologies, but I must ask if my son is the father of that child?"

It was Haylee's turn to look like a deer, frozen in place, gawking into bright headlights. Shaking her head, "No sir. Josh isn't the father." Her cheeks bloomed bright; she focused on adjusting blankets around Serena.

"Oh dear, I've made a fool of myself. It's just that the last time Josh was OK; he was staying at your house...and now you have a child that appears to be about the right age." Jason's neck flushed, he ran a finger around his collar.

After coffee was topped off, menus were handed out, giving the group a chance to recover from the excitement. Ting...ting...ting... The sound of spoons blending ingredients in mugs seemed loud to Haylee.

"We didn't come all this way to put you into coronary arrest," Gene apologized.

Nervous laughter echoed around the table. "We came because we think we might have found a way to bring Josh out of his coma," Glori stated.

This time, Jason drew in a long, very slow breath that expanded his chest. "Surely, you would not say such a thing in jest?" he asked.

Haylee saw his eyes widen slightly. She watched his hands clench into tight fists before he moved them under the table.

"I would not," Eugene said. "If I weren't certain that we could deliver, we wouldn't have come." He met Glori's eyes. "By the time we leave, you'll have your son back, Jason."

Blinking rapidly, Josh's father pushed his glasses up on the bridge of his nose. He looked back and forth between Gene and Glori, "Seeing Glori like this, I don't doubt it, but I have to ask how it's possible? Every doctor we've been to has given us zero results."

Glori, compressing her mouth, nodded, "Gene went through the same thing. The solution to the problem doesn't have anything to do with doctors."

Through the conversation, Haylee watched Jason's eyes grow red. He sniffed, wiping his nose on the back of his hand. Finally, he pulled out a handkerchief, blowing.

Jason rested his chin on a fisted hand, "Then, how....?"

"Honestly, we don't know how it works," Gene responded, "but Haylee found something— while she was away— that did the trick."

All eyes moved to Haylee. She nodded. "I can't answer how it works either. I'll need a couple of hours alone with Josh. Once we're gone, the family can help him begin his recovery." She hesitated, swiping at moisture that had collected in her eyes, "I just wanted to say how sorry I am..."

In her peripheral vision, Haylee saw her dad's body tense. "...that this tragedy struck our families."

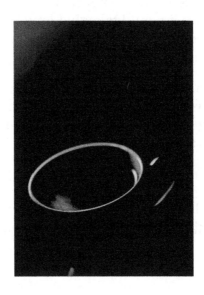

❧10❧
JOSH'S THOUGHTS

HAYLEE WALKED AROUND THE room taking it in as the grandfather clock chimed three.

This home was so different from her rustic, country style house. Antiques arranged into cozy groupings filled the large living room. Books lined the entire back wall. Haylee felt like an intruder.

She'd asked Mr. Herkowitz for two hours with Josh. It wasn't because it would take that long to revive him—that part would only take about twenty minutes. It was because she needed time to get ready to let Josh go.

The thoughts and memories she absorbed with each of her victims took focused work to keep quiet. If she wasn't careful, they could overwhelm her and make her feel as if she was about to implode.

Josh was different. His thoughts were the only ones she wanted to hear. As a Psychology graduate student and as her logical, quick-minded best friend, his sensibilities were grounding. They kept her steady when she felt defeated.

He tailed her that night on her most excessive hunting excursion. She'd dressed in a black leather jacket and skirt. Wearing high heels, she roamed the streets with an insatiable appetite. She'd been aware that he had been following her; she could smell him; she tasted the sourness of his fear. Had her victims not been so plentiful, he'd have been in severe jeopardy. She allowed Josh to believe that his presence remained unknown.

He'd watched her play coquette, luring men into her personal space, enticing them with provocative words and body postures. Once she had them where she wanted them, she'd thrust her arms back. The gossamer webbing that appeared didn't look frightening—until it clamped over the nose and mouth of her victims. Josh had seen her arch with pleasure as the person beneath her thrashed with a desperate need to fill burning lungs.

He'd been horrified and sickened by her actions—yet he remained by her side. He believed her when she told him she was trying to find a way to stop; he bravely joined her on a trip home to search through her mother's things.

Haylee wandered over to the fireplace mantle. Framed family photos lined up like train cars. Josh's younger brother, Spencer, and their mother shared many similarities. Haylee smiled, running a finger along the base of a photo of Josh at age seven or eight, grinning widely, with missing front teeth.

She knew that he lay just a few doors down the hallway. Glori would be sitting by his side. The urge to go to him was strong—but not yet. Haylee walked to the window. She pulled aside the sheer curtain. A sparkling blue pool filled a large, neatly manicured yard. Off to the side, her dad held Serena. He handed her leaves that she mangled, dropped, or stuffed in her mouth.

Haylee wandered into the kitchen. Opening a cupboard, she stared at the rows of neatly stacked bowls. *I wonder which is Josh's favorite cereal bowl?* She could have retrieved the answer if she'd wanted to—but not yet.

On the day that she'd attacked him, she learned about his deeper feelings. Once Josh's body grew still under her hand, his thoughts flooded her mind like water, seeping into the crevices of a sponge, until it was saturated. He felt fresh and clean.

During the first night he'd spent at her home in Elverta, he shamefully admitted to himself that he was in love with her. These feelings caused hours of self-debate. He didn't understand how they could exist at all—especially after having witnessed her revolting actions.

Sipping on warm tap water, Haylee called Josh's memories forth. *Never accept what appears to be obvious. Question everything, then ask more questions. Two brains are always better than one.*

Even after she'd found Reece, a man who turned her bones to liquid fire, the father of her child, there was always Josh. Caustic comments or remarks he would have made about a variety of topics would make her smile. The pull to return to restore him always remained persistent. He was her best friend. He needed her. Now, finally, here she was.

Settling herself for the task, Haylee walked with heavy steps to Josh's room. As soon as she reached the threshold, a wave of familiarity overcame her. She knew every crack and cranny of this space. Blocking out all those sensations, her eyes darted to the still form lying in the center of the bed, she glanced at Glori, then back to Josh. The bed was new. Rails on both sides kept him from falling out. Haylee also noticed a wheelchair parked in a far corner.

Her heart was lodged high in her throat as she approached. His glasses, so much a part of him, were nowhere to be seen. Josh's mop of unruly curls was cropped close. The angles of his face looked sharp. His hands and forearms were thin.

"Glori, I need a few minutes alone with him before I start. Could you step out? I'll call you when I'm ready."

"Are you OK, Haylee?"

"Fine...everything will be fine," she answered woodenly

Once Glori was gone, Haylee sat in the place she vacated. The seat was still warm. She pulled one of Josh's hands into her own, bringing it up to rest against her cheek. She turned her face into his palm. "You loved and trusted me, Josh. I betrayed you. You'd never believe where I have been. I'm sorry that it took me so long to get back." Haylee ran gentle fingertips across his forehead. She leaned over placing a kiss at the corner of his mouth.

She got up, then, to make a circuit around the room. Opening her mind to him, she regarded his mementos and special objects. Touching the base of a swimming trophy, *That was a good meet. Those guys from the Stockton team were fierce competitors.*

Haylee felt his glow of pride over having won that championship. Wandering over to his bookshelves, she picked out some of his favorite titles. Lifting a hand, hesitating with uncertainty, she raised up on tiptoes, reaching out to her right. Pulling down a thick hardcover volume of Gulliver's Travels, Haylee hefted it in her hands. It felt lighter than it ought to. She smiled. Haylee opened the cover to reveal a square hole in the middle of the inner pages. A secret hiding place Josh had carved out with a pocket knife when he was twelve.

Fortune cookie fortunes, bottle tops, and friendship bracelets filled the cavity. Haylee stirred them around. A stone-like piece of chewed gum caught her eye. "Ha!" Haylee huffed. She picked it up, *A reminder to not let hormones overrule critical thinking...*his words echoed in her mind.

Dropping the gum, Haylee dug in her pocket, fishing out a folded piece of paper. "I hope that by the time you find this, you don't hate me too much." Dropping it in with the other items, she closed the book, returning it to its spot on the shelf.

Haylee was already feeling the sting of loss. "I hate those minds crowded inside," she whispered. "I work so hard to keep them silent. If I drop my guard or get stressed, the walls crumble, then they trample me, like crowds of desperate people running to escape a fire." She reached up to wipe away a single tear. "You wouldn't believe how difficult it is to stuff them back inside once they've gotten out," she laughed, harshly. "But your thoughts were not like that, Josh. Instead of hounding me, yours were soothing. They wrapped me in a warm blanket from home, encouraging me to ask questions, to learn more. It sounds ridiculous to say that I will miss you—but I will."

Haylee called to Glori, "I'm ready."

ꙮ11ꙮ
HE'S AWAKE

"MY BOY! MY BOY!" the sobbing repeated.

What the hell? Josh wondered. Cracking an eye open, a stabbing pain shot through his head. Frowning, he clamped it shut, attempting to turn away.

"Oh! He moved, Jason—did you see that?"

"I did, Frances, it's just like they said."

"They....?

"Never mind. Look! He moved again. Josh, son, can you hear me?"

I hear you, Dad, why is everyone so agitated? Josh thought. "Uh..." he groaned. *Where's my voice?*

"Oh, my goodness, Jason! Did you hear that? He made a sound."

"Shhhh....shhhh....shhhh," Josh said while raising a single finger.

"He can hear us!" his mother screeched, "Jason, he's responding!"

"He is— but look at him. We might need to tone down our excitement. He's been out for such a long time; this might be too much activity."

Out? What does that mean? Josh tried opening his eyes again.

"Oh look!" his mom whispered loudly. 'He's reacting to the light. Jason, go close the curtains."

"Duh…" Josh croaked when he meant to say, *Dad, what did you mean when you said that I'd been out?*

Josh felt his mother stroking the side of his face. "Oh Honey, my sweet, sweet boy. Keep working to get back to us, Joshua."

Farther away, Josh heard his dad. "I think we better let him rest."

"I'll call Dr. Rose to tell him the wonderful news. He'll want to come over to have a look. I must call Spencer too. He'll want to come home as soon as he hears."

Josh dropped into an exhausted sleep.

Two days later.

When he woke up the next time, Josh could open his eyes. He could see the light fixture on the ceiling. It was blurry, but he knew what it was. Turning his head, he could see things on the nightstand. *A box of latex gloves?* Next, he noticed the silver railing along the side of the bed. *What the?*

When Josh tried to lift a hand to reach for it, he discovered that it felt like it weighed thirty pounds. Anxiety began working its way through him. He wanted to call for help, but his voice wasn't there. Feeling his heart race, Josh realized that he was on the verge of a panic attack.

It helped to close his eyes. *Blocking out the visual stimulus affects my physical stress responses.* Testing his voice again, only garbled whispers came out. Josh tried wiggling his toes. Those checked out. He could move his fingers. With his tongue, he probed inside his mouth. *All my teeth are there.* The rest of him was as inert and unfeeling as a sack of cement.

What is going on? His breathing quickened. He reminded himself, *stay calm. Adrenalin subverts clear analysis. Piece it out. What do I know? I can blink and breathe; there are micro-movements in my extremities. My mind seems to be intact.*

Resuming his efforts to move an arm, Josh unintentionally hit the call button. The repeating bell tone was annoying. He wished he could figure out how to turn it off. Eventually, he heard footsteps.

"Oh, my goodness, Joshie!" commented his mother, "I'm sorry that it took me so long to come—I didn't realize what the buzzing was for. "She paused, staring down at him, wearing a goofy grin.

"It gives me chills every time I see you looking back at me. It's the best gift a mother could receive. How are you feeling? Can I get you something? Are you thirsty? Hungry? Do want light in the room?"

Josh wanted to respond, he wanted to tell her to give him a chance to answer, but she kept talking like she didn't expect one.

"Wa...water," he finally got out.

"What?" She seemed startled to hear his voice. "Oh! You're thirsty?"

He nodded. "Real thirsty," his voice sounded like his throat was clogged with gravel.

"Of course!" Frances replied as she went to fetch it. She returned shortly holding a tall glass of water with an orange straw. "Let me raise the back of your bed, so you'll be more comfortable."

He nodded. He wanted to see more clearly. "Glasses?"

At first, she looked perplexed, then, "You want your glasses?"

He nodded. Holding the water up so he could sip, she replied, "It's been so long since you wore them. I don't know where they are. Are you done?" she asked when he stopped.

"They've got to be around here somewhere." Frances began pulling out drawers, rummaging through their contents.

How could she lose track of my glasses? I never go anywhere without them.

A cold, sinking feeling began in the pit of his stomach. It spread, gripping his mind. *Was I in a car crash? It would explain the hospital bed, why I can't move or talk.*

What is the last thing I remember? The blankness frightened him. Frenzied, he searched his mind, grasping for strands of certainty. His childhood, this room, his parents, and his brother; those connections seemed intact. College, swimming, friends at school, his apartment; that was there too.

"Ah Ha! There they are!" he heard his mother say. She unfolded the black frames as she approached. Placing them on his face, she leaned back, "That's better. You're starting to look like your old self again."

Now that Josh could see clearly, his alarm levels raised another notch. *What happened to her hair? It was brown. Now it's gray. She's lost at least twenty pounds. He'd never thought of his mom as old before, but now, she looked like his grandmother. She said that I don't look like my old self. Am I mangled, disfigured?*

Frances studied him closely. "Josh, are you feeling alright? You're sweating."

He moved his head from side to side, his eyes darting at her, then away. He was blinking rapidly.

Grasping his hand tightly, "Josh, do I need to call 911?"

'No,' he looked at her, his eyes wide with alarm, "Tell me—" he croaked, *what happened.*

Frances plopped down in the chair. She had a medium, athletic build. A lifetime of outdoor activities kept the extra pounds off her midsection that many of her peers carried. But she looked drained, unanimated, not like herself at all. Frown lines etched around her mouth; she fiddled with her wedding ring.

When he thought he couldn't stand waiting any longer, she raised her gaze to meet his. Her eyes were over-bright but direct, "The doctor's instructions are to go slow in every aspect of your recovery, including new information. All I am going to say right now is that you have been very, very sick. But you are on the mend now, and I know that you are going to make a full recovery."

Josh shook his head, "Not acceptable."

"You're still my same Josh." A sad smile played about her lips, causing the frown lines to deepen. "Dr. Rose said that recovering patients sometimes have personality shifts."

"Mother...."

"I'm sorry, Honey. I know you must have many questions. I promise that once the doctors give the 'OK' we'll tell you everything we know."

Frances got up, beginning to pull clothes out of his drawers, laying them at the end of his bed. "I can't tell you what a relief it was to give up your spot at Sunnyside. I made a point to say goodbye to everyone who told me that my belief in your recovery was a waste of time."

Josh grew frustrated at her endless prattle and his own inability to respond.

"Canceling your maintenance care appointments was sheer delight. We have you scheduled for a full battery of physical and cognitive therapy sessions in the next few days— I'll be back in a few minutes, sit tight dear."

Josh wondered what she was doing.

She walked back in, carrying a large bowl of steaming water, a towel draped over her shoulder. Smiling, she set the bowl down on the chair she'd sat in earlier. "It's bath day," she stated. She froze as a new thought occurred to her. Her eyes grew wide, meeting Josh's equally broad stare.

He pulled his blankets up to his chin; his cheeks flushed.

"Oh.... Josh.... uh.... I'm sorry. I'm so used to the routine. I didn't stop to think. Oh, baby, I'm sorry!"

Frances hurried out, calling down the hallway, "Jason! I need some help in here!"

⁂12⁂
THRONE OF OCEANUS

IN ANCIENT GREEK MYTHOLOGY, Oceanus, a Titan, is an ocean-stream, located at the Equator, that continually flows around the world. To the east, the sun rises from it; at the west, the sun returns to it.

Spencer sat in the chair next to the bed. Josh had begun to think of it as the Throne of Oceanus. Everyone who sat there had an endless amount of knowledge that he wanted.

His parents blockaded him from the facts surrounding his condition. Josh understood that they meant to protect him, but that didn't stop him from feeling frustrated.

That he was *still* unable to speak as quickly, and as fluently as his thoughts gave people the impression that he wasn't capable of comprehension. When he'd been able to articulate questions, every visiting therapist and physician had refused to elaborate. As his body grew stronger, Josh's mind grew restless.

I'm a grown man. They treat me like I'm a twelve-year-old invalid!

"Dude, I can't believe that I'm having a conversation with you," Spencer said enthusiastically.

Josh eyed him without uttering a sound.

"Even if we aren't conversing, it's still pretty cool, seeing you giving me the stink eye."

Josh grinned. Over the weeks, the brown stubble on his face had filled in, covering his chin and jaw with thick straight hair. He refused to let either his parents or the visiting nurse groom it. "Spence, the folks... *are staying pretty tight-lipped about my situation*....won't talk about it." As usual, the words weren't keeping pace. "I need...*some explanations*...to know...*before I go flipping crazy!*"

Spencer grimaced, worried. He got up to glance both ways down the hall before returning. "They said that we aren't supposed to talk about it because you are psychologically fragile."

Josh snorted. He turned to look out his window while shaking his head in disgust. "What do they think will happen?" he was slightly surprised, and more than a little pleased that all his words came out.

"I get it...but, Josh, what if they're right? Taking it slow is probably a good idea."

Raising a hand, Josh pressed the muscle at his eyebrow that had begun to twitch. Spencer was his best bet to get information. But he knew from experience that if he pushed too hard, Spencer would clam up.

When they were little, Spencer was clueless about his looks. Curly blond hair framed skin that bronzed at the first hints of the sun in the summer. In his teenage years, Spencer's jaw and neck widened, his voice deepened, his muscles developed burly contours that never ceased to impress members of the opposite sex, heck, members of the same sex too.

Josh realized, early on, that his little brother would garner attention solely from his classic physique. He loved him but resented the ease with which life's pleasures came to him. To compensate, Josh had developed and honed his mind. He'd chosen swimming as a sport because Spencer played baseball and football.

Josh had gotten in the habit of ridiculing his brother whenever he did something stupid, which was frequent. They were comfortable in those roles, but now Josh wondered if he'd been selling Spencer short.

Josh stared long and hard into his brother's eyes willing him to understand fully. "You know how I am. Currently...my words are halting, slow. But my mind is there." He held out a hand for Spencer to clasp. "It's all still there, man."

The pressure of their grip and their eye contact shifted something between them. "Do you agree, that it's best to keep me in the dark?" Josh asked.

Spencer's expression looked pained. He got up to recheck the corridor. "Oh man—what do you want to know?"

Yes! I knew that I could count on you! Josh held the signs of his triumph inside. He composed the first question that had been uppermost in his mind. "Was I in an accident?"

Spencer leaned his elbows on his knees, whispering, "No...but you've been in a coma."

Josh nodded. "How long?" Swallowing hard, he tried again. "I don't know...When it is...now. How long?"

Spencer leaned back against the seat. With an arm crossing his chest, the other elbow resting on it, he pressed a hand to his mouth. Indecision was written plainly on his face. He shook his head, beginning to look worried. "Maybe we shouldn't do this, Joshie. The professionals could be right about it being a shock."

Josh could tell that he needed to salvage the situation, "Please, Spence," he begged. "I can.... handle it."

Nodding slowly, Spencer grabbed hold of the bed rails. Leaning close, he whispered, "You're not going to like the answer."

Josh squeezed his eyes shut, willing Spencer to continue, "Need... to know. Have...to know."

"OK," he sighed heavily, "It's been fifteen months."

Josh's eyes flew open; he met his brother's gaze. They regarded each other soberly, in silence, as seconds turned to minutes.

Spencer, gripping the rail with white knuckles, studied his brother carefully.

Josh stared at the ceiling, eyes glazed, blinking slowly, the edges of his eyes grew red.

"What are you thinking?" Spencer asked, his voice shaking.

Josh's face had grown hard, horizontal wrinkle lines raised on his forehead, "I'll tell you what I'm thinking, FUCK!" Grasping and squeezing his blankets, Josh's fists were hard, tight, compressions of bone, tendon, and muscle. He shook his head as if trying to clear muddled thoughts. "How did it happen?"

"No one knows. They got a call from Sacramento. When the folks arrived, you were already gone. They had you transported back here."

Sacramento? "Why was I there?"

"Mom is convinced that something happened at the Garrett house. The wife of the guy who called us also came down with the same thing."

A look of terror came over Josh's face; it drained of all color. Spencer's reference to Glori Garrett started a crack. It fractured, sending runners in every direction, breaking apart the wall of blankness, crumbling, it disintegrated. In the choking dust plume, every memory returned at once.

Haylee, a new student at school; he'd been drawn to her– powerfully. Her aloofness and defensiveness only made it worse; she was like a Dr. Doolittle with animals; he'd fallen hopelessly, unreasonably in love with her. He'd stalked her, and while doing so, he'd discovered her terrible secret. Her behavior revolted him, but he'd tried to help; then she...then she...

Josh was having trouble breathing. Sucking in great gulps, wheezing, struggling to free himself from the restrictive blankets.

"Oh, shit! Josh!" Spencer reached for him.

All Josh could see were hands, big hands, coming at him, "Get away!" he screamed, "don't touch me!" His arms flailed, his legs kicked.

⁓

Worried that Josh would hurt himself, Spencer lowered the rail. Holding out his hands, he tracked the movements of his brother's swinging arms, making sure his timing would be right.

Spencer's motions seemed to push Josh over the edge; his screams went higher in pitch, his movements were wild, erratic.

Spencer wondered where his parents could be but couldn't stop to find out. Reaching out in a quick gesture, snatching Josh's wrists, he climbed on top of him, using his body to restrain his brother.

Bucking, Josh cried.

It ripped a gouge in Spencer's heart, seeing his big brother, so out of control.

"I can't breathe, I can't breathe," Josh repeated.

Keeping his voice even and calm, Spencer countered each repetition with, "Yes, you can." When Josh quieted, Spencer, remained in place. He asked, "Josh?"

"Spencer."

"You know that you're still breathing?"

"Yes, you can get off me now."

"You sure you're alright?"

"Get off!"

Slowly, Spencer loosened his hold, pushing up, he looked down at Josh.

With eyes still red and leaking, Josh met his brother's gaze. "Thanks, buddy," he said sounding self-conscious, "sorry you had to see that."

Shifting his weight, Spencer climbed back down over the side of the bed. He watched Josh, glancing at the door.

"If Mom and Dad, somehow, missed that, I'd be grateful if we kept it between us."

"What the hell was it?" Spencer ran a hand through his hair, also looking over his shoulder, thinking about their parents.

"I remembered something, something that happened right before my 'accident.'"

"Are you going to tell me? What happened to you, Josh?"

Covering his face with both hands, Josh shook his head, "No, but I can assure you that it's not going to happen again."

After Spencer had left, he realized that he didn't know what Josh had meant. What wasn't going to happen again? His 'accident' or his flip out?

♣13♣
SYMPATHETIC DAD

Five months later.

JOSH SAT IN THE front seat of his dad's car as they drove to the Anaheim Aquatic Center. He stared out at the city buildings, the bald hills, the grayish cloud of smog that perpetually hung over the city.

Today was different because it was his first day using a cane instead of a walker. Progress—not as fast as he would like, but progress none-the-less. As his strength returned, his relationship with his mother grew increasingly strained. His father had started filling in for services that his mother previously performed. He liked spending time with his dad. They'd even resumed their ongoing chess game. This was a multi-month activity that they'd been working on... before his life-altering encounter with Haylee.

Josh had been alone at the house that day—another first— when he shuffle-walked, with his trusty metal stability system, into his father's study in search of a book. His eyes landed on and held at the side table where the chess game remained. The knights, rooks, pawns, and royalty looked petrified, covered with layers of dust. Memories of their times together playing suffused him.

His dad hadn't touched it. Josh sat in the chair on his side of the board staring at the black and white terrain. All his frustration, helplessness, anger over what his parents had been through rose to the surface. During his emotional storm, he momentarily thought about swiping all the pieces off the board. Instead, he waited until he was calm again, then found a dust rag.

Returning to the present, Josh dug around in his backpack. Bringing out his notebook, he asked, "Dad will you tell me again about your last interactions with the Garretts'?"

Jason gave his son a pleading glance, "We've already been over this. What do you hope to gain by repeating it?"

"I'm correlating the information you've given me with my own experiences with them. It's helping me remember."

Nodding, Jason commented, "You've always been tenacious about problem-solving. When you were a boy, I used to imagine that you'd become a detective."

Josh smiled, "A psychology major isn't that far off." He raised his eyebrows, holding up his pen expectantly.

His father complied, "Since your illness, I'd been keeping in contact with Gene. His wife, Glori, came down with a condition identical to yours. We visited them when we went to Sacramento to get you. Another doctor approached us there too, a really tall guy. He said he had a patient— a young male— who'd presented similar symptoms the year before. He was investigating causal relationships between that and the environment. He gave me his card. I never heard back from him, and, frankly, we were too busy arranging your care, to follow-up."

"I'll take that card if you still have it," Josh said.

"Sure," Jason replied, offhandedly. He continued his narrative, "Eight months ago; I received a phone call from Eugene saying that they might have found a way to end the ordeal. He said that Glori had awoken; they wanted to come here to see if they could help you too."

"I met them at a restaurant in Anaheim, and sure enough, Glori Garrett was there looking as healthy and robust as a person could." Jason's voice had grown thick; he took a moment to recompose himself. "Eugene's daughter, Haylee, was there too."

Filling in the backstory, Jason said, "The daughter had been missing since you, and Mrs. Garrett got sick. There were newspaper articles speculating about what happened to her—many of them cited a possible kidnapping or a run-away situation. At the hospital, Eugene said that you'd known her at school, that you became friends, and that you'd gone home with her to spend the holiday."

"I couldn't imagine dealing with a wife in Glori's condition, and having a missing child too," Jason's empathy showed. "The poor man didn't have a support system. I wanted to do what I could to help. I believe that a fondness developed between us during that time."

Josh nodded, "Eugene is a good man. I'm glad that you reached out to him, Dad."

Leaving out the part where he questioned Haylee about the baby's father, Jason said, "Eugene introduced me to Haylee and his granddaughter, Serena."

"How old was the kid?" Josh inquired.

"I can't say exactly. It's been so long since you and Spencer were little. You forget these things. If I had to guess, I'd say three or four months. In retrospect, I should have asked Eugene about his daughter's reappearance, but I was so focused on the possibility of your recovery, that I didn't."

"Eugene said that Haylee found something when she was gone that would affect a cure. They asked for time alone with you."

"Did that strike you as an odd request?"

"Of course, it did, but Glori was right there, smiling, and talking. I'd have done anything they wanted if it meant that the same would be true for you. We're lucky that they weren't shakedown artists. If ever there was a time in my life where I was ripe for the picking, it was then!"

He glanced at his son, grinning, "You wouldn't believe the multi-faceted plan that I had to concoct, to get your mother out of the house for that stretch of time," his tone softened, "she loves you very much and has done a lot for you, you know?"

"I know," Josh sighed, "I've been trying to be more patient with her." He finished catching up on his notes; he looked up, expectantly.

"They were gone when we got back home. By then you were already starting to come around."

"You haven't spoken with Eugene or any of the others since?"

"It has felt strange, not communicating with him. But things have changed."

Josh's mouth turned down when he responded, tersely, "Yes, they have." He clicked his pen, putting away his notebook, "Thanks, Dad."

They pulled up to the curb. Josh had convinced his father that he should be dropped off and left to navigate his way to the therapy session. As Josh struggled to exit the vehicle, then lumbered toward the entry, it irked him that he was still so clumsy. In the water, it was another matter.

As soon as they'd begun hydrotherapy, his recovery had taken a leap forward. His therapists said that his body remembered when he'd been a championship swimmer. His speech had returned to normal not long after the water activity began.

Josh felt whole again in the water. It was there that he'd decided to approach his dad about driving practice. He was making plans to reclaim his old life.

❧14❧
DECISIONS & SACRIFICES

JOSH AMBLED AROUND THE kitchen. He left his cane leaning on a nearby counter. His mom was home, trailing after him like she was prepared to catch him if he took a wrong step.

"Can I fix you a sandwich?" she asked.

"No, Mom, I can do it myself. You heard the physical therapist. She said that I should be doing all of my day-to-day activities, now."

"I know, Honey, but once a mama, always a mama."

He responded in clipped, cryptic statements. "Except, that I'm not a child, or an invalid, anymore!"

Frances backed away; she looked injured, "OK...well, I'll be in the other room if you need me."

Slamming his open hand on the counter, Josh yelled, "I am so flipping tired of being taken care of! I need space, Mom! I need to get back to my life."

His mother's eyes glittered, they were sharped edged diamonds, with soft feelings radiating out from behind them. Her mouth formed an 'oh.' Inclining her head, she spoke in an even, quiet tone. "That's good, Josh. You've come such a long way. I think you're ready. But before we start working to transition you back to Berkeley, I need you to know a few things."

"When you were at the Sunnyside Nursing Home, the ward you were on was called the 'vegetable patch.' The doctors wanted us to accept that you were gone. They wanted us to consent to withhold food and water. They said that starving you would be the most humane thing to do."

Frances blinked, keeping her tears from spilling over. "I worked at the University Department of Labor Relations for twenty-six years. I only had three years left to retire. I took a leave of absence to become a full-time caregiver. When my leave ran out, I chose not to go back, but to stay home with you, Josh."

"I never asked you to do that, Mom!" he screamed.

"I did that because I believed in you. I still do, son." Her voice was raspy as she gathered her purse and car keys.

"I don't know what you want from me. I didn't ask to be in a coma, and I didn't ask you to stop living your life to wash my hair and wipe my ass, I never asked to be born in the first place. Those were decisions you made."

"This is true," she stated. "We make decisions for our children, sacrifices are part of the job. Life isn't pretty, or even happy sometimes, but, still, we can't give up, we must carry on."

"I know that you are putting all of your energy into recovery," she said. "But it would be refreshing to be noticed, maybe even appreciated for the difficult work that I've been doing...for you."

Josh stood there watching his mom clutching her purse like it would protect her from further abuse. He swallowed passed the dirt clod lodged in the back of his throat. "I am grateful, Mom. You have no idea how much I appreciate what you've done. I've just been so furious and angry, feeling like a cripple, and a burden, I guess I've been taking it out on you. I am sorry."

She nodded.

"Please, Mom would you stop making me the focus of your every waking moment? Can you get back to living your own life?"

Frances nodded again. "I'll back off, but I'll always be there for you, Josh, no matter what." She held her head high, walking through the kitchen, and out into the garage.

Josh heard the car engine come to life; he watched from the window as she maneuvered the vehicle onto the street. Closing his eyes, pressing his fingers to the bridge of his nose, Josh forced himself to breathe.

Grabbing a beer from the refrigerator, he took it into the backyard. Limping along, he approached a lawn chair. As he settled into it, he groaned. Shifting around to face the sun, he leaned back, closing his eyes. The heat, warming his skin, and the orange blossoms that he hadn't noticed, scented the air with a heady sweetness.

He let his mind wander. There was a pool at the Berkeley campus. Dr. Peterson, his boss, had assured him that he'd have a job waiting for him as soon as he was able. For the first time in a long time, Josh felt that things might work out alright.

It had been a mild surprise to learn that Spencer was living in his apartment. *I don't think he'll protest too much, once he discovers that he's about to have a roommate.* Josh smiled.

✎∽◯∾✎

Josh awoke from his catnap with a start. What was it that brought him abruptly back? He'd been dreaming about Haylee. They were involved in a charged discussion. He'd gotten her to shut up when he leaned in to kiss her. He'd had this dream many times, so what was different?

He sat up straighter when he realized what it was. It was her response. She'd kissed him back! Unsettled by the depth of feeling that the dream evoked, Josh got up. He prowled around the yard, then the house, and, finally, his room.

Finding boxes, Josh began packing for his move. Maybe if he kept busy, the Haylee, crazy-making thoughts would go away.

After an hour, he looked at what he'd accomplished. *There isn't much here that I want to take with me.* He remembered when he'd set about packing for his first move to Berkeley. That felt like eons ago. Fresh out of high school, he'd anticipated the independent life that was his for the making. He had to hand it to himself. Once there, he'd busted his butt to make the grades. He'd strategically chosen internships and employment opportunities that would get him closer to his goal—psychological profiler for Innovative Medical Advancement Technologies. He wondered if this latest 'hiccup' in his plan would help or hurt his chances of eventually winding up with the job he wanted. *I guess I am going to find out.*

Josh sat down at his desk; his eyes wandered to the bookshelf. Zeroing in on the spine of Gulliver's Travels, he smiled. He reached for his treasure book.

Before he even opened the hardcover, he was already going down memory lane as he inventoried the items inside. Anticipating views of long remembered mementos, it came as a shock to see them covered with a fold of paper that didn't look familiar.

He knew before he knew, who had put it there. His hands trembled as he held it. *I should toss it! Not even tempt myself to look.* But the memory of her heated response to his kiss warmed and stimulated parts of his body. Curiosity, too consuming to ignore, had him unfolding the paper and reading her words.

Dear Josh,

I found some of the answers that you were trying to help me find.

I betrayed you and let you down in the worst possible way. Saying 'sorry' can't even come close to expressing the regret that I feel for what I did to you. I don't blame you if you never want to see me again!

I wanted you to know that all the time I was gone, you were with me— your thoughts talking in my mind. It was scary, at first, being somewhere, foreign, where I didn't know how to behave, always worried that I'd make a mistake. You kept me from being petrified with fear. You kept me asking questions.

Not a day went by that I didn't think about you. Even if we never meet again, you are, and will always be, my friend.

Haylee

Josh swallowed passed the constriction blocking his throat. Carefully he refolded the letter, putting it back in his stash. He closed the book adding it to the box that was marked to go.

☙15☙
BACK TO 'NORMAL'

INTERSTATE FIVE NORTH OF the Grapevine is a flat, monotonous drive. The city gives way to desert; the desert gives way to farmlands. The only exciting things to see are the mountain ranges to the east and west, and the other vehicles sharing the road.

About halfway through the trip, Jason asked Josh if he wanted to take a break. "I'm OK, Dad." Josh smiled over at him. "I appreciate the company, but I would have been fine on my own."

"I know, but your mother—"

"I know."

"I think you are doing the right thing, Josh. I'm proud of you."

"Thanks, Dad, I'm proud of me too."

"There's been something that I've meant to ask."

"Shoot."

"This girl, Haylee, is she important to you?"

Josh's immediate reaction was to respond saying that they were nothing to each other, but he thought better of that. "She's trouble in ways that you can't imagine...I don't understand why I feel the way I do about her. I can't get her out of my mind."

Jason sucked in a breath, "I was worried about that. You know, a relationship is challenging enough when it involves two people. When you add a child, and that child's parents, things get complicated, quickly."

Josh didn't intend to snap, but his father had hit a sensitive nerve. "I'm not stupid, Dad! I am not planning to pursue her."

His dad changed the subject, "Have you found out where she'd been all those months?"

"I haven't spoken to her at all." Josh's grip on the steering wheel turned his knuckles white. "She wrote a note that said she'd been traveling."

"Oh.... with the baby's father?"

"She didn't say," Josh scowled.

Jason raised a hand, "I got it, Josh. Enough with the questions. You're a big boy— the captain of your ship, and all that."

A hint of a smile lifted the corners of Josh's mouth, "I know that you, and Mom, have my best interests at heart. I promise that I'll be OK *and* that I won't be making any fatal errors."

...any more, Josh thought to himself.

Josh had been able to move back into his old life. The weeks slipped by, turning into months.

He was teaching classes and had resumed his administrative duties for the family trust. A rigorous swimming routine gave his muscles definition and his mind even greater clarity. He kept the beard that he'd grown as a symbol of strength and independence.

He and his brother had had moments of aggravation as they'd worked out their routines, schedules, and apartment cleaning responsibilities. But they'd found their happy medium and often spent time socializing with each other's friends.

One area of contention remained—Josh's sex life. Spencer was rarely without female companionship. Being the thoughtful brother that he was, he continually offered to find hook-ups for Josh.

"Spence, you are being a PIA. I'm not interested."

"Josh, you're the one who's being a pain-in-the-ass. You're a healthy, decent looking guy. I don't get why you don't want to— get some."

Josh glared at his brother, "Grow up."

Spencer hesitated, "Oh man, I'm sorry! I thought that you were recovered, but maybe you aren't. Is your soldier not able to salute anymore?"

Disgusted with where the conversation was going, Josh bent down, grabbing a dirty sock, flinging it at his brother's face. "Pick up your laundry, Spencer, and get your nose out of my business."

Stalking away, Josh muttered over his shoulder, before slamming his bedroom door, "There's nothing wrong with my soldier."

He could hear his brother's footsteps following. Through the door, Spencer hammered home his point. "If you count all the time that you were sleeping, it's been a long time, Josh! That's not normal. Unless your swimming or hand jobs are releasing your...ah...tension.... you're going to explode. Sooner or later, it's going to happen. I can find you a little hottie who'll take care of you tonight— just say the word."

"Go away, Spencer!"

Josh tossed and turned. Sheets twisted around his legs. Struggling to sleep was the worst part of his day. Nothing helped—not warm milk, chamomile tea, staying out late, or drinking too much. It was always the same.

Josh's thoughts dwelt on Haylee.

She knew I wanted her.

She pushed me away.

She did that to protect me, didn't she?

She thought she could control herself—that she wouldn't do IT to me.

But she did.

There was nothing I could do to stop it.

Josh remembered the terror of being caught in a life and death battle....and losing. Seeing, first hand, that the girl he loved was gone. In her place was a predator. She was incredibly sexy, inhumanly strong, and entirely without emotion. Her cold, callous eyes, looking down at him, observing with detached interest, as she drained him. He could feel himself slipping, even as he fought against it, an unseen force pulling him below the murky waters of consciousness, until, he didn't care.

Josh's heart hammered. A cold sweat sent chills rippling across his skin. He sensed Haylee in an intimate way he could not explain. He knew the shock and disgust that she felt about herself. He could hear her cries of anguish and feel her desperation to make things right again. He didn't know where he ended and where she began.

Through it all, his soldier remained ram-rod straight. He imagined taking her angrily, making her pay for the hurt and damage she'd caused. He was grabbing her hair, yanking her head back, exposing her neck, listening to her whimper, then he put his mouth on her neck, his teeth exposed, ready to clamp down, prepared to draw blood.

Instead of putting his teeth on her, he touched her with his tongue. His grip loosened, he was cradling her, a shudder of desire rocketed through them, they clung to one another. He kissed her, passionately, as an ardent lover. Her whimper, now, was one of longing, she wanted him. And he wanted her. His shaft throbbed with savage intensity, needing to press into her slick, womanly, cavity, needing to connect, needing to find release.

A sarcastic, mocking inner voice, broke the spell. *She felt guilty about me, yet while I lay in a coma, she met another guy, slept with him, and had his kid. She never loved me.*

Josh ripped the covers off, padding into the bathroom. Staring at his haggard face in the mirror, he commented, "This is ridiculous. What am I so afraid of? That she'll kill me all the way the next time? This has got to stop."

❧16❧
REALLY?

GLORI WAS IN THE middle of changing Serena when insistent knocking started at the front door. "What in the world?" She said, smiling at the squirming child.

Serena gave her a sunny, gummy smile.

The knocking continued. "They're just going to have to hold their horses, aren't they?" Glori commented as she fastened the diaper. She hoisted the little girl up and onto her hip, "Because I can't stop in the middle of this important operation or leave a squirmy girl, alone can I?"

Glori widened her eyes while tickling the tiny tot. A delighted squeal came from Serena. "No, I can't!" That changed the squeals into full belly laughs as they waddled through the house.

When the door swung inward, Glori looked at the person standing on her doorstep with a question. When she recognized who it was, she exclaimed, "Oh my goodness! Josh, come here!"

Josh's mouth hung open, but he didn't speak. His gaze moved from Glori to the baby, then down to regard Glori's blooming lower half.

With her free arm, she pulled him into an embrace, smashing him up against the wiggly child. Glori's enthusiasm caused Josh to break out in nervous laughter.

Losing her hold on Serena, "Oh! Oh.... help, Josh, she's slipping!" Glori cried in alarm.

He reached out to grasp the child, lifting her up and out of harm's way. Josh found himself peering eye-to-eye with one of the most attractive toddlers he'd ever seen.

"I'm sorry about that," Glori said, winded. Rubbing her belly, she reached out a reassuring hand to Serena. "The farther along I am, and the bigger this one grows, the more complicated it is to manage everything."

Josh was captivated by Serena's large green eyes framed by a forest of thick lashes. He noticed her waves of soft brown hair that created whirling patterns. "It looks as fine and soft a spun cotton candy," he commented.

Glori laughed, nervously, "Josh, this is, Serena, Haylee's daughter."

With that statement, the tender expression on Josh's face was replaced by a hardened, resolution. He carefully and deliberately returned the child to Glori.

"Let me get Serena set-up in her playpen so we can catch up," Glori's smile didn't reach her eyes, her tone sounded forced. She made small talk while she gathered toys to keep Serena occupied. "The beard caught me by surprise; I almost didn't recognize you."

Josh nodded, "I get that frequently."

"You look terrific; whatever you have been doing seems to agree with you."

"When my PT discovered that I used to be a competitive swimmer, he made swimming part of my therapy. I've kept it up."

Glori nodded, standing up straight. Their gaze locked. She inhaled deeply. "Will you join me in the kitchen?"

With his hands clenched into fists inside his pocket, Josh took another glance at the baby before following Glori. He watched her moving around the kitchen as she prepared two cups of herbal tea. "When are you due?"

"Almost there, two more months to go," she smiled, walking carefully, bringing two steaming mugs to the table. "I don't want to talk about me; I want to know how you are."

Josh took a hesitant sip then leaned back against the chair, arms crossed, feet spread wide. Turning his head, he gazed toward the living room where Serena making industrious noises, "Physically, I'm fine. I'm back in Berkeley, working at my old job. Mentally...." He shifted to regard Glori. "I didn't think that I would ever return to where it happened. I didn't think I'd ever want to see Haylee again—or you."

She nodded, "But here you are."

"Here I am."

"What can I do for you, Josh?"

He glanced around, "Is she here?"

Glori shook her head, "No, Haylee went with Gene to a growers meeting. One of the farmers had a dog that he wanted Haylee to ...talk to."

"Ah..." Josh nodded. "It's just as well; I'd like to talk with you—if that's alright?"

Leaning his elbows on the table, he gave Glori a hard stare, "The last time I saw you, you were laid out on a bed down there," he nodded in the direction of the hallway. "Do you remember what happened?"

Glori stared at her hands, folded in her lap. "No," she shook her head.

Josh threaded fingers through his hair looking away. "Unfortunately, I *do*."

Her head snapped up, so her eyes could meet his, "Oh...."

"Yea....'oh'...." he replied sarcastically. "Is she still.... doing it?"

"She's not, but I think that's something that you'll have to hear from her."

"She left me a note saying that she traveled in time."

Glori pressed a hand over her mouth. She nodded.

"But that's impossible. How can you sit there and nod like you believe it as fact?"

"The certainty Haylee has when she talks about it? That she presents no other outward signs or symptoms of psychosis?" Glori lifted a hand to point into the living room, "That little girl in there."

Josh looked incredulous, "Really? Glori, you don't have to time travel to have a kid."

Glori rolled her eyes, "I am aware of that." She leveled a glare at him. "She was wearing clothes from the period."

"Easily accomplished with a costume shop."

"They were full of soot; holes were burned in the dress and bonnet, the burn patterns on the cloth matched burns on her head, neck, and back."

Josh paled, he swallowed with difficulty. "Was she hurt?"

"Yes. She'd been in a fire. Haylee's recovered, now."

Shaking his head as if bring himself back to the task, "Fire, injury, pregnancy, kid, old clothes— still do not prove time travel. Unbelievable!" He got up, beginning to pace.

"I know how it sounds. Last year, I would have been on the exact skeptical page as you. But I've seen and heard enough to convince me that— I can't be sure about it anymore."

"OK, I'll bite." He looked at Glori, with exasperation. "When? When did she say she'd gone to?"

"She was in San Francesco, in 1850, when the first Great Fire broke out."

Dropping back in the chair opposite Glori, Josh leaned heavily on his elbows. Suddenly, he was exhausted, drained, it took a concentrated effort to keep his eyelids open, and his eyes focused.

"Haylee described wooden buildings and boardwalks going up like matchsticks, hundreds of people desperate to escape, men attempting to douse flames with water buckets and dynamite, and the casualties. Her post-traumatic distress symptoms are genuine. Her nightmares are consistent with what we see with burn victims."

Glori was quiet. Noting his skeptical expression, she continued. "I looked up every possible verifiable fact. It checks out, Josh."

"It could be an elaborate story, concocted from a detailed study of history."

"You're right," Glori agreed. "But why? Why would she go to all the trouble? Is Haylee the kind of person who would burn herself to make a story believable? Or, maybe, the truth is standing right in front of us."

❧17❧
IMPOSSIBLE

I'M NOT SURE WHAT I expected. Josh pressed a thumb against an eyebrow where a headache began to throb. He tried taking deep breaths to open airways that felt cemented shut. A hot sting of tears prickled behind his eyes; he blinked rapidly. He got up, walking away from Glori, gripping at his emotions like they were something he could hold.

This isn't happening. This was a miscalculation of gargantuan proportions. Josh stopped near the edge of the playpen. The little girl inside was on her hands and knees swaying.

Looking up at him, Serena mirrored his expression. She didn't move while their stare held, lengthening into something substantial, and earnest. Raising her delicate hand, dainty fingers reached, greedily, as if to pluck a mouth-watering fruit, she uttered, "Dada."

A blast of emotion, like a downdraft at the entrance of a walk-in refrigeration unit, hit Josh. *That didn't happen. She didn't say what I think she did!* He had the urge to reach in there and pick her up; to hold her close, inhaling the scent of her hair. Josh took several, stumbling, steps back.

The front door opened. Eugene walked in, followed by Haylee.

A moment, where time elongated and warped, gripped everyone.

Gene was the first to pop the bubble, "That was Josh's car parked out front! We didn't recognize it. You look great, son, I'm delighted to see you!" He strode forward holding out a rough, work-worn hand.

On autopilot, Josh reached out to clasp and shake it. A tight smile formed as he met the other man's eyes. "Thank you, sir."

"You came," Haylee whispered, from behind her father.

Eugene stepped out of Josh's line of sight. Glori swooped in to lift Serena. Together, Gene and Glori left by the back door. Josh found his arms filled with Haylee.

"You have hair all over your face!" her voice trembled.

A torrent of tears flowed through them both. It was as if they were the only two occupants aboard a ship on an angry, churning sea. Riding the waves, they clung to one another. Gradually, the winds died, the sails luffed, and calm waters returned, once more.

Josh, resting his cheek on the top of Haylee's head, gently held her. He was reluctant to let go.

Haylee filled her lungs, heaving a sigh. Pulling back, she swiped at the remaining dampness on her face. With a soft laugh, she said, "I must look a sight."

He followed suit, "If you do, then I must too," he moved to put space between them.

"I like the beard. You look good —healthy, robust."

"Thanks."

"I...I don't know what to say, Josh. I thought that you'd never want to see me again."

He shoved his hands into his pockets. He glanced down at his shoes. Only partially looking at her, without fully raising his head, "Truthfully, Haylee, I didn't. But I'm having difficulty sleeping. I think you're partly responsible."

Surprised, she muttered, "But how can I....?" She rephrased, "Of course I want to do whatever I can to help, what do you need?"

When they'd first met, the banter between them had been fast and furious. Their usual game of his outrageous flirtations, followed by her deft sidestepping had been a source of appeal and enticement. An opening like this was a checkmate move. He pounced on it without thinking. A flash sparkled in his eyes, a mischievous grin turned up one corner of his mouth, "Do I have to spell that out?"

Haylee's eyes grew wide; she quickly moved farther away, "You came here because you want to...?"

Her reaction caused violent thoughts that crashed around inside his mind, surprising and troubling him with their strength. Had he been alone, Josh would have struck out—at a wall or a piece of furniture.

"I need to get some water," Haylee said while turning to trot into the kitchen.

Josh watched her go up on tip-toe, looking outside over the sink. *What does she think I'm going to do? She's afraid...*

Josh followed her. In the doorway, he stopped. Slamming an open hand on the door frame, he yelled, "You did it to me, Haylee! I naively believed that you wouldn't take me down—not *me.*"

He gripped the doorjamb, with talon-like fingers. Josh's voice cracked, growing hoarse, "You were killing me. You looked right at me as you were doing it—and you wouldn't stop—and I loved..." His voice broke; he turned on his heel, striding away.

Haylee heard the front door slam. Sobbing, she ran after him. "I'm sorry! I can't tell you how sorry I am. I couldn't control it. I tried, Josh. I thought about that every day until I could get back to help you."

His eyes were red, blazing. He turned toward her. Sarcasm and bitterness laced his reply, "Yea—were you were thinking about me when you slept with some other guy and got pregnant.

"How dare you!" she snapped.

"How dare *me*? I was the one laid out like a corpse while you were...." Wiping angrily at the tears and snot on his face, he continued, "Did you know that while my parents were exercising me, feeding me, and washing me that the medical support staff was telling them that they should starve me."

"I didn't know." Haylee looked aghast. Her expression softened. "Oh, Josh, I'm so...."

He held up a hand, "Don't say it. I'd don't want to hear 'sorry' from you."

"Then what *do* you want?"

"I want the time back. I want my parents not to have gone through that. Damn it, Haylee! I want answers!"

"I learned a few things while I was gone. I'll tell you whatever you want to know."

Running a hand through his hair, Josh walked away, and then came back. "Glori said that you stopped attacking people, is that true?"

"Yes."

"How? How did you accomplish that?"

Haylee tucked hair back behind her ears. She sighed. "Some of the answers are long. Do you want to listen?"

He simply nodded.

Haylee led them outside to an old picnic table under a walnut tree. Sitting opposite one another, she began, "The pendant that I got from my mother is involved. It started getting hot. I passed out. When I woke up, I was in a strange place. It led me to someone who had a crystal that looked like mine, but much larger. Reece used it to burn away the webs between my fingers."

Josh rested his chin between his thumb and forefinger. He stared at her silently. Wearing a grim expression, multitudes of questions and heaps of skepticism splintered off in every direction in his mind. Deciding to keep it simple, he asked, "And Reece is?"

Haylee looked away when she replied, "Serena's father. I attacked his brother, Edward. He was the first person I restored once I learned how to use the larger crystal."

Ignoring the stab of jealousy that pierced him, Josh continued, "According to Glori, these people lived in—?"

"It was 1850 when I left," Haylee said softly.

"Time travel?" his voice was tense and curt, "How did you return?"

Sending him a wounded look, she continued, "I'm not sure—"

Josh sat up straighter, shaking his head.

"I told you that I had *some* answers. I don't have them *all*. Do you want me to keep going or not?"

Placing his hands flat on the table, Josh moved to get up, "I'm done. I can't do this anymore."

Before he got too far away, Haylee called out, "You said that you thought I was responsible for your not sleeping. What did you mean?"

He paused on his way to his car, turning back to her, "The letter you left in my book."

Haylee nodded.

"I thought you went to Canada or Mexico." A harsh laugh escaped before he continued, "You said that I made you feel safe and that you couldn't stop thinking about coming back to me."

"It's true."

"But wasn't enough to keep you from sleeping with another guy," he muttered, dropping into the driver's seat, slamming the door. Without giving her another glance, he started the engine and drove away leaving a plume of dust engulfing her in its dusty wake.

❧18❧
SWEET DREAMS

FOR THREE NIGHTS AFTER visiting the Garrett farm, Josh slept peacefully. Waking up refreshed improved his mood, made his work days more relaxed, and enhanced his regular workouts. Josh congratulated himself for having faced his unhealthy attachment for Haylee and released the latent trauma from the attack.

Josh's success didn't leave him feeling as light-hearted or as buoyant as he hoped. A hollow sadness settled around him like atomic radiation from a mushroom cloud. He was bad-tempered with his colleagues, cross with his students, and combatant with Spencer.

"What is with you, Josh?" Spencer complained. "Ever since last weekend, you've been a major PIA, no, more like a gargantuan PIA. Did something happen that I should know about?"

"Nothing happened," Josh grumbled. "I went to visit friends— that's all."

"Maybe you're having a relapse. Should I call mom?"

"You've played that card too many times, Spencer."

"Look, Josh, if I can't stand you, you're probably pissing off other people too. You can only go on like this for so long before people start complaining. I know we give each other a hard time, but I'm willing to listen if you want to talk."

Josh frowned, "I'm not pissing people off," he mumbled as he stomped into the bathroom, slamming the door behind him.

On the fourth night after his confrontation with Haylee, Josh tucked a bookmark in *The Bourne Supremacy*. He felt a connection with the main character, who only had partial memories from the past. The CIA plots and international espionage were well-written, action-packed, escapist entertainment.

Fluffing his pillows and straightening his blankets, Josh leaned over to turn off the bedside lamp. Yawning, he settled in, closing his eyes, he waited for sleep to gather him in her waiting arms.

Thirty minutes later, he heard, *'Josh?'*

His eyes popped open, his body jolted. *Did someone say something?*

'Josh, it's me, Haylee.'

"What the...?" he cried out, fumbling for the light.

'I'm going to talk to you for a few minutes. It'll be quick.'

"Haylee? Where are you?" Josh scanned the room; it was empty. Throwing off the blankets, he crouched to peer under the bed.

'The first place your mind is going to go is that you must be crazy. Right?'

There was a ring of humor in her voice. But, in fact, there was no sound at all. His pounding heart warmed all his extremities. *I must be...* Josh stopped himself from completing the thought. *How is she doing this?* he wondered. Anxiety clamped a hand around his chest; it was compressing into a fist.

'There were a couple of things that happened with Ed and with Glori, that made me wonder if, when I return someone, they can hear <u>my</u> thoughts...at times, like when I feel strong emotions. I am testing out a hunch to see if you can hear me.'

'All those months that you were...asleep, Josh, I heard your thoughts inside MY head. You didn't speak to me directly, but I listened. If you hear this, I want to assure you that you are not crazy. Good night, Josh, over-and-out.'

"Over-and out?" Josh shouted, raking his hands through his hair. He sat there, at the edge of his bed, for an hour, holding his hands out, watching to see if he could get them to stop shaking.

Spencer's key jangled as he entered their apartment at 1:15 a.m. When he saw his brother wearing sweatpants, sitting in a pool of lamplight with a beer in one hand and a book in the other, he paused to observe, "Dreams keeping you up again?"

Josh held up his bottle in a salute before draining the last swig.

Day Five

He'd spent the day convincing himself that he'd imagined it. He'd worked out doubly hard, making sure that his body was ready to drop into sleep as soon as his head hit the pillow. He worried, *What if it wasn't my imagination?*

At the same time as last night, he heard, *'Josh?'*

As before, he startled, his eyes popped open. He hadn't been asleep, only going through the motions. "Where are you?" he raised his voice, turning on the light, getting up. He repeated his activities from the night before, looking under the bed, in the closet, out the window, and out into the empty hallway.

'Don't worry; I'm not planning to 'haunt' you or anything. There are a few things that I wanted to say before I leave you alone for good.'

Back on his bed, Josh wedged himself against his headboard, crossing his arms. He focused on breathing and calming his hammering heart. He tried not to pay attention to the prick of pain that her statement 'leave you alone for good' caused.

'My dad saved the genealogy research that you brought back from the library all those months ago. I found it last week. I think I figured out what you wanted to show me.'

Until this moment, Josh had forgotten about that. He'd been gathering data about Haylee's mother and her kin. For a moment, curiosity blocked his incredulity over this, bizarre, information exchange.

'As far back as you went, every woman in my family only had one daughter. They all died young. That's it, isn't it? Thank you for that. Over-and-out.'

Josh threw up his hands. "Haylee! Haylee, can you hear me?" He waited, but there was no reply.

Sleep was impossible. Not because he was upset with the evidence of his 'brain damage,' but because she'd been right.

Josh could feel the familiar pull of a problem that he was primed to solve. *What in God's name are you thinking, Herkowitz?*

Day Six

Tonight, Josh waited. He thought about calling her; he'd picked up the receiver at least a dozen times. But he'd decided to wait and see what would happen.

'Josh?' She was right on time.

'I was sent there for a purpose. My function now, with regard to this 'legacy,' is to wait for the Traveler who comes next.'

There was a long pause. Josh was on edge, "And?" he said out loud.

'That's it. Over-and-out. I'll leave you be now.'

⚜19⚜
RECLAMATION

THE CONSTANT DRONE OF the VW engine helped relax Haylee as she became enveloped by traffic. *I used to love driving to the city,* she thought. She glanced over at Serena in her car seat. She was asleep; her head lolled over to the side like her neck was boneless. Haylee's grip on the wheel tightened. *Now that I'm responsible for her, I'm scared all the time!*

While keeping her attention riveted on the speeding hunks of metal, glass, and plastic, Haylee let her thoughts dwell on the conversation with her folks this morning.

"Haylee, we'll help, if you will be patient for a few more weeks," Her dad pleaded.

Glori nodded in agreement while resting her arms on top of her, much extended, belly. "This isn't something you can do alone. You have to have support for the after effects."

They were talking about her plan to find and return the souls of the people she'd attacked while she'd been a student at UC Berkeley. "I can't wait—I need to get their thoughts out of my head. Their families can't wait any longer either." Haylee turned to Glori to further plead her case, "What if some of them are considering withdrawing life support treatments?"

Haylee had been frustrated when she'd learned that her very first victim, Curtis Carter, had been moved to a care facility in Denver. This discovery made the urgency to locate her victims even stronger.

"I understand," said her father, "but we can't go with you until after the baby comes."

"This is something I have to do on my own." When they were about to protest, Haylee stopped them, "I won't be doing any soul returns today. I am just going to research— to see if I can find the others. I'm also going to stop in to see if Dr. Jamison wants me to work for him again."

She knew what they were about to say, so she continued, "I know you want us to stay with you. But you guys need your space. It's important for me to start taking care of my own little family. Please say you understand?"

Haylee smiled as she recalled the looks on their faces. *They couldn't say anything after that.*

Three hours later, Haylee was still smiling as she slowly drove through her old Berkeley neighborhood. She loved the giant trees that lined the edges of the streets and all the old houses that sat in between them.

Dr. Jamison had welcomed her. He'd told her about his worry over her disappearance and her father's efforts— Gene had come to visit him as he tried to piece together Haylee's life in Berkeley.

The veterinarian admonished her for 'running away' but admitted that he'd often had similar feelings and wished that he'd had the guts to follow through with it.

When Haylee asked if he was interested in having her do intuitive pet readings again, he didn't have to think it over. "Can you start today?" he'd asked. He already knew her skills and the accuracy of the information that she supplied.

Haylee was basking in her small success as she neared the smoothie shop—the place where she'd met Josh. She parked the car and unbuckled Serena. Walking toward the outdoor tables, Haylee chattered to her daughter who straddled the side of her hip. The empty child carrier seat swung from her free arm. "This was one of my favorite places. You can watch all kinds of people walking down the street. The smoothies are so yummy! I'll get us my favorite—yogurt, wheat grass, spinach, carrot, and apple."

When the thick drink arrived, Haylee leaned over, taking a long draw on her straw. Smiling and murmuring, Haylee made the sound, "yuuuummmmm," with evident pleasure.

Serena watched her mama with sparkling eyes. She reached toward the object of their attention. Haylee held the tall glass down so that Serena could reach it. Once the drink hit the toddler's tongue, she made a face that looked like she was hurt. The green liquid dribbled down her chin when she spit it out.

Haylee giggled. "Oh no! You silly! This is good stuff." Haylee hurried to wipe away the goo before it could stain Serena's clothes.

After clean-up detail was complete, Haylee ordered Serena's standard: apple juice. The two girls shared a few happy moments as they sipped their drinks. Haylee leaned back against her chair to marvel at the miracle that was her daughter. Serena looked so much like her father with bits of herself sprinkled in too. Haylee, again, felt the bone-weary pain of separation from Reece. But their daughter supplied her with tremendous amounts of strength. Haylee had to carry on, building a life for the two of them. Reece would expect nothing less.

Glori told her once that, "Serena only has one life. It's up to you to make it a good one—whether she has her father or not." Haylee had taken that advice to heart. It was why they were here. She couldn't help herself from glancing over at the steps leading to Josh's apartment. *What are the chances that he came back to live there?*

Josh has probably already got all the information about those guys I attacked at the frat house. If I tell him what I am planning, he might be willing to help.

It was this thought that had Haylee knocking on the familiar door ten minutes later. She was surprised when it swung inward. A familiar face greeted her. Haylee stood there; mute, while Spencer eyed her. "Can I help you?"

Shaking herself, "Sorry, I was surprised to see you."

Spencer gave Haylee a doubtful look, "Have we met?"

"No...but I've seen...pictures of you. I'm a friend of your brothers. Is he around?"

A smile cracked his face. Spencer stepped back to hold the door open wider, "A friend of Josh's you say? Come in!"

Haylee entered, enchanted with the warm welcome. "This is my daughter, Serena."

"She's a cutie," Spencer responded, leaning out into the hall. Is her dad coming too?"

Haylee stammered, "Oh...ah.... her dad isn't... We're not together."

"Is that right?" he responded. Spencer sounded a little too cheerful. "I'm sorry to hear that. Have a seat," he indicated the couch, "Can I get you something to drink?"

Haylee shook her head. She liked him; he had a natural smile and friendly face. He was slightly shorter than his brother, but he had a stockier, more muscular build.

"How do you know my brother?"

"I used to be a student in one of his classes."

"Well if Josh showed you pictures of me, you must have known him a little better than a student would know a teacher."

She laughed. The brothers had that in common. They paid attention to details and liked connecting the dots.

"I'd say we were friends," Haylee alluded.

"Ah.... friends as in pals or friends as in.... *friendly* friends?" Spencer wiggled his eyebrows.

She laughed nervously, "Why do you want to know?"

Spencer leaned in giving her a conspiratorial look, "The entire time I've been living with him, he's been acting like a monk. For the last few weeks, he's been impossible, irritable, short-fused, in a bad way. He won't tell me why. Suddenly I'm wondering if *you* might be the reason."

"Me?" Haylee squeaked.

Just then, the door opened. Josh filled the frame. He paused to notice all the occupants. Spencer turned in his brother's direction, "Hey Josh...."

Spencer's smile died when he saw his brother. Josh had gone completely pale. He clutched at his left arm, crumpling to the floor.

"Josh!" Spencer and Haylee cried in unison. Reaching his side first, Spencer leaned over, "What's wrong?"

Josh squirmed, his eyes wildly going back and forth between them, "Stay.... away!" he gasped. "Don't let her..."

Serena, surprised by the loud voices, had begun to wail.

Shaken and confused, Spencer looked to Haylee, then to the baby.

"I know CPR," Haylee nudged him away. A medical emergency on a human isn't that different from an animal crisis. Josh's skin was ashen, but his breathing was unobstructed. His heart rate, although fast, was steady. A gut instinct told her that he wasn't in imminent danger of dying. With authority, Haylee directed Spencer to take Serena outside.

He reached for the handle on Serena's carrier, then paused, looking back.

"He'll be alright, Spencer," Haylee said, "I just need her out of here for a few minutes."

Once they were alone, Haylee turned back to Josh who still clutched at his arm and remained wild-eyed. "Josh! Look at me," she patted his face.

"No....no.... not my brother," he mumbled.

"Your brother is fine! Everything is alright.... Josh! Take some deep breaths." Not making headway, Haylee held Josh's face firmly between her hands. "Look at me!"

His eyes wouldn't focus. Not knowing what else to do, Haylee leaned down. Meeting his lips with her own, she kissed him, hard. There was a shift in his body. Still holding his head, she lifted so she could speak, "Come on, Josh, focus." She met his lips again, pressing, tasting. His tension drained, his breathing calmed, a free hand came up to cradle the back of her head.

As Haylee continued kissing him, all thoughts ...everything...left her mind. This was a freedom she rarely experienced. There was only the feel of his lips beginning to respond, the warmth of his mouth, the smell of his skin.

Josh wove strong fingers in her hair; he pulled her toward him to deepen their contact. Mouths opened so that tongues and teeth could gently explore, "I've missed you! I've missed you so much." Josh whispered between kisses. He twisted their positions so that his body covered hers.

The feel of his erection pressing against her filled Haylee with a compelling desire. She clung to him, pulling him closer.

"Harrumph.... It looks like I was right about one thing," Spencer observed from the door.

Josh and Haylee scrambled apart.

Mortified, Haylee bumbled to her feet.

Josh, in a similar manner, dashed for the bathroom, calling, "Don't leave!" he over his shoulder.

❦20❦
IS IT PITY?

WITH HANDS THAT WERE unsteady, Haylee put a fresh diaper on Serena. Haylee's mouth was a straight line. Finishing, she lifted Serena, hugging her. "I love you so very much. I love your daddy too, with all my heart." Haylee whispered in Serena's ear.

The three of them sat in awkward silence, waiting for Josh. Spencer kept glancing at his watch. Finally, he sighed, saying, "I've got a class. It was interesting to meet you; I hope that we'll see you again."

"Likewise," Haylee smiled. "Thanks for looking after Serena."

Spencer gave her a wink, "Thanks for taking care of Josh."

Haylee rolled her eyes. Her stomach was in knots; her hands were still shaking, palms sweaty, she kept wiping them on her jeans. If she didn't need Josh's help, she'd have left too.

It didn't take long for the quiet apartment to lull Serena to sleep. A clock ticking somewhere, echoed, its sound bouncing off surfaces making Haylee's skin crawl. The longer she waited, the more agitated she became. Walking over to the bathroom door, she called, "Josh, are you OK in there?"

"Yes," was his terse reply.

"Are you planning to come out?"

He opened the door, leaning an elbow high on the door jamb, he looked down at her. Haylee thought he looked mad. Meeting his eyes, she felt her cheeks growing warm.

"I'm sorry I came," she started, hesitantly, "I didn't mean for that to happen..." She still couldn't look at him. In her peripheral vision, Haylee saw his hands balling into fists. "I..." she glanced up at him. He still looked angry. "I came because I.... thought...you might be able to help me find them— those guys from Alpha Sigma Phi."

She heard him swallow; his voice sounded forced. "So, you didn't come because you wanted to see me?"

"Of course, I wanted to see you."

"The thing is," Josh raised his free hand as if to touch her, then dropped it back to his side. "You are a problem, Haylee. Whenever I'm around you, there are problems."

Still not looking at him, Haylee said, "I don't mean to be."

He lifted a hand so that he could place a single finger under her chin. Tilting her head up so he could meet her eyes, he said, "Every time I think about moving forward with my life, something keeps bringing me back to you."

"I don't understand," Haylee said. "I haven't seen or heard from you since...."

Josh raised his finger from her chin, pressing it against her lips.

The intimate contact had the blood rushing to her face again.

"Let's go sit on the couch," He indicated the piece of furniture. They both turned to look at Serena, sleeping in her car seat.

Leaning on his knees, Josh scrubbed his hands over his face. His gaze took on a faraway quality, "I heard you those nights."

"You did?"

He turned to regard her. "That was cruel and unusual."

Haylee's eyes grew wide, "I wasn't sure if it would work."

A faint smile started at corners of his mouth. "I thought I'd handled my anger issues after seeing you at your house. But I was kidding myself. Spencer could tell you about what a jerk I've been lately."

"You called it right," Josh continued, "I spent a long time questioning my sanity. It was a good thing that you weren't anywhere close. It made me realize that I had a lot more baggage to sift through. I spent so much time at the pool, beating out my frustrations, that I could have turned into a green, shriveled pickle— Vlasic variety." He grinned.

"Once I acknowledged the cause of my fury, I could separate my personal feelings from the information that you gave. It all came back after that. What we were investigating before.... My sense of discovery, something extraordinary, a mystery that no one has seen yet."

"I never, ever, looked at it that way, Josh," Haylee commented.

"I know," he quipped. "Communicating with me mentally, presenting me with a puzzle, and telling me that those guys can be cured. You didn't think that I could ignore that, did you?"

Haylee mirrored his faint smile. "You don't have to get involved; I can figure out how to take care of it on my own."

Sighing, like he was admitting to a monstrous error, he shook his head, replying, "I'm in, Haylee. For them, and for me."

She nodded, pressing, still trembling hands, to her mouth. "I wasn't expecting— this."

He nodded, "Me neither."

"The first thing I have to do is locate them."

"I'll start on that first thing Monday."

"I got my job back with Dr. Jamison. I'm going to start looking for a place in town. Once I'm settled, I need to plan for what to do with Serena. She'll need looking after."

He regarded her steadily for a few moments before saying, "OK."

Haylee got up, beginning to pack Serena's diaper bag, "Can I call you next week to see where you are on the location research?"

"Sure— "he replied distractedly. "Haylee, about that kiss..."

She halted, meeting his eyes. Nodding in resolution, she sat back on the floor, her legs crossing under her. "It was the only thing I could think of to do."

Josh nodded slowly, "Was it a pity kiss or was there something else behind it?"

Haylee blinked back tears that threatened. She hesitated, "To be perfectly honest, I'm confused." She looked over at her daughter, "I love her father, Josh. A part of me feels like it died when I returned to a place where I'll never see him again." Haylee wiped at a single tear trickling down her cheek. She turned back to him, willing him to understand. "The only time I don't hurt is when I'm with you. Was it a pity kiss? No— It was an 'I need to help my friend kiss,' and 'I was curious what would happen' kiss."

Raking a hand through his hair," At least you aren't trying to spare my feelings," he replied sardonically.

Haylee felt like she couldn't breathe, "You're pushing me." She started to cry.

Moving over to her, Josh gathered her in close, murmuring apologies.

Burying her face in his shirt, she whispered, "I can't say that I liked it, Josh, because if I say that, then I am being disloyal to Reece."

HERE & NOW

❧21❧
GLORI'S TESTIMONY

GARRETT, GLORI - Entry #2

UTERINE HEMORRHAGIC DISORDER - This is the diagnosis that Dr. Carlie Lester entered on Haylee's chart when she first presented at Sacramento Regional Hospital on 14 November 1984.

I was the first staff member to see Eugene when he brought Haylee in. My initial assessment was that they'd been in a car accident. Both Haylee and Gene were covered in blood. It was not clear who had sustained injuries.

I was in the exam room several times when they were working on her. I could tell from the rapid-fire directives and fast-paced life-saving actions that they thought Haylee was in critical condition. They'd been about to take her into surgery to find the bleeder when the lead doc called a halt. "Her heart rate is coming back...respiration too...BP is— normal."

The philosophy of ER care is to patch it up and discharge when possible. The next phase is to stabilize before hospital admission or pass it off to a specialist.

Once Haylee had been admitted to the general care ward, the ER docs didn't give her another thought. Dr. Lester, me, and possibly a handful of the nursing staff were the only ones disturbed by Haylee's dramatic illness, and her, unusually rapid recovery.

The idea of initiating a Child Protective Services investigation was being discussed before Haylee ran away. When she turned up at home, the hospital held its breath waiting to see if the family would file charges. CPS notification never happened and it was strongly discouraged.

Haylee, mystery that she is, brought Eugene and me together. I didn't understand the full extent of her unusual behaviors until after Gene and I were married.

It is an intensely odd to learn that you have been incapacitated, having no memory of it, but observing the results of your weakened body. It is equally odd to learn that the person responsible for that condition is your step-daughter, that she traveled through time to pull you out of it, and, finally, that a long-time dream has been fulfilled.

I have a new husband—and a child that I never thought that I'd conceive. Was the price I paid worth the reward? I wouldn't give it up.

I am not afraid of Haylee; I don't think that she is dangerous— anymore. I believe that something happened that compelled her to perform those grievous activities. I know that she is remorseful about what she did. She is determined to find and bring back each one of her victims. We've seen evidence that she can, in fact, do that. Eugene and I support her in this. We will do whatever it takes to see it through.

She's a kind and loving mother to her child.

Her father believes, fervently, that she needs to be protected, that keeping her condition a secret is critically important. He's concerned that too many people already know about it...

----Testimony End----

Josh, writing with efficient all-caps, continued pressing hard on the notepad, moving his hand across the page. Catching up, he paused to look at her. "What do you think?"

She nodded to the tape recorder; it was still running. "On the record or off?"

Josh reached over, hitting the 'off' button.

"I don't know if it should be a secret. I think Gene's right if we start investigating too openly, gaining access to those students could get complicated— fast." Look what we did with you," Glori lifted a hand gesturing toward him. "If Eugene and your father hadn't already established a relationship, you might still be in the same position as those poor boys."

Josh tossed his pencil down. Leaning back in his chair, he pinched his lower lip. He nodded, slowly, as if he were asking and answering questions in his mind. "Something else has been bothering me."

"Yes?"

"She attacked us on the same day. There were a couple of months between when she woke you up and when she came for me."

Glori nodded.

"A couple more months in a coma can't alter the body that much, can it? Why was your recovery time so much shorter than mine?"

"I've thought about that too. The body continues to deteriorate when it's not moving, but you're younger and in better physical shape... Is 'coma' even the correct diagnosis?"

Josh huffed, "More questions."

"I admire what you are doing, Josh. Maybe, eventually, it will lead to answers, but for now, the more we look, the more questions come up."

"I have a personal, off-the-record question. You don't have to answer it if it makes you uncomfortable."

"I'm a nurse, nothing makes me uncomfortable," Glori smiled.

"Ahhh...." Josh could feel his face heating up. He ran a hand through his hair, starting to feel like an a-hole for even bringing it up, "I couldn't help but do the math..."

He could see the direct, open expression on her face beginning to close. *She has a few things of her own that she doesn't want laid open on the table,* he thought. Did he want to get back at her for getting on her feet faster than him? Was he upset that she didn't seem to share her husband's protective feelings for his daughter? Was it the comment about Child Protective Services? Josh couldn't pinpoint what it was that made him forge ahead with his query, "I know that you're pleased about that baby and all, but aren't you feeling a little 'used' knowing that your husband, took liberties with you when weren't aware of what he was doing?"

Glori blinked as if he'd slapped her. Planting her palms on the table, she hauled her heavy body into a standing position. Leaning over her hands, she glared at him. "I'm not going to answer that. Not because I'm uncomfortable talking about a sensitive subject, but because I expected better than that from you! This interview is over," she started walking away.

"Glori, I'm sorry," he got up to follow. "You're right; I was out of line." He was surprised to see she was crying when she turned to face him.

"I can't talk any more, just.... leave, Josh."

When he was alone in the room, he mumbled, "Shit," while unplugging the tape recorder. Unzipping his backpack, he shoved his notepad and other items inside.

Thinking again he sat back down, pulling out his notepad. Ripping off a fresh sheet, he scrawled a note that he left on the table.

❧22❧
SOMEONE TO
WATCH OVER HER

"THEIR BLADDERS ARE STRONG. They can easily wait," Haylee told the dog owners. "Perry wakes up first because he hears a rooster crowing. He gets restless; then he wants Earl to play. I think if you put them in separate kennels, both would go back to sleep."

They'd done everything they could think of, short of having the dogs sleep in bed with them, to curtail the daily round of barking at 5:15 a.m. After receiving a letter of complaint from Animal Control, Ron Truitt, a hospital administrator, who thought a pet intuitive was another term for 'scam artist,' consented to his wife, Trudy's, plea to meet with Haylee Garrett. Ron was surprised and skeptical when Haylee told them that the behavior had more to do with Perry being a light sleeper rather than a demand to go pee.

When he heard the rooster's call the next morning, Ron waited, expectantly, to see what the 'boys' would do. "I'll be darned!" he said, shaking his head when the dogs remained silent. He looked over at his wife who wore a grin. That his phone wasn't ringing with neighbor grievances validated Trudy's solution.

Perry, Earl, Trudy, and Ron, had become regular clients. When Trudy heard that Haylee and her daughter were looking for a place in Berkeley, she jumped at the chance to have them rent the granny unit above the garage behind their house. "If you'll do regular sessions for us and the 'boys,' I'll only charge half the rent."

～～～～

During the move, Josh had made a point to ride with Eugene in his pickup loaded with furniture and household items. "Once she gets settled, Haylee's planning to find the other people she attacked in Berkeley. I've gotten the addresses of four of the families."

Gene wore a grim expression. His hands adjusted on the steering wheel, "Glori and I want her to wait. This is not something that she can do by herself—afterward; she goes down. Someone needs to take care of the baby, and keep an eye on Haylee."

"Oh?"

"Haylee was out for seven days after she did that thing with the crystal for you. When she did it for Glori, it was five days." Gene glanced over at Josh.

"She didn't tell me about this."

Gene drew in a long breath, "I was worried that she hadn't. She's so focused on repairing her mistakes that she's not thinking everything through. That's why we want her to wait—so Glori and I can help."

"My parents never said anything."

"Your parents didn't know."

"But— "

Eugene shook his head vigorously. "No. There are too many odd things about my girl. If your folks had seen—any of it—they'd have asked too many questions."

When Josh remained silent, lost in thought, Gene continued, "You're wondering about me, I suppose, why I haven't been asking questions. I can't, honestly, say. Glori and I have been talking about this too. It's a gut instinct, something I don't consciously think about— to protect my daughter and her mother. "

Josh turned his head abruptly, regarding Eugene, he was frowning.

The older man chuckled, "So I'm not the only one." Another long a pause stretched out as they drove. "Well— I'm glad for that," Gene commented.

"Tell me what happens to her when— After she's done the 'crystal thing.'" Josh repeated crossing his arms over his chest.

"She's not in distress." Eugene began, "No fever, aches, or pains. She looks like she's sleeping, but there's nothing that'll wake her up. She gets up once a day, somewhere between two and three in the morning, to use the bathroom, scarf down anything she finds to eat, then she drops back to sleep."

"Do you think she's sleepwalking?"

"That's what Glori thought at first, but it doesn't follow any of the classic signs. Haylee talks sometimes, but in very different voices, accents, languages even."

"What do you think it is?"

"Me?" Eugene sounded surprised that Josh would ask. "I think that it takes a lot of energy to put someone back. I think that the deep sleep is a recovery process."

"Did you watch her— do her thing— on me?"

"I watched her with Glori. I was keeping Serena occupied when she did you. We got Haylee out of there before your parents returned. When Haylee goes down, she goes down hard."

"So— it occurs instantly?"

"More or less."

"You drove her home like that, from Los Angeles?"

"Nah, I booked a hotel ahead of time, not too far from your house."

"You stayed there for a week?"

"Yes, at first Glori and I alternated taking Serena out while one of us stayed behind with Haylee. Once we realized that her waking moments kept to a specific pattern, we went out together. Serena had a grand time; we took lots of walks in the park. We visited museums. You'll have to do that too, look after Serena, if Haylee plans to go forward... before we're ready."

Although it vexed him, Josh knew that Eugene spoke the truth.

❧

After unloading the truck, Eugene was ready to head back home. Glori had given birth to Haylee's little brother, Byron, the week before. Haylee knew that her dad would want to go. She ordered a small pizza, his favorite kind, extra sauce, cheese, mushrooms, tomatoes, and sausage, that she handed him so he could eat while driving.

Eugene hugged and kissed his granddaughter, shook hands with Josh and Spencer, then turned to say goodbye to Haylee. "Josh and I talked on the drive."

Rolling her eyes, but smiling, she replied, "When he asked to ride with you, I thought that was what he was hoping would happen."

"I know you want to fix those other boys."

"Dad—" Haylee looked over her shoulder.

He glanced in the same direction. "If you are going to go ahead, you can't be keeping things from him. It's not fair to your daughter, and it's not fair to him."

Abashed, Haylee didn't meet his eyes, "I know," she admitted.

"Listen," Eugene put his hands on her shoulders, "I support you, how ever you want to do this. But don't leave things to chance, especially your daughter."

"I wouldn't."

"Be careful, Hay Hay, and let us know if we can help."

They hugged.

⬥⬥⬥

Spencer wolfed down four large pieces of pizza and gulped two beers, hastily, while observing his brother. Haylee had joined them briefly, then went to another room to start getting beds made.

Clinking his empty beer bottle on the table, he gained Josh's attention. "What's up? Something happen between you and her father?" he asked his brother.

"Not really," Josh shrugged, he gave me a few more things to think about."

"Wanta share?"

Looking Spencer up and down, Josh grinned slowly. "I see childcare looming in your near future," he crooned.

"Aw, crap!" Spencer leaned back, "I'll never live that down."

Sobered, Josh replied, "That's not a bad thing, Spencer. It's a useful skill you'll be glad to have, eventually." Josh glanced at the bottle, "Drinking and kid sitting don't mix."

Standing up abruptly, Spencer grabbed his jacket. Yelling down the hallway, he announced, "I'm outa here girls!"

❧

On the first morning in their new place, Haylee bundled up Serena, packed her stroller, diaper bag, warm milk, hot tea, oatmeal and a scrambled ham and egg sandwich, and sand toys into the car. This early in the day, the traffic was light. It only took them eight minutes to get to the toll booth on the Bay Bridge. Tossing seventy-five cents in the change basket, Haylee started whistling when the striped barrier arm raised, letting them pass. Treasure Island came into view, inspiring a sea shanty theme.

Crossing into downtown San Francesco, Haylee concentrated on the road signs. Unable to enjoy gazing at the tall skyscrapers, she changed lanes, switching from Interstate 80 to Highway 101. Turning off at Geary Blvd, they navigated through the business district that gave way to tightly packed row houses. At the entrance to the park, Haylee glanced up in the rearview mirror, grinning at Serena, "We're almost there."

Driving passed the Cliff House, a tourist destination, and restaurant, perched on the rocks at the edge of the sea, Haylee thought about the changes that happen to a place over time. She'd picnicked at Ocean Beach on many Sundays when she'd worn long skirts, petticoats, high-necked blouses with full-length sleeves and wide-brimmed hats.

Parking in a lot with drifts of sand, Haylee talked while she loaded the stroller with all their supplies, tucking Serena in last. "Your dad used to bring me here. That was before that building over there was built. Back then, this was just one long stretch of beach."

Haylee kept to the paved bike path that paralleled the road, pushing the stroller at a brisk pace. The wind off the water was cold, whipping loose hair about her face. Zipping up her jacket and hood, then checking to make sure Serena was warm, they continued. Spotting an outcropping of rocks that would be a good windbreak, Haylee set up a mini-breakfast picnic camp.

After two hours of building sand castles, eating their food, throwing bread crumbs to the seagulls, and making forays out to play in the water, Serena was fast asleep, spread out on a blanket, still clutching a piece of driftwood. Haylee leaned back against a rock, stretching her legs out, crossing her ankles, she rested a hand on Serena's back. Sunglasses shielded her eyes from the elements.

The even rising and falling of her daughter's chest lulled Haylee into relaxation. She'd been resisting the emotions that clawed under the surface of her 'even-tempered Mommy, pet intuitive' veneer. Letting her masks slip out of place, silent tears streamed, in a steady flow, from beneath her Ray-Ban's.

From a floating place, warmed by the sun, Haylee jerked back into wakefulness. What had startled her? Serena was still dozing. All the animals and people on the beach were far away. Taking her sunglasses off, she rubbed at the crusty remains left from dried tears. Haylee noticed it, then, something— not right. It was a sound, but not audible; it vibrated down the entire length of her spine. Careful not to disturb Serena, she stood. Staring out over the sun-sparkled water, she raised a hand to protect her eyes. She noticed that the gesture increased the sick feeling.

Holding both hands in front of her, palms down, Haylee walked to the water's edge. The feeling got worse. When a cold wave lapped over her bare feet, she jumped. The vibration down her back had turned to a silent shriek.

Running back to their day camp, Haylee rushed to collect their things. By the time she woke Serena, changed her diaper, and loaded her in her wheeled chariot, the rise of Haylee's troubling sensations had subsided.

Haylee was irritable and off-kilter for the rest of the day. Josh called, asking if she wanted help unpacking, but she put him off. When Serena was down for the night, and Haylee was, once again on the fringes of sleep, the kernel of what had been bothering her popped into her mind.

The last time she'd been on Ocean Beach with Reece, Edward and Polly, something similar had happened. A vibration that was a sound, but wasn't, her hands behaving like radio antennas. What she'd felt, then, wasn't unpleasant, it was like the rhythm of Serena's sleeping breath, it was vibrant; it was a song.

☙23☙
STAKEOUT

HAYLEE SETTLED INTO HER new work routine at the veterinary clinic. Serena thrived at her new daycare center. They started having Josh practice taking care of Serena on his own.

As soon as Josh could handle Serena, Haylee would be ready to restore her next victim - Thomas Milani. He'd been a Mass Communications student at Berkeley. He had been living at the Alpha Sigma Phi house on the fateful night of Haylee's rampage. Now he was housed in an adult care facility in Milpitas close to where his parents lived.

After several overnight stakeouts, Haylee had discovered that there was a gap in staff coverage between 2:30 a.m. and 4:14 a.m. On the night that she'd made this discovery, Josh had joined them. They'd split a medium sized whole wheat vegetarian pizza while Serena munched on bananas and turkey dogs in the back seat.

The car was quiet once Serena nodded off to sleep. For a while, Haylee and Josh observed a decreasing stream of people who came and went from Bay Care's main entrance. In a notebook, they recorded the time and number people. Covered in thick blankets, they were cozy and warm. Somewhere around 11:30 p.m., Haylee awoke to a light touch tickling her face.

Josh was leaning on his side tracing the contours of her eyebrows and temples. He smiled, hesitating when she opened her eyes. When Haylee didn't make a move to stop him, he continued, "You are beautiful," he whispered. "Your skin is soft, and your eyes are so deep. I've never known anyone like you."

Haylee's breath caught in her throat. The heat from his touch traveled all the way down to her toes. A waiver of hesitation, on her part, was so slight that he didn't notice. She reached up to lay her hand along his neck. It felt warm, solid. Haylee saw the pulse in his artery, "Your heart is racing," she whispered.

Josh closed his eyes.

Afterword, Haylee couldn't remember if she moved onto his seat or if he lifted her over to him, but suddenly she was snuggled under his blanket lying on top of him. Their lips met, softly at first, hesitant, exploring, asking for permission. Open mouths and darting tongues turned the kiss forceful. Their movements were pressing, demanding.

Haylee moaned a breathy sound, from the deep recess of her throat, when Josh's hands slipped under her t-shirt, touching bare skin. Her response was to grind her pelvis into his.

Her bra came loose. She moved, giving better access to the places he wanted. When he cradled her soft flesh in the palms of his hands, lightly stroking his thumbs over the sensitive, nubby skin, they both tensed. Realizing that the tide was high and that they were quickly approaching a point of no return, Haylee let her full weight press against Josh, efficiently stopping the movements of his hands. "We have to stop; we can't," she whispered, even as she tasted the lobe of his ear.

"I know, he growled, "but I sure want to!"

Haylee giggled. They lay together, like exhausted sprinters, glistening with perspiration, as their breathing calmed after the exertion. They regarded one another, smiling.

Josh, reluctantly pulled his hands away, tugging Haylee's shirt back into place. Still holding her, but cool now, he resumed his tracing patterns on her face. "Haylee, I...," he whispered.

Shaking her head 'no,' she turned her face into his palm, kissing him. "Not yet. I am so very close, Josh, but not just yet..." To ensure that he didn't feel hurt by her statement, she made eye contact, then ran her tongue up his thumb. When she got to the end, she pulled it into her mouth.

"Oh good, God!" he bucked under her. His face scrunched, as if in pain.

Immediately releasing his digit, Haylee shushed him so that he wouldn't wake Serena.

From their bucket seats, under their blankets, they held hands off and on for the rest of the night, not daring to kiss again. It was then that they discovered the information that they would need for Haylee to return.

⚬≈≋≈⚬

"Trudy mentioned, several times that she'll be happy to watch Serena when I want to go grocery shopping. I haven't taken her up on it yet, but I guess I should..." Haylee chewed on the end of her thumb, watching Josh fumble with a squirmy Serena on the couch during a diaper change. "If you do that on the floor, she won't be able to fall anywhere."

"I just realized that," Josh responded dryly. He finished fastening the ends, lifted the little girl to her feet, keeping her close to the couch so she could hold onto it for support. "There you are, Serena." Josh declared. "That wasn't so bad, was it?"

Serena laughed, jostling up and down on chubby legs. "Pee!" she yelled. The diaper fell to her feet, making a weighty thud. A stream of yellow urine soaked her socks. "Pee! Pee! Pee!" she sang in delight.

Twenty-five minutes later, Josh pushed Serena down the sidewalk in her stroller. She giggled every time they went over a bump. "More!" she cried until Josh realized that she was asking to emphasize the movements. Serena named a few things as they passed. "Doggie." "Key Key." "Tree!" Josh wore a lingering smile. He couldn't remember having laughed so hard.

Small children must have the same attraction qualities as puppies, Josh thought as they stopped for a second time so that a woman could admire the baby. The females seemed to be having a lively two-way conversation. It ended when Serena fished a Cheerio out from under her seat, holding it out to the woman. Accepting it as if it were the Hope Diamond, the woman exclaimed, "Thank You!" with an exuberance befitting the wondrous gift. "I'm going to keep this someplace special, and I'll think about you whenever I look at it."

"What a darling little girl!" The matron crooned, smiling at Josh. "Your daughter has your eyes," she commented.

Josh opened his mouth, then shut it. He nodded, "Thank you."

For the rest of their outing, Josh felt like his feet were floating several inches above the pavement. The interaction replayed in his mind on a continuous loop. Like trying on a new sports jacket, he tested the weight and feel of a new role.

He hadn't planned to think about that for a long time, yet, here it was, presented with simplicity, without fanfare, a remarkable moment.

The jacket fit, surprisingly well, it didn't restrict or bind, it was comfortable, familiar, like something he'd been waiting for, but didn't know it; it made him feel like the person who was Joshua James Herkowitz had become...larger.

༺24༻
MY WIFE

THEIR PLAN WAS READY to execute. They would visit Bay Care on Monday. Since it was Friday, they had a few days to kill. Haylee suggested a hike and picnic to take their mind off waiting.

It was a beautiful, sunny day. The rolling hills, carpeted with fragrant fresh grass and wildflowers smelled green and alive. Dotting the mounds of earth were oak trees and scrub redbuds. Warm, sweet, heady scents of spring uplifted their mood. Josh laughed as Serena wound bits of his hair around her fingers. "Come on, leave that alone." He playfully brushed her hands away.

Shifting his weight, he adjusted the straps that were digging into his shoulders. He continued the narrative he'd begun. "My family moved to the Los Angeles Basin in the 1930's. I came up here to go to school because we have business ties here."

"Thank goodness for ties," Haylee said. "If you hadn't gone to Berkeley, we would never have met."

"Right," he smiled, looking down at their entwined fingers. He gave her hand a gentle squeeze.

"Where are you taking me?" he wanted to know.

"You'll see. We're getting close...I think." She peered around, working to get her bearings.

As they hiked, he couldn't bring himself to tell her that he was already very familiar with this place.

Josh thought about how much he loved her. He fully admitted it to himself, although he had yet to say those words out loud. He loved her mind, her enthusiasm, and all her wild stories. He loved her smile and dedication to doing the right thing despite the perils. She was a good mother, daughter, and friend.

Today, Haylee's expressions were tinged with something else...worry perhaps? *I want to spend the rest of my life watching her,* Josh thought

"Oh! I think I see it!" Releasing his hand, Haylee raced ahead to a rock outcropping. Laughing, he jogged behind her, causing the cumbersome backpack to bounce in time with his footfalls.

A delighted giggle broke out from behind his head. "Horsey!" Serena chirped.

"Neigh! Neigh!" responded Josh. He elongated his gait to give her more of a rolling motion.

Josh watched Haylee in the distance, searching for something. He hadn't told her yet about the grant he'd won from the Université de Lyon...it included a cute little two-bedroom house in a neighborhood with lots of young families. The position he wanted to take would open next year. He grinned.

Haylee found what she was looking for; he could tell by the way she stiffened then reached out with a purpose. She was on her knees, looking somber as she poured over an assortment of things in her lap. "What's that?" Josh asked when he arrived.

Placing the items inside an open metal box on the ground beside her, she got up to help Josh remove his backpack. He glanced over at the container. He could see the edges of what looked like a stack of papers.

Haylee adjusted the expanding part of the child carrier frame so that it would stand up on its own. From one of the side pockets, she fished out a sippy cup and a Tupperware container filled with Cheerios. She opened them, handing them to her daughter.

Coming back toward Josh, pain was visible on Haylee's face. "Do you remember when I told you about my time jump?"

He rolled his eyes, "Not this again."

"I can prove it."

Taking in a patient breath, he sighed. "Alright, I agree to suspend all logical arguments, sit here quietly with my hands folded nicely, while you show me proof." He nudged his glasses farther up his nose.

She nodded with a grimness that suggested he should be concerned.

❦

Forty-five minutes later, Josh was the one wearing an expression of dazed confusion. She'd brought him to the place where she said she first arrived in 1849; a place where she'd stashed all the twentieth-century items she had on her at the time.

Haylee's hands were trembling as she pulled things out of the box. "This is the keyring Dad gave me when he surprised me with the Bug. This was a pack of gum that I had in my pocket. There are lots of other things in here." Her voice was hoarse, Haylee sucked in an unsteady breath. Peering inside, she said, "Reece did this.... the box." She sighed, "I remember those from the safe." Lifting out a small cloth sack, she held it out, dropping it in Josh's hand.

He was surprised by the weight. It was heavier than it looked. Untying the string, he spread the cloth wide. Inside were twenty to thirty pea-sized gold nuggets. Josh shook his head. *You'd think with all the extraordinary things I have witnessed with Hay, I'd be used to this by now.*

He heard her make a painful utterance, like a wounded animal. "There are letters in here. Lots of them, addressed to me." She reached in, carefully, bringing up a stack of envelopes tied together with twine.

She knelt there, reverently, holding the letters, like they were sacred. Haylee, brought them up, pressing them against her chest.

Raising red-rimmed eyes, she met his gaze. "I have to go," she squeaked, getting up, she moved off, away from them.

The farther she went, the colder Josh felt.

Serena coughed, calling his attention to her. Moving automatically, he patted her back, removed the conglomerated mess of food from her hands, wiped her face with a washcloth and refreshed the water in her sippy cup. All the while, his eyes darted to where he'd last seen Haylee.

When it didn't look like Haylee was coming back anytime soon, Josh's curiosity got the best of him. He returned to the box, peeking inside. A large, legal sized folder caught his attention. Scrawled across the front were the words Wild Cat.

The hair on the back of Josh's neck and along his forearms stood up. He reached for it.

If everything that had already happened today wasn't enough to liquefy his brain and have it oozing out of his ears, the paper clutched in his hand could have done that all on its own. It was a document he'd heard about but never believed existed.

It was part of the trust that his family had administered for well over a hundred years. Management responsibilities were the primary reason he'd chosen to come up here to go to school. The trust governed an enormous piece of open land surrounded by houses and business parks—land that they had been hiking on.

A clause in the trust verbiage stated that if a specific document was produced between 1985 and 1992, the instructions upon it were to be followed to the letter. If the document never surfaced, then the remaining heirs could sell or dispose of the property however they saw fit. Proof of its validity would be provided.

The paper in Josh's hand read, *If this document is presented by my wife, Haylee Louise Garrett Keener, on or before the year 1992, then the entire tract of land known as Wild Cat Canyon is to be transferred into her ownership for the express purpose of providing for her, and for my daughter.*

It was signed by Josh's great-great-great-great-great grandfather, Reece James Keener. The date on it was June 8, 1869.

Josh's stunned gaze traveled first to the cherubic angel with a fist buried in her mouth, a child he'd recently begun to think of as his own. Then his eyes, once again, went to where he'd last seen Haylee.

❧25❧
SEVEN YEARS

ALL JOSH COULD THINK about was that someone was coming between them. It was as if a wall were being built brick by brick, impenetrable.

Haylee had been coming around. She'd been affectionate, open to his advances. Now Reece was back. All Josh could focus on was Haylee, the stricken look on her face, and the stack of letters she'd clutched over her heart.

The words....'my wife' pierced him. The blade, razor sharp, hit dead center, decimating that tender organ into pieces of jagged shrapnel. *She'd married him. She'd gone willingly into his bed.* Josh closed his eyes. He heard the injured animal sounds Haylee was making from somewhere in the distance. He couldn't bear to witness her grief.

Turning on his heel, he backtracked on the trail, far enough away so that all he could hear were bees and birds. He needed distance. Josh paced as his thoughts ran amok. *He doesn't exist. He's only an idea. Ideas can't hold her or...*

Forcing himself to unclench his fists, he sat on a rock. *This is real.* He nodded in resignation. *She really did what she said. She traveled back in time.*

Josh's thoughts shifted into a more personal vein. Reece Keener was <u>his</u> ancestor. Not only had the man been responsible for creating offspring that eventually led to his mother, but the investments that he made had grown and provided a sizable income for his family— for generations— revenue that would now, in part, belong to Haylee and Serena. *Serena is the man's direct descendant.*

When Josh heard a screech followed by a yelp and high-pitched cries, his body tensed. He jumped up, dashing back toward the picnic spot, charging into the clearing.

Haylee was on her knees clutching Serena tightly. "Oh my God! Oh my God," she repeated, rocking the screaming child.

"What is it?" Josh yelled. "Are you bit? Is Serena bit?"

Seeing that Haylee was incapable of answering, he pulled Serena away. "Show me where!" He frantically began checking the little girl's extremities. Josh's hands shook as he removed Serena's shoes and sweatpants. Mentally he thought through how long it would take to retrieve his snakebite kit; he'd left the damned thing in the car! He calculated the child's body weight, how fast poison would circulate through her system, and how long it would take them to reach help. Finding nothing physically amiss with Serena, he set her on top of their picnic blanket, turning to Haylee.

Josh pulled Haylee's boots off, then her socks, checking for puncture wounds. Not finding redness, or swelling, he was at a loss for where to look next. When she continued screaming, he grabbed her by the shoulders, shaking her. "What is it?" he shouted.

Haylee shook her head in a 'no' response. "It can't be! It just can't be!" she sobbed...

He assessed her eyes. Her pupils were not dilated. He put his hand on her forehead noting that she wasn't cold or clammy.

Haylee calmed under his touch. Josh sensed it when her focus shifted to his actions.

"What are you doing?" she asked.

Heaving a sigh of relief, he regarded her. "I thought that one of you had a snakebite."

Haylee shook her head, "No... there wasn't a snake."

Not knowing how to respond, he remained silent, feeling his heart rate calm.

Serena crawled up into his lap. Josh pulled his jacket off, draping it over her. The little girl took catchy breaths as she settled in. Giving her a reassuring hug, he rubbed her back. She relaxed against him.

The expressions on Haylee's face changed as she watched her daughter. "You left her here— alone."

"I wasn't thinking."

"Neither was I," Haylee admitted. Leaning back, she blinked slowly. Attempting to smile, her lips twitched, tears rimmed her eyes. "Serena feels safe with you," she observed.

Josh returned Haylee's hesitant smile, willing her to tell him what was bothering her, but not wanting to hear what she would say.

Haylee heaved a sigh. "He lied."

"Who lied?"

"Reece."

"Oh—" *Maybe I was jumping to the wrong conclusions,* Josh thought.

"When we were on the Dicey, Emis wrote down how to send me back. He was supposed to have done it that night. That night, Josh! Do you know what that means?"

"I don't—"

"I was there for nearly a year. That entire time, Reece knew that I wanted to return, but he chose not to send me—until the fire." She swallowed.

Josh hugged Serena, resting his cheek on top of her head. He could feel a sting at the back of his eyes.

"He left all that stuff back there because he felt guilty. There was something *else* he'd kept from me." Haylee got up, grinding and baring her teeth; she wore a murderous look. Pacing, her fists were tight balls of stone-like muscle and bone. She thrust them out, making an exclamation, before stomping back toward him.

Serena burrowed inside Josh's jacket. He wrapped himself around her while keeping his eyes on her mother.

"Travelers attack people." Haylee spit out, turning, she stomped away. Coming back, she shouted, "They jump through time— if you haven't already guessed," she laughed sardonically. "I am one. Lucky me."

With long strides she paced away. Turning around, she stood looking at him, across the distance. Her shoulders drooped. "Travelers in the lineage are rare, but all of the women in my maternal line share something." She stated, walking back, standing before him. Her chin and lips trembled, her voice quivered, "They die seven years after giving birth. That's what happened to my mom." Silent tears coursed lines down Haylee's face, "It'll happen to Serena too." Her voice trailed off.

Pressing her fingers over her eyes, she scrubbed her face as if scouring it with sandpaper. She let out an abrupt, furious utterance. "For Travelers, there's something more."

Sinking to her knees, directly in front of Josh, she shuddered. Clutching her elbows, she looked like she was trying to keep herself from falling apart. "He was hoping...." She laughed. The sound was abrasive, brittle. "That I'd come find this box before I did what I came back to do."

"Haylee?" Josh felt goosebumps forming on his skin. His scalp was growing tight.

"No!" Her eyes were wide, glassy. Her head and neck bobbled on her shoulders. She held up a finger, 'shhhh-ing' him. "No! Josh, it gets so much better!"

"Every time the crystal is used to return a soul—" she sounded crazy, maniacal, like Jack Torrance in The Shining. "One year is deducted from the seven!"

❧26❧
WHAT IF IT'S TRUE?

A LIFE-AND-DEATH, emergency, with straight-forward decisions to make would be preferable to.... this, Josh thought.

Haylee hadn't spoken since she'd given him her pronouncement. As she knelt there, staring at him, he could see that her mind was a million miles away. When she, finally shook herself out of it, she collected Serena, checked and changed her diaper, re-dressed her, hefted her up and placed her in her carrier. Moving the entire contraption onto a boulder, Haylee made sure it was stable before turning around to slip her arms and shoulders, one-by-one into the straps. Hoisting the weight onto her back and adjusting it at her waist, Haylee began walking down the trail.

"Haylee, wait!" Josh had called.

She didn't respond but kept going. Josh looked over the trash, the blanket, and the box with all its contents. Hastily, he sorted and gathered everything stuffing it into the backpack Haylee had worn while he packed Serena.

Jogging to catch up to her, he let her continue ahead, keeping his distance but keeping her in sight. He couldn't stop himself from analyzing facts. Haylee appeared to be perfectly healthy. Serena was also a picture of vitality. Surely, if anything was wrong health-wise, they could find a solution.

Josh refused to let his mind tangle with the idea that Haylee might have a limited life span...made more so by the act of rescuing him and the others.

As they hiked, Josh could tell Haylee was getting tired. Her pace slowed, she shifted the straps, redistributing the weight. After an hour and a half, she stopped. Finding a log, she leaned back, letting it support the carrier while she slipped out of it. Setting it on the ground and stabilizing it, Haylee dug in a side pocket, pulling out her canteen. Josh could see sweat dripping along the sides of her face and neck.

Haylee made eye contact with him while wiping a sleeve over her brow. When he took a step toward her, she gave him a murderous look, pointing in his direction, indicating that he should stay away.

Packing up his Nissan Stanza, was also a silent affair. Haylee climbed in the back, buckling herself next to Serena. When Josh tried talking, she shook her head and closed her eyes.

On the road, he glanced at their reflection in the rear-view mirror. Serena was sleeping soundly. She'd never know her father, what would happen to her if she lost her mother too? The band of constriction, around Josh's chest, started squeezing again.

When he remembered the research he'd done, it tightened another two notches. His hands ached from clutching the wheel. The records had shown a history of women with early deaths.

He had to focus on less emotional topics, so he could drive safely.

Josh thought about the Wild Cat Board of Directors. It was the managerial body that made recommendations and decisions about the family's landholding. The board consisted of four members of the community and himself. For the last six years, Josh had met with them once a quarter to discuss the economy and land use issues. They'd leased portions of the property out to the County for recreational purposes.

He'd learned a lot about business, city growth, and land stewardship. Josh wrote up annual reports and signed the board member compensation checks. He also knew that each board member had a personal interest in the land— if it ever became available.

The old boy had amassed a valuable set of holdings in his day. They'd appreciated at astronomical rates. Other properties, in downtown San Francesco, were still owned by his descendants.

He'd done as well as anyone could, leaving a legacy. The family certainly didn't need...more. They had stayed true to the original intent that Keener had stated for Wild Cat Canyon. He wanted it to remain open and free. He'd been a part of San Francesco in its infancy. The canyon, then, was miles away from city development. But he'd guessed that it wouldn't always be that way. Josh admired that the man had been such a forward thinker.

Wild Cat had remained separate. Everyone who knew about the unusual 1982 stipulation thought it was either a joke or evidence that Keener suffered from delusions. Josh had been one of them. He'd joked with the board members saying that the likelihood of a document surfacing after all this time was less than zero.

Now, here he was, in possession of said document well within the years that Keener had predicted. Not only was he in possession of the paper, but he also had the man's *wife* and his daughter to look after.

A war was beginning to rage inside Josh. His belief system, in the orderly, understandable workings of the world, was swaying on its foundation— not unlike the behavior of buildings in the city when the ground quakes under their feet. The woman he loved was pulling away. Another man, that he had no way of confronting or fighting, was asserting his claim on her.

Josh glanced in Haylee's direction. She had no idea that she was about to become a target for heavily armed lawyers who would be circling her, testing the water for blood, their sharp teeth ready, at a moment's notice, to sink into soft flesh.

Strong, undeniable, feelings of protection assuaged Josh. Right then, he promised to do whatever it took to stand against the backlash. He would follow Reece's wishes.

Turning on the exit ramp off the freeway and onto the surface streets, the clamp around Josh's heart cinched smaller again. Restricted, he couldn't take full breaths. *What if it's true?*

He'd been blindingly furious with her for betraying him, stealing time from him, setting him back. The evidence, what there was of it, appeared to support her claim. Haylee was undoubtedly behaving as if she believed it.

What if it's true? his mind screamed inside, "What have I done?" he whispered so quietly that no one heard. His lips barely moved.

❧27❧
WILL YOU HAVE ME?

WHEN THEY ARRIVED AT Haylee's place, Josh helped unload the picnic and baby gear as well as the box from Reece. Haylee stood in the middle of the kitchen staring at it sitting on the table.

Part of her wanted the world to go away so she could lose herself in a lifetime of words that Reece had managed to get to her. Another part of her wished that she could find her way back so she could scream at him. *YOU kept me there! You lied to me almost the entire time we were together!*

That box made his death, so very long ago, real. *I'll never see his face, hear his voice, fight with him, or make love with him ever again...*

Haylee felt utterly alone. She turned desolate eyes toward her daughter who was starting to fuss. *She's hungry.*

Haylee was incapable of moving or even asking for help.

❧

"I'll feed Serena if you want to go take a bath or a shower." Josh offered.

Haylee looked at him like he was a stranger. Woodenly she nodded, "That's a good idea."

⟡

Josh listened to the water running as he held out another spoon of chicken and rice to Serena. At first, the little girl grabbed handfuls, smashing it into her mouth. She smeared it all over her high chair tray and rubbed it in her hair. Her big eyes looked lovingly at him as she daintily took the bite of food offered from the utensil.

"Mmmm, gud," she grinned showing off her new. "More pease."

Josh chuckled, fulfilling her request. His mood lightened. "You are going to need a bath yourself, young lady."

"Ba!" Serena squealed.

⟡

It was late by the time Josh had Serena clean, diapered, jammied and sleeping in her crib. Haylee had gone straight to bed, falling asleep the moment her head hit the pillow.

Josh straightened the kitchen, snacking on miscellaneous leftovers. He fought a bone-deep weariness as his thoughts fixated on their discovery. He eyed the rusty box. He picked it up, turning it around in his hands, studying its construction. Sitting down, still holding it, he ran his thumb over the clasp.

He bit a corner of his lip, hesitating. It was a time capsule. It contained information he could use to arm himself for what was coming. Sucking in a breath, feeling the clamp on his chest tighten again, he opened it. In the silent room, the rusty-hinged creak sounded amplified. Freezing, Josh looked up, checking to see if he was still alone.

The codicil was still there, right where he'd left it. Beneath it, he could see the letters Haylee had shown him. Sure enough, the very first one had her name scrolled, with flourishes made by a steady hand.

He wanted to reach in, but he remembered the feelings he had when he'd discovered that Haylee had been inside his Gulliver book. Sure, the note she left held meaning, it was a logical place to put it, somewhere she was sure only he would find, but knowing that she'd seen his most private things.... wasn't good. He huffed when he realized her going through his things felt more invasive than her access to all his thoughts.

Pursing his mouth, Josh closed the lid, placing the box back in the center of the table.

Instead of locking up and going home, Josh decided to shower and camp out on Haylee's couch.

❦

Haylee turned to look at the clock. It was 12:45 a.m. Her heart still thundered from the dream that had woken her. For a brief time, she'd been back in the middle of the fire. Polly, held tightly in her arms screamed for her maman. Haylee's mother, Doris, told her to remember the pendant.

Blinking into awareness, Haylee remembered what had happened earlier in the day. She shivered. Wrapping a blanket around her shoulders, she got up to check on Serena. She found her daughter dreaming with the hint of a smile. Haylee echoed that expression. *She's amazing. How is it possible that in the middle of confusion and chaos, something as beautiful and wonderful as Serena happened?* Haylee leaned down, kissing her daughter's smooth cheek.

On her way to the kitchen for a glass of water, Haylee stopped in mid-stride staring at the lump on her couch. *He stayed.* The ice at the edges of her heart thawed. Thankfulness for Josh's steadfast presence seeped into it.

In the kitchen looking at Reece's box, memories of events that happened with Emis replayed in Haylee's head. The hostage situation, and stealing Edward's soul. Reece being forced to watch. Emis placing her face in Haylee's webbed hand. Her drowning and what Reece had had to do after that.

Emis had spoken hatefully of ancient ones who'd enslaved their bloodline. Haylee had never taken the time to think further on that topic. After Emis had forced Haylee to take her soul, intense headaches had interfered with her ability to read Emis's thoughts. Recently, small bits of information had started to trickle through.

Haylee knew, with a certainty, that her own life would end soon. If she continued with her plan to return every soul she'd stolen, she'd have even less time. *It's not fair! I've only just begun to sort out this mess. How can I possibly choose between the people I've hurt and Serena?*

Their plan for tomorrow, to return Thomas Milani, would have to wait. Haylee's heart hurt as she looked back toward Serena's room. Closing her eyes, Haylee didn't want to think about that right now.

She ran a finger along the edge of Reece's box. "I'm so mad at you, but I still love you," she whispered. "I love Josh too. I want to be with him...I *need* to be with him. Forgive me." Haylee kissed the tips of her fingers, pressing them to the metal lid.

She tiptoed over to the couch where she perched on the edge. Josh lay under a crumpled blanket; one arm flung over the top of his head. Her eyes followed the moonlight as it highlighted the contours of his brow, nose, and cheeks. She fought the urge to touch his beard and run her hand down the side of his neck. *How could I have not realized this before?* she wondered.

Haylee leaned down to kiss the hand that rested on his chest. She inhaled the clean, fresh scent of him. Haylee scooted herself into the crook of his arm, stretching out next to him. Instinctively, he took hold of her. He turned to bury his nose in her hair while mumbling. Haylee reached up, tracing a finger along his cheek. Josh's eyes fluttered before opening.

When the realization dawned on him where they were and what she was doing, he frowned, rising on an elbow, "Haylee? Are you alright?"

Haylee knew that he was attempting to move away so that she would not feel his growing reaction. Reaching down to hold his hips in place, she pressed herself against him. "Kiss me Josh.... please?"

A pained look crossed his face. Gazing deeply into her eyes, he said, "Are you sure this is what you want—that *I* am who you want?"

Haylee nuzzled his neck "You are my best friend."

Josh was still, he looked like he was fighting a fierce battle.

She kissed him, nibbling at his ear. "We've been inside each other's heads, Josh. I know you...and you know me." Haylee reached between them, pressing against his rigid manhood.

Josh sucked in a breath when Haylee unzipped his pants, "You're sure?" his voice was strained, his eyes beginning to glaze over.

Haylee stretched up to place a kiss on his lips. "I love you, Josh. It's you I want to be with if you will have me."

He leaned down to claim her lips with a purposeful acceptance of her words and meaning.

❧28❧
THE CODICIL

THEY'D SPENT HOURS making love last night, dozing, then repeating. At first, their motions were hungry, frenzied, almost rough in their greediness. The need to know each other's scents, textures, sounds, likes and dislikes was savage. As dawn drew near, they shifted into smoother, more flowing expressions of tenderness. At last, curled around each other, they fell into a restorative, dreamless, sleep.

With her hands in a prayer pose resting beneath her left cheek, Haylee woke. Josh's knees rested behind hers; his arm draped over her waist. It was still early. Serena would be asleep a while longer.

Haylee shifted so that she could look at him.

Stirring, he moved to make it easier. "You're awake," he stated while running a hand up her arm.

"So are you," they smiled, tentatively. Haylee's expression faltered. A frown line appeared between Josh's brows. The light of day illuminated the tremulous thoughts hovering under the surface of calm waters.

"Hay—" Josh inhaled, disengaging.

"Shhhh...," she placed a finger over his lips. Pulling him back, she hugged. "It feels so good to have you close. I don't want to let you go, yet."

"I'm not going to let you go, you know," he said, rolling over, so she was beneath him. Josh used his lips, tongue, and touch to show her how he felt.

Haylee responded with sighs, making sounds of encouragement. She eagerly entered the zone of focus that lovemaking claims. It blocked out the variety of other disturbing places her thoughts could go. She wished that they could remain within their hedonistic bubble indefinitely.

Josh hovered over her, their bodies primed to meet, primed to mate. He paused in that vulnerable position, meeting her gaze, "I love you," he stated.

Haylee nodded, reaching up to bring him to her for a wet, sensuous kiss, "I feel like I've loved you my entire life, Josh." Tilting her hips upward, she welcomed him, smoothly. Their breath and sighs mingled as their bodies joined.

≈≈≈

An hour and a half later, they sat in a restaurant booth waiting for their breakfast order to arrive. Reece's metal box was locked in the trunk of Josh's Nissan. Spencer had agreed to join them for breakfast, then watch Serena for a couple of hours.

Spencer arrived, slipping onto the bench seat opposite them.

Josh winced in pain as a sudden, sharp headache came on, "Ah!" he yelped, pushing the palm of his hand against his throbbing temple.

"What's the matter?" Haylee turned to him, alarmed.

"I'm alright; it's just another headache. It'll pass."

Haylee's worried frown met Spencer's.

"If I didn't know better, I'd think it was triggered whenever Haylee and I are in the same room with you."

"Don't be ridiculous," Josh complained.

"Test my theory bro," Spencer said, getting up and walking outside.

Haylee watched Josh's expression clear. A look of surprise crossed his face. She observed, carefully, as Spencer slowly made his way back to their table.

Spencer and Haylee waited to hear Josh's pronouncement.

"Ok, Spence, there is something to it" Josh admitted, "but we don't have time to think about that, will you just sit down so we can talk?"

When they continued staring, Josh claimed, "It's alright. Really. It's just about gone now. Let it go—"

Spencer leaned back glancing, suspiciously, between Haylee and Josh. A slow smile broke out on his face, "You two look cozy, relaxed." Staring at his brother, he raised an eyebrow. "It's about time!" he enthused. "Way to go Haylee! I knew it had to be you."

Josh ignored his brother's jibe. "Spencer, we found something yesterday that I need to tell you about."

Josh reached for Haylee's hand. Picking it up, he brought it to his lips. "Haylee, there's something else that you need to know, but I wanted to tell you when we had Spencer here too.

Haylee's back stiffened, she pulled her hand out of his. "Not you too!" She looked frightened.

It didn't take Josh long to realize why she was worried. "No!" he grabbed her by both shoulders, looking intensely into her eyes. "I haven't lied to you; this is something that I read in the document, yesterday." His hands tightened on her when he thought about the *other* part of what he'd seen.

"Josh, you're hurting me," Haylee complained.

"Sorry!" he loosened his grip but didn't take his hands away. He rubbed his thumbs over her shoulders. "This isn't bad news."

Concern reflected in Haylee's eyes, "What more can there possibly be?" She glanced at Spencer quickly, then returned to Josh. "I don't think I can take much more, besides," she lowered her voice, "I'm not comfortable sharing."

The conversation was interrupted by the arrival of their food and coffee refills. The moment that Josh's plate arrived, he reached for the Tabasco sauce. Unwinding the top, he upended the bottle, shaking it over his food like it was Parmesan cheese. Haylee looked sideways at him, her eyebrows raised.

"What?" he asked innocently.

"You're going to eat that?"

"Watch me," he grinned.

Haylee got Serena set by cutting a banana into bite-sized chunks and giving her part of her Denver omelet. She took her first fork full of eggs. "This tastes good!" she exclaimed. "I didn't realize how hungry I was."

Spencer raised his eyebrows, nodding. Haylee's cheeks bloomed. She hunched forward, concentrating on her food. Josh reached to take her hand again.

When he began to speak in formal tones, it was a welcome distraction. It reminded her of when Josh was teaching her Psychology class. "Haylee, you've heard me mention the board meetings that I attend."

He watched her nod, then continued, "Spencer works with them too, it's part of a service that we do for the family business. The focus of the meetings is land management of a piece of property that is in a trust. There's a clause in the original charter that states that ownership may change hands."

Spencer sat up straighter. He set his coffee cup on the table with a clunk. Dark liquid sloshed over the side. "But that's an old wives' tale."

Josh shook his head, "I thought so too."

"I don't' understand what you are talking about," Haylee said.

"I don't either," Spencer said. "I think he's about to tell us."

"The *Keener* Family Trust owns all the land that we were hiking on yesterday."

"What?" Haylee was baffled. "But your name is Herkowitz…"

"Josh, where are you going with this?" Spencer leaned forward. His voice lowered.

Looking directly at his brother, Josh said, "The codicil mentioned in the trust charter has surfaced. It names Haylee as the beneficiary."

"What?!" Haylee and Spencer exclaimed together.

Josh turned to Haylee, "We're Keener descendants, on my mother's side."

Tears filled Haylee's eyes; she brought up a trembling hand pressing it to her mouth.

A crash behind Haylee turned everyone's attention to Serena. She'd managed to reach a water glass on the table, turning it on its side. "Da, da, wa!" She bellowed.

☙29☙
LEANING TREE

JOSH SAID THAT HE'D wait outside while Haylee decided what to leave in the safe deposit box. But Haylee asked him to join her. The cubicle they stood in was cramped. It was over warm; the air was stale and unmoving.

Josh placed the metal box he'd been carrying onto the table. Haylee stepped forward, putting her hands on the container. She looked at Josh for reassurance, he nodded.

The codicil was the first to come out. She scanned it, then handed it over to Josh. The stack of personal letters went into her purse. Haylee also kept a handful of nuggets that they would sell at a gold exchange. The rest would remain at the bank. As Haylee reached the bottom of the rusted container, she pulled her hand back as if she was burned. A stricken look settled in her eyes as she put her hand back inside, pulling out a simple golden ring.

"It's my wedding— ring," her voice caught on the last word. "I was sure that it didn't survive the fire." She positioned her hand to slip it on when she stopped herself. Glancing over at Josh, she saw the pallor of his skin, the creases between his brows.

Attempting to mitigate the hurt she'd thoughtlessly caused, Haylee bent her head so that her hair covered her face while muttering, "I'll just put that in my pocket."

They walked next to each other along the sidewalk. There was much to say, but neither wanted to be the first to break the silence. Haylee watched green leaves overhead teeter-tottering on thin stems. Such a delicate connection to the life force that sustained it. A few of the unlucky ones separated from the branch, floating away with the wind. *Is that what will happen to me? Will I disconnect and disappear?*

Growing up on a farm, Haylee watched life coming and going. Haylee also had first-hand experiences with a mind being separated from a body; she still had a few of them inside of her. While she worked diligently to keep them at bay, she wondered if she could focus on them instead. *Will their bodies die when I am gone?*

Emis was one victim that was different from all the others. When Haylee was trapped, unable to move, Emis had intentionally pushed her face into Haylee's webbed hand. She was fully aware of what would happen next. Emis had rigged it so that once she was 'gone,' she was swept away into the water. She was beyond saving, even though Reece had tried, valiantly. *If anyone had answers, it would be her. No matter what I try, I can't reach her thoughts. Is it because she's dead?*

More than anything, Haylee didn't want Serena to experience life as an orphan. Haylee swiped at a tear that escaped.

Noticing the gesture, Josh offered Haylee his hand.

Their intimate relationship was still so fresh that Haylee felt awkward. She'd seen him naked; he'd seen her that way too. Haylee could feel her face heating up; more tears stung her eyes. *I'm a married woman. I cheated on my husband,* she thought miserably. Glancing at him, wearing a pained expression, Haylee jogged ahead. She stopped at a tree, leaning her back against it. Sliding down onto her bottom, Haylee pulled her knees uptight. She leaned her forehead against them, hiding her face.

Haylee could hear his footsteps approach. Out of the corner of her eye, she saw him squat beside her.

"I..." he sounded uncertain. "I'm at a loss, Haylee."

"Me too," she sniffed. "Josh, I don't want to die," she said raising her head.

"I've been thinking about that." He sat down on the sidewalk, one hand leaning on the ground, an elbow resting on a raised knee. He chewed at his lower lip. He looked everywhere but at Haylee when he started to speak. "We can't take someone else's word, accepting it as fact."

She laughed. It was a harsh, cutting sound. "Like that's going to happen. How do you imagine that 'facts' are findable?"

Josh's voice sounded strained, "Just because things might appear to have no answers, doesn't mean that they don't exist. There are *always* answers, Haylee. When I look at you right now, do you know what I see?"

"No, what do you see?"

"You are a beautiful, healthy young woman. Your heart is beating. You're breathing, and you're thinking."

"But for how much longer?" she wailed. "I can't stand the idea of Serena not having a mom around.... like I did."

"And I can't stand...." Josh stopped in mid-sentence. He got to his feet, leaving the storage box on the ground, he shoved his hands down into his front pockets.

Haylee remained sitting, the tree supporting her. She watched him shift uncomfortably.

He cleared his throat, "The first thing I think we need to do is suspend the plan for you to return more souls. At least until ...."

Haylee stiffened, banging her head against the trunk, "Argh!"

"What?" he exclaimed.

"Reece said the same thing. It's— because— he— knew!"

"I don't think he knew, any more than we do. He was trying to play it safe."

"How could you know what he was thinking?"

"I don't. But I would have done the same thing, given the circumstances."

Haylee's face looked tortured, a mask of disbelief and hurt, her mouth hung open in an 'o,' "Would you have lied about it too?"

Pulling his hands out of his pockets, he spread them wide, his shoulders bunched up toward his ears. "I don't know... I..."

Haylee gathered herself together, then regained her feet. Still leaning on the tree, she looked at him shaking her head, "I feel really confused. I don't know which way is up or down. With that look on your face, it's almost like I can see Reece standing there staring back at me. Right now, Josh, I can barely keep myself from railing at him, at you."

"I can understand," he said in a softer voice. "We're not getting anywhere with this conversation. I think we need to calm down and regroup."

"In case it is true," Haylee replied, bitterly.

Josh nodded.

❧30❧
MOMENTARY CONFUSION

"WE SHOULD BE GETTING back to Serena and Spencer," Haylee said as Josh led her into his apartment.

"We gave him the bank's phone number and asked him to leave a message here if he needed anything." Josh walked over to check his machine. "See? No blinking light," he said as he walked back to her.

Haylee smiled uncertainly. "We told him we'd only be gone a little while; I don't' want to take advantage of him."

Josh slipped the strap of her purse off her shoulder, setting the bag on the floor. He removed his glasses, tossing them on a side table. "Spencer can handle Serena for a little while longer."

"What are you doing?" She put her hands up to his chest as he stepped in close. "We shouldn't," she pushed against him slightly.

He cupped her jaw, Josh tilted her head, lowering his own. "I disagree." His warm breath breezed over her mouth.

Their lips came together in a light, tentative touch. Groaning as desire swept through him like a flame contacting prime tinder, Josh forced himself to take it slow.

Haylee's arms wound around him. She made a reluctant sound, even as she returned his kiss, straining forward, coming up on her toes.

Josh would never admit to Haylee that he was afraid. Afraid of having their time cut short, afraid that her issues were too big or complicated to resolve, and afraid that she didn't love him the same way he loved her.

One hand, at the base of her spine, pressed her against him. The other, between her shoulder blades, hand open, cradled the back of her neck. Firm pressure and his kisses attempted to stamp out thoughts in her mind .... about her husband.

Josh released his hold. He would have pulled away if Haylee hadn't said, "I want you, Josh. I need you." Her breathing was heavy, laced with arousal.

Thunder and lightning crashed within. His shaky, desperate hands fumbled for her buttons. Haylee unfastened her jeans. She threw off her t-shirt, then her bra. Together they scrambled with Josh's clothes until he was standing, nude, and at full attention, before her.

Haylee stepped into his arms. Josh buried his hands in her hair, kissing her with abandon. Coaxing her lips apart, he tasted the sweetness of her.

Her tongue moved against his, exploring.

He felt full, powerful, and ready to burst. Lowering a hand to her hips, he held her in place as he eliminated the space between them, almost as if he wished they could merge into one body. His erection, cradled between them, was warm. Its hard length throbbed with need.

Backing off slightly, they knelt, stretching out on the floor. Haylee sighed as Josh moved from her mouth to her earlobe where his breathing tickled her sensitive shell. "I can't get enough of you, Haylee. I want to cover you, dig deep inside you, feeling you all around me."

Haylee threw her head back, sighing. As a flower unfolds its petals, reaching for the heat and light of the sun, Haylee gave free access to his touch.

Josh's fingers, gently prodded the center of her womanhood. Dipping into her sweltering wetness, he circled the folds of skin like a tongue moistening chapped lips. Keeping a tight rein on the desire that raced through his blood, Josh focused on the slight movements Haylee made, responding to his ministrations. When he discovered the pressure and stroke pattern that had her pressing against him, he continued, steadily, leading her to ever increasing plateaus.

"Ah!" Haylee's body bucked. "Josh!" her fingernails dug, painfully, into is shoulders. He smiled. Slowing his strokes, he lightened his touch. With a final outburst, the pent-up steel of her muscles relaxed into a mass of pliable taffy.

Chuckling, Josh kissed her lightly. He rolled her on top of him. She adjusted herself, so he slid inside of her. Laying back, he closed his eyes, thinking, *This is a moment is ultimate perfection.*

Grinning, Haylee propped herself up on straight arms while straddling him. Her hair, falling around their faces, enclosed them in their private world.

His hands gripped her as she began to move. Enjoying his pleasure, Haylee followed their subtle movements as if he were conducting a personal symphony. At his peak, Josh, whose eyes were closed, popped open. He let out a verbalization. It was surprised, animistic, quenched.

"Thank you," she said when they languished in a haze of gratification. Her head on his shoulder, a blanket from the couch thrown over them to ward off the chilly draft coming in from under the front door.

"What for?" he brought a finger up, lightly tracing the line of her jaw.

"For reminding me to live in the moment."

Josh ran his hand behind her neck, urging her toward him. The full length of their bodies, meeting at every surface, ready to go into action, they spiraled back into the wellspring of desire. The scent of their lovemaking still infused the air as their mouths met.

As before, their encore performance didn't include underlying notes of worry or desperation. It was a careful, unhurried, act of acknowledgment, an act of kindness and of courtesy.

They traveled, ever upward, together. Reaching the summit, their crescendo rang out, like the sounding of a church bell, their voices exalting praises of satisfied desires.

Josh rolled away, still breathless, "Haylee, darlin, you nearly drive me insane."

❧

At those words, Haylee's eyes flew open. Her heart suddenly felt like it had become wedged in the back of her throat. Moisture that lingered on the surface of her body abruptly turned cold. With goosebumps puckering her skin, Haylee shivered.

"Hay?" Josh looked at her with alarm.

With swift movements, she scrambled to her feet, gathering her clothes, she raced into his bathroom.

With shaking hands, she clung to the lip of the sink willing herself not to be sick. Anguished eyes reflected at her from the mirror. *I couldn't have heard that right.*

"What's wrong?" Josh knocked, calling through the door. He wiggled the knob —it resisted.

Backing away, Haylee responded, "Give me a minute!" She turned on the hot water in the shower letting the room fill with steam. Adjusting the temperature, she stepped inside. The water cascaded over her felt like hot needles. Haylee hugged herself tightly, letting the heat thaw the block of ice she had become.

When she stopped shaking, Haylee braced herself against the wall, directing the spray to the top of her head. "It's Josh. It's only Josh," she repeated.

For an instant, when Josh had spoken the words, "Darlin, you nearly drive me insane," Haylee had thought— that Josh was Reece.

❧31❧
LOVE IS A CROWDED INTERSECTION

JOSH LEANED ON THE wall opposite the bathroom. Barefoot and wearing jeans, he crossed his arms over his chest. His lower lip, clamped between his teeth, pinched, almost to the point of bleeding. He didn't know what had caused her to bolt. A queasy feeling settled in his stomach. A headache was coming on from not wearing his glasses, but he refused to leave his post.

When Haylee opened the door, a cloud of steam billowed out. She was dressed, running fingers through wet hair. Coming face-to-face with Josh, she stopped short.

The hint of an embarrassed smile at the edges of her mouth gave him courage. "Do you want to talk about it?"

"Not really," Haylee shook her head looking down. "I used your bath towel." She brushed passed him. Locating her shoes, she sat on the floor to tie the laces.

Josh grabbed his shirt and shoes as well, "I'll drive you."

❧❧❧

They didn't say any more until they were in the car. Haylee looked out the side window when she said, "I think Serena and I need to go home for a while."

"Home as in your apartment, or home to the farm?"

"—to my Dad's."

Josh pulled his lip between his teeth again.

She turned toward him. "I need to go through Reece's letters."

Seeing his compressed expression, she continued, "See? That's exactly why I need to do this. I want to put my wedding ring back on," her voice wavered. "And I don't want to see that wounded look on your face when I do."

Clamping down on his lip, Josh, tasted blood. "It's not logical, is it?" he said. "That I'm jealous of your— "Josh's voice cracked on the last word, "husband." There, he'd done it. He named the hairy mammoth that had become his loathsome, constant companion. He slammed a hand on the wheel.

Haylee flinched.

Josh was about to open his mouth to apologize, then changed his mind.

After a few moments of silence, Haylee spoke. "I am sorry that you feel that way. I can't change the past. And honestly, if it *were* possible, I wouldn't." Her short laugh sounded sad. "I haven't' told you how I first met Reece."

Josh shook his head, "You don't need to— "

"I think I do." She pressed a hand along his thigh. "It might make a difference."

Josh nodded, reluctantly.

"I'd cut my hair, wrapped my breasts, and wore pants and boots. I don't know if I was all-the-way convincing, but most folks accepted that I was a man. Do you remember me telling you about that?"

"Yea."

"Edward, Reece's younger brother, had hired me to work at their store. One of my jobs was to carry purchases home for customers. I had a couple of heavy sacks balanced on my shoulders while following the man who'd bought them. Reece, who was driving by with a wagon load of supplies, stopped to talk."

"When I first saw him," Haylee reminisced, "I stumbled and fell. The load landed on top of me, cracking a rib. It was the injury that led me to Emis. They took me to her to wrap my ribs."

"The reason I stumbled, Josh, was because when I first saw him, for an instant, I thought he was— you."

What?" Josh glanced in her direction.

"It's around the eyes, especially. In one way or another, it hurts to look at the both of you. When he said something a certain way or was in a mood, there you were, plain as day, staring right at me. It's going the other way too..." Haylee paused, pulling a tissue from her purse, wiping it under her nose.

He nodded, thoughtfully, "Is that what happened?" He swung his head, indicating the direction from which they'd come.

"Something like that," she admitted.

Josh's swallow was audible.

Haylee touched his shoulder; he tried not to flinch.

"There was a strong connection between Reece and me from the start," she said. "He was upset because he thought he'd turned gay. I was worried that I wanted him because—" She stopped, running a hand through her hair, flipping it off her neck. "Despite everything, we found our way to each other. Eventually," her voice dropped so that Josh had to strain to hear, "when I couldn't figure out how to get back here, I started to feel like that place was my home."

Haylee put her hand on the window crank, digging a thumbnail into the grooves of the rotating handle. "There was *some* consolation, having part of 'home' living inside me."

Josh looked at her, incredulous, "You mean me, and Glori— the mechanic from that night, and all those guys at Alpha Sigma Phi House? You think *that* makes me feel better?"

"I wasn't saying that to make you feel better. I was trying to explain what was going on at the time, so *maybe* you could understand what's going on right now," she retaliated.

A stony silence disrupted their glowing emotions for each other. When Josh was about a mile from her house, Haylee had settled, returning to her mood to explain. "I think with us ..." she said, "there wasn't enough time between events. I mean, you and I were friends at Cal. If I hadn't been keeping walls up ... "Haylee let the statement dangle before continuing. "In between where we started and where we are now, there was Reece. He meant everything to me...and then he was gone...or I was."

Haylee wiped at tears leaking out of her eyes. "When I was there, I didn't think it through. I knew that I needed to get back. I didn't realize what it would mean, for Reece, if I made it." She blew her nose into the tissue. "It bothers you that I still love him and I'm resentful because he, *obviously*, found someone else, I'm jealous too!"

"But if that someone hadn't been there Josh, then *you* wouldn't be here. I couldn't stand that—if I came back to find that you never existed."

When Josh opened his mouth, Haylee held up a hand, "Please let me finish. Even through all the confused feelings, there is one thing that I know—"

Josh parked the car, turning off the engine. He twisted in his seat, facing her, "And that is?"

"That I love you, too—" Haylee's voice shook. She kneaded her tissue until it started falling apart. "I am so grateful that you haven't washed your hands of me, or turned me in to the police...that you even want to touch me after what I did to you—"

He reached over, brushing a wisp of hair from her face. With a sad smile and a look of resolution, Josh replied, "My wanting you isn't logical, or sane. But it feels—necessary." He leaned forward, resting his forehead against hers while rubbing a thumb up and down her neck. He kissed her lightly, then moved away. "I'll give you the space you want. But I request two things," he said, holding up his fingers.

"What?"

"One, if you find anything in those letters that have to do with your condition or with the property bequests, you'll let me know."

She nodded solemnly, "And two?"

"Try not to take too long. If you do, I'll be coming for you." Pulling her into his arms, his kiss was tender, possessive, long, and wet. When he pulled away, her eyes were heavy, her hair was messy.

For as unsettling as it was for Josh not knowing, exactly, where he stood with her, he knew that if he could affect her this way, there was hope.

"You're not making this easy," she commented dryly.

"Then you got my point." He gave her a long look. They straightened their clothes before getting out of the car. "Let's go see how Spencer and Serena got along."

❧32❧
DOMESTICITY

SERENA WAS STILL NAPPING when Haylee and Josh came in. His eyes followed Haylee as she quietly stepped into Serena's room to check on her.

Spencer took a long, assessing look at his brother. "How'd it go?" he asked, glancing at the clock, Without giving him a chance to reply, he said, "You were gone longer than it would take to stop at the bank. By your rumpled clothes, I can see that you've made good use of your time."

Shaking his head, Josh said, "We took care of what we needed to—thanks for baby minding."

"No problem," Spencer replied. "Why the long face?"

"She's decided to go home for a while."

"Oh— "Spencer looked concerned. "Are you two—?"

"We're alright, I think. Everything is just...extremely complicated." Josh reached up to massage the side of his head that had begun to ache.

Haylee came back. "How did everything go with Serena, Spencer? Did she give you any problems?"

"Not a bit." He answered in similar, hushed tones. "She was happy to ride in her stroller while I went for a good long run on the bike trail. We had lunch at the park where she splashed in the water at the fountain; then we hung out for a while in your yard playing with your landlady's dogs. She ate good and then passed out as soon as I put her down."

Josh nudged Haylee's shoulder, "I told you he'd be alright with the kiddo."

"I'm impressed, Spencer," Haylee commented, opening her purse.

"Nah," Spencer waved. "This one's on-the-house." He closed his open textbooks with a muffled, *muhmp,* starting to shove them in his backpack. "Besides," he winked, "my time here was an investment in peace and harmony. Josh should be much easier to live with, now. I should be thanking *you.*"

Haylee pinked, she coughed, covering her mouth as well as, possibly, her embarrassment.

Josh rolled his eyes. "My car's here, I'll give you a ride," he said.

"No, thanks. I'll catch the bus. You guys look like you still have things to work out."

⌘⌁⌐⌐

After they said goodbye to Spencer, Haylee poured them each a glass of sun tea. They wandered out into the yard, easing, side-by-side, into the hammock. Laughing as they balanced their glasses, trying not to spill.

"When do you think you'll leave?" Josh asked.

"In the morning."

He nodded, "—so soon."

They finished their drinks. Josh grabbed the empties, leaning out, with his long arms, he set them on the ground. He laid back pulling Haylee alongside him. Holding each other, they stared at the branches overhead. He kissed the top of her head, "Going to miss you."

Haylee nodded, snuggling closer. She breathed a contented sigh.

The quiet afternoon, the rocking motion, the emotional upheaval, and the intense lovemaking had taken its toll. Soon, they were fast asleep.

⮞⮜

A banging noise coming from inside Haylee's apartment startled them awake. When they arrived in Serena's room, they found her clanging a plastic cow against the bars of her crib like a prisoner inside a jail.

"Mama!" the little girl beamed up at her mother, raising her arms.

Josh noticed that Serena had dried crud on her hands and face—that it had gotten on the crib sheet and the blanket.

Haylee lifted Serena out of her confinement, the child's bulky diaper sagging between her legs, "Whoa!" Haylee said. "You've got a load there, little Missy."

"Woad!" Serena echoed.

"Haylee, I'm sorry— "Josh started.

"Hey," she looked at him, smiling. "She's happy. She had a grand day. A little dirt and a full diaper won't cause lasting damage."

Josh shook his head, "I'll talk to him about it if he sits for her again."

"He did a great job, Josh. How is it that he's so comfortable with children?"

"He used to babysit for my aunt's boys when he still lived at home."

"That explains it," she said.

"What can I do to help?"

Haylee paused as if surprised by his offer. "Could you bathe her? Do you know how?"

Reaching out for the toddler, Josh gave Haylee a look that said, *Of course, I can, how hard can it be?*

While Haylee stripped the crib, she listened to the chatter and animal noises coming from the bathroom; she couldn't suppress a smile.

⌇⌇⌇⌇⌇

Dinner was prepared and the laundry in progress when Haylee tiptoed to the bathroom. Josh was bending low, so Serena could carefully pile bubbles on top of his head. Haylee bit the nail of her thumb to keep from laughing.

"Ya know, Serena," Josh said, "we're going to have to get you over to the University pool once you and your mama come back. We should get you started with swim lessons."

Haylee's gasp had Josh swiveling in her direction. "She's too young for swim lessons."

Sheepishly, he scooped off his bubble crown, handing it back to Serena.

"More!" the little girl squealed.

"She's not." Josh looked at Haylee. "I taught infant water safety classes when I was swimming seriously. I had even younger students."

Pleased that Josh was concerned for Serena's safety *and* making plans, Haylee smiled. "We'll think about it. Dinner is ready if our mermaid can come out and dry off."

Josh turned over that chore to Haylee while he splashed a little water on his hair, then washed his hands.

Rinsed and bundled into a towel, Haylee set her daughter in her crib while she pulled clothes out of her dresser. "You've had an eventful day today."

"Bubbles!" Serena proclaimed.

"Right," Haylee agreed. "An outing with Spencer and a bath with Josh. You hardly need Mama anymore, do you?"

Once Haylee finished helping Serena get her arms and legs into her sleeper, she zipped up the long, body length zipper. When Haylee picked her up, Serena wound her little arms around her neck, squeezing tightly.

"Sena loves Mama."

Haylee hugged her back, "I love you too! More than all the stars in the sky and bigger than the universe."

They met Josh in the kitchen, wearing smiles.

❦

Haylee and Josh took turns putting little food chunks on Serena's tray throughout the meal. Serena seemed more boisterous than was her norm, Haylee had the impression that her daughter was competing with her for Josh's attention.

Josh gladly encouraged Serena's behavior by telling stories with dramatic and silly expressions. When Haylee began to feel left out, she slipped a shoe off, reaching under the table to place it on Josh's knee.

At the contact, he paused to regard her.

Wearing an impish grin, Haylee inched her foot forward along the inside of his thigh.

Color crept into his face. Lowering his chin, he stared at her, meaningfully.

In her mind bloomed a detailed and erotic scene of the two of them together. This mode of communication included feelings from the sender. It was not unlike how she communicated with animals.

Blushing, Haylee removed her foot, sitting up straighter. "Can you stay?"

"I can."

"Good," she replied.

❧33❧
UPHOLDERS AT McDONALD'S

ABOUT AN HOUR INTO the drive, Haylee stopped at a McDonald's. She used the bathroom, then changed Serena's diaper.

They zig-zagged through the zee-shaped path to the counter where Haylee ordered a Big Mac and chicken nuggets with Ranch dressing. While they waited for her order, Haylee let Serena scoot around the edges of the play area, keeping an eye on the older kids—she didn't want them crashing into her toddler.

McDonald memories with her parents brought a wistful smile to Haylee's face. Life seemed so simple and uncomplicated when she was a child.

Haylee recalled a day that they'd spent at the Sacramento Zoo. It was spring. She and her mother had worn pink pedal pusher pants with matching blouses. Her dad thought that taking their picture in front of the flamingos would be fun, since they all were, roughly, wearing the same colors. Haylee still had that picture of the two of them, posing, balanced on single legs with arms that had turned into wings. They'd stopped at McDonald's for dinner on their way home. Haylee could still see her mom leaning back into her dad's arms smiling across the table. Haylee tried to ignore their comments about what a lovely, thoughtful daughter they'd produced.

Not for the first time, Haylee wondered about her mother and what secrets she took to the grave. *Did she know she would die when I turned seven?* Haylee clutched at her pendant, bringing it up to tap against her lips.

A blinding flash of light obliterated her vision. Dizzy, Haylee wobbled, throwing out her arms. It was followed by a searing pain that tightened her scalp, making her hair feel like it stood on end. Haylee dropped her face into her hands, then slumped to the floor.

She didn't see Serena turning toward her, wearing a look of alarm, or hear her begin to wail.

While she lay on the ground, unseeing, cramped with pain, she wondered if she was having a stroke. *Do I have emergency contact information in my purse?*

As abruptly as it started, the physical discomfort passed, replaced by a dense, green water-like fog. Sounds coalesced, then focused, gaining in clarity and volume.

A group of four indistinct, shadowy figures materialized in the distance. She could see them approaching, growing larger, moving in a way that was unnatural. They had high, whispery voices that sounded like a chorus performing a rap song. With each word, Haylee felt vibrations in her bones and joints, in every organ, and across the surface of her skin.

They seemed, hauntingly, familiar. With a certainty that Haylee didn't question, she knew that it was important to remember what they said.

The time has come for the re-delivery of ancestral information.

Travelers and all their lineage serve the original pledge made to the Upholders.

Listen, daughter. Hear the song. Teach it to your daughter so that she may teach it to hers.

A drum thrummed deep in the distance. Each beat caused a corresponding vibration in Haylee. The colored fog dissipated, the figures went with it. A night scene, dotted with twinkling stars above, came into view.

Haylee heard cracking and popping. She could see flickering light. Her vision zoomed in. Flames, hot, red and greedy licked along tall branches arranged in a tall cone shape. A woman stepped into a dancing ring of light. Her outline was crisp and sharp. She stood, poised before a gathering of women. Illuminated by the flames, their faces were pale, round. The woman's hair, like those of her audience, was dark and thick. It flowed down her back. Her blouse hung low on her shoulders. Her skirt, gathered at the waist fell to her ankles. Bare toes peeked out from under its hem. She stood tall and proud, making eye contact with each person, nodding and smiling when they acknowledged her. She raised an arm as if beckoning them to follow. Her throaty voice rose up in song.

From the Heart of the Dawn

Haylee recognized the words. She was surprised. How did she understand the language?

Keys to survival birthed in stone

As the 'n' sound elongated, a young girl stepped forward. She was thin, her long, dense hair woven into a braid that hung down her back. The whites showed clearly around her dark eyes. Her steps to the front were halting, hesitant. She clenched the object that hung around her neck from a cord.

The singer moved her free hand to rest atop of the girl's head. The action was familiar. The youngster released tension she'd been holding in her shoulders.

The smaller travels a straight line

When the hands of the little girl fell to her sides, Haylee could see what was hanging around her neck; it was the same thing she'd been tapping against her lips a few minutes before.

The larger is passed by the hands of the Travelers alonnnnne......

The singer held something in her hand, high above her head. Her gaze scanned, intently, over the watching faces. Someone else stood. It was a woman; her back was to Haylee.

Haylee sucked in a quick breath, her body jerked. This woman wore a dress resembling a ball gown. Hooped skirts, a tight bodice, cinched at the waist, three-quarter length sleeves molded to her arms were fringed by lace.

With a turn of her wrist, and a flash of blue, white light, Haylee knew what the woman at the center of the circle had; it was the large crystal.

The assemblage chortled high pitched calls, tongues rolling, giving a quick succession of undulating sounds.

With the calls still ringing in Haylee's ears, darkness faded. A glaring light and Serena's frantic cries brought her back into the moment.

"Mam!"

Someone was nudging her shoulder, Haylee blinked several times. When her eyes focused, she saw that she was on the ground, a group of people stood in a circle looking down at her.

"Can I call someone for you?" asked a large woman, kneeling at her side, wearing a badge that read, 'Helen, Manager.'

Groaning, Haylee rolled onto her side. "No...I'm alright.... I.... ah.... just spaced out for a second." She sat up.

Serena was in the arms of another McDonald's employee. Climbing to her feet, Haylee made sure her balance was stable before taking her daughter in her arms.

The manager squinted as she peered, closely, into Haylee's eyes. She leaned in, sniffing.

Haylee backed away.

With a stern, yet resolute expression, Helen turned toward the group of on-lookers. Raising her voice, she said, "Nothing to see here folks. Go about your business."

To Haylee, Helen motioned with a nod, "Bathroom's down the hall if you want to see to your kid."

Keeping her eyes on the floor, Haylee hustled Serena in that direction.

She made a big deal about running the water and cranking the arm of the paper towel dispenser. With an overly cheerful voice, she said, "See? Everything is alright." Haylee continued to chatter as she wiped down Serena's face, touching her reassuringly, "I know that must have been scary. But it's over now."

Haylee stepped away, doing a little pirouette. She bowed with a flourish. Serena hiccupped, a start of a smile played about her mouth.

Haylee would have skulked straight out to the parking lot if Helen hadn't been waiting outside. Handing her a to-go bag, Helen said, "Look out for yourself—?"

"Haylee," she supplied, feeling her face grow warm. Accepting the bag, Haylee commented, "Let me get my wallet."

Helen held up a hand, "No need. But be careful. This little one— "Helen reached out, squeezing Serena's foot, "can't take over for you if you feel unsteady behind the wheel."

"I understand."

❧34❧
YOU CAN'T EVER GO
ALL THE WAY HOME

HAYLEE STOOD AT THE living room window watching Serena offer toys to Oscar in her playpen outside. Oscar looked up to meet Haylee's gaze across the expanse. Haylee sent him a message. *Can you keep her occupied for a little while longer?*

He blinked at her leisurely in response. *She will run out of patience soon.*

Can you at least—try?

Tuna?

Making an aggravated verbalization, Haylee nodded.

Alright, Oscar thought back, *but if she pulls my fur— I'm leaving.*

"You're not very helpful, you little extortionist," Haylee muttered.

"Did you say something?" Glori asked from behind her. Glori sat next to Gene on the couch rubbing his back. Gene had his face cradled in his hands while leaning on his knees.

Haylee glanced over her shoulder, shaking her head, 'no.' She returned to the lounge chair opposite her folks. She didn't know what else to say.

Haylee spent the last hour filling them in. Her dad lost it when Haylee told them her suspicions about her mother's death.

"No! I would have known if your mother had anything like that!" Eugene yelled.

"Would you?" Haylee asked.

They stared at each other in silence, each lost in their thoughts.

Glori pulled her hand away from Eugene. Bringing it on her lap; she tapped a fingernail on her wedding ring.

"Dad," Haylee hated the words she was about to speak, "I *have* to ask you this. Would you— please— tell me how she died?"

Eugene sat up straight, leaning back into the couch like he wanted it to suck him inside. The whites of his eyes were pink beneath puffy lids. He adamantly shook his head, no.

"I know this is hard—" Haylee glanced at Glori, meeting her eyes.

Glori shrugged, looking sad.

Gene blinked rapidly. Leaning toward her, in a jerking motion, he rested an elbow on a knee. "Do you think the same thing is going to happen to you?" He searched her face.

Haylee broke the gaze between them, glancing toward the front window where Serena played. "I do," she whispered. She didn't have the heart to tell him how much time she thought she had left.

Gene pressed a hand over the straight line of his mouth. He sucked in a deep breath. He stood, abruptly. "I need to be alone for a while," he said, his voice choked with gravel. He strode outside, letting the screen door slam in his wake.

Haylee started to follow but stopped at the window. She watched him walk to the playpen, pick Serena up, and kiss her, tenderly. He set her down next to the cat, then walked toward the barn.

Haylee turned toward Glori. "Should I be worried about him?"

"No— He wouldn't—" Glori started. "It's a lot to take in!" Glori trotted in Gene's footsteps stopping at the door. "Does Josh know?" she asked.

"He does."

"There *must* be a rational explanation."

"Josh agrees."

"And you, Haylee?"

"I wish—"

Rustling sounds and small, fussy cries came from down the hall. Glori looked torn.

"I'll get him," Haylee offered. "Go after Dad."

Hesitating she asked, "You and Josh are fairly sure that—whatever it is— it's from your mother?"

Haylee blinked, her heart constricted. She took a step back as if she'd been struck. Her smile held no humor when she replied, "As sure as I can be. Byron won't get it, Glori, but I can't say the same for Serena..."

Glori's hand flew to her mouth. "But she's just a baby!"

"Yes, she is," Haylee's eyes filled. "We found letters from Reece. We think he may have written about Polly. There might be something in there that could help."

"That's incredible!" Glori rejoined. "How?"

Haylee shook her head, dismissively. "He put them in a place he knew I'd go back to."

Byron was starting to make loud demands.

Glori took a couple of steps in that direction, but Haylee put out a hand, stopping her. "Please, let me. Diapers, I've got, talking sense into my dad is something only you can do."

"Very well," Glori sighed. "You're planning to stay?"

"Just a few days, until I've read the letters."

Glori nodded. She stepped outside, holding a hand on the door, guiding it, so it closed softly.

Haylee brightened when she walked into her dad and Glori's room. "Hey little man, we haven't forgotten about you," she leaned over the bassinet, smiling as she watched her brother wave his arms and legs.

Pulling out fresh supplies, she placed them on the changing table. She kissed him. Putting him on the operations surface, Haylee's hands were sure as she unsnapped his onesie, hiking it up along his torso. Haylee unfastened the corners of his diaper, letting it fall open. Seeing, and smelling what he'd left there, she pulled back. "Whew! Your system is in proper working order," she exclaimed waving a hand in front of her nose.

Byron giggled as if he were proud of his accomplishment.

Holding his small ankles between her fingers, she raised his bottom with one hand, keeping him elevated so she could wipe him down with wet ones. After the fourth go-around, he was clean. Adding the wipes to the center of the bulk, she slid it away, replacing it with a clean one. Taping it snugly around Byron's waist, she pulled his onesie down, snapping the snaps. Haylee made sure his squirming feet stayed clear of the dirty pile.

Picking him up and putting him back in his bassinet, Haylee talked while she worked, "Stay there for a minute, brother while I clean up." Tightly winding the edges of the heavy diaper around itself, Haylee attached the tape edges, creating a heavy round ball. Carrying the load to the trash in the bathroom, she thought about a statistic she'd heard at school, "Disposable diapers now constitute 1.1% of municipal waste."

For a moment, Haylee envisioned every disposable diaper in the world, piled into a tall mountain range, congealed with superabsorbent particles, plumped to carrying capacity, dripping excess that oozed a fetid stench.

Holding the plastic packaged wad of guacapoopie suspended over the waste can, a shiver went down her back. For a moment, she felt the rattle in her bones, the edges of her vision clouded with green water-like fog. Startled, Haylee released the parcel; a weighty thud sounded when it hit bottom.

Shaking her head as if to clear cobwebs, she washed her hands. Slathering soap bubbles, Haylee flashed back to a visit from her grandmother. She was small and holding onto the cold edge of the toilet. Haylee had to stretch to peek over into the bowl.

With her hands immersed in brown water, Grandma plunged a dirty cloth diaper.

Haylee gagged.

"It's only guacapoopie," Grandma had said, "part of the circle of life."

Haylee pushed against those thoughts, sending them fluttering away like locusts on a feeding mission.

"Your niece is waiting outside for you." Haylee chimed to Byron as she approached him. "The fresh air will do us all some good."

Oscar was waiting on the front porch when they came out. *Tuna?* He sent.

"Alright, you've earned it," Haylee agreed.

Setting Byron down in his playpen, she told Serena, "Keep an eye on your Uncle while I get Oscar what he wants."

"Oker, good key, key," Serena smiled at her mom.

"Yes, he is."

❧35❧
REECE'S LETTERS

WITH BLANKETS, A CANTEEN of water and a basket of snacks, Haylee set up a day camp in her favorite contemplation spot—near the old tractor at the far end of the equipment lot.

Oscar trotted after her. Haylee wasn't sure if he was joining her because he thought she could use emotional support or if he was curious to see what was inside her picnic basket.

Finding a shady area at the base of one of the big tires, Haylee stomped down a patch of tall weeds. She spread her blanket over them. Putting off the activity she came to perform, Haylee carefully arranged everything on her blanket. She peeked at the food, took a few bites here and there, and poured herself a drink.

She placed the stack of letters on top of the extra folded blanket beside her. Her gaze was glued on them while she sipped. Propping her back against the cracked tire treads, she thought, *If I never read a word, I'd always have something to look forward to.* Her chin and lips trembled. *That's 'the end' right there.*

Oscar placed his front paws on her thigh, beginning to knead. Tiny pricks stabbed into her, making her jump. Haylee sent a thought question, *Why do you have to do that?*

Because, he replied indignantly, *I am a fe-lion. It would be unseemly to ignore preparations before gracing you with my presence.*

Alright, Haylee huffed, bracing herself to brave out the completion of his arrangements. Once his heavy, warm weight settled in, Haylee ran her hand over him from head to tail. Oscar's responding rumble *did* calm her conflicting emotions.

Even with her confidence firmly fortified, Haylee's hand shook as she reached for the first letter.

September 7, 1850

My Dearest Wife ~

When the fire broke out, I thought we were all safe. I was laboring in the fight; man, against nature. Shouting through my speaking trumpet, directing crews setting dynamite.

Then I heard you. But that can't be right. A fearsome, howling wind ripping down the streets sounded like the belly of the beast had burst open. You called me, across a space that should have been impossible to hear.

The last time I saw you might have only been minutes. But those minutes have re-played in my mind many times, I am resigned to living with them. I wish I could erase the sights and sounds from that day.

Haylee nodded, her lips twitched. She felt the same. Reading his words brought his voice to mind, its deep timbre, his rolling r's and soft vowels.

The Drake Hotel was slipping from its footing. Engulfed in flames, it behaved as if it were alive, swaying, groaning; it took a step off its foundation. It was on its way down! That throng of crazed humanity was doomed to die beneath the building's blazing surrender to gravity.

I gave you the only chance possible. I didn't stop to question, until much later, if the damned crystal might have kept you safe.

The ground shook when The Drake collapsed. A wave of scorching air singed my, mustache and eyebrows. I stood there as still as a statue and as empty as a corn husk from last year's harvest. The unfortunate ones who weren't crushed on impact, screamed as they burned. Time stopped.

I don't remember what happened after that. For a while, I lay upon a pallet in the corner of our warehouse on the wharf. With a bottle of whiskey always at hand, liquid forgetfulness could drown turbulent thoughts.

Song came. He greased my burns with a foul smelling ointment. He said nothing about my resistance and profanities. In his quiet, efficient way, he took care of me.

Later, I learned that the fire had raged for more than ten hours. A total of eighteen blocks, in the heart of the business district, had been lost. Over 1,700 homes too.

Edward had taken charge of recovery efforts. Along with many our friends from the port, they fenced off the mercantile plot while the ruins still smoldered. He sent Song hurrying to Sacramento to purchase timber and supplies before word of the fire inflated prices.

I don't know how long I lie there. Time was marked by Jakko, pushing his muzzle into my hand for scratching, and the sounds of his conquests. Jakko's a Bull Terrier, a ratting breed. Song found him wandering the docks, homeless. He brought him to the warehouse to look after me. If it weren't for that dog, the vermin would have gnawed me down to bones.

Jakko announced the quick, heavy steps of a horse before I heard it. Someone shouted my name. I turned away from the racket, pulling the blanket over my head. Shards of bright light pierced my eyes when my covering was yanked away. I responded with an angry swing of an arm and fist.

"Hey! Look out!" Edward complained. "Good news, Reece, Polly's come back!"

"Wha...?" I replied, still fuzzy in the head.

"It's a miracle!"

That got my attention. I am sure that I looked a sight— pasty lashes framing pink tinged eyes. The backs of my hands and arms sporting burns, shiny with the sticky stuff Song had put there. My eyebrows were gone, and the hair on my head felt like nappy sheep's wool. Still stinking of soot and sweat, my voice cracked when I tried it. "Back?" I croaked.

"Papa, Reece." Polly knelt close. "I found my way home."

"From where?" I blinked attempting to moisten my eyes, for I was sure that I could not be seeing what was right in front of me. Not a charred skeletal specter, but my entirely intact, adopted daughter.

"I don't know. One minute I was in the fire and the next, I woke up in the hills."

I reached out, unsure if she would welcome my touch. Polly leaned forward. Her face was smooth, unblemished. When I, finally, understood, I asked, "Haylee?"

Polly shook her head. "I was hoping to find her here."

Polly's return altered my cloud of despair. If she made it out of the fire, then, maybe, you and the baby did too.

My body channeled my emotions with sweat, cursing, and hard labor; lifting and carrying timbers, sawing, hammering, and finish work.

We were moving stock onto shelves the day the Pool's came in. The place still smelled of raw wood and varnish. Mrs. Pool held a tiny bundle close to her breast. It was her infant daughter, Stella.

I must have made a sound because Ed, Song, and Polly stopped to watch. I fear that I moved with a lurching gait, toward Mrs. Pool, like Mary Shelly's monster. "May I hold her?"

Mrs. Pool stared at me, unsure how to react. Edward stepped near her husband, whispering that I'd lost my wife and child in the fire.

"It's alright, Martina," Mr. Pool whispered kindly, in his English accent.

She handed over the infant. I took her, so carefully, holding the head securely as Mam had taught us. When the wee beour looked up at me, I had the strongest feeling that I was looking into the eyes of our Serena. "A stór," I whispered, "My treasure."

At that moment, I knew, with an unfathomable certainty, that you and Serena were still alive.

All My Love, Reece

Haylee carefully refolded the aging paper, sliding it into its envelope. She set it aside, leaning her head back so her gaze could get lost in the puffy, slow-moving, clouds overhead. Without conscious thought, her hands stroked Oscar from his head to the tip of his tail. He started purring. Haylee was grateful for his company.

She'd been so wrapped up in her agenda and her loss that she hadn't spared much thought to what *Reece* had experienced.

A light breeze lifted the ends of Haylee's hair, blowing it across her nose. Reaching up to wipe it aside, she remembered the blistering gale that stung her eyes. Leaving the mercantile, Reece, Song, Polly and herself had stared, in terror, at the wall of flames a short distance away. Plank walkways, alight, looked like squirming tentacles reaching for purchase.

Haylee remembered grabbing onto Polly, running. In her panic, the voices of her victims rose, blocking out all rational thought. She'd stopped short, looking this way and that, but not focusing on anything. Polly's terrified cries got her moving once again.

Getting caught up and almost trampled in a terror-struck crowd had cost Haylee her life no matter how she looked at it.

She knew, logically, that Polly had to have survived. But until she'd read Reece's words, she hadn't fully felt a sense of relief. They all made it. Her family was OK...

Haylee's fingers didn't hesitate this time as she reached for the next letter.

❦

October 5, 1850

My Dearest Wife ~

Everyone agrees that lack of organization and the means to combat fire is a danger to our town.

Incendiary construction methods with wood and canvas, plus high winds make the threat of additional fires more than a possibility; it's a probability.

I joined the Town Council with Brannan, Davis, Harrison and John Geary. Preventative measures were the topic of lengthy debates and discussions. We established three fire departments and made some resolutions.

We will supply the fire companies with hooks, ladders, axes, ropes and other necessities.

A Police Chief, with enough men, will guard burned districts to protect the property from squatters.

Every enterprise and household will be required to keep at least six water buckets in readiness for future fires.

Another interesting topic is the growing interest in the construction of fire-safe buildings. Some merchants have been building with bricks—making the walls three feet thick while others have imported stone and metal materials from Europe.

When I recall the extraordinary nature of this fair city that you described in your time, I feel confident that we have made the first steps in a long journey toward that future.

All My Love, Reece

October 28, 1850

My Dearest Wife ~

There have been two more fires since the last time I wrote. Damages are thought to exceed "15,000,000.

Thankfully, the mercantile survived; however, plenty of our friends lost their homes and businesses. The city, like a Phoenix, continually rises again and again from the ashes.

The personal toll that such repeated destruction meets out is harsh. Remember the Pool family? After their home caught fire for the second time, Alfred escorted his wife Martina and their small daughter, Stella, into the street. In a state of utter despair, he shot them both; and then he shot himself. He was found lying on top of them.

I am grateful to have spared you and Serena these experiences.

Haylee set the paper down abruptly. A hand flew to her mouth. Alfred Pool! Homer! He'd changed his name to Alfred when he came abroad. He'd been her first victim in 1849. She'd taken care of him until she found a place for him at the sailor's home.

After Edward, he was the second person she'd brought back with the crystal. His dearest wish was to marry Martina. He'd done it! And they'd had a baby.

Haylee had to keep herself from crumbling the letter in a fit of rage. She'd given up a year of her life for that man. "Homer, you idiot!" Haylee screamed. "I didn't save you so that you could kill yourself...and your family!"

Knowing what had happened to Alfred, Martina, and Stella was almost more than Haylee could bear. It took several hours and an iron will to pick up reading where she left off.

One of our warehouses went up in flames in the last conflagration. Losses were minimal since we spread inventory evenly between them.

The Jenny Lind Theatre has succumbed in every fire. My poor friend, Thomas Maguire, jokes that one day he will write a play about it. I appreciate his humor. I pray that it runs deep.

The crystal in your possession and the fragment in Polly's pendant have occupied my thoughts, lately. In that terrible moment, when I spoke the words that sent you back, did I think that I might condemn Polly to death? I did not.

Until she returned to us, I did not know that I had come to love her. She is my last, tenuous, tie to you.

Is it common for a guilty parent to make amends for things the child never knew of?

Two months ago, Polly fell off the wagon when the hem of her dress caught on a nail. With howls of pain and the cock-eyed angle of her arm, I knew what was wrong. Even as I sent Song for the doctor, Polly begged me to bring her the pendant.

When she had a hold on it, her cries reduced to whimpers. The Dr. assured us that the injury was merely a bad bruise.

If a tiny fragment of stone is capable of that—what kind of power must the large one possess? I hadn't forgotten the force of the thing when I touched it for the first time. The blast nearly split my head open. Why was I able to hold it after Emis was gone? Had she done something to affect it?

Unbeknown to Edward and Song, I experimented on them with the pendant. When Ed held it, nothing appeared out-of-sorts. He wondered why I wanted an appraisal.

Song had a different reaction. When I dropped it into his hand, he reached out to steady himself as if he'd felt dizzy. His face lost color. He let it fall on the nearest tabletop. Regarding me with suspicion, his voice was tense, spoken in a rush, "Ms. Emis had powerful magic. She gave that to her child. One risks being cursed by playing with things that one does not understand!"

After that, he would not speak to me for weeks. This damaged the friendship between us.

All My Love, Reece

☙36☙
THREE MORE YEARS

HAYLEE HAD BROUGHT HER reading back to the house. Helping with dinner and getting the kids down, she cut her visiting time with the folk's short. Gene and Glori would be watching Bob Newhart, Moonlighting, and Matlock on TV.

Haylee hugged them goodnight. She put a tall-backed chair close to Serena's crib, draping a blanket over it to keep her bedside light from disturbing the baby.

With Reece's stories still fresh and his voice still echoing in her mind, she settled in to continue.

July 15, 1851

My Dearest Wife ~

Rather than waiting for another fire, we've decided to rebuild the store with brick. While nothing appears to be 100% fireproof, the brick seems to offer enough to make it a worthwhile investment.

Ed and I have also diversified with properties spread throughout the city. We're experimenting with specializing goods and services in those locations. The income from them minimizes fire losses in all places and subsidizes rebuilding costs.

I bought a house up in the Russian Hill district. It has too much room. Ed and Polly want to fill it with borders.

Song's going to work at the Sam Yap Company. He will be helping to manage Chinese work crew contracts. There was a break in our relationship since the pendant business. Nothing I said could bridge the distance between us.

Polly started attending a school for young women. More and more of her free time is spent with me at the stores. For her, saying goodbye to Song wasn't as painful as I'd feared. We will miss him, but I think he will be satisfied with his work there. I wouldn't be surprised to hear that he returned to China one day.

Mistress Blanchette, Polly's teacher, is from a region in France near where Polly lived with her mother. Polly has been speaking French again and doing an excellent job with needlework and etiquette. As part of her training, we have been attending theatrical performances and dining in restaurants.

She's developed an interest in the Ready-Made clothing store off Franklin Street and has begun selecting merchandise. She's got a real knack for it.

I think of you and Serena, often. I imagine what we would be doing if you were still here. Serena would look up to her older sister, Polly. Oh, how I would enjoy seeing you attired in the latest European fashions...all the while listening to your complaints about their lack of comfort.

I imagine us riding home in a hired carriage, huddled together holding hands under mufflers while watching the city lights. We'd arrive at our grand home and check on the girls, tucking in their blankets, before retiring to our room. We'd laugh over how much our living style has changed in such a short time.

With the essence of those dreams lingering in my thoughts, I climb into my big, lonely, bed.

Holding this letter, do you feel my thoughts spanning the distance between us? Do you lay hands upon yourself, imagining that those hands belong to your lover?

I love you and miss you, always.

Reece

~~~

June 3, 1852

My Dearest Wife ~

In a few weeks, our home will be full of family!

Polly is excited and nervous about meeting her aunts and grandparents. She asks Edward endless questions about them and has been helping to choose furnishings for their rooms.

Polly has made the acquaintance of a Madame Cassini. She runs a collar shop two doors down from our dry goods store on Market St.

This is disturbing. The woman's operation is a ruse. (Polly was exposed to enough immoral behavior at the Union.) As she grows into womanhood, I don't want her anywhere near that—thank goodness, my parents, and sisters will be here soon!

The unusual nature of their relationship is that M. Cassini claims to foretell the past, present, and future. Polly must be drawn to that because it is familiar. M. Cassini claims to have known Polly's mother when they served the July Monarchy.

Polly has begged, most convincingly, to be allowed to visit Madame. I have agreed to let the relationship continue so long as the woman honors her promise to shield Polly from the illicit activities that go on behind her doors.

It was during a terse meeting with Madame that she told me I would 'be sending information of utmost importance to a love that transcends time.' More on this later.

Ed has recently taken to courting Miss Agatha Flannigan, daughter of our newly appointed Fire Chief. You'd like her. She has an abrupt manner and is not afraid to challenge convention. I can just imagine the sparks flying when my sisters meet her.

All My Love, Reece

Feeling melancholy, Haylee ran a finger over his last sentence. Reece had already gone through many changes. Polly was growing up. Edward had fallen in love. Haylee refolded the letter.

She searched her memory for when she'd possessed Edward's mind. She could see Reece's sisters. Briged, the eldest Keener, was tall and commanding. She had a quick mind, helped to make financial decisions for the family, and was a force to be reckoned with in their Roman Catholic social circles. Rayenne was next in line after Reece. She was the 'odd' one with milky-white skin and a head full of fiery auburn curls. She was an artist and a musician. Einin, only fourteen months younger than her sister, had a willowy build, long, straight dark hair and flashing green eyes. She was a talented seamstress with a strong desire to explore. She often wandered the hills around their home, gone for hours at a time. The youngest of the Keeners were Edward and his twin Deirdre; she was a quiet, bookish sort, a puzzle solver with a golden voice. When Ed joined Reece out west, the separation from Deirdre had been painful. He never stopped missing—as he thought of it—his other half.

Knowing them, yet having never met them, Haylee felt wistful. She remembered Reece telling her how much fun they would have when the boisterous group arrived. She wished she could have been part of that. *Serena will never know her aunts and uncle.*

Emotionally drained, Haylee lay on her back, closing her eyes. Too restless to sleep, she continued reading.

January 1, 1853

My Dearest Wife ~

During the conflict with Emis, we were critical of her motives. I have, since, come to understand them better.

I am afraid that if you were successful in restoring Glori and Josh—as you were so determined to do— then you will be in a similar situation as Emis with a young child in need of a guardian.

I've watched Polly continue to grieve for her mother. I remember your feelings about the loss of yours.

I understand the pain and remorse that you have for the atrocities you were compelled to commit. I also guess how tempting it is to atone for your sins.

But there is more to consider, my Darling. What's done is done. Our daughter is innocent. She deserves to know her mother.

I have been working out a way that I might provide for Serena. Once it is secure, I will write to give the details.

Know this. When your time comes, go without fear. Whether you are still in the spring of your life or a faded autumn leaf, I will be there to greet you if God grants me that wish.

All My Love, Reece

With a trembling hand, Haylee dropped the letter. It floated to the floor. She pulled a tissue from the box on her nightstand. Blowing her nose, she wiped away her tears.

He'd hit too close to home. He'd spoken directly to her heart and her most significant worries. It drove her nearly insane to not be able to talk to him, to feel his arms wrapped around her.

November 13, 1853

My Dearest Wife ~

Today is your birthday. You occupy most of my thoughts on this day.

How do you fare? My wish is for you to live your life to the fullest. Love our little girl, enjoy the warmth of family, and do whatever it is that makes you laugh and smile. A further wish is for you to let go of things that cannot be changed.

I celebrate your birthday today even though it will be many, many years before you are born.

I think about you holding this letter. When it rests in your hands, I will be long gone from this world. Every single day is the anniversary of someone's birth or death. Perhaps the celebrations or remembrances of those days are not what is essential but the living that goes on moment by moment.

Still— I wish I knew what day Serena was born. In lieu of knowing, I think of her for an entire season. She is my fall child. Fall is a lovely time of year. Harvests come in; a chill is in the air; fires are in the hearth. It's a time for gathering and appreciating friends and family.

Although I'm writing to you, Haylee, I hope that, someday, Serena reads my letters. I hope she knows how much her father loves and cares for her.

There is a final wish that I have for you. One I could not express a few years ago. I hope love is part of your life. Not the love of your father and daughter, but romantic love.

I have been a widower long enough to entertain the idea of loving again. The thought of you living without someone to share your sorrows and your joys pains me.

Happy Birthday, Haylee

All My Love, Reece

There were more letters to be read, but all Haylee wanted to do was weep. Knowing that Reece wanted her to find love again made her sigh. *If he suspected my feelings for Josh, he'd forgive me.*

Can I forgive him too? For the secrets and the lies? For finding someone new? Turning the light out, Haylee pulled up the blankets; she adjusted her pillow. *He forgave me for hurting people... Why can't I forgive myself?*

❧∿◦∾❧

To Haylee, it seemed that she was living in two worlds. In her mind, she was roaming the places she remembered in 1850, the shop, the stables, their living quarters, the kitchen, their bedroom. She watched members of her family moving about, remembering the jokes and endearing mannerisms.

In her field of vision was the bedroom of her childhood, decorated with interests from her teens, Shaun Cassidy and Andy Gibb, a cozy haven for the lonely times when she needed to be invisible for her dad. Her daughter, Serena, stood in the crib, rattling the bars, waiting to start her day.

"There they are!" Glori called from the stove when she heard Haylee and Serena come in. Glori's eyes met Haylee's, "Everything alright?"

Just then, Gene walked in carrying Byron. Both had wet hair and looked freshly scrubbed. "Hey girls," Gene smiled. He squinted at Haylee as if he was searching for clues.

"Breakfast's just minutes from ready," Glori said. "Gene, will you set the table?"

Haylee sent mental thanks to Glori for buying her a few more moments.

The distraction of getting the little ones set up in their high chairs and preparing the meal helped Haylee settle in and process more of what she'd been taking in.

Garden scrambled eggs, and hash browns hit the spot! As soon as they started eating, Haylee realized how famished she'd been. With Glori's help, they kept the conversation confined to kid stuff and crop forecasts.

When breakfast was over, the adults washed, dried and put away the dishes.

"Did you find anything?" Gene's deep voice penetrated their introspection.

Haylee shook her head. "Lots..." she sighed, "nothing that directly relates to what's going on now. I still have more to read. It's slow because he's telling me about his life." She blinked, turning her face away. "It's ... difficult."

"Aww, Haylee," Glori said sympathetically. She put an arm around her, squeezing her.

"I have something, important, that I need to ask you guys," Haylee set down her drying towel. Leaning against the counter, she regarded them.

"What's that, Hay, Hay?" her dad asked.

Haylee knew that her next words would be difficult, but they had to be said. Swallowing passed the lump in her throat, she said, "Ahhhh.... we think...."

"It's OK, Haylee," Glori encouraged.

Haylee looked at Glori, thinking, *I'd make the same decisions if I had to do it all over again. Glori will be here for Dad and Serena when I can't be.* Reaching out to press Glori's outstretched hand, Haylee turned back toward her father. "When I return souls to their rightful owners, I.... reduce the time that I have left to live."

Haylee watched the reactions bloom on their faces. She continued before they had a chance to say anything, "If I'm a short-timer, I need to make sure that you guys will take Serena when I am gone."

❧37❧
TEXTURE OF
MEMORY & DREAMS

WHEN HAYLEE WAS OVERLY tired or emotionally drained, she struggled to keep the restless thoughts of her captives muted. Some of them were dark, mean, and chilling. Others were apprehensive, crowded with self-doubt. The most distressing, were the ones filled with hope. They imagined themselves returning, triumphant, to family back east. Reece had known what to do when Haylee felt this way. Early in their relationship, he'd discovered her holed up in a closet, trembling.

"Tell me what's the matter," he urged, squatting next to her, rubbing a gentle hand up and down her back. Once he understood the problem, he'd scooped her up, carrying her back to their bed. Wrapping her in quilts, he sat beside her while murmuring endearments. He went to the kitchen to make her a cup of tea.

"Letting yourself get overwrought can't be good for the baby," he said, kindly, keeping an eye on her as she sipped the heated liquid.

"I know— I can't help it sometimes. You don't know what it's like having all that stuff inside."

He took her teacup, setting it on the nightstand. Framing her face between his palms, he urged her to meet his eyes. "I need you, Haylee. Our baby needs you. We love you."

"Thank you—"

Moving slowly, he whispered so that she tasted his breath. "Focus on me right now, Darlin' "Teasing the edges of her lips, his slick tongue coaxed hers open.

Becoming absorbed in the pleasurable sensations that Reece always ignited, Haylee could feel tension releasing like a warm flowing river, spreading tendrils over soft earth. Her tongue twirled and brushed against his. The heat of desire warmed her skin. Haylee pulled him back with her onto the bed. They spooned. He reached over to stroke the hard roundness of her belly. She sighed. His hand continued down toward the apex of her legs. Moaning, she moved, giving his fingers access to the silken, sensitive folds of her womanhood.

Reece kept his touch feather-light and teasing. When her breath began to catch spasmodically, he shifted his tempo to match her mood.

Casting a glazed look at him, Haylee turned, smiling. Her arousal and touch soon had Reece in his own state of single-minded focus. Tugging at his buttons, Haylee couldn't stand anything blocking access to each other. Pulling back, they hastily removed their clothes. The fresh air on their skin, damped down the flames of desire, slightly, as they fit themselves together under the covers.

Reece made growl-like sounds as he playfully bit into the soft flesh of her shoulder. Prolonging their pleasure, he began to move against her, letting his tightly engorged organ play an adagio against her wanting, sensitive flesh. He inched inside her, giving her a hint, then pulled away. He repeated this tantalizing stroke until Haylee wiggled in frustration.

She knew that he wanted to plunge deeply, but he held back. Inch by pleasant, agonizing inch he filled her. When he could go no further, he stopped. They shuddered in unison.

Shifting into a smooth, long pattern of piston-like action, Reece gave himself over to the full range of her receptive length. He led them, confidently, over the pinnacle of their yearning quest, Haylee and Reece lay in each other's arms perspiring and satisfied.

In the blissful haze of post-lovemaking, Haylee understood that the gift he'd given her was more than physical pleasure.

Glori and her dad had taken the kids to the YMCA for infants and tots pool time. Haylee was alone in the house, alone in her room, laying on her bed, thinking.

Reece's letters brought back feelings of separation and loss. She squeezed her eyes tight; tears trailed down the sides of her face, absorbed by the pillowcase. She could hear his whisper, "Relax and feel me, next to you, Darlin'."

Forcing her breath to slow, Haylee concentrated on the echo of his voice. As she calmed, her lungs filled completely. Her exhales expended every ounce of pent-up air. She could, now, imagine his eyes, filled with affection, looking at her. A dark eyebrow quirked upward. His lips mirrored the movement. Haylee loved it when he looked at her this way. She desperately wanted him, wanted to be encircled in his strong arms. She wanted to feel him touching her in her deepest places.

Her breathing focused. It became him— his rigid manhood gliding into her with every inhale and, out, with every exhale. Momentarily surprised at her response— aroused, slick, quivering.

Yielding to her instincts, she released self-judgment. Reece... In and out, her imaginings felt solid. Haylee's muscles tightened, her back arched, her breath shifted. Clutching sheets in tight fists, Haylee turned her face into the pillow, muffling her cries.

Sleep claimed her. She could feel Reece, lying next to her, holding her.

⸙

Moments before Haylee opened her eyes; she luxuriated in a feeling of peace.

Stabbing pains across her scalp were followed a flash of white. Pushing the heels of her hands into her eye sockets, Haylee scrambled blindly into a sitting position. She recognized these sensations. As she fumbled to find her notebook, the pain subsided. A green water-like fog, that muffled all sound, focused Haylee's attention. Indistinct figures formed at the edges of her vision. With high, whispery vocals, their separate voices merged into one until the sentences became understandable.

Like before, the words felt like they were delivered directly into the buzzing cells of her tissues.

Haylee had her notebook and pen ready.

From the Heart of the Dawn

Keys to survival birthed in stone

The smaller travels a straight line

The larger is passed by the hands of the Travelers alonnnnne.....

Haylee recorded the words and phrases as fast as she could, hoping that her writing would be readable.

Remember the story of our past

When tomorrow's child repeats it

The future remains steadfast.

Progress of the flesh disturbs the seed

Welcome the Traveler and wish her Godspeed.

Upon the Traveler's shoulders, the world of men depends

Her hastened life is a sacrifice

That pays the ultimate Upholder price

By these signs, you'll know

that the verses we sing are true.

A mother who never ages

A single soothsayer child

A locket that cannot be beguiled

Little girl child remember

Remember these words

Sing them to your child before she reaches her seventh year.

A heavy silence followed the verses. Haylee's heart thumped. The figures remained before her, undulating as if they were gazing through a span of deep, blue water.

"Are you there?" she called out.

"We stand before you."

"What are you?"

"We are Upholders and not Upholders."

"What are Upholders?"

"The Upholders have always been."

The figures began to recede. Haylee tried, once more, "What is that song?"

Three of the forms continued to fade, one remained. The voice that answered was feminine. "The song of the Traveler has been restored to your lineage, my dear."

Haylee was startled to recognize the movements of the figure's arm. The woman touched her forehead, chin, and heart. Extending her hand in front of her chest, she flattened it. From the center of the palm, tiny lights floated up, drifting toward Haylee.

"We honor your service to the Upholders."

Haylee watched as the minute orbs circled, slowly, above her head. One by one, they dropped from their position, raining down on her shoulders and chest. A pleasant spark of heat pricked her skin where they made contact. They clung to her, like stickers. Haylee felt no sense of alarm. Slowly, they dissolved, melting into her, warming the area around her heart.

When her vision cleared, Haylee was startled to see the empty room around her. She reached up, holding a hand on her chest. Haylee noticed a sense of heat, still there. She smiled.

Seeing legible words on her notepad, Haylee was relieved. The warm feelings were replaced by a rush of adrenaline when she imagined handing her notepad to Josh.

⚜38⚜
WAIT OF UNEASE

JOSH TAPPED A PEN on the edge of his knee nervously. His foot wiggled in time to the beat playing in his head. A careless stack of graded papers lay on his desk; his book bag covered a pile of tabloids. Pinned to his corkboard was a grant agreement contract, with vacant blanks, and an imminent deadline. His eyes returned to the student paper directly in front of him.

It was a disservice to grade papers in this mood. But they were slated for return this afternoon; he couldn't put it off any longer.

Kendra Cherick's paper began with a quote from research by Brainerd & Reyna, "It is fundamental to differentiate false memory from the more recognizable concept of memory fallibility. Most people understand that memory is a flawed storehouse of our experience... False memories refer to situations in which we are positive that certain events took place when they didn't actually happen."

Josh, tossed his pen aside, leaning on his elbows, he pushed his fingers under his glasses, massaging tired eyes. *Stress causes all kinds of brain malfunctions. How many of my memories about Haylee are real and how many are false?*

It was useless trying to concentrate. Josh stood, unbuttoning the dress shirt he wore while teaching. Peeling it off, separating it from his t-shirt, he tossed it over the back of his chair. He scratched his scalp as he inventoried the jumble of projects he should be working on. His eyes kept returning to the book bag....and what lay underneath.

When he first discovered them in the newsstand, his instinct was to run down the street, grabbing every copy. Logic prevailed with the understanding that this idea was not executable.

Raising his arms to lace fingers on top of his head, he elevated and lowered his shoulders. Shifting his weight from foot to foot, he let his mind wander.

It had been two days since Haylee and Serena left. He'd promised not to bug her. *Who are you kidding? She's reading love letters.... from him.* The waiting was driving him crazy.

Josh had been questioning everything lately. His chosen profession, where he wanted to live, what he wanted to do with his life. Before Haylee, those questions had been simple. He didn't like uncertainty.

What if she does die in a few years? Wouldn't it be less painful to walk away now?

Leaving them was not an option! With an undeniable determination, Josh knew that he'd see this thing through to its conclusion.

He dropped his hands, reaching for the contract. A lifetime ago, he'd applied for a grant to join a research team in Lyon, France. Scientists there were going after brain tissue analysis, linking it to specific behaviors. Their studies had progressed beyond lower life forms. They were beginning to work with humans. The enthusiasm he'd felt when he first applied wasn't there anymore, but the thought of moving to France held appeal.

After everything that's happened is there any way that I could convince them to go with me?

Not for the first time, Josh wondered if his interest in this field of psychology had to do with Haylee...unlocking the keys to her unique biology.

He'd read the reports that Eugene and Glori had completed. When he'd begun taking steps to launch this research project, he had no idea where it would lead. It was past time that he composed his own entry.

The lab in Lyon is state-of-the-art. Access to it might be our only hope of learning something new.

At the bottom of his list of concerns was dealing with the trust business. He was reluctant to tackle that; the backlash could be significant.

If I am committing to Haylee and Serena, then I should accept all that entails, including facing my parents and the trust board.

He'd had a heated discourse with Haylee before she left. "Throw the paper out!" she'd said of the codicil. "I wouldn't know what to do with that land."

"It says that it's for Serena, you can't turn a blind eye to that."

"The gold he left will take care of her for a lifetime. She doesn't need land too! Plus, it has been in your family for generations. No one ever believed that they'd have to give it up."

"Except for Reece...."

That stopped Haylee in mid-sentence.

"The value of that property is considerable," Josh replied sternly. "Serena is too young to speak for herself. It's up to you...or us, to make sure that we do right by her."

"I don't want to deal with this, Josh! I have other things to think about."

"Haylee, what if we set funds aside that would cover care and upkeep costs for your— casualties."

She stared at him, wide-eyed, blinking, "They won't need upkeep if..."

He hated to say it, but he ground out the words, "What if they do?"

No more was said on that subject. *France sounds better all the time!*

Josh took a break, walking down the hall to the vending machines. Putting coins in the slot, he waited for the spiral arm to unwind a bag of Cool Ranch Doritos. It hit the bottom shelf with a thud.

Shoving three chips in his mouth, he crunched his way back to his cubicle wondering if Spencer had gotten anywhere with the favor he'd requested.

The sight of Lucinda O'Connor, sitting in his chair, leafing through the *Investigator* stopped him in mid-stride.

"Hey Josh," she looked up, smiling.

He'd dated Lucinda, briefly, two years ago. The way his mother told it, Lucinda had been a frequent visitor at his bedside in the hospital. This was partly why he usually went out of his way to avoid her.

"I didn't know you went in for the 'Alien Kidnaps Innocent Children' stories."

"Uh," he snatched the paper out of her hands. "I don't. These are for a research project."

She leaned over to study the one on top of his desk. Waves of sandy blond hair covered her face, "Are you planning to study those poor students at the Alpha Sigma Phi house?"

Josh noticed that his book bag and dress shirt had been moved to the empty seat of the extra chair. "Ahhh...." he hurried to move the topics of conversation out of sight, "something like that."

The phone's ring interrupted the conversation. Josh, grabbed the handset from its cradle, "Joshua Herkowitz, Assistant Professor, Berkeley Psychology Department," he answered. He listened for a few moments nodding. Glancing over his shoulder, he saw Lucinda motion a phone sign by her ear, pointing at her chest with her other hand. He gave her a wan smile, nodding like he intended to follow through. He breathed a sigh of relief when she left.

"... his best friend." Spencer's words only just began to penetrate.

"What? Spence, say that again?"

"We found the guy who wrote the *Investigator* article."

"Tell me."

"He's best friends with Candy's brother's girlfriend's cousin."

"Who's Candy?"

There was a long pause on the other end of the line. "My *girlfriend*, you met her last week."

Hitting his hand against his forehead, Josh looked skyward. "Right, sorry. Can we arrange to meet him?"

"Already done."

❧39❧
PEACE MADE

HAYLEE'S DAY-CAMP WAS set-up, again, next to the old tractor. Puffy clouds responded to breezes that swept them across the sky. With letters in hand, Haylee climbed onto the hood. Settling in, she leaned back against the windshield. Solar power provided a heated seat.

April 23, 1854

Dearest Wife,

I used to feel envious— Your having Serena with you. I still do sometimes. I wish I could have seen her sweet face.

I have finally made peace with our separation. It still hurts, but it is a soreness now rather than a bleeding wound.

It has been nearly a year since my sisters and parents arrived. Apologies for my lapse in writing.

San Francesco continues to change almost daily. Many more wives and children have joined their husbands. They bring a gentle refinement that was lacking before.

Mam, Da, and my sisters have been finding their places in society.

Edward, Polly, and I have made stoic adjustments. There is more noise and commotion but also more laughter, music, and food.

It's been a difficult transition for Polly. She changed her mind about wanting them here once my sisters were competing for the privy and telling her how to clean-up properly. I am afraid that Ed and I were not strict about that. I've taken to including her more often on my store visits and purchasing trips.

Do you remember Happy Valley near Mission, Market and First Streets? It's become a metropolis of industry and production. We now have iron foundries, breweries, boat builders, timber, and flour mills!

The South Market area has also seen much development. We have upholstery shops, saddle makers, book and shoemakers, letterpresses and binderies. And not to forget Da's favorite, the billiard table makers.

He can't convince me to start selling billiard tables. They take up too much space and don't have a good return on investment. Most of the other industries springing up have cut supply costs for the items we do sell.

Until Next Time.

All My Love,

Reece

June 20, 1854

Dearest Wife,

Deirdre and Aggie have become joined at the hip. Did I mention that Deirdre and Edward are fraternal twins? Whenever Ed is at work, those two are working on the house we bought for the engaged couple. It's on Union Street. Ed doesn't seem to mind having those two working on feathering his future home.

Edward and Agatha married on June 2nd at Saint Patrick's. Both bride and groom were nobly attired and looked blissfully happy. There were nearly two hundred guests in attendance!

The ceremony took place at 10 AM, followed by an outdoor luncheon across the street in Yerba Buena Park.

Brigid cornered me during the reception to ask more about our wedding. The Family's been respectful of my wish not to bring up painful memories. Though, I've not been deaf to their whisperings and hushed conversations.

An unspoken agreement kept all tongues silent. Sometime last spring, Polly blurted out during dinner that my baby would be three, had she lived. The girls were all set to clamp down on her when Da hushed them all, "Son," he looked at me solemnly, "everyone sitting at this table has your best interests at heart. We will honor your wish not to speak. However, I'd like you to consider sharing Haylee and the baby with us. We're all sad that we never knew them, but they are as much a part of our family as you are. I think it would do us a world of good if you'd speak of them now and again."

Da was right, speaking openly about you, helps. They all think that you perished in the fire on that terrible, terrible night.

Briged's questions brought back our small, sweet wedding. Do you remember how we laughed at Father Flannigan's pronunciation of, sur-ah-money? How surprised we were when Song, Ed, and Polly rowed us out to the scrubbed and decorated Dicey for the wedding night. I still chuckle when I remember our efforts to conceal our feelings when Ed told us that he'd bought it as a wedding gift. And I smile at how none of that mattered by the time we left.

Ryanne has been courting with a fellow from over Marysville way. She invited him to the wedding as her guest. Cooper Hollowell is his name. They met at a church social. Ryanne played violin in a quartet. Cooper asked Da for permission to wed her in six months' time. Rayenne is already dreaming about making her new home up the valley even if Polly is put out by the idea of her leaving.

Polly's become quite an accomplished fiddle player under Ryanne's tutelage. They played together for the wedding, to everyone's delight.

Rather than being fitted at the dressmakers, Polly chose to wear a gown from 'her' store to demonstrate the quality of our new ready-made wares. She was thrilled when a society reporter asked for a quote. I don't know if it was the dress or the young woman wearing it, but Polly never had a shortage of admirers.

Ed and Aggie will be spending their first night of matrimony in their new home.

All My Love,

Reece

December 6, 1853

Dearest Wife,

I have found what I have been searching for; a vast swath of land on the eastern side of the cove. It is some distance from town. Because no surveyor marked the geology as gold-bearing, I acquired it at a reasonable price. It's called Wild Cat Canyon.

Since I've made a habit of property investments, I've employed a lawyer to manage my estate. The family is ever growing. But this piece of land is for one specific purpose. It is for Serena. Mr. Hayes is confident that he can draft a binding document that will hold it for her until she comes of age. Wouldn't I love to be a fly on the wall when it comes time to execute it!

Briged has taken it upon herself to see to the needs of our aging parents. I have criticized her for not allowing us to hire a servant to help. If her eyes could shoot flames, I'd have been burned to ashes when I accused her of deliberately becoming an old maid. (She already is!) She could have suitors if she'd allow it. Plenty of fellows from St. Patrick's have asked about her. She says that she'll consider saying 'yes' to suitors as soon as I turn my eyes to available women.

As much as I love my sister, her ~~meddling~~ *well-meaning intentions and her prodding grow tiresome. I have been traveling more, searching for new items to sell in the stores— and to be free of Briged's harassment.*

Madame Blanchette's nephew, Dantan, has arrived for a visit. He is three years older than Polly and has spent much time in Paris. I am afraid that Polly has grown too fond of the boy too quickly.

All My Love,

Reece

February 12, 1854

Dearest Wife,

I have sad news this time. My Da passed last month. He took to his bed with a fever — said his jaw was burning like Dublin's Hellfire. This same affliction has come and gone with him before.

We summoned the doctor when he grew so chilled that no amount of hot tea, blankets, or warmers helped. The doctor was there when his convulsions started.

He slipped away from us in the wee hours of the morning.

Brigid and I are worried about Mam. She's stopped eating and won't speak. Even Father Flannigan can't get a response.

Polly has been corresponding with Dantan. He is ill; she's begging me to take her to visit. Maybe once Mam starts to come around we'll go. We could use some time away from the grief and sadness in the house.

Some happier news — Ed and Aggie are expecting their first child.

Brigid has invited a widowed friend of hers, from the home country, to visit with her young son. She says that we all played together as children, but I don't remember. Brigid hopes that Mam will perk up once they get here. They are planning to arrive in the spring.

All My Love,

Reece

May 17, 1854

Dear Wife,

Mam is better!

I think that hearing the fresh-off-the-boat burr of Mary Kirkpatrick and her seven-year-old son Niall, or the laughter and reminiscing about bygone days in County Fermanagh breathed new life into her old bones.

The boy seems to get on well with Mam. They enjoy playing rounds of checkers; he likes telling her about his studies.

Their arrival, though enlivening for mother and Brigid, has become a source of irritation for me. All my sisters and my mother seem to think that Mary should accompany me on my social outings.

I haven't written of this, Haylee, but there are women who I escort in town at times. Several of them have become outright disrespectful of Mary.

Though she is beautiful to look at, she's spent most of her life in a small seaside town. Her husband was a ship's mate. They were hard working, salt of the earth folks. I never paid it heed before, but the women of San Francesco society carry airs with an international flair. Poor Mary is floundering.

No pun intended. ...Well, maybe a little.

Polly says she thinks Mary and I could be a good match if only I would regard her with an open mind. She's informed me that Madame Cassini has mentioned seeing us together.

I am considering moving back to the apartment above the original Keener Brothers.

All My Love, Reece

July 6, 1855

Dear Haylee,

Mistress Blanchet's nephew arrived back in San Francesco several weeks ago. He seems quite recovered from his illness last year. He and Polly say they are in love with each other.

I did not follow through with my plan to move back to the Mercantile. I find that I am resistant to write these next words...

The change in how Reece addressed this letter shook Haylee. When she re-read his last sentence, a cold sweat broke out over her neck and arms. Her hand trembled. She pressed fingers against her lips.

Gripping them tightly, Haylee lowered her arm into her lap. She gazed across the open farmland and orchards. *If I never left, this wouldn't have happened. I wanted him to be happy...but...*

Jumping down off the tractor, Haylee scrambling on her knees, shoving Reece's letters back into their storage box. *I can't do this!*

Rolling the blanket into a wad, Haylee didn't bother stowing away her food. She shoved all remaining items into her pack, flung it onto her back then walked around in circles. She wanted to go somewhere but didn't know which direction to take.

Joey parted the tall grass, stalking toward her. *You cry,* he said in her mind.

"I'm not crying," she spoke out loud. She sat down in the grass, setting aside her burdens. She welcomed his weight in her lap, even his kneading claw pricks.

Inside, he replied. Oscar purred, pushing his face against her hand.

"I love you, Fur Face," she whispered. "Thanks for coming to my rescue."

Feeling steadier, Haylee walked toward the house. The mangled picnic blanket leaked lemon aid on her feet. The dishes inside it clanged against her shins. She didn't care. Hearing additional voices inside, Haylee paused. *Farm hands must be visiting.*

In the doorway, she took in the scene of Josh and her dad, sitting around the table, holding babies, laughing. Josh's eyes lit up when he saw her. He shifted Serena around so he could stand to greet her.

Haylee thought she was OK until he pulled her into a one-armed hug. Her waterworks broke loose. Vaguely, she was aware of her dad and Glori taking Serena. They ushered Josh and Haylee into the yard.

Josh held her without speaking.

Haylee clung to him thinking about how good he smelled and how warm it felt pressed against his chest. Through hiccups, she said, "I told .... you.... not to.... come. But I'm.... glad.... you did."

Pulling away, he brushed hair out of her face. "I couldn't stay away."

❧40❧
TAKING NOTES

THEY WERE HOLED UP in the kitchen pantry whispering back and forth in a heated exchange.

"I am not going to allow him to stay in the same room as my daughter!" Eugene said.

"Gene, that's silly. They're practically living together in Berkeley."

"I can't control what they do when they are on their own, but in my house, they don't sleep in the same room unless they are married."

"It's not as if Haylee is an innocent and you have to protect her virtue."

"It's not right, Glori."

"Josh is committed to her and the baby. Haylee needs emotional support. There's only so much you, and I can do. Do you want to deny her that?"

Gene pressed his lips into a grim line. Crossing his arms over his chest, he regarded Glori without reply.

Pressing her advantage, she continued, "Haylee, and the rest of us, are experiencing something we don't understand. But we do know it that it is an emotional strain. Every one of us needs to take comfort where we can. Screw moral conventions; they don't serve a practical purpose here."

He stood there for a few moments staring at her. With a little nod, he exited, slamming the screen door behind him on his way out.

⊷∾⋅∾⊶

Stretched across Haylee's bed, Josh relaxed, his fingers laced behind his head. He looked around Haylee's room. She had a few of his favorite authors on her bookshelf; Stephen King, Tom Clancy, and Terry Pratchett. Like his room at home, remnants of her childhood lingered around the edges. A stuffed Kermit posed next to Miss Piggy on top of a lampshade.

Important material held prominent positions on or near her desk; infant and parenting books, reams of printouts from research libraries, animal biology textbooks, and some of the items they'd found in the box that Keener had left.

Josh intentionally redirected his thoughts away from Keener. *Eugene seemed short tempered. Was he upset that Glori put me in here with Haylee?*

Serena began making fussing noises in her crib. Josh tiptoed over to check. She wasn't awake, but her expression looked pained, she kicked her feet. Josh rubbed her back making soothing sounds.

When Haylee came in from the bathroom, he held his index finger to his lips. Haylee leaned over to view her daughter, then turned, smiling, to Josh. Taking his hand, she led him back to her bed. Once they were under the covers and snuggling, she gave him a long kiss. "Thank you, again, for coming," she whispered.

He reached for her, running his hand over her stomach and upward. Haylee responded, making explorations of her own. Against his lips, she murmured in a Porky Pig type voice, "We have to be very, very quiet."

⌒⌒⌒⌒

Haylee and Glori were planning to take the children to the park in town. Before they left, she briefed Josh about what she learned.

Pad and pencil in hand, he took notes while she spoke.

"I left off reading at 1855. Polly's grown and in love...." Haylee glanced out the window. She crossed her arms tightly. Her gaze took on a faraway look. "I think he was about to tell me that he's fallen in love again." Haylee's troubled eyes turned Josh's, "I don't want to.... I can't read anymore. Do you mind?"

With his thumb and forefinger clamped tight, Josh rubbed a thumbnail along the outer seam of his jeans. He didn't want to mind. Something deep inside was wary of touching the man's things, reading his words, seeing what was in his heart. "I'll do it," Josh said with resignation. *What was I expecting?*

With a steaming cup of coffee in hand and a quiet house, Josh approached the box of letters that Haylee had left out for him. As he did so, he recalled the heated phone conversation he had with his mother earlier in the week. One of the Wild board members briefed her about the happenings at their last meeting. Josh had presented copies of the codicil for inspection. He'd also invited the lawyer he'd hired to attend. He was still smarting from her vehement tongue lashing.

Josh sighed. *I won't get passed this unless I get started,* he thought.

July 6, 1855

Dear Haylee,

Mistress Blanchet's nephew arrived back in San Francesco several weeks ago. He seems quite recovered from his illness last year. He and Polly are genuinely taken with each other.

I did not follow through with my plan to move back to the Mercantile. I find that I am resistant to write these next words.

When we said our marriage vows, we said, 'until death shall part us.'

Once I realized that you'd escaped the fire and traveled back to your own time, I let myself believe, for a while, that you'd return to me, someday. I rejected the idea that our marriage had ended. I still felt that I was your husband and that you were my wife.

But I was fooling myself. We are parted as surely as if death had claimed us.

If I were in your place, would I want to hear this from you? I would not want to hear it. But I would need to...

Mary has agreed to become my wife.

Polly was right about her. It's taken a long time to feel happy again, Haylee, but I do. I hope you can find it in your heart to ... ~~forgive me?~~ Accept that my life has continued...and be glad that it did.

I still love you and I always will, my Darling.

Reece

The aged paper crinkled in Josh's hand as he carefully set it down. He wiped at the layer of sweat that had gathered on his upper lip. The cold coffee in his mug rippled with the trembling of his hand. Taking a swig, Josh attempted to grab hold of his turbulent emotions.

Of course, he wanted her back. She wants him back too.
They can't be where they want to be— together— so they settled for the next-best- thing?

Shaking himself, Josh pulled a notepad toward him. He jotted down his first note. This refocused his mind and calmed his rattled nerves.

Without giving himself a chance to wonder further, he picked up the next letter.

May 28, 1857

Dear Haylee,

Mary and I married on the 14th. We'll be honeymooning abroad for a month.

Our trip will conclude in Lyon, at Dantan's family estate, where we will attend Polly and Dantan's wedding.

Reece

July 5, 1857

Dear Haylee,

Polly's wedding was a fairy. Dantan's home on the outskirts of Saint- Étienne in south-central France. The estate is old and traditional. The bride and groom wore clothes that once adorned the Blanchette ancestors who were members of the royal court. The couple arrived at the rose garden in a handsome cab decorated with flowers and ribbons. It was pulled by pulled by a majestic fawn colored Percheron, high-stepping its way up the lane.

Although Polly speaks French fluently and was born here, she is still considered an American. Dantan is besotted with his young wife.

We are so happy for Polly and delighted to watch her start her new life as a married woman.

I worry about the next natural event in her life. Do I warn her?

Emis's actions sought to alter the unfoldment of the lineage, yet you arrived here with the same issues— Did she change anything?

Struggle as I may, I feel that I must honor the last known wishes of her mother. Silence.

None of us knows how much time we have on this earth. We cannot live in fear of what <u>may</u> happen but must grab hold of all the happiness that comes our way.

Reece

As Josh read, he could smell the sweet aroma of the plump yellow roses blooming in the garden. How did he know that the ribbons streaming behind the handsome cab were deep blue? It was one of the colors featured in the Blanchette family crest.

He could see sweet Mary Keener, elegantly dressed as a merchant's wife, with her laughing blue eyes urging him to join the dancing. Josh's heel bounced in time to the music he heard playing.

Holding up a finger with cake frosting on it, Mary giggled, daring him to lick it off. The taste of it had been buttery, sweet carrying a hint of lemon essence.

Josh leaned far back in his chair, stretching. He took off his glasses. Massaging the bridge of his nose, he laughed uneasily.

March 4, 1858

Dear Haylee,

Mary is expecting our child in September.

I am delighted.

Reece

November 9, 1858

Dear Haylee,

—Babies must be in the air.

We've had word that Polly and Dantan had a baby daughter. They named her Joanne. Jo Jo is what Polly calls her.

Mary gave birth to Johnathon Joshua, a little earlier than expected— on August 22nd. Johnathon is after Mary's father. She asked me if Joshua was after one of my relatives. I told her that it was not. I did not say that was the name of your good friend. I hope that you could bring him back, as you did Edward.

I am glad to report that all the mothers are doing well. The children are also in good health.

Reece

"I'll be damned, Keener. You are a better man than I am." Josh muttered as he began recording the names and dates of the live births.

January 10, 1860

Dear Haylee,

Mam died in her sleep last week. Her funeral service was well attended.

Mary, Jon and I have moved into a house I bought on Stockton Street. Mary's eldest son Niall has moved back to Ireland to serve an apprenticeship with an uncle on his father's side. He'll be working in a shipyard there.

Reece

February 15, 1861

Dear Haylee,

Torrential rain and flooding have been on everyone's mind. Sacramento, the new state capital, has been hard hit. It is located at the confluence of the Sacramento and American Rivers. With the onslaught of water, levees built to protect the city have crumbled. Newspaper reports say that the town is under ten feet of water. The only mode of transportation is by rowboat. Furniture and dead animals are afloat everywhere.

Our new Governor, Leland Stanford, was inaugurated at the Capitol building, even while the floodwaters were rising at a rate of one foot per hour. When the ceremony was over, he rowed to his house, entering through a second story window.

A few weeks later, the city was still submerged. The legislature has since moved to San Francesco to wait for the waters to recede.

Rayenne, Cooper and their children have come to stay too. Marysville is under water. They've lost the farm and a hundred head of cattle— to starvation and drowning. Cooper says that the entire valley is under water from the Coastal Range to the Sierra Nevada's. Mail delivery has ceased, the Telegraph is unreliable.

We'd been so worried about them. Their losses are distressing, but they have their lives. I am glad that we have a haven for them. I have teased Rayenne, that eventually when the hurt has passed, her feelings about the great floods will play out in her music.

Reece

May 8, 1861

Dear Haylee,

Brigid has finally married — thank heaven!

Randall has been after her for years, but she's always had her reasons to say 'no.' I guess her reasons ran thin or he put his foot down.

Ed and Aggie are about to have their 5ᵗʰ child.

Rayene and her husband have three children.

My own Mary is pregnant again. It was a surprise. We thought we'd reached an age where we were done having children. Jonathan, at three years old, is a handful and lively enough to equal more than one child. Mary is in good spirits. The doctor assures us that we have no cause for concern.

I am blessed.

Reece

June 27, 1865

Dear Haylee,

Mary and I have been planning a trip to take the boys to visit Polly, Dantan and Jo Jo. It has been over long since we have visited Polly. I wish I could say that it has nothing to do, what-so-ever with the timing of Jo Jo's seventh birthday...

Reece

❧〰❧

Josh sat up straighter as he read the last sentence. Placing the delicate paper on Haylee's desk, he leaned back, tossing his glasses on top of his notepad.

Glancing at the sparse notes he'd jotted down so far, Josh stood up, stretched his arms behind his back then cracked his knuckles. Dropping into a plank position, Josh did what his swim coach taught him to do whenever he needed to sort out his thoughts— push-ups.

His jealousy, unreasonable but real, had been replaced with a quiet feeling of connection. Curiosity about his ancestor's life had taken root and flourished.

At Reece's mention of his siblings and their activities over time, Josh's thoughts had wandered to his brother. *How much time I spend with Spencer directly correlates to the personality of his current girlfriend. Will we still hang out after we're both married?*

At thirty push-ups, Josh reflected on his parents and their divergent attitudes toward his relationship with Haylee...and with Serena. "Lucinda would never threaten our family legacy," his mother had said in their last, terse phone call.

Josh gritted his teeth, doing fifteen furious counts. The more his mother pushed, the more Josh understood that there was no question about his sticking by Haylee and Serena. In fact, he'd even begun to imagine raising Serena by himself if Haylee's questionable assertions came true. If that ever happened, he knew that people in the family would speculate about his motives.

His dad and Spencer seemed to be the only ones who understood that his feelings for the little girl ran about as deep as they did for her mother...but in a completely different way.

Josh finally came to rest, sitting on the floor as he thought about the years Reece had taken care of Polly. *What if it's true?* A sick feeling in the pit of his stomach felt like a rock wedged in there.

Part of him didn't want to read what came next. Josh breathed deeply, closing his eyes, pinching the bridge of his nose. He couldn't avoid it any longer. This was what they'd been searching for.

⊰⟋⟍⊱

July 7, 1866

Dear Haylee,

We were touring through northern Spain when word came of Polly's illness.

As beautiful as ever, Polly reached for my hand, "Papa, thank you for returning from your holiday with such haste."

Around the time she was ten, she dropped my first name. I was flattered and pleased I felt when she first did that.

Surrounded by feather pillows, Polly looked small and waif-like.

"Papa," she squeezed my hand, "may I confide in you?"

"Haven't you always?"

She smiled sadly, "Not always..."

"What is it Dear-heart?"

"The doctors assure Dantan that the malady is only in my head. They say that I should be dancing again in a month's time."

"That is wonderful news," I replied, even while grief wedged in my heart like a lead ball.

She looked solemn." When I try to imagine myself dancing again, I can't."

"Why is that?"

"Do you remember Maman and her visions?"

I nodded, how could I forget?

"I've never thought such a thing about myself before. But I do now..."

"Tell me."

"When I dream about the future, all I can see is my body surrounded by flowers, Dantan in despair."

I didn't try to argue with her but pulled her into my arms so that she wouldn't see my tears. "What do you want me to do?"

"Stay— please. Until after... for Dantan and Jo Jo."

"Of course."

"Ask Mary and the boys to look after my daughter."

"Anything you wish."

≈≈≈

As the weeks past, Polly's skin lost its healthy glow. It became waxy and taught. Her hair began falling out, her bright eyes grew dull, sinking into her head.

"How do you feel today?" I asked every time I came to see her.

"It doesn't hurt, Papa, it feels like the bright, shiny light that was my life just grows dimmer every day."

I noticed that Joanne now wore that damn pendant.

Polly was slipping away. Her lips receded, her nose thinned. It was like all the water in her body was drying out. Still, nothing pained her.

She only spoke in a whisper now, "I am more gone than here. I can't see anything ahead— all I know is that I have to go."

I cried in despair, "Fight it, Polly! Stay with us!"

"No, Papa." She patted my hand as I leaned close to hear what she was saying. Her voice was faint. "It is going to be alright. You held onto her longer than you should have—"

At first, I didn't know what she was talking about. Had she gone addled? Then I realized that she was speaking of you.

"—don't' repeat that. Promise."

I nodded, I didn't care if she saw me crying.

"Help take care of my family...then let me go...and tell them that I said for them to do the same."

I nodded and kissed her forehead. Closing my eyes, I stayed like that for a while, knowing that this would be our last goodbye.

It was only right that the last of her strength was spent with her husband.

After Polly had passed, Mary took the children on many picnics and outings. I joined them sometimes.

We brought Jo Jo home with us while Dantan took some time. He planned to collect her in San Francesco in about three months.

❧⁓⌖⁓❧

While we were aboard the ship, I thought about taking the necklace away from Jo Jo. It would be so easy to do when she was sleeping. I wanted to throw the accursed thing in the water and let it rot on the bottom of the ocean floor.

But then I remembered the fire and the daguerreotype...and I remembered that one day, in a future that I can't even imagine, it will come to you. It would bring you back to me.

There's too much pain in this world. Sickness, wars, and the struggle for survival. We had our share of it, you and me. If I took that necklace, I might be able to spare us a lot of pain, but we'd also miss out on the happiness and joy.

I realized, on that trip, that the pendant is a link to you. You'll know what decision I made.

All My Love,

Reece

September 11, 1868

Dear Haylee,

Jo Jo is nine years old this year. We haven't seen her in some time, but her father writes often. They are doing well.

My boys— JJ is ten, and Daniel six— are healthy and thriving. I've got them working in the stores when they are not in school.

Mary has found my box of letters. I won't go into details about how she came to discover them or about the noisy discourses that followed. I will say that I have realized that my continued attention to you is unfair to her. She is my wife now. I love her deeply. I do not wish to cause her hurt. My writing (and thoughts) have done what I have not intended.

It is time to say goodbye, my Dearest.

Reece

October 1, 1888

Dear Haylee,

It's time to make one last trek through Wild Cat Canyon, to make a special delivery. I'll be thinking and dreaming about my girls with every step.

Do you remember my mention of Madame Cassini all those years ago? The fortune teller who befriended Polly? She told me that I would 'be transmitting information of utmost importance to a love that transcends time.' What I didn't tell you then was that Madame Cassini described the picnic that we went on with Polly, Ed, and Song in such detail, it was as if she were there with us. She told me about 'astonishing items' that you'd hidden in the rocks and that this was how I would communicate with my love that 'time has taken.'

She said one more thing. That I was to include these words in the last letter that I would write: "Since the Dicey, my blood carries attachments to Travelers. The crystal carriers now have consorts. Joshua of the swimmer's team will know what to do when the time comes."

I love you still,

Reece

❧

"What?" Josh yelped when he read that. He stood abruptly knocking over the chair. He couldn't get out of the house fast enough! His mouth turned to cotton. He thought he would puke. "This isn't possible he repeated. "That can't mean *me*..."

⚜41⚜
WHERE'S JOSH?

HAYLEE AND GLORI RETURNED from the park. Both little ones were fast asleep in their car seats. The house was quieter than expected when they trundled in with the children and all their paraphernalia.

A chill went through Haylee when she went into her room and saw her desk chair laying on the floor. She got Serena transferred into her crib then went to investigate.

She looked outside toward the walnut tree where Josh parked his car in the shade. It was gone.

Looking down at the letter lying on top of her desk, she read until she saw the part that must have freaked him out.

Glori knocked lightly on the door frame. "Is Josh gone?"

Haylee nodded. She followed Glori into the kitchen, "You're never going to believe this, there's something in this letter that is about *him*."

"May I?" Glori asked, holding out a hand.

Haylee hesitated, then held out the letter.

Glori read it out loud from the beginning. "A fortune teller?" she repeated. She continued. "Is all this true about the rocks and where he placed his time capsule?"

Haylee nodded.

"Blood attachments and crystal carrier consorts? What do you think that means?"

"I don't know."

"Joshua of the— Ohhhh." Glori's eyes widened, "I see—"

Haylee clamped her lower lip between her teeth. "I'm worried about him driving when he's upset."

"Do you have any idea where he might go?"

"I don't!" Haylee started pacing. You'd think, having had him inside my head, that I'd know something like that. But I haven't a clue." Haylee's voice continued to rise with every sentence.

"Listen—" Glori grabbed Haylee's hand, tugging her over to a chair at the table. "We need to stay calm. Josh is no dummy; he's rational and reasonable. I can understand that he would need some space to sort out something like this."

"He's already dealt with so much."

"He has, and it hasn't scared him away, has it?"

"Not yet..." Haylee sounded hopeful.

"Do you trust him?"

"Yes."

"Then trust him enough to know what he has to do to take care of himself. When he's ready, he'll be back."

Haylee inhaled a deep, calming breath, "You're right."

"Shall I finish reading?"

"I'd like to," Haylee said, holding out her hand. Scooting the chair up close to the table, she leaned on her elbows holding the fragile paper. Clearing her throat, she began.

I've convinced Ed to join me on this excursion. He is the only person who knows the whole of your story. I told him about the pendant and time travel. He's been a great friend and support. He's always willing to reminisce about you and Serena. Of course, we stopped doing that after Mary came into our lives. But we've taken it up again....

Edward and I are living with each other. After he lost Aggie to apoplexy in '86 and I lost Mary in '87 from Scarlet Fever, we decided to team up to keep out of the way of the youngsters. We miss our dear wives, but we are doing alright.

Ed's been making noises about wanting to enter politics. I keep trying to convince him to move to Belize. There's a fresh Gold Rush going on down there. When I told him that we could afford to keep our comforts and hire young men to do the hard labor, I could see him giving the thought more consideration.

Little Jo Jo's engaged to be married. JJ and Daniel are twenty-nine and twenty-six, both married with children, managing their own stores."

Haylee paused to explain, Ed, you've heard me talk about, he's Reece's younger brother. I don't know who these other people are that he's talking about.

"My sisters and their husbands are showing wear and tear— like me. I wonder what you would think of me if you saw me now? A crotchety, old codger with thinning hair and a few too many pounds. You'd probably laugh at Ed too.

It's funny how I can remember you, Polly and all my siblings so young, vital, and bursting with plans. Those of us still here are the same on the inside, but we are slower and unsightly on the outside.

You have always been in my heart, Love. I expect you'll remain there till I'm done.

It's been a hell of a ride. A good one.

Reece

Haylee huffed, a smile hinted around her mouth. "Belize!"

Glori was smiling, "It sounds like he lived a full in interesting life."

"It does," Haylee agreed. She placed the letter on the table, tracing a finger over his sentence about losing 'Mary.' "His wife's name was Mary." Haylee was surprised that the idea of him, older, and married didn't hurt...it was...nice. "What was scarlet fever like?"

"It's caused by a strain of streptococcus. In the nineteenth century, it was most common among children; entire neighborhoods could become infected. It usually starts with a strep throat. Fever, chills, body aches, nausea, and sometimes vomiting are symptoms. What gave it its name is the rash that develops on the throat and neck. Tiny, itchy bumps at first, merge, spreading over the entire body. Inside the throat and the tongue can develop bumps, open sores, and peel."

Haylee leaned back; her expression was alarmed.

"I'm sorry," Glori apologized. "I've been away from work for too long."

"That's alright," Haylee replied. "I was imagining Reece taking care of her, watching her suffer. How that was treated?"

"Bed rest would be the first thing; then keeping the fever down."

"I remember now," Haylee said. "No solid foods. Rennet and whey were popular liquids to drink when sick."

"Yes, they would have also used Epsom Salts, and nitrate silver."

Haylee shivered, "It sounds like a painful way to die."

"It must have been difficult."

"Poor Reece."

"Poor Mary."

❧42❧
CEASE & DESIST

IN ELEMENTARY SCHOOL, spelling tests, recess games, and PE had driven Josh to express his anxiety one bite at a time. The ends of his fingers curled around abbreviated keratin.

When his mother caught him gnawing on a toe, she began a cease campaign, in earnest. She tried everything she could think of to get him to stop. Results from that had been the development of a lustful relationship with Tabasco Sauce and a hostile attitude toward his mother.

Frances enrolled Josh on the swim team. Lane drills and more than a few 'man-to-mans' with the coach re-channeled his nervous energy into the pool. When his nails had grown out, he found a renewed pleasure in scratching, but he had to watch that too, it could get out-of-hand.

While reading Keener's letters, Josh scratched holes in his jeans. He needed to find a pool!

He knew speeding was stupid, especially in his current mood, but pressing down hard on the accelerator felt like a release. He allowed himself this temporary act of absurdity because the country roads in Elverta were lightly traveled. His reaction times were sure; he felt confident that he would make correct decisions if the need arose.

Spotting a phone booth, Josh took a sharp turn into a dirt parking lot. He slammed on the brakes. Dust plumed around his car. He hopped out, heading straight for the blue box. It was hot and smelly inside, despite the folding door standing wide open. Someone had used it to relieve their bladder. Holding his breath, Josh swung the heavy phone book up from its hanging pendulum. Dropping it onto the steel corner shelf, it clattered into place. The desire to put his fingers in his mouth was strong, but germs and the will to resist kept his nails intact.

"Come on!" he urged himself to go faster.

Under normal circumstances, Josh would never defile a book— even a phone book. Finding what he was looking for, he took a quick glance around before ripping out the page, folding it, and shoving it in his back pocket.

Knowing that he was on his way to swim calmed him enough to resume his typical driving habits. He could keep his thoughts from troubling him through a quick stop at JC Penny where he bought a Speedo and swim goggles.

When the YMCA street sign came into view, Josh breathed a sigh of relief. In the locker room, the smell of sweat and mold, as well as the metallic clanging of locker door latches lifting and dropping brought on a further sense of calm.

Stepping into the sticky, humid, environment of the pool room, sucking down a lungful of caustic chlorine infused air, Josh's focus sharpened onto the cordoned off swim lanes. Two were open. Approaching the one he'd chosen, he pulled goggles over his head, tightening the straps to hold them in place.

Slicing into the water, Josh's relief was immediate. Five freestyle laps had him warmed up enough to pour all his might into powerful butterfly strokes. The stopper came out of his bottled-up emotions.

It's one thing to be a victim and bystander in Haylee's drama; it's something else to be directly involved.

When I had the chance to get away, what did I do? I walked right back in.

Am I being manipulated?

I don't think so.

Do I want to leave?

Why is it every time I get scared, I contemplate leaving?

When I think about what my life would be like without Haylee and Serena, the answer is, 'no.'

Josh let his mind go back to the times he and Haylee made love. She seemed happy. In those moments, he didn't have doubts about her feelings.

It was difficult watching her mourn for another man. It shook him, made him question their relationship. *Is her pain, and my jealousy a deal breaker?*

Whenever he felt vulnerable and uncertain, he had a strong urge to organize everything, categorize it, line it up in neat, predictable rows.

In this situation, as soon as he felt like he was making progress, control slipped out of his grasp. It was frustrating, frightening at times, but it was also interesting.

Josh switched to the backstroke. The long, pulling windmill-like strokes and propelling kicks gave his muscles a rest.

He daydreamed about a day or a week, where an emergency wasn't breaking out, when they weren't worried about someone dying, or re-seeding souls. He dreamed about a time when Haylee's past wasn't hanging over their heads.

He envisioned a little outdoor cafe, sitting at a table covered with a red and white checkered tablecloth. Wine glasses in hand, soft, stinky cheese, crackers, olives and thin salami slices were on small plates in front of them. They were relaxed and secure with each other, bantering like they used to do when they first met. They didn't have things to do or looming responsibilities. He pulled her hand toward him, kissing her fingertips, smiling, winking. He could have her whenever he wanted to, and she would say 'yes.'

Doing a summersault turn at the end of his lane, Josh continued with a breaststroke, pulling himself up and out of the water with each propulsion.

The Cassini woman said that Reece's blood carried attachments to Travelers...since the Dicey. What is a blood attachment? If there was no blood connection before the Dicey, what happened on that ship to change it?

Note to self: Schedule blood tests, search for unusual characteristics, anomalies. Get a sample from Spencer too. What are the chances of getting Mom to do it? Could I talk Dad into being my control test?

How is Cassini connected? She knew Emis in France. Did she follow her to California, targeting Polly for some purpose? Was she a Traveler? Are there more of them out there?

'Joshua of the swimmer's team will know what to do when the time comes.'

What the hell is that?

Reece's son was a Joshua, did he swim?

If it was me mentioned in that letter from 1888, what does that mean about free-will and destiny? Have my actions, Haylee's actions already been scripted?

That thought stopped Josh in mid-stroke. He swam over to the pool's edge. Resting his elbows on the side, wiping the water out of his face. Cocking his head and frowning, he said, "It's preposterous to think that every event in life is determined. There are too many variables." He mumbled. "Could a derivative of that be possible? Events that present themselves for interpretation of free will?"

Could this be one of those moments?

Too unnerved to think about it anymore, Josh returned to freestyle. When his fatigue, reached maximum capacity, he wondered, *What would happen if I stopped fighting all these things that I hold onto so strongly? Would my life be more straightforward?*

Part Three

A POINT IN TIME

⚜43⚜
TRAVELER ARRIVES

OVER A REMOTE SECTION of rolling hills on the valley side of the Coastal Range, a ball of light rocketed across the sky. Of the stargazers who observed the phenomena, most assumed that a meteorite had entered the Earth's atmosphere.

As the blazing ball slowly lowered, its circular shape elongated, the unconscious occupant inside unfolded. The snapping and crackling on the exterior reduced, turning to tiny specks of rainbow lights. They moved from the bottom to the top, before winking out. Fizzing sounds shifted to a gentle hum as the exterior thinned, growing increasingly transparent. The ball shape disappeared.

Laying on the ground, the waif-like figure did not move. Dressed in nothing but body conforming film, the surface of the material glowed a gentle pink, pulsing rhythmically, precisely matching the beat of the girl's heart.

Her eyes fluttered, she gazed, blankly, at a familiar cluster of stars overhead. As memory returned, she frowned, taking a deep breath, testing the unfamiliar scents. The air itself felt different, wetter. Unused to being satisfied with the simple act of taking a breath, Norah inhaled a few more. Her mind cleared. Her muscles engaged.

Flexing, first, her aching hands, she lifted them for a visual inspection. They looked like regular hands, but the memories of what she'd done with them troubled her— as did the intrusive thoughts that now inhabited her mind.

She felt around her neck contacting the hard surface of her pendant. Clutching it, Norah took comfort in the warmth it emitted.

Slowly, she turned, maneuvering herself into a sitting position. Looking intently in every direction, she noted a grassy field and trees making skeletal black shapes in the distance. She was startled when a hoot, hoot echoed. Something about the size of a basketball separated from the deep shadows. It barreled straight toward her at an incredible speed.

With heart racing, Norah scrambled backward as the thing closed the distance. Turning over, she got to her feet and ran. A screech pierced the darkness, a whoosh of air dropped over her head. Norah raised her hands, crying out.

"What was that thing?" she muttered as she watched it move away, climbing into the sky with undulating motions. Shaking herself, she looked down. Her skin fabric glowed bright red with blue splotches over her internal organs that were flooded with blood and hormones. She didn't need the colors to tell her that she'd been frightened and had reacted with a flight response. Checking to make sure that the thing in the trees was not returning, she focused on calming her heart rate.

Her optical device scrolled data across her visual field. Animal: Bird: Order Strigiforme: Nocturnal: Species, Barn Owl: Prey consists of small mammals and insects: Extinction: May 13, 2112.

Additional area scans showed no large life forms in the vicinity, though it was distracting to see small ones EVERYWHERE! They were in the air, clinging to the grasses and in the soil. Norah shivered with disgust. The surface of her skin prickled with the thoughts of those things crawling all over her.

Norah ran. She had no plan for which direction to go, but getting away seemed like the right thing to do. Eventually, she came to a clearing where the grasslands parted near a stream. Norah stopped, catching her breath while initiating another scan. The tiny life forms were still present, but the clearing afforded a reduced number.

Her directives began to reassert themselves.

Disorientation may be experienced upon arrival. The sensory input system will compensate. Remain calm.

Check atmospheric recording application to verify travel event data. If it captured information, back it up. If backup is not possible, memorize.

Assess survival conditions. Adapt as necessary.

Inhaling more of the delicious oxygen, Norah squeezed her hands into tight fists, releasing them, she flexed her fingers. Relax. She began an internal dialog. You knew that the adjustment period would be traumatic. You've had every inoculation that could be anticipated. None of these life forms should cause problems nor should any of the local humanoid diseases. I'm fine...I'm not in mortal danger at this minute. Breathe!

Jogging in place, she noticed that the bottoms of her feet were overly tender. She stopped her exercise to hobble to a rock. Sitting down, Norah removed the thin layer of material that covered the bottom of her foot. She tilted her ankle so that she could look. The surface was dark and slick. Even after rinsing it in the stream, she couldn't tell if the slickness was blood or wet earth.

She scooped up a handful of dirt. It was cold and slick. It smelled of plants and decay. It didn't taste like much — metallic — the texture was gritty. She spit several times, clearing her mouth. How am I going to function here? she wondered. I've never been outside of an environment before. I haven't moved from my arrival destination, and already my foot covering is faulty.

Two things happened simultaneously. A tremor began in her middle. It sent vibrations through her extremities, and her pendant started to burn.

The tremor shook Norah for more reasons than its physical force. She knew to expect it, had experienced light versions of it in the lab. When it happened at home, her techs had immediately provided means to satisfy the need.

This one was visceral and raw. The hunting urge came close to overriding her thinking. Losing control and running wild in this foreign time frightened her more than the strangeness of her surroundings. Grinding her teeth, Norah focused her energy on resistance.

Ripping a length of Second Skin from below her knees, Norah stuck it to the bottoms of her feet, reinforcing the thin lining. With a few thoughts, she changed the material's structure to reflect her surroundings. Except for her head, hands, calves and the tops of her feet, Norah became invisible.

Picking stalks of grass, she squeezed them. She'd seen a documentary about aboriginals using plant material for dye. Extracting color proved more difficult than she'd anticipated. Grabbing more plants, she took the bundle to a grouping of rocks by the stream. Bunching them up on a flat surface, she began beating them with another stone.

The crystal began to insist, strongly. Norah rolled her hands around in the fibrous mass, rubbing juice onto exposed extremities.

Optical scans did not indicate a direction she was to go, but she knew enough about the ancient, yet sophisticated, technology within her pendant to realize a bearing would be forthcoming.

It wasn't long before Norah discovered that the crystal diminished its temperature when she moved in a north by northeasterly direction. At first, Norah tried hopping over the thick vegetation that scratched and irritated her legs. She let out squeals of annoyance, until another tremor rolled through, efficiently focusing her thoughts on a single directive.

In some ways, it was a relief to give herself over to instinct. Her strides stretched and grew longer. Her body became tense and hard with powerful energy.

Grasslands gave way to tree cover that was difficult to see through. A full moon rose to its zenith, dappling everything in a silver light. A trail came into view as Norah ran. Her light colored, chin length hair floated on the night air in the wake of her jet stream. She swerved to follow the trail's course as it offered an unimpeded path. The crystal did not object.

Covering more ground, Norah detected a new scent. It stung her nose and made her stomach growl. She headed toward it. People would be near.

At the next trail rise, Norah stopped to catch her breath. Below was a tiny settlement. A half dome, illuminated from inside showed two human forms. The more massive would be a male, the smaller with a ponytail would be female. Norah wondered if the increased strength afforded by her condition would be enough to overwhelm those two.

A shiver of anticipation snaked its way down her spine. With a fluid, practiced movement, she threw her hands out to her sides, spreading her fingers wide — thwap! Her fingers followed each other in a wave as she tested the resistant membrane filling in the spaces between her digits. Raising an arm toward the sky, she looked at the moon through her webbing.

It refracted off the transparent surface, glowing in pleasing multi colors. Bringing her hand toward her face, she rested the heel under her chin, feeling the slight pulsations under the surface. Not for the first time, she replayed the memories of the victims she had suffocated with these webs.

Closing her eyes, she apologized. Dropping her hand and her concerns, she returned her attention to the settlement.

A ring of stones near the dome was the source of the smell that had drawn her. Small wisps of smoke climbed like ghosts released from tombs. A box-like contraption sitting on four wheels was located nearby.

Norah's ears pricked up when she heard, "Crap! I gotta go take a crap," in a low voice. Laughter erupted, "Ever since I was a kid, I've always had to do my business right after I eat. You going to be alright while I go?"

"I'm not scared of the dark," responded a female voice. "Do you want me to escort you to the outhouse? I'll hold the lantern."

"I got it," the male replied. Norah watched as he bent down, kissing the female before exiting the shelter. A narrow beam of light speared out in front of him.

Norah knew that this was the opportunity that she needed. Creeping forward, she stayed in the bushes as she approached. The woman inside was busily arranging things, humming to herself.

Keeping a watchful eye on the rectangular structure that the male entered, Norah wondered where it led and how long he would be absent.

The female had bedded down by the time Norah crept near the fabric structure. An opening flapped in the slight breeze. A twig snapped under Norah's foot. "Jango? Is that you?" the female inquired.

Norah sprung through the gap with as much force as she could. Hands out in front of her, she landed on top of the woman with a thump, not quite hitting her mark.

"What the...." Came a surprised expletive as Norah frantically struggled, getting into position. The female kicked wildly from inside a sheath of thick, slick material.

Norah had the advantage of surprise and unrestricted movement. She pushed a webbed hand toward the woman's mouth and nose, using her feet as leverage to press it into place. Upon contact, the webs adhered to every surface like a second skin. They throbbed as they bonded.

Sweet, relief flowed through Norah. Filling her chest, it radiated outward. Inhaling deeply, she pulled the luxuriant oxygen into her lungs while she drew the essence of Maya Rodriguez into her muscles, tissues, and body fluids.

The taking of a life force was gratifying. As necessary as the act was, it was equally horrifying. Instead of abandoning herself to the sensations, Norah met the eyes of her victim. No longer fighting, Maya's gaze was direct, searching for understanding even as the last vestiges of consciousness drained from her mind.

Norah watched awareness fade from the girl's face. Before it was gone completely, she leaned in, kissing Maya's temple.

When it was done, Norah pulled her hand away. It made a dry, scratchy, sucking sound. Sitting on her haunches, she stared at Maya's features. Brown skin, thick-lashed eyes, and full lips were lovely. Maya was huge! Norah lifted one of the girl's limp hands. Placing her own against it, it was twice as big as hers.

Maya's thoughts, foreign and stout, percolated to the forefront of Norah's mind. She understood that this tiny settlement was a 'campsite,' and that it was a temporary dwelling for recreational purposes. Further, Jango was someone that Maya felt intimate toward. She'd planned to have intercourse with him tonight. Norah whispered Maya's words for that, making love.

With the reminder of Jango, Norah had to make a quick decision about what to do next.

❦44❦
TOGETHER SLEEPING

WITH A RELAXED BLADDER, Jango stopped by the water pump to wash up and brush his teeth. Hiking back to his campsite, he whistled while thinking about Maya. *If she zipped the sleeping bags together, there'd be no question. If they are side by side, then...*

"I'm baaack," Jango sang quietly outside while toeing out of his shoes. Ducking his head, he stepped inside. He paused, taking in the layout, puzzled. The lantern was still on. Maya was balled up in her sleeping bag already asleep. He frowned, tapping a finger against his lips.

"Humph," he muttered, turning off the light while stripping down to his underwear. He slipped into his, separate, sleeping bag. Laying on his back, he folded his hands, resting them on his chest. He wasn't tired. *Did I do something to piss her off? The silent treatment isn't like her. Last night she said how much she was looking forward to this trip.*

Jango rolled on his side, "Maya, are you asleep?" he asked. He wiggled closer so that they were spooning. Her hair was loose, the way he liked it. Nuzzling in, he thought that her shampoo smelled like tropical fruit, coconut, pineapple mango. Carefully, he put his arm around her, waiting to see if she'd respond.

When she didn't move, he retracted his arm. Petting her like a cat, from shoulders to hips, he began rubbing her fanny. He'd nosed his way through her hair, getting down to the warm skin on her neck. He kissed her, his own body responded.

By now, she's usually more encouraging. What is up with her?

Norah had made a severe error. Feeling Jango's hand roaming over her buttock, she froze. Her sensors flashed crazily. Wedged in behind Maya, she had no way to retreat. Jango was even more enormous close-up. If he got a hold of her, Norah's chances of escape would be small.

Mentally, Norah turned to Maya for help. She queried how the woman would put an end to Jango's overtures. The answer was immediate. Bunching up material from the 'sleeping bag' and pressing it over her mouth, Norah did her best to mimic Maya's speech patterns. "Jang, cut it out! I don't feel good. Give it a rest till tomorrow, OK?"

He stopped, sounding disappointed, "Oh? I'm sorry. Is there anything I can get for you?"

"Nah...thanks. All I need is a good night's sleep."

"Oh, alright. Sweet dreams, then, Maya."

Norah had to hold back a sigh of relief. Jango moved away, shifting around on his side of the tent. As his breathing slowed, her paralyzing fear subsided, but she remained alert, listening to every change in his resting patterns.

When Norah was sure that Jango was asleep, she slowly peeked out. Illumination from the moon was enough to see the tent interior. She waited to see if he would stir. Growing bolder, Norah wiggled free. She stood, looking down at the slumbering man.

Norah wasn't compelled by an overpowering force. But she felt terrible for Jango. *Will he be very sad when he sees Maya? Will he be held responsible?*

Slowly, Norah gathered the loose material at the opening of his sleeping bag, she knelt on it, pinning his arms inside. Flicking her hands, she waited to see if the sound disturbed him.

Easing her thighs alongside his head, she pressed both hands over his face, the webbing fastened, leaving no space for air pockets.

Asphyxiation can be a terrifying experience. Every instinct kicks in to fight.

Jango's eyes popped open. "It's a dream! It's only a dream," she spoke urgently next to his ear. Pressing, harder, with her thighs and her hands

When Norah had begun taking consciousnesses, she realized that the most humane way to do it was by surprise— to get it over with as quickly as possible.

Long ago, it was discovered that nutrients pass energetic qualities to those who consumed them. Qualities such as how they had been cultivated and processed for ingestion. It is evident to Norah that Jango's essence was pure. There hadn't been time enough for him to register fear.

Norah allowed herself the freedom to delight in the physical sensations that inundated her now, especially with two new procurements.

Unrestricted, her lungs filled with the fragrant aromas of plant matter. Her extremities felt charged with compact strength. Norah wished she could run in her exercise sphere at six rotations per second!

Norah's insecurities evaporated. Her comprehension of how to function in this primitive environment expanded with Maya and Jango's knowledge.

Studying, listening to historians, watching vids and even practicing with tactile virtual reality, didn't adequately prepare her for her mission. She was immensely grateful to her two ill-fated victims.

Norah slid Maya and Jango's heavy forms next to each other. She pulled Jango's arm away from his side, positioning it so Maya's head was cradled against his shoulder. She gently closed their eyelids.

The idea for how to 'cuddle' them was from Jango's thoughts. The notion of sharing a sleeping environment with another living creature was strange to Norah. But as she observed them, she could almost believe that they'd come together that way on their own. It was pleasing.

Maya and Jango's feelings of pleasure associated with the heat of arousal, skin to skin contact, penetration and moving against each other during coupling were in direct opposition to Norah's revulsion for those concepts.

Sex was eliminated long ago. It was not an efficient way to reproduce. History showed that free will to choose sexual partners led to substandard genetics, troubled family groupings, and unbalanced offspring. Human engineering had solved those issues by dampening down the instinct for touch, substituting it with a heightened desire for mental rewards.

⁂

As her additional strength faded, Norah's confidence ebbed with it. The sun made its first appearance over the horizon. Norah sat at the entrance of the tent, wearing Maya's over-sized coat, staring. *This environment is entirely random. Nature, evolution, and natural selection are wild and unruly. Anything could be out there!*

When she couldn't delay any longer, Norah rummaged through the couple's food supplies. She was pulling from their minds, how this or that was consumed. Settling on something easy, Norah chose cereal and milk.

Taking a bite of *Raisin Bran*, Norah savored the flavors and textures bursting in her mouth. Crunchy flakes mingled with chewy, raisins. Sugar! was delightful. When she finished her bowl, she dug through the rest of the cereal box, searching for raisins, putting them in her mouth, sucking on them.

Where she lived, nutrients could be taken by mouth or infused directly into the stomach. They were perfectly balanced for the bodies changing daily needs, and they were tasteless. Most citizens opted for direct infusion. It saved time and increased efficiency. Ingestion by mouth was a hobby.

Elimination was treated much the same way, except in reverse.

So, it was with building interest that Norah eyed the rectangular structure called an 'outhouse.' With Jango's recent experiences, Norah understood how the little building was used. While she chewed, putting off a bathroom visit, Norah called up the data logs from yesterday. It was with surprise and delight that she learned that her atmospheric recording application was full!

Unfortunately, the information was indecipherable. If she had access to Institute research tools, the translation would be easy. However, now, she'd have to find other ways to access it or at least keep it safe until she returned.

Her Second Skin stored all her technological assistance. The fact that it had a knowledge base saved within it, provided a level of comfort. However, the longer she was here, the more likely it was to run out of power or shut down completely. This terrified her. Acquiring the crystal wasn't the only thing with time constraints.

The temperature had climbed to sixty-three degrees Fahrenheit, an antiquated unit of measurement commonly used. The time was 11:45 a.m. Maya's concerns about vacating their site before 'check-out' time, had Norah scrambling.

She straightened up the campsite as well as she could, packing everything usable into Jango's Jeep. She raided their wallets for cash and helped herself to Maya's ID, just in case— though no one would believe that Norah was Maya Rodriguez.

Covering her Second Skin with Maya's borrowed clothes was dreadful. Not only was the fabric hot and irritating, but it also dampened many of the Skin's information receptors. Having to rely on her eyes, ears, nose, and hands made Norah feel like she was partially blind.

The last thing to do was learn to operate the vehicle.

Ignition keys were in the front pocket of Jango's pants. Finding the proper placement of it had been easy. The sound of the engine turning on had been a surprise, Norah rolled with it. She had a certain level of satisfaction when noting that the fuel tank was full.

☙45☙
SMOKEY'S BALLS

HAYLEE'S REPUTATION AS AN intuitive animal diagnostician had grown. Referrals and endorsements from Dr. Jamison had established a solid client list in the Bay Area. Whenever she came home for a visit, it wasn't long before the phone started ringing.

Locals had been calling her since she'd been a teen. Her dad's friends, who thought Haylee's animal communication skills were cute at first, had come to rely on it.

When Haylee first started 'hiring out,' she'd accepted fruit, nuts, and garden produce in trade. Once she moved to Berkeley, she'd taken cash as payment. Her initial fee was $35 per visit with an additional charge for mileage.

Today's fee would be $95. It amused Haylee that the level of respect her clients gave her directly correlated to the prices she charged.

Communicating with animals was much more direct and honest than doing the same with people. Helping them function better in their captive environments made Haylee feel like she was making a positive contribution to the world.

Her client this morning was Smokey. He was a repeat customer, a rescued Golden Retriever. Smokey's human was Dr. Hill, an anesthesiologist from the hospital, one of Glori's friends. Smokey had suffered from various forms of anxiety that they'd worked through when he was younger. Once he learned to trust his owners, he'd blossomed into a happy, reliable, member of the family.

Dr. Hill came out to meet Haylee as soon as she parked at the curb. "Thank you for coming so quickly!" he exclaimed, reaching forward to shake her hand.

"What's going on?"

"Smoke's been acting lethargic. He usually inhales his food, but he's only picked at it since last night. I can't find anything wrong with him, but he isn't acting like himself."

"Alright, let's go see what I can find out."

The Dr. led Haylee through the living room and kitchen into the laundry room that doubled as Smokey's den. Haylee could tell right away that Smokey didn't feel well. He lay on the floor looking up with mopey eyes. "Hey there, fella," Haylee cooed, laying down on the floor next to him.

The Dr.'s wife and fourteen-year-old son, Peter came to watch from the doorway. Haylee saw adoration for them written in the dog's gaze, but she also knew that his desire to please would get in the way of him telling her what was wrong.

Stroking a paw gently, Haylee looked over at Smokey's people. "Can we have a few minutes?"

When they were alone, Haylee rested her chin on folded hands. Smokey looked at her sorrowfully. He *harrumphed.*

Sorry that you don't feel well. Do you hurt?

Tummy.

Are you hungry?

Hungry, yes, hungry. But it Tummy hurts.

Did you swallow something that wasn't food?

As the whole story came out picture by picture, Haylee's expression grew increasingly dismayed. When Smokey finished, she rushed out to consult with the family.

"You need to call your vet right away!"

"What did he tell you? Mrs. Hill asked anxiously.

Haylee tried not to glance in their son's direction. "Peter and one of his friends were putting in the backyard. Smokey was excited to be 'helping' by chasing the balls...."

"And?" they asked.

Placing a comforting hand over Mrs. Hill's, Haylee looked pointedly at the family. "Not all of the golf balls made it back into the golf bag."

Mrs. Hill's expression, "Oh no!" was followed by her husband's, "Peter! What have I told you about Trent?"

Haylee interrupted, "Dr. Hill, Smokey needs attention immediately. Your vet may not take my – or Smokey's word – for what's happened; he'll want to perform an X-Ray. The longer it takes to get Smokey help, the longer he's going to suffer.

Haylee helped the Dr. and Peter load Smokey into the back of their station wagon while Mrs. Hill phoned the vet's office letting them know they were on their way.

Haylee waved good-bye, saying a prayer for Smokey as they departed.

Six hours later, Mrs. Hill called to report that the surgeon extracted four golf balls from Smokey's stomach. She thanked Haylee profusely, promising to include a sizable tip with their payment.

Calls like this were no longer surprising. Repetition and success built confidence. Compared to her peers, Haylee was ahead of the curve. By accident or fate, she was born with a skill that was unique and in demand. Working with her dad on the farm had taught her money and customer management skills.

Living in Berkeley exposed her to professionals, with pets, who were willing to pay top dollar to diagnose problems with their pseudo-children. Like Dr. Hill, a few of them tipped more than her service fee. Haylee was doing well financially. She had no worries about her abilities to live on her own, take care of Serena's needs, and manage her finances.

She knew she could easily charge three times what she did now, but she wanted to remain affordable for most people with animals.

Before she came home, Haylee had been approached by the National Education for Assistance Dog Services – Dogs for Deaf and Disabled Americans - organization, NEADS for short. They'd heard about her through the grapevine. They wanted to know if she'd consider contracting with them exclusively. She'd gone in for an interview and met with some of her potential clients.

When service dogs have health issues, they are usually more complicated than their cohorts. Working closely with humans, they also have a lot that they want to say when given the opportunity.

Haylee had met a few war veterans and folks with hearing and developmental disabilities whose lives were transformed by these animals. She'd already made up her mind that she wanted to work there when she met Owen and Melissa.

Owen was a black Labrador Retriever, a service dog to Melissa. Owen and Melissa were not part of Haylee's interview; they were passing in the hall. The dog walking at the side of Melissa's wheelchair, approached Haylee, plopping down in front of her.

"Owen!" Melissa said, surprised.

"It's alright," Haylee reassured the woman. "He's not going rogue; he knows that I...sort of...speak his language. He has something he wants me to tell you." Haylee squatted next to Owen, "Is it alright if I touch him?"

The staff member, Andy, who was showing Haylee around, introduced them. "Melissa, this is Haylee Garrett, the young woman we were talking about at the staff meeting— are you alright?"

Melissa stared, wide-eyed and open-mouthed at Owen and Haylee. Glancing up at Andy she nodded. Turning back to Haylee, she said, "We usually don't distract them when they are working, but it's alright with me if it's alright with Owen."

Haylee held out a hand, Owen licked it, nuzzling in. She looked thoughtful and a little sad while they communed. Nodding, Haylee stroked his head and neck, before standing. "The first thing he wants to say is how much he loves you. He's enjoyed working with you."

Melissa and Andy, blinked, speechless.

Haylee continued, "He says he remembers Gus, the old dog you had when he came to you as a youngster."

Melissa inhaled sharply, tears rimmed her eyes, "I know what he's going to say!"

Surprised, Haylee paused, "I think you do... but let me say it for him since he stopped me for that reason."

Melissa nodded.

"He says he's been feeling tired, it's getting harder to keep up. He knows that you still need help. He says it's time for him to be Gus, and for you to bring in a new Owen."

Seeing that Owen and Melissa were deeply affected by the communication, Haylee excused herself to continue down the hallway.

Andy was attempting to clear his throat when they entered a meeting room. "I think any last vestige of doubt about hiring you is gone. That dog you were just talking to belongs to Melissa Taylor, our Chief Financial Officer. She was the only staff member with reservations."

⚜46⚜
BIRTH DEFECT

EUGENE KNELT NEXT TO his farrowing sow, a somber expression wrinkled his brow, clouding his eyes. Six perfect piglets were already suckling at their mother's teats. His hands were gooey with blood and amniotic fluid; in them, he held a squealing, squirming baby. Gene sat motionless staring at it. The sow was working herself around, so she could see what all the fuss was about, even while she panted and delivered number eight.

The piglet was about the size and shape of a Nerf football. It's front two cloven hooves gyrated in mid-air. From the youngster's ribcage to its tail, it tapered into a point at the anus and reproductive organs. Smooth, cavernous sockets, where its hind legs should have been, were empty.

A lot of time had past since Haylee fought with him about slaughtering their pigs. He'd never been able to obliterate the memory of the look on her face when she'd screamed at him with all the fury that a little girl embodies. Gene understood much better, now, why it had been so challenging to teach his ultra-sensitive daughter about animal husbandry.

He was pleased with how she'd developed her skills into a going concern. What she was doing with it in the city was terrific. When she told him about her job offer from NEADS, he was as proud as he could be. He had several war veteran buddies who got service dogs from them. Her talent was an asset.

Right now, however, it was damned inconvenient. If Haylee weren't home, this little anomaly would be a non-issue.

Gene never *liked* slaying animals, but it was a fact of farming life. *This pig will never make it. Letting it live would be cruel. It'll take up resources that the healthy ones need. If I get rid of it, Haylee will know... She'll look at me the same way she did back then.*

Footfalls crunched outside. The barn door groaned on its hinges. A bright light streamed in, spotlighting dust floating in the air. "Hey, Dad," called Haylee softly, "Glori says that we have piglets! I brought Serena to see." Setting Serena on her feet, Haylee let her toddle on her own.

Gene tensed. He searched everywhere looking for an escape route he knew didn't exist. His face was a mask of pity when he met his daughter's eyes.

Haylee saw what he held. "Oh no..." she murmured. She rested her hand on his shoulder, kneeling beside him.

Serena, who'd been admiring the sucklings, came around from the opposite side. The high-pitched squeals coming from Grandpapa's hands drew her attention. "Oh noooo...." She echoed her mother's sentiment, "Feet."

Gene began wrapping the piglet in folds of his work shirt, "I'll just get this little girl outa here..."

"Wait, Dad," Haylee said, putting a hand on his arm. She glanced over at the new mother. "Alice wants to nurse her baby."

"But..."

"*Please,*" she pointed her chin in Serena's direction, "for her, but especially for Alice. She knows. It's *her* baby. Don't take it away from her."

"It's broken. If I let it live, it will only make it harder later," he implored.

"I understand. If it's just an investment then that makes sense. But, Dad, it's more than money, it's a life. Alice would notice if her baby went missing, it's part of her imperfect family. Although she might not show it in a way we would understand, Alice would grieve...it could affect her milk production." Haylee paused, gauging to see how he was taking her words. She continued, "That little one looks broken, but she's not."

About to protest, Gene relented. He squeezed his eyes closed, letting Haylee take the baby. Like the tines on a rototiller, the piglet's front legs twirled. Once on the ground, she scooted efficiently to the chow line and wiggling into a spot between her siblings. Latching on, she grunted as she nursed. Alice relaxed back into her bed of straw.

Haylee turned to share a shaky smile with her dad. "See how she's right in the middle of everything seeking what she needs to make her grow? Nature is a strong driver. It knows what it wants, even if we don't. If we let the piglet be, she'll figure out her way."

Moisture gathered in Haylee's eyes, "I'm like that piglet, I'm broken too—"

Eugene interrupted, "Haylee, it's not the same."

Raising her eyebrows, she regarded him, "You know it's true. I was born— different. I like the part of me that helps animals...and I hate the part that hurt people. You've given *me* a chance; can't we do the same for one tiny little pig? She'll be alright. You'll see," Haylee said.

Eugene frowned, regarding his daughter, "Are *you* going to be alright?"

Haylee's eyes filled, she looked over at Serena, "I don't know, I hope so..." Brightening she turned back to him, "Josh said something that made me think. He said that I'm not dead right now."

Gene smirked, then nodded, thoughtfully.

Haylee continued, "Do you know what that makes me do?"

"What?"

"It makes me pay attention. My mind isn't wandering in a million directions, worrying about making plans, or what I'm going to be doing tomorrow or next year. I see you, not wanting to admit that you're afraid. I see Serena taking delight in those little pigs. I see Alice, tired after the work of bringing life into the world...and I'm thinking about how grateful I am that you guys are here for us, that you'll be there for Serena if she needs you. I'm grateful that I've had the time and space to think about Reece, and that Josh is here."

Too choked up to answer, Gene nodded. He got up slowly, striding over to the sink to wash. Lathering his arms, he listened to Haylee and Serena laughing at the newborns. Keeping himself in check, with an iron will, he fiddled around the barn cleaning supplies he'd used for the birth.

When he was done, he walked quietly outside, to the farthest corner of the barn, where he leaned against the wall pressing a fist against his mouth so that the sound of his sobs wouldn't reach the girls.

⚘47⚘
DR. HERKOWITZ

NORAH HAD BEEN BORN and raised at the Institute. She led a sheltered existence in a strictly controlled environment. Systematic tests and examinations were a routine part of her life. She'd learned the basic knowledge of her genetic line; their lifespan, reproduction, and healing abilities were different from the rest of the population.

Near her eighteenth birthday, Norah's biomonitors started showing signs of Traveler transformation. Migraine headaches, body pain, tremors, and unusual hormonal activity were just the beginning.

Suddenly she'd been required to train with equipment and technology that she had no idea existed. Fluid tests, brain and body scans, and nutrient elimination examinations happened daily.

The Haylee archives were opened for study. Watching Dr. Herkowitz, in his archive videos, made her smile when she didn't realize she was doing it. Norah scribbled his name in her notebooks, resisting the urge to dot his 'I's with hearts. When she pressed the button that sealed her sleeping pod at night, it was his face that she imagined when she closed her eyes.

The thought of meeting Dr. Herkowitz, in person, gave Norah another goal, one that helped push against her fear.

Norah had been so inundated with personnel hovering during her waking hours that the isolation she experienced now made her restless and apprehensive. Being cut off from the net com – that ever-flowing stream of communications – also had Norah feeling off kilter. *I need to stop letting my mind drift. Focus on the next step!*

Unlike Haylee's travel event, Norah had arrived with a grasp of her situation. She knew that her pendant would guide her to Haylee. She would return home with the large crystal. Some of the volunteers that the Institute recruited for her to 'drain' would be 'repaired' when she returned.

Whenever Norah thought about the travel event data she'd had stored in her Second Skin, she grew excited.

※

Wearing one of Jango's ski caps to cover her white hair and a pair of Maya's sunglasses, Norah did the best she could to disguise her appearance. The information that she acquired from the couple indicated that her looks would draw unwanted attention.

Before attempting to operate the Jeep, she hiked around the campsite in a full circle, gaining a clear signal from her pendant about which direction she was meant to go.

Even with the learning to drive memories, Norah struggled to make the vehicle move in the way she thought it should. The problem was her size. She wouldn't be able to reach the operating pedals *and* see out. Pillows from inside the tent solved the first complication. After rummaging around through Jango's supplies, she addressed her second dilemma with firewood and duct tape.

The first tap on the accelerator sent the vehicle jumping forward. Norah yelped as the Jeep came to a sudden halt when the front tires hit a concrete parking stopper. She rushed to put it into park, swiping at the sweat that discharged on her face and in the palms of her hands. Norah wasn't used to the moisture gathering. Her Second Skin usually wicked it away so that it never collected. *The outer clothing must be hampering its performance. What ELSE is going to go wrong?*

Norah tried a circular breathing technique to calm both her mind and thumping heart. She refocused, trying again. Keeping her foot on the brake, Norah slipped the shifter into 'R.' Looking behind her, she gently let her foot up.

She moved in a squiggle line as she got the hang of backward steering. Fortunately, the road was wide, and Norah was going at a mollusk pace. She put the Jeep into park, letting the engine idle as she took a moment to enjoy a small measure of success.

A green transport moving on the opposite side of the campground caught Norah's eye. Her stomach cramped. Her breathing became jerky. She queried Maya. This would be the Forest Ranger – the person who would discover the incapacitated shells of Jango and Maya.

Without thinking, Norah called up her net com and sent, *Adult male and female in campsite number fourteen require assistance. Please respond...*

A red blinking dot in her field of vision reminded her that she was no longer connected. Norah closed her eyes, pressing her palms against them, "I don't think I can do this," she whined. *I'm not prepared. I won't be able to transport myself. I will be captured or attacked by wild creatures. I will contract a disease. I will eat poisoned food. I will make a social mistake that causes violence. The pendant will burn me up. I might as well admit defeat, accept failure. I want to go home!*

A visual memory of Dr. Herkowitz surfaced. It was one of his Institute video interviews. "I've promised not to use your name, Traveler." He took off his glasses, winking as he leaned toward the camera. "I won't sugar coat it. Your journey is going to be difficult."

His deep voice and kind blue eyes sitting in a comfortable nest of wrinkles soothed her. People didn't age anymore. It was nice to be reminded that at one point in time, you could approximate where someone was on the spectrum of their life cycle.

"It is reasonable to expect that you are afraid." He paused, nodding, "But know that you made it. You overcame the challenges and obstacles you faced. We owe you our lives." Dr. Herkowitz slipped his glasses back into place. He rested his chin in the palm of his hand. "You are very dear to my family and to me. The time we spent together affected us in ways that lasted lifetimes. I hope when you share the same memories that I have, that you feel the same."

❧48❧
LOST LIKE DAD

JOSH'S PURPOSEFUL STRIDES HALTED in mid-step when he saw Haylee in the barn. He did not comprehend what he was seeing.

She was on her elbows and knees. Between her hands was a piglet she was balancing upside down. "Come on Hanna; you can do it," Haylee coaxed, wriggling backward, bunching up straw behind her. The tiny animal struggled to remain upright on its two legs as it precariously attempted to follow.

"What are you doing?" Josh startled her.

When she let go, Josh noticed that the piglet was missing body parts. It scooted away dragging its torso, making a small furrow in the straw and dirt.

Haylee looked embarrassed. "Hanna's going to get sore if she keeps that up, especially once Alice starts leading her litter outside. I thought, if I could teach her to balance, she'll be able to keep up with everyone else."

"You think she can?"

"Absolutely," Haylee responded enthusiastically.

Shaking his head, Josh switched gears, "If you're finished, there's something I need to talk to you about."

Getting to her feet, Haylee brushed at her pants. "I was starting to get worried about you— when you left, suddenly— without a word."

"Never mind that, I've been thinking about something. It's important."

"Josh—"

"Hear me out," he said, taking her hand, pulling her outside. He kept holding her hand while he walked toward her tractor.

When he remained silent too long, Haylee spoke, "What's this all about?"

He stopped, turning toward her, taking her other hand. Josh leaned in, lowering his head. He kissed her gently at first, teasing, playful, then he grew serious. Without question, Haylee followed his lead.

He pulled away. His blood was simmering. He thought about eating Doritos, the bag's annoying crinkle when you struggle to open it, the dusting of 'cheese' that clings to your fingers, the first taste and crunch when you bite down...

"Ahem, Josh? You said you wanted to talk?"

Clearing his throat, he asked, "Do you love me?"

Haylee looked surprised. "Of course, I do. What's this all about?"

"I think that we should get married."

"What?" she squawked.

"Hear me out."

"Where did that come from?"

"I've been thinking about it for a while now. Let me explain."

When they reached the tractor, Haylee scaled one of the oversized tires. Grabbing a side-view mirror, she swung herself up on top of the hood where she perched, cross-legged looking down, "I'm listening."

Hands on hips, he searched her face, then nodded. "We love each other. Do we agree on that point?"

She nodded.

"I want you and Serena to come with me to France next year if I accept the residency."

"That's not a good reason to get married." Her voice was flat.

"It's only one of a few on my list."

"Tell me the others.... Does this have anything to do with the Wild Cat business?"

"No— "Josh paused, thinking, "But it would be another point in favor."

Haylee rolled her eyes.

"I'm in Haylee. All the way, better, or worse. I want to be with you every day. I want to help raise the kid— I want to be her daddy."

"But Josh— "she paused, "There are so many unknowns...I already asked my Dad and Glori if they would take her...once I'm gone."

Josh wasn't sure what he was expecting, but it wasn't this. "You— how could you do that without talking to me? I thought we were working together?" His tone had risen.

"We are— It's not easy being a single parent. You have a full-time job. I wasn't sure if you even liked her, at first."

He blinked as if she'd slapped him. "Haylee, when I learned you were back, and that you had a kid—" He stopped, turning in a circle. He brought the edge of a pinky finger to his mouth, biting. Clamping onto the nail, ripping it, the hard crescent came free. Spitting it out, Josh stated, "But she's mine!"

Shocked, they stared at each other. Josh glanced everywhere but at Haylee. He reached up, scratching his neck. "I don't know where that came from," he blushed. "But I *do* love her... It hurts to think of anyone else having her." Lowering down on one knee he asked, "Don't you want to marry me?"

He watched her face crumple. Haylee descended the machinery, coming to kneel in front of him. She reached up, holding his face, "Oh, Josh, don't ever think that! If I were going to marry anyone, it would be you."

He covered her hands, "But—?"

"It wouldn't be fair. I want so much more for you than what I have to offer. I want you to find someone you can love for your whole life, someone you can grow old with, someone you can have children with."

He pulled her hands down, keeping hold of them," You're not giving me credit for knowing what I want. I want you, Haylee. Will - you - marry - me?"

"Does this have anything to do with the crystal carrier thing?"

Josh shook his head, "No.... I don't know...maybe. It doesn't matter. Will – you – marry – me?"

"I don't know what to do!" Her voice sounded muffled.

"Do you trust me?" he asked quietly.

"Yes, it's not that."

"Tell me, then."

Haylee's chin trembled. Her eyebrows raised as she took a deep breath. "When I think about how I want it to be— when I die. You are always in that picture. Like when I was gone, you were inside, telling me that everything is going to be alright."

Josh swallowed passed the obstruction in his throat. "And?"

"It's selfish to want you there at the end. I don't want you to live with that memory, of me...no longer me. It was awful seeing you after— I still hate thinking of that! I'm worried that you might end up like my dad was after he lost my mom."

"You think that if we aren't married, I'll feel less sad?"

She didn't say anything for a while, then, "If I can save you from pain, I want to."

His laugh was humorless. "Haylee, if you are willing to die with me, do you think you could live with me until then—?"

Tears filled her eyes. "If you're sure."

"Is that a, yes?" he asked, hopefully. "As in 'yes' you agree with what I said, or 'yes' as in you'll be my wife?"

"Yes, Josh, it would be an honor to marry you."

❧49❧
BARGAINS WITH GOD

EUGENE WAS WORKING LATER, farther out in the fields. He monopolized dinner conversations and went to bed without watching TV.

Glori joined him this evening, getting ready for bed. Clad in her cotton mid-length nightgown, she smoothed lotion over her arms. It smelled of roses. Fine ground glitter in the formula, gave her skin a glowing sheen. Padding toward their bed, she commented, "I know what you're doing. So, does Josh."

Glori crawled in, pulling up the covers. Sitting back against the headrest, she eyed him. "He asked me to talk to you."

Gene took a deep breath. He scratched behind his ear while looking up at the ceiling. "The thing is...."

Glori put a hand on his arm. "Would it make it any easier if you say it to me first?"

"Nah," he shook his head. "I don't want to go through it more than once."

"After my brother died, it took years to stop wondering if I could have changed the outcome by visiting more often, or calling, asking myself, 'What if I had taken food over when I heard he was coming down with something? I bet you've already gone through it plenty of times, mentally. You said that she was sick for a while. It must be excruciatingly painful, watching someone you love slip away.'

He blew a puff of air, "Yep. Many helpless, inadequate feelings. I did my fair share of bargaining with God— for all the good it did."

"People do it all the time. Talking about it might release some of the emotions behind it."

"Maybe," he was noncommittal.

"What's really bothering you, Eugene?"

He looked directly at her, the whites of his eyes were turning red, his voice was husky, "I'm afraid. I don't want to break down. In front of you, or Josh."

Glori softened, "Oh Honey...."

"I don't want to talk about it," he said, hunkering down, pulling the covers over his head.

Glori leaned over him, resting a closed fist on his shoulder. She set her chin on top of it. "Eugene, no one will think less of you. I won't. I'll think that you are brave."

He didn't answer.

"Strong emotions are normal. There's not a bit of shame in expressing them. It's a medical fact that keeping them bottled up is detrimental to one's health."

He whispered, "I know."

"I'll be there with you if you want me— "

"I do. Love you, Glo."

"I love you too, Eugene," she sighed. "We'll talk to Josh in the morning?"

"Alright." He reached up, turning out the light.

In the dark, Eugene pulled Glori into his arms. When they were settled comfortably, she said, "It's a big step. I'm proud of you."

⁂

Eugene was usually the first one up in the morning. The smell of coffee reached him as soon as he opened his eyes. When he walked into the kitchen, Haylee was sitting on the counter; Josh was standing between her legs. They were wrapped in a tight embrace, kissing too intensely for his comfort. "Hey! Knock that off!" he ordered in a tone like one would command a dog to 'sit.' They jumped apart. Haylee looked self-conscious.

As he poured his first cup of strong, black coffee, Gene saw Haylee nod in his direction. Josh shook his head, murmuring, "Later."

"Later what?" Gene asked, turning, leaning a hip against the counter.

"Nothing," Josh said. "Gene?"

"I know—" he cut him off. "I'm ready."

Josh looked surprised, "OK... Now? I'll grab my notepad."

Gene halted him with a raised hand. "After we're finished with breakfast is soon enough," his voice sounded strangled.

Haylee poked Josh lightly, nodding in her dad's direction. He sighed, "Haylee wants to sit in on the interview."

"No!" Gene's eyes widened. His grip on his mug tightened, his fingertips and knuckles were white.

Glori walked in carrying Byron, "Haylee, Serena's up jabbering in her crib."

Haylee nodded, hopping off the counter without a word.

Glori regarded her husband, "What's the matter?"

"Haylee said she wants to listen."

Glori took a deep breath, "Oh Eugene—" she walked toward him, holding Byron out toward his father.

Like a Rube Goldberg machine, Gene set his cup on the counter. He moved to the table, slid the silverware and condiments out of reach, then shifted, reaching out to receive his son. The warm weight and clean smell of the little boy went a long way toward soothing his clashing nerves. Gene kissed his temple, then wiped at a rivulet of dribble using his bare hand, drying it on the leg of his jeans. Looking for something to occupy Byron, he grabbed a coffee mixing spoon.

The baby's eyes grew large and round. Stretching forward, his mouth in an 'o,' his little fingers grasping.

"Gene! Don't give him that!" Glori admonished from the refrigerator.

Too late, Byron popped it into his mouth. "Mmmm....mmmmm!" he verbalized enthusiastically. Everyone laughed.

Gene let Byron bang the spoon. Josh came to the table, sitting opposite, keeping his coffee safely out of busy boy range. Gene eyed Josh. "It's going to be difficult enough, dredging up all those memories. This is her mother we're talking about. When it was happening, Doris and I agreed that Haylee needed to be shielded from it as much as possible."

Josh nodded, "How old was she at the time? Six, seven? She's a grown woman now; she wants to know. Given the situation and the pertinent information in Keener's letters, I think she has a right to know. "

Gene was about to interrupt, but Josh stopped him, "You'll get full disclosure. I need to record your information first. I don't want you to be influenced by the nineteenth-century material."

Silence filled the room, except for Byron's spoon banging. "Fair enough," Eugene admitted, quietly, reluctantly.

"I don't want Haylee hurting any more than she already is," Josh conceded. "We'll handle it as sensitively as possible."

❧50❧
SYMPTOMS

EUGENE AND GLORI HELD hands. Josh and Haylee walked on either side of them as they headed toward the barn. Back at the house, the kids were being looked after by a friend of Glori's. Feeling the gravity of what they were about to do, no one said a word.

They entered through a side door into a room with creaky floorboards. The workshop smelled of grease and gasoline. A center work table was covered with machine parts. Bar stools were scattered here and there. Along the edges of the countertops were clamps, vises, screwdrivers and dirty rags. Pegboards on the walls held both tools and empty spaces.

Two dirty, cobweb-encrusted windows let in a limited amount of natural light. Overhead fluorescent shop lights hummed to life chasing away the shadows in the far corners.

"Well!" Gene clapped his hands, dismayed to see his space with a fresh perspective. "I'll make us some room, so we can work," he said, pushing things to the side.

Haylee pulled the stools in place, while Josh located an empty box. He broke it down, making it flat, laying it on the table so they'd have a clean surface. Glori went to the refrigerator, looking inside. She pulled out three Squirts and one Dr. Pepper. Popping the tops, she set them out, then went to the side entrance. Searching, she found a large rock. Propping the door open, a refreshing, warm breeze followed her back into Gene's man cave.

"This place hasn't looked so clean in... ever," Gene laughed nervously. He eyed Josh as he set his yellow legal pad on the table, writing the date and time. When the boy pulled out a mini-cassette recorder out, situating it the middle, Eugene's mouth dried out. He grabbed the Dr. Pepper, taking several long swigs.

Josh leaned over, pressing the start button. He pushed up his glasses and looked around the table. Everyone was waiting for him. "Ok let's begin. Today is June 27, 1987. It is 9:38 in the morning. This meeting is taking place in the workshop of Eugene Garrett located at 4398 Rural Route #36 in Elverta, California. Present are myself, Joshua Herkowitz, Mrs. Glori Garrett, and Haylee and Eugene Garrett."

"I am about to interview Eugene. The information we will be recording are the symptoms and stages of his late wife's illness that led to her death in 1974."

"Mrs. Garrett is a registered nurse. She will clarify if we have technical or medical questions." Josh looked at Glori who nodded. "Please respond so that the tape recorder will pick it up," Josh requested.

Glori cleared her throat, "Yes, that is correct."

"Thank you," Josh replied.

"Now, Eugene, I'd like to start by asking you to describe what Doris was like before she became ill. Did she work on the farm? And what kinds of things did she do?"

The question surprised him. He blinked as he ordered his thoughts. "Yes, well, she worked on the farm, she was raised here. We bought the place from her folks after we graduated from Berkeley."

"I didn't know that," Haylee chirped.

Gene nodded, smiling, "Grandma Millie wanted to move closer to her sister in Florida. She eventually succeeded in convincing Grandpa Herb to go."

"Millie was Doris's mother?" Josh asked. Because Eugene swiveled toward Josh, he didn't see Haylee sit up straighter.

"Millie was her step-mother, but she raised her." Gene suddenly went pale; he slouched forward. "I never met Doris's natural mother, Sylvia."

Everyone watched Josh making furious notes. He looked up, crinkling his forehead. "Please continue, what kind of things did she do on the farm after you'd bought it."

"Oh.... well, she interned on a farm that was doing experimental work with water conservation. When she came back here, she invested a lot of time implementing what she'd learned. It was a heck of a lot of work removing the old sprinkler system, replacing it with drip lines. We did most of it ourselves because we didn't have any money to hire help. Doris sold all the pipes and sprinkler components to Larry next door. He thought we were crazy kids back then. Once the system was going, it started saving money right away. In lean times, it saved us."

"Really?" Haylee said, smiling faintly.

"Really," Gene replied proudly. "Did you know that your mom built the pond at the far end of the property?"

Shaking her head, "No," Haylee replied with wonder. "It's not natural?"

"Oh no, Doris did that. It was a safety measure so that we wouldn't have to rely on municipal water. She used to joke that she filled it up the first time."

"How did she do that?" Haylee asked.

Gene was enjoying himself. Watching the light of curiosity in his daughter's eyes made him wonder why they'd never talked about this before. "No," he chuckled, "The system was designed to capture rainwater. She claimed that she made it rain."

"What?" Josh chimed in, his hand still writing even as he asked more questions. "Do you have stories about Doris doing other things like that?"

Gene glanced at Glori, concerned. "Things like what, Josh?"

Continuing to scrawl, he didn't look up when he replied, "Unusual things—like Haylee communicating with animals—did Doris do anything else with rain?"

"That was a joke, Josh. Doris couldn't control the weather."

"Weather? You said rain."

"Right. We joked about her being able to influence the weather. People can't control that stuff."

"You're sure about that?"

Gene took another gulp of his Dr. Pepper, setting it down carefully. Glori put her hand on his thigh, giving him a reassuring pat. When he looked at Haylee, she shrugged her shoulders.

Josh turned a page and looked back at them. "We can come back to that later if we need to, can you tell me about the first time you noticed that she wasn't feeling well?"

Eugene closed his eyes' he rubbed them while nodding. Leaning forward on the table, he clasped his hands. He stared at them while he spoke, "She started dropping things. Stuff in the kitchen, a carton of milk, a jar of applesauce. Then, it got worse."

"We made appointments with neurologists who assured us that her central nervous system was fine. They didn't find indications of infection."

"Her regular doctor kept telling her to rest and take it easy. 'The body will naturally heal itself', he said, even while he continued sending us to specialist after specialist. Honestly, I don't think he knew what to do, but he wouldn't admit it. After the specialists, we tried every alternative health practitioner and faith healer on the west coast."

"I wouldn't let Doris drive anymore after she got lost a few times. She fought me over that one something fierce. Having her husband show up in the pick-up line at school was one of the worst blows for her."

Gene stood up to wander around the edges of the room pausing to lay a hand on one thing or another, "She said...." He cleared his throat, "She said if she was going to waste away and become useless that she didn't want to try anymore."

"By then, she was having trouble sleeping. She couldn't make it through the day without a nap."

"We'd seen too many doctors to count. Everyone told us that they couldn't find anything wrong— "He paused, turning to look at Glori, "That's why I didn't push Haylee to return to the hospital after she ran away."

Glori nodded. "I didn't know, Eugene."

He shook his head, continuing. He walked over to the doorway, standing with his back to everyone. "She was wasting away," he said. "Her hair started falling out. Her comb would come away filled with hair and then Doris pulled it off her head in chunks." Gene's shoulders began shaking; he braced his hands on the door frame.

Haylee would have gotten up to go to him, but Glori put a hand out to stop her.

Josh glanced up with concern but remained focused. He returned to taking notes.

"She didn't want me to see her like that," Gene stated raggedly. "She refused to leave our room, she wouldn't let Haylee come near her either." His voice broke.

"My world was falling apart, and there wasn't anything I could do about it. My wife was losing weight; her eyes wouldn't focus. Her voice was nothing more than a whisper."

"Her general practitioner started making house calls. When he told me how sorry he was, I lost it. I came close to beating the shit out of him." Gene laughed dryly. "It must have been Dr. Fowler who called Millie—she must have gotten hold of my sister, Sara."

"The next thing I knew, they were here taking us in hand. Sara took Haylee home with her, and Millie sat vigil with Doris."

"I don't remember any of that," Haylee whispered. Glori took her hand.

"Millie sang soft songs, held her hand, and wiped her face. I sat beside Doris when she was asleep. She looked like one of those mummies that you see on TV, shrunken, dry."

Gene shook his head, wiping at his eyes. "I was with her when she stopped breathing. At first, I couldn't believe she was gone." He inhaled with jerks, "and then I was glad. —Fuck!" He looked up at the ceiling, "I was glad that she didn't have to endure another minute." Looking down at his feet, Gene declared, "I'm done." He stomped outside.

Glori got up, following him.

Josh blinked rapidly, "Shit." He reached over, turning off the tape recorder.

Haylee, looking down, nodded and sniffled.

❧51❧
EGOCENTRISM

JOSH WALKED AROUND BEHIND Haylee, resting his hands on her shoulders.

She resisted at first, then gradually relaxed against him. "There could be worse ways to go…" Haylee commented sarcastically.

He pulled her into his arms. Tossing his glasses on the table, he squeezed tight, rubbing his face in her hair.

She inhaled, sighing.

❧

Returning to the house, they relieved the sitter and spent the next hour sitting on the living room floor playing with Serena and Byron. Stilted, hushed exchanges flowed between them.

"Is that the what happened to Polly?"

"Pretty much," he replied grimly. "Reece was thorough in his observations."

"You haven't called him by his first name before."

Josh nodded. He watched Haylee demonstrate sharing for toddlers by passing a ball from one to the other. "Haylee?"

"Yea?"

"Polly told Reece she wasn't in pain."

"Well.... that's a relief." Haylee looked tortured. "I feel like I've known all along— that this is real."

Josh wouldn't meet her eyes but nodded grimly.

"Do you think that If I brought all of my victims back, I might go differently than my mom and Polly?"

Josh turned green. "I think you should stop where you are."

"How can you say that? If it weren't for me, they wouldn't be in the situation they are in," Haylee spoke intensely. "If I had listened to Reece, you and Glori would still be like that!"

The little ones stopped playing, regarding the adults. Serena frowned. Byron shoved a fist in his mouth.

"Don't you think I know that?" Josh stood abruptly. "I've spent the last few weeks setting up trust accounts for them."

"That's because you are trying to assuage *your* guilt at asking me to stop!"

Josh looked stunned. Blinking, he shook his head. His voice was quieter this time, "My attitude could be a form of egocentrism."

"It's easy to do when you don't know the people involved," Haylee admitted. "I know them— too well." Haylee crossed her arms, running hands up her biceps. "Think about this," Haylee stopped, facing him, "what if Spencer had been one of those Alpha Sigma Phi guys?"

Josh paled. His expression turned into a grimace, he clutched at his temple.

Serena and Byron started crying.

Haylee scrambled over to Josh, "What's wrong?"

For a moment, he looked dazed, like he didn't recognize her. "No," he held up a shaky hand, "not Spencer, don't hurt my brother."

Haylee knelt beside him, alarmed, "I wouldn't—"

"Edward."

Haylee nodded, tears filling her eyes. "I'm not a threat, anymore."

Blinking, Josh's eyes cleared. Nodding he lowered his hands. Turning to the distressed children, he rubbed Byron's back.

"Everyone I hurt is someone's family." Haylee continued. "If there's something I can do to help, I have too."

Josh shifted to his knees, facing her. "I understand," he rested back against his heels, "But we can't ignore your other obligations, especially if you lose more time with each return." Josh looked troubled. "Spencer has been moving assets into the accounts... By the time we get back, the only thing left to do is to have you sign them."

Haylee stood up to, picking up Serena who was still crying. "If I do that," Haylee raised her voice while patting her daughter's back. "I'm sentencing them to stay the way they are!"

Glori came rushing in. "I could hear the crying all the way outside!"

"Everyone's upset," Haylee replied tersely. She pinched Serena's diaper. "She needs changing." Turning on her heel, Haylee retreated.

Josh handed Byron to his mother. As he was settling down, he rested his head on his mother's shoulder.

"How's Eugene?" Josh wanted to know.

Glori glanced toward the front door, "He's pretty torn up, but I think he'll be alright."

"He got through it," Josh replied grimly. "What he said helped."

Glori nodded, "Did it?" She met Josh's gaze. Her eyes were dark. "It's a heavy legacy that they carry... That we're all carrying," she corrected.

Josh didn't know what to say.

"My life was simple before. I didn't realize how nice it was."

"I could say the same."

"You could still walk away, Josh."

"I could."

"But you're not going to?" Glori smiled slightly.

He shook his head, "It doesn't look like you are planning to go anywhere either."

Glori rolled her eyes, "Nope, but there are days...."

"You're a good person, Glori. I hope eventually, we'll have a conversation about how glad we were to have stuck it out...whatever 'it' turns out to be."

Cupping her son's head, she kissed him. "I hope you're right. We need a nap."

♵52♵
SHORT TEMPERS

"I'VE GOT TO get out of here!" Haylee handed Serena to Josh, slamming out the door. He looked concerned as he followed her with his gaze. Had she overheard his conversation with Glori? Josh looked at Serena.

She smiled around a hand in her mouth, pulling it out, she planted it on his cheek.

Making a face, he said, "Uck!" Josh could hear Glori talking in her room. He wandered in that direction.

Muttering in a pleasant, but false tone, Glori vented. "First it was putting my job in jeopardy. Then it was helping her date when she attacked that kid— who is still in a semi-comatose state. When I got in her way, she took me out," Glori looked up, noticing Josh leaning in the doorway. She continued, "Then she went after you!"

Josh nodded.

"Granted it was difficult for her to bring us back. Granted that she's...both of you...are doing everything you can to find out why she behaved the way she did, but I'm tired, Josh. Tired of watching two kids, tired of following Haylee around on missions. Part of me wishes that she'd disappear again and not come back...." Glori stopped as if she'd only just heard what she'd said. She clamped her mouth shut, her cheeks flushed.

"I don't know what to say, Glori," Josh said, worried.

"Please don't repeat that. I'm overtired."

Haylee found her dad working by the barn. His shirt was off, and he was sweating as he pitchforked manure mixed with straw into an open trailer. "Hey, Dad," Haylee approached anxiously.

"Huh," he commented without looking at her. He kept shoveling.

Haylee grabbed another pitchfork, joining him in the task. They worked silently for a while until Haylee tried talking again, "I never knew any of that...how mom passed. Thank you for sharing."

Eugene stopped. He stepped on the back end of his tool, so the tines dug into the dirt. Reaching to grab his t-shirt, he mopped the sweat from his forehead and chest.

"Can I ask you something?" Haylee said. "When you first met my mom, was there anything weird about her?"

Pulling his undershirt over his head then grabbing his snap-up shirt, Gene threaded his arms through the holes. Smiling slightly, he shook his head. "Nah, nothing weird, Honey. She was just one hard working farm girl."

"But did you have a stronger than normal attraction when you first met?"

Gene huffed, looking down, clicking his shirt snaps together. "When you fall in love...you just fall. How you fall, or the strength of the feeling is as different and varied as there are combinations of people."

Haylee nodded, looking thoughtful. She started toward the barn door, urging him to follow with a nod of her head.

The little piglets began squealing as they approached. Haylee went to the refrigerator, filling a bucket with creep food; yogurt, cottage cheese, and breadcrumbs. She stepped over a low-strung hot wire to their feeding area. Before spreading it for the little guys, she fished Hanna, the deformed piglet, out, handing the squirming bundle to her dad.

Hanna was not happy at all about being removed from her drift. She let them know quite loudly. Haylee shoved a finger in the pig's mouth to keep her quiet until they got to the training area. Haylee sat down cross-legged, letting Hanna eat a little bit of the creep food. Gene squatted beside her.

Setting the piglet down, Haylee gave her an 'up' command while lifting her torso over her shoulders – so Hanna was holding a headstand. "Good! Good girl," Haylee enthused. She repeated this, giving Hanna treats.

Next, she encouraged the youngster to take steps while in the 'up' position, stepping toward her treat.

"I'll be darned!" Eugene laughed.

"Here," Haylee reached over, handing her dad some food, "let's see if we can get her to walk between us."

They held their breath as they watched expectantly. Hanna took unsteady steps, then more as her confidence grew.

"She's doing it!" Haylee exclaimed happily.

Gene grinned, "So she is."

They let Hanna rejoin her brothers and sisters. Haylee stretched out her legs, leaning back on her arms.

Gene turned his gaze to his daughter, "I know that I haven't told you this enough, Haylee, but I think you are an amazing young woman. I admire you."

She heaved a sigh, returning his look. "Do you think Josh is right? That I shouldn't repair the other people I hurt?"

He shook his head, "I can't say. You're the only one who can make that decision. If your mom had known anything about this, I'm sure she would have gotten the information to you." He shook his head again, "Or she would have said something to me. In the end, she wanted to make sure you'd be looked after once she was gone."

Seeing that self-recriminating expression on his face, Haylee said, "You did look after me, Dad. I always had clothes on my back, a roof over my head, and food to eat."

He snorted.

Haylee smiled, "Do you know what?"

"What?"

"I think one of the reasons that I like helping animals is because they are simple. When treated well and understood, they are loving and kind. They don't stress out about the future. They live in the moment and that's enough."

"Being human is complicated."

"I'm going to go back to Berkeley, tomorrow. I've got a long waiting list of clients asking for appointments and I need to give Josh and Serena time together."

"Josh and Serena?"

"He wants us to be together as a family," Haylee said getting up. "I want that too, Dad." She knelt behind him giving him a hug.

"I see," he said putting a hand on top of hers. "I like Josh."

"Me too. Besides, I think it's time that you, Glori, and Byron get back to your own routines."

"You'll let me know if…" he whispered.

"Of course. But until then, I'm going to live my life."

⚜53⚜
DRIVER SCREAMING

NORAH LET OUT A high-pitched squeal when a blue Datsun passed in the opposite lane. It looked like it was coming straight at her! She was only going ten miles per hour, but she swerved to the shoulder, slamming on the brakes. A cloud of dust enveloped the Jeep. Airborne particles affected her oxygen intake! Her visual monitoring system flashed warning signals. Her heart felt like it was thumping in her head.

She coughed, her throat and eyes were scratchy. With each forceful spasm and expel, Norah noticed that an equal intake of oxygen followed. Between succession six to eight, she realized that her ability to breathe was becoming more comfortable, her warning signals communicated airborne particles, not that she was asphyxiating.

Norah wiped sweaty hands on her borrowed jeans. She flexed fingers that had been gripping the steering wheel like claws. Learning her head against the wheel, she willed the muscles in her neck and chest to decompress.

Norah hadn't gone far from camp. At this rate, transporting herself in the vehicle wasn't faster than traveling on foot. It was highly dangerous. She considered abandoning this course of action.

The population center grid layout— from Jango and Maya's thoughts — changed Norah's mind. Bipedal transit would be cumbersome, take copious amounts of time, and would be fraught with native interactions.

Nothing in the material that she studied said if the time trip would take hours, days, months, or years. The Institute had prepared her for all possibilities, but she'd been fantasizing that her stay would be extremely brief.

She started whimpering. The sheer amount of open space here set her nerves on edge. The tall land-dwelling humans were intimidating. She looked down at her body. It was slim, small compared to the people she'd come across. Norah was of an age to be recognized at council meetings, a sign that full mental maturity has been reached.

She felt out-of-sorts. Her people had been bio-engineered for maximum efficiency; her size was a perfect complement for the undersea biopods she inhabited. It regulated the resources needed to sustain life and the amount of waste that was generated as a result.

Norah needed to regain her emotional equilibrium. She didn't know what would happen if she utterly failed at her task. She reached up, rubbing a finger across the pendant hanging around her neck.

Another soothing technique was reciting Dr. Herkowitz's Traveler Summary Report. "The small crystal in the pendant and the larger appear to be made of the same material. They attract each other at certain intervals in time. They have protective and destructive qualities; protective for the women who carry them, destructive to others who touch them."

"The larger of the two can be used to restore damages caused by a Traveler when she is in the webbed state of development. However, the choice to do so has serious consequences."

"A set of actions occurs when the large crystal is transferred from one Traveler to the next. Records from 1849 and observations from the 1987 Travel Event show that the large crystal is used to burn away webs on the Traveler's hands."

Norah paused. She regarded her hands, fingers splayed. Flipping them away, as if shooing an insect, her webs appeared. They were flexible, offering a slight resistance when she moved. Bringing her right hand to her face, she covered her mouth and nose. Norah wondered why they adhered to the faces of others but not to her own. Blowing into them, the webs inflated, like a balloon.

Will it hurt to have them burned away? Norah wondered. She wasn't sure that that was an experience she wanted.

Unlike Haylee, Norah wasn't troubled by the people who relinquished themselves to the Institute's experiments— web absorption. Knowing that the need for volunteers would eventually arise, the Institute had been well prepared. Long-lived and very wise members of society, scheduled for culling, were offered highly coveted travel passes and elevated living quarters in exchange for their submittal to Norah's hands when their cull date arrived.

As a result, Norah had been honored to receive their accumulated knowledge and glad to have provided an opportunity that enhanced their lives. About Maya and Jango, she valued the current-day information they provided. She suspected that she'd spared them pain and anguish, but she also felt a level of unease. Perhaps she'd taken something that they valued? They hadn't been given a choice as the elders back home had.

A warning signal began to flash. This was a unique adaptation in her optical sensors that had been developed specifically for her. Norah realized that she'd need to feed again. She didn't have the physical strength necessary to subdue a person if they resisted, she'd have to figure something out in that regard.

I've accumulated information that no other traveler has collected. I cannot fail!

"I have to get to Dr. Herkowitz and to Haylee," Norah stated, putting the car into reverse. She maneuvered it back on the road.

 Norah discovered that frontage roads paralleled the interstate highways. Not as many cars were on these streets. She drove slowly at first, being careful to steer her vehicle between the white and yellow lines. She still jumped and screamed when other cars sped passed at velocities that made her break out into a sweat. After a dozen of those experiences, that she survived, she stopped screaming and picked up speed.

Navigating through intersections, when others were doing the same was harrowing. Norah waited over long to take her turn, jumping and yelping when drivers tooted their horns. Moving forward, she stepped on the gas, closed her eyes and hoped for the best.

She hadn't crashed yet. The pendant told Norah that she was moving in the correct direction.

For the first time since she arrived, Norah began to think that might have what it would take to survive in this hostile and foreign land.

❧54❧
ON THE MOVE

AT 2:00 A.M., at a fixed reference point, fourteen cars pass on westbound Interstate Eighty. Twelve hours later, that number climbs to two-hundred-forty-three. With the harrowing inconsistencies of individual drivers controlling thousands of pounds of mass moving at high speeds, it didn't take Norah long to decide to travel in the deep hours of the night and to find alternate side roads.

Moving at night was not a problem. Her optical enhancers corrected for low light conditions. She was careful to follow every posted traffic regulation.

Many of her training sessions had been devoted to avoiding law enforcement officers. It was the 'force' part of that word that worried Norah.

'Cooperate and be docile if captured. Speak with a high pitch. Say you're lost and need to find your parents. Look for and execute an escape route at the first opportunity. Use webs if necessary.'

Since she looked nothing like Maya Rodrigues, Norah was deeply afraid of crossing paths with highway law keepers. She would keep the Jeep and use it if she felt safe. It would provide cover, protection from the elements, and it would store her food supplies. Norah looked down at the measurement gauge. She'd been watching the needle approach the empty line. *What will happen if all the fuel is used?*

Jango supplied the answer with an image of sputtering followed by loss of power. The steering wheel was difficult to maneuver. Cursing came next. Then he remembered walking for miles to the nearest service station to purchase a portable red container that would provide enough fuel to drive back to the service station...

How did these people ever get anything done?

Norah spotted a corner fueling station ahead. Breathing a sigh of relief, she parked she could make observations before attempting the interaction.

She watched several people behave differently once they moved their vehicles in place. On the side that said, 'self-serve,' people parked, got out, and opened the fueling port. They pushed a button on a coffin-like box, removing a handle and squeezing a trigger. They watched a display until it beeped. Then they removed the nozzle, replaced the fueling port cover, and passed currency to the attendant.

On opposite side – 'full service' – the vehicle driver drove over a black rope-like object that signaled a bell. The engine was turned off. An attendant approached, asking, "Fill 'er up?" A nod was all that was needed for the young man to take care of the hose tasks. He then re-approached the window asking, "Do you want me to check the oil or fill your wiper fluid?"

Norah observed half a dozen of these interactions. When she was reasonably sure that she could respond appropriately, she started the car and pulled into place. She was pleased to hear the bell chime when her tires rolled over the rope.

She kept her hat pulled down low, and her sunglasses on when she responded to the questions. The boy hesitated longer at her window than he did with the others. Norah lowered her voice when she told him, "I'm in a hurry."

"You didn't seem like you were in a hurry when you were spying on me."

"That's none of your business!" she squeaked, "I just need gas for my vehicle, the gauge shows that it's almost out."

"Sssalright," the boy raised both hands so that she could see them. "I didn't mean to scare you. It gets boring on the night shift."

"I am a lawful citizen taking care of a vehicle maintenance task for this Jeep Cherokee that belongs to me."

The boy nodded slowly, backing away, "Is that right?"

Norah nodded, "Yes, that is correct and completely accurate."

Standing at a distance, the attendant announced the service fee. Norah's hand shook as she riffled through Jango's wallet, searching for the correct currency.

When she was taking too long, Norah noticed the attendant rise on his toes as he watched her. She turned to face him.

"The twenty, right there," he pointed, "will work, I'll make change."

Norah handed him the bill. Once he took it, she started the engine. Pulling away, she heard him yell after her. A glance in the rear-view mirror showed him waving paper currency over his head. Norah stepped on the gas.

Once the fueling station was out of sight, Norah relaxed into the backrest. Tossing her hat and sunglasses on the passenger seat, she grinned. "I did it!" exclaiming gleefully.

She drove, slowly, feeling better every minute. When the sun began to rise, Norah left her directional travel and started searching for a place to 'camp' along the side roads. She found a grove of trees near a waterway. Although it looked like cars had stopped there before, the space was empty now. She parked so that greenery screened the vehicle from the roadway.

Satisfied that she'd been successful thus far, she got out, stretching. Her stomach reminded her that she needed something to put in it. *Another thing to remember...*

Norah rummaged in the supplies, finding a breakfast bar. She wandered to the bank of the water, munching, while she watched the sparkles of sunlight winking on its glassy surface.

Norah wondered what was happening with Maya and Jango. Had they been taken to a medical facility where attempts were being made to repair them? A deep sadness overcame her. She knew from her studies that Haylee had returned consciousness to her victims, including Dr. Herkowitz.

Maybe Haylee would instruct Norah how to do the same for those two.

A yawn reminded Norah that it had been too long since she entered a sleep cycle. Wondering if she'd be able to function outside of her rest chamber, she arranged a sleeping bag in the back of the Jeep, stretching out.

With her hands crossed over her chest, Norah tapped an index finger, thinking about everything that was wrong. The ambient air temperature was twelve degrees off; her olfactory perception detected repellent aromas; sounds from the outside were a distraction; the inside of the vehicle had sharp corners, and she was surrounded by clutter.

Norah longed for her sleep chamber, a peaceful egg-shaped container that suspended her weightless at its center. Norah closed her eyes, attempting to recreate it in her imagination. Filled with light, in the beginning, it gradually dimmed, the walls disappeared as soon as it sealed. She could envision any scenery she desired. Tonight, she would float among clouds.

Norah selected a piece of ancient, classical music that she often enjoyed; Beethoven's Für Elise. Her eyes closed, as the first notes of the piano played.

❧55❧
WATER ESCAPE

NATURE'S CALL AND A shaft of bright light woke Norah. In her semi-conscious state, she'd been contemplating redistributing her Second Skin. If she did that, some of it would need to be stored.

There wasn't enough room in her small travel pack, but one of the backpacks in the Jeep would work. The Skin was such an integral of life that was extremely rare for a citizen to remove it for more than a few minutes. The idea of taking it off and keeping it off brought on, yet another, wave of unease. Separation from the information it fed continuously to her optic system was dangerous. She'd need it in its entirety to retrieve the travel event data. Dividing it into smaller portions felt risky.

Norah thought through her reasons for altering it. It was incredibly irritating wearing clothing on top of it. Textiles disrupted the streaming information, creating static that caused headaches. Although it could virtually make her invisible, unless she kept it in that mode, its body-conforming properties made her conspicuous.

Norah crawled out of the Jeep's hatchback, hauling an aluminum-framed backpack with her. She walked a little way away from her 'camp' to 'take a piss' as Jango called it.

When she was finished, she pinched the Skin's neckline, folding her fingers beneath it, gaining a hold. As the material disengaged from her epidermis, it made a wet, sucking sound. Its strong adhesion made her removal activities strenuous. Norah's struggles diverted her attention from hearing the crunch of tires in the parking area.

She had the Skin pried away from her arms and torso when the slam of a car door, followed by a series of beeping tones froze her in place.

A crackling white noise ceased when a deep voice spoke. "Twelve, suspicious vehicle on Mare Island Road."

Norah heard a faint response but could not understand it. She squatted low behind a bush, hugging the backpack to her bare chest. Fresh air blowing across sensitized skin, made her tremble.

"Dispatch, run a registration check on 2 RIT1Niner Zero."

Alarm bells went off inside Norah's head. Her training said that she'd have approximately four minutes before the Law Officer retrieved the information he was seeking. Likely, he was already scanning the surrounding area and taking in details both inside and outside of the Jeep.

She couldn't make it out to the road. It was too open; she'd never be able to convince someone to accept her into their car. She'd be discovered once the officer widened his search area. If other officers arrived, there'd be more eyes searching.

Norah ripped off enough of the Second Skin to cover her head, neck, and shoulders. Applying pressure over her eyelids caused it to remodulate so she could open her eyes. She did the same for her ears, nostrils, and mouth. If she could make it into the water, she could use the skin for disguise.

She remolded the torn edges around her hips, rolling the excess into a ball and tossing it into the backpack. Pulling out a shirt, she pulled it on.

On hands and knees, Norah stopped to check where the officer was. He was opening doors and beginning to inspect the Jeep's interior. Norah made it to the riverbank. Securing the backpack in place, she slipped into the water, diving down as deep as she could manage. She didn't have a direction in mind but knew if she swam against the current, she'd be moving closer to the population area.

When she surfaced for the first time, she looked back to see how far she'd gone. It wasn't nearly as far as she'd hoped. She could see the officer moving around at the edges of the greenery. Taking another deep breath, she dove again, kicking with all her might. Spotting an overhang of branches, Norah came up for air beneath it. She hung onto a gnarly wood snag under the water's surface, pulling herself into a tight ball so that even if he spotted her silhouette, it wouldn't resemble a human form.

Norah heard a motor; a water vehicle was approaching. Sticking up out of the center, was a long straight pole with a tiny flag on top. From her vantage point, Norah could see that the uniformed officer noticed it too. He came to the bank, waving.

If she could find something to act as cover under the water, Norah could break away, letting the current guide her to the 'boat.' She could latch on to the far side; it would move her to safety. She'd need to act quickly while the boat people conversed with the man on shore.

Breaking loose a large clump of grass, Norah spread it out. She wound strands of it onto the backpack straps. Flipping her hands, she engaged her webs. Giving a strong push, Norah launched. Pulling and kicking against the resistance, she moved toward her goal. Norah remained alert for sounds of alarm, indicating she'd been spotted.

The ship to shore conversation was well underway as Norah surfaced near the boat. She could hear snatches of communications, "No, we didn't see anyone downstream. It's marshland.... ...looking for anyone dangerous? Are we safe?"

When Norah got closer, she could see that the boat had two halves with an open section in the middle. A flexible cloth floor covered the span. Several lines hung down into the water. She felt sure that she'd be able to grab hold of one.

"It's only a precaution," the officer answered. "We've got an abandoned vehicle here and would like to locate the owner. If you see anyone who looks suspicious, call 911."

Norah dove down, pulling hard, clearing the hull to emerge in the open center.

"Will do!" she heard the reply from the top deck. The engine roared to life. Norah grabbed the line wrapping it around a wrist. Once they started moving, she had to hold tight to resist the pull. She breathed a sigh of relief.

The water was cold! She wished that she hadn't taken off most of her Second Skin. Her visual indicator began flashing temperature warnings. If she shouted for help, the boat's 'captain' would surely call the law enforcers.

Norah extended her arms so that her body rode out of the water. This position increased the drag on the backpack that looped over her shoulder. She took stock of her surroundings. There were a couple of places under the 'hull' where she might be able to crawl up, but it was risky. If she missed and lost hold of her line, she'd be shredded by the 'propellers.'

What is my most significant chance of success? Pleading with an unknown person, or risking injury to stay concealed? I doubt that even the healing powers of the crystal could repair that damage.

The directive, 'Do not let yourself become restrained or caged. Use your webs if necessary,' came to mind.

Norah stretched as far as she could, using her feet and the current to bounce up and down. *This could work!* She needed a little more line to reach the ledge.

Struggling out of her shirt, Norah tied one end to her rope. She tugged on it making sure it was secure. She held on and let it gradually take her weight. *It held!*

Giving herself the added length she needed, she was directly under the ledge. Her body filled with adrenaline as she wiggled her arm out of her backpack. The water was cold; she was beginning to lose feeling in her limbs. The lights in her vision flashed with ever-increasing warnings. Kicking up and out of the water, she tested the weight of the soaked contraption. If she got her hand under the metallic part of the frame, it would give her a more extended range. Holding her breath and kicking, she hauled herself and the backpack up, pushing with all her strength.

It almost made it, but then the weight came back down toward her, "No!" she shouted scrabbling to regain a hold on it. Her fingers twined on a loose line and held...just. "Off! Cancel! Stop!" She shouted to shut down her optic sensors. Using all her will, Norah reclaimed the mass, hugging it for dear life.

I'm going to have to call for help. I can't do this.

Then she looked up at the ledge again. One more try. Norah gave each hand a turn out of the water to warm up and stretch. She let herself, once again, flow up and down with the current kicking her feet to increase her momentum. On her fourth swing, she kicked and shoved the pack. When it sailed up and onto the shelf, she let out a groan, almost losing her grip on the shirt.

Next, it was her turn. She would have to let go of her lifeline and grab onto the lower edge of the shelf. There was no room for error. She hoped that she had enough feeling left in her hands and force to pull herself out.

A final time, she sent herself swinging into a pendulum-type motion. Keeping her eyes on the target, she kicked on the upswing, letting go and reaching out.

She got it! But the current dragged on her feet, threatening her grip. Closing her eyes and willing everything to go as planned, Norah scissor kicked, gaining ground. The ledge was a storage for rope and other equipment. She could see hand holds about twelve inches away. Another mighty kick and she got one hand in, the other flailed. "Ahhh..." she cried. A hand fell onto the rope. Catching hold, it provided that last bit of leverage she needed to haul herself out.

Norah lay there gasping like a landed fish. She might have fallen asleep, but startled back to awareness sometime later. Shivering, she crawled into the pile of rope, pulling the strands over the top of her. It provided warmth, protection from the wind, and best of all, it was dry.

Wearing a smile, she fell asleep secure in the knowledge that she'd survived another trial and that she was still heading in the right direction.

⚜56⚜
MARTINEZ MARINA

HER BOAT WAS DOCKED, and the occupants had left ages ago by the time Norah decided that it was safe to come out of hiding. She didn't want to get wet again, so she explored the top of her shelf. She found a recessed latch; it opened with ease. Norah climbed a ladder into a living space. This water transport appeared to be personalized, like the Jeep.

The curtains were closed. The light inside was dim, but she could see well enough to make her way around. It felt safe and quiet. The stress of the previous night and most of the day had taken its toll. Even though she had dozed below, she still felt incredibly tired.

Dropping her backpack, it landed with a thud. Norah squatted to remove the Second Skin from around her face and head. Adding it to the balled-up material inside her pack, she got up to tour the tiny spaces of the craft. Finding dry clothing in a drawer, she pulled a large, warm sweatshirt over her head.

Covered and comfortable, Norah discovered that she was hungry. It surprised her to realize that her optic sensor hadn't signaled before her stomach did. She remembered that she'd shut the sensor down when she was in the water. Norah almost reactivated it but changed her mind.

Tentatively, Norah walked through the tidy kitchen. "Lights and refreshment please," she stated. Nothing happened, her shoulders drooped. Norah let out a drawn-out sigh. She began opening doors. The cold box only contained a few items; mayonnaise, mustard, relish, and a few cans of beer. A dry cupboard contained rounded cans with photos of food. Norah chose one that said, 'SpaghettiOs.'

"Open"

She banged it on the counter, "Open."

There must be more steps involved... She pushed on each surface, shaking it. Rummaged in every drawer, she could not find anything that looked like it would open the container. Giving up, Norah found a box of crackers and a jar of peanut butter. They were quite delicious even if they were not as beautiful as the little circle O's.

Norah returned to the living room where she unpacked her backpack. She'd lost the sleeping bag, food, money, and licenses. Deeper inside the bag, she found soggy maps.

Norah carefully unfolded them, spreading them out over a low table near the couch. Last, she checked her pendant. It was still pleasantly warm.

Her full stomach and the gentle movement of the boat soon had her yawning. Not in a hurry to leave this haven, she went to a tiny sleeping space, climbing into one of the lower 'births.' Opening a 'porthole' to let in fresh air, Norah dropped off to a dreamless sleep.

~~~

The cawing of birds and a racket outside woke Norah the next morning. Running over to peek out a window, she watched an extra-large vehicle with a robotic arm reaching toward a huge box. On the side of it was a sign that read, 'Trash only no recyclables. 'With a loud, high-pitched whine, the arm lifted the box, tipping it over its top. Debris fell out and into the cavernous space below.

Norah turned on her sensor to query; 'trash.' It replied with, 'something discarded; worthless or useless; rubbish; refuse; garbage.'

Her next query; 'recyclable' 'to treat or process (used or waste materials) to make suitable for reuse.'

Norah deactivated her sensors, nodding thoughtfully, "They haven't understood, yet, that resources created with chemical processes contaminate the biosphere." Fighting a strong urge to change the course of history, Norah backed away, returning her focus to the interior of the water transport.

She inspected the contents of the closets in the sleeping areas closely. There appeared to be multiple operators of this boat. She found several, distinctly different sizes and styles of clothing. She was excited to see that there were items she could wear that would not be loose and baggy.

Another intriguing discovery was the books. There were so many! They were all lined up like data blocks in a row. She'd only seen them in museums behind glass. Picking up a fat one, Norah tested its weight. The texture was hard near the 'spine,' pliable at the outer edges. It made a crackling sound when she opened it. Fanning through many pages at once, Norah inhaled the unusual old-paper scent. Turning a single sheet, she was struck by its delicacy. The wood-based material was thin, but not transparent.

She found similar things in the bathing room. Sitting in a shelf pocket near the 'toilet' were book-like items. They were larger than what she had scrutinized before, lighter in weight; the pages were shiny. Images rather than words dominated these. The front pages read, Vogue, Time, Rolling Stone and Vanity Fair.

Norah couldn't help but become absorbed in her observations of clothing, hairstyles, and 'make-up' applications. Maya's thoughts informed her that, 'magazines were consulted for fashion tips.' She looked from the page to her reflection in the mirror. *This explains why people behave as if they've never seen anyone like me! My mannerisms must contribute to the formation of perceptions. Those are more difficult to correct and will take practice, but modifying my appearance is something that I can do with little effort.*

Someone named Madonna seemed to be the leader of Punk Rock style. Norah, eagerly turned pages until she found something she thought she could replicate. Three hours later, she'd spiked her hair, applied thick eyeliner, and shadow. Norah shaped her eyebrows and put a beauty mark at the side of her nose.

⚜

She wore a tight, sleeveless T-shirt, a short jacket, jeans, and a choker around her neck. The transformation was stupefying. As appalling as the outfit made her feel, the 'tennis shoes' that matched her foot size were a most welcome addition. 'Tying' the laces were another challenge that she finally solved by referring to the encyclopedic knowledge base housed in her optic tool.

Checking to make sure that the items going into her backpack were dry, Norah went about packing it. The Second Skin went to the bottom, the safest place for it. She selected a few other items of clothing that she could change into if needed. Crackers, more peanut butter and a jar of jam went in.

She straightened up in every room she'd occupied. *This is time-consuming,* she thought. But since she wasn't that keen on leaving, it didn't bother her. Norah started feeling anxious again when she thought about the close call with the law enforcers. She realized that she no longer had identification or currency. Another thorough search of the sleeping quarters turned up seventy dollars and some coins.

Once the kitchen was clean, and the sleeping area tidied, she was ready.

Dusk was coming on when Norah stood on deck, observing her surroundings. Taking a deep breath, she carefully stepped from the boat onto the floating walkway. Hefting her backpack onto her back, putting sunglasses on, she attempted to stride with purpose and confidence.

She passed a few other boaters. Some sidestepped, continuing their way, a few merely nodded. She returned the greeting.

Once on solid ground, Norah congratulated herself. Her pendant was mixed in with other beads and chains hanging around her neck. She held it while she walked. At the end of the boat service area, close to where she came off the 'dock,' it started to grow warm. She stood there looking with longing at her secure haven.

Her perimeter check indicated south. If her optics were correct, Haylee's last known address was South and West of this location; it was only twenty-six miles from there.

Spotting a group of similarly dressed youthful people loitering around in front of the 'Marina Office & Store,' Norah approached. "Excuse me? Could you tell me how to obtain transport from here to Berkeley — specifically to the University of California at Berkeley?"

They laughed. Looking at each other, making their eyes go cross-eyed. A tall female wearing a long net shirt over shorts and a 'bikini' top, stepped toward Norah. "Aren't you a little young to be wandering around all by yourself?"

"I am fully mature."

The female raised her eyebrows, "If you say so."

"Do you know how to direct me, or shall I inquire inside?"

"You're not from around here are you?"

Mimicking the expression she observed, Norah raised her eyebrows.

"OK. Sure. The San Joaquin train leaves in half an hour. That goes to Richmond. From there you take BART. We're waiting for the shuttle bus to the train station, now. You can tag along if you like."

Norah wasn't at all sure what most of that meant, but she responded, "Yes, please. Thank you very much."

The girl who'd spoken was Katie. Her friends were Chris and Laura. Katie worked at the marina. She nodded toward the others, "We're all 'Cal' students. Do you go to Berkeley too?" she asked.

"Yes, I'm going there."

"Are you an exchange student?" Chris chimed in.

"Exchange?"

"You know, from another country? Are you a German prodigy or something?"

Norah paused, glancing up as she accessed the meaning of those words put together in that way. "Ah, — I understand. Your question is because my speech and language patterns are foreign to you, and my complexion is fair. Yes, you may consider me a prodigy."

"What are you studying?" Laura tried.

"Sociology. I have been studying sociology for some time."

Katie smiled, "I'm Psych. These two are Engineering."

"Psych?" Norah inquired.

"Psychology."

"Oh! Then you may know my — Uncle. Dr. Joshua Herkowitz."

"Sure, I know Dr. Herkowitz."

The shuttle bus arrived. Chris and Laura climbed on board. Katie helped Norah pay the driver. The two girls sat next to each other.

"What's he like?"

Katie laughed, "He's *your* Uncle, shouldn't you be telling me?"

Norah was confused. Of course, Katie was correct. Nodding, Norah stalled for time while she composed an appropriate response. "I meant as a teacher. I've never seen him in a classroom setting."

Katie seemed to relax. She smiled as she leaned back into her seat. "When I first got to Cal., I wasn't one-hundred-percent sure what I wanted to study. I thought teaching might be something I'd like because that's what my mother does. I helped in her classes sometimes, and I liked working with kids. *Then* I attended a lecture that Dr. Herkowitz gave about psychology applied in school settings. I knew right then that that was what I wanted to do — be a school psychologist. Dr. Herkowitz has been helping me find internships. He wrote a recommendation letter so that I could work with a psychologist at a middle school. I am a huge fan of your Uncle!"

Pleased, Norah smiled in return. "Has he lectured about his memory issues research?"

"No....," Katie gave her a strange look, cleared her throat, then glanced back at her friends. The shuttle bus arrived at its destination. The exit door opened with a hiss. Chris and Laura passed by, "Come on Katie," they encouraged.

She turned to Norah. A look of indecision played across her face, "We're only going as far as Richmond. Once we get there, I can show you to the BART station and help you get tickets."

"Thank you very much, Katie. Do you mind if I continue gathering information about my...Uncle, in his professional capacity?"

"Sure," she grimaced.

⁂

Once they were settled again, Katie tried striking up the conversation, "So you're from Germany?"

"No," Norah corrected. "I did not state my point of origin; I merely confirmed that my appearance is similar to a person who lives in that country."

"Oh..." Katie nodded, "my mistake."

"It was a misconception that I chose not to correct. Have you had an opportunity to meet Dr. Herkowitz's wife?"

"Wife?" Katie blurted, "He's not married."

Norah's eyes grew round, "It is possible that they kept the marriage a secret."

It was Katie's turn looked surprised, "I didn't know he was getting married. Are you going to the wedding?"

Blinking rapidly, Norah nodded, "Yes, that's exactly my plan."

"Who is he getting married to and where are they having it?" She sounded wistful, "I love weddings!"

"Oh — his wife is, I mean, will be, Haylee Garrett. The ceremony took, I mean, will take place, at the municipal courthouse." In her mind, Norah recited the rest of` the information regarding the address, date and time. Surreptitiously, she looked at the date stamped on her train ticket. The wedding would take place tomorrow!

She'd never witnessed a marriage ceremony. *It is something that a stranger could attend? Are there acceptable forms of dress?* How could she ask Katie about it without sounding more out-of-place than she already did? "Tell me about some of the best weddings you've been to."

For the next twenty minutes, Katie went into detail about dresses, bride's maids, reception decoration themes, and menu planning. "It is one of the most momentous occasions in a young woman's life. You get to be a princess for a day. I've been dreaming about and planning my own for years," Katie sighed.

"Have you already been paired with a compatible mate?"

"Not yet," Katie's smile created dimples.

"What happens after that one day?"

Katie slumped, "Oh...well you go on a nice honeymoon, then go back to work and start planning to buy a house and thinking about how many kids you want."

"Where I come from, our work contributions over time are the most prized aspects of our young adulthood. If we are very fortunate, our work assignment is matched with someone who is already noteworthy in their field."

Katie was giving Norah a look that made her uncomfortable. It was a relief when the announcement stated that they were about to arrive in Richmond and to, "Check your seating area so that you have all of your belongings."

⁂

Norah cross-referenced coordinates for the Alameda County Courthouse with the Bay Area Rapid Transit (BART) station maps. She found a station located just a few blocks from her destination.

Norah had to change trains a couple of times to follow the correct line color. She noticed that most of the humans were engaged in selective perception; a cognitive state where only specific things gained attention. If she didn't do anything unusual, like trying to talk to someone, it was easy to remain unnoticed.

At home, something like this could never happen. Living pods were limited to one hundred and fifty. Everyone knew each other's names. Remaining aloof when in public was improper behavior, a cause for a series of mandated therapy sessions.

The train decelerated, coming to a stop. Automatic doors whooshed opened. A stream of people flowed out, Norah flowing with it. Exiting the station, the assemblage of train riders dispersed. Norah was overwhelmed at her first sight of the bustling antiquated city. Cars zoomed passed, turbulence in their wake caused dust and rubbish to float into the air. People of all colors, sizes, and ages walked like they were in a hurry.

Small, red warning lights flashed in her vision when she observed stationary people; sitting on the sidewalk, or leaning on walls, their eyes following the movements of passers-by.

In her living environment, stillness was an invitation to connect with random pod members on a deeper level. Approaching someone with a friendly expression was an acceptance. These stationary people didn't make Norah feel like approaching.

Taking social cues she'd learned on BART, Norah avoided eye contact and walked with a deadline-like pace toward her goal. She joined groups of people waiting for the red, yellow, and green lights that would indicate when cars would stop.

Approaching a tall multi-storied edifice, Norah read Alameda County Court House on the side of the building. Triumph! She'd found it. Congratulating herself, she noted the time. In less than twelve hours, Haylee and Dr. Herkowitz would be here.

Norah took a seat on an empty concrete bench to wait. Lake Merrit was across the street. It had greenery along the banks, plenty of places to seek cover once it turned dark. For now, she eyed a food truck, it was 'Taco Tuesday.'

Her stomach groaned. Looking down, she rubbed it. She rather enjoyed the activities involved with appeasing that physical craving.

⚜57⚜
ECHO'S ANXIETY

HAYLEE WAS FASTENING A delicate buckle on her sandal when the phone rang. Her hair, done up in soft round curls, woven through with ribbons, brushed against her bare shoulders as she reached for the phone.

"Don't answer!" Josh said urgently, but too late. He stood in the doorway, wearing a gray sports suit. He held Serena on his hip. She had a purple ribbon in her hair, Pebbles-style, and wore a matching sundress. Josh held her sandals in his free hand.

Haylee eyed him while listening to the frantic voice on the other end of the line. "Uh, huh," she nodded.

Josh heard every few words, 'stable,' 'all my horses!' 'contagious.' He shook his head, 'no' at her while pointing at his watch.

"The vet's already been out? "Haylee asked while sending Josh a pleading look. She showed him the tiny space between her index finger and thumb. She compressed her lips before responding to her caller, "I can't stay long, I have an important appointment that I can't miss, but since you are on my way, I'll be there in a few minutes."

"No!" Josh roared when she hung up.

Haylee slipped off the sandal and went to root around in her closet for her cowboy boots. She hiked up her long white dress, securing it with a belt, "We'll take two cars. You take Serena. I'll meet you there."

"Unbelievable...."

Haylee stopped in front of them. She leaned down to kiss her daughter, "Sweetheart, you look so pretty! Keep Josh company till Mama gets there, OK? "

"Haylee..."

She halted his words with a kiss. Haylee smiled tenderly. "Besides YOU, the best wedding present you could give me is to let me do what I do best – guilt free. There is an entire stable of horses that I might be able to help."

He sighed. "Don't – be – late!"

"I won't!"

In twenty minutes, Haylee arrived at the Happy Hollow Horse Ranch. The manager was waiting at the gate when she arrived. "Thank you so much for coming! "Erica Rainwood called through Haylee's open window.

As soon as Haylee stepped out of her car, Erica stopped short. "You didn't say your 'appointment 'was a wedding! "

Haylee smiled, "No, I didn't. "

The forty-something woman held out her hand in greeting. "I've heard nothing but good things about you. Bless you, for coming. "

Haylee got right to it, "So you've got some cribbing going on with how many horses? "

Haylee knew that cribbing is when a horse bites onto a hard surface— a wooden structure or drinking trough— arches its neck, and sucks air.

"It started with two, but now I've got twelve! I think they're teaching each other! If my boarders start pulling out, I'll be ruined."

Haylee nodded as she walked quickly toward the barn. "What did the vet say? "

Dryly, Erica stated, "He said that there's no medical reason for them to be doing it. It's an addictive habit. It makes them high, and it's just about impossible to stop. He said that he isn't an animal psychologist."

"I've seen it a couple of times. How many horses do you have total? "

"Twenty."

When they arrived at the stable, Haylee glanced down its long dark tunnel. She asked Erica if she'd wait at the entrance while she got acquainted with the horses. No one was cribbing now, all but a few of the curious animals were peering out at her.

Haylee did a walk through, scanning for the best communicators. Her first choice was a handsome Morgan Horse. The nameplate identified him as Regis. He told her that he felt well, his human familiars took him out for trail rides often. He liked most of his stall mates, and he was ashamed to have started his bad habit.

The next one, Jazzy, a pretty Paint with black and white spots, nuzzled Haylee's hand, taking advantage of willing pats and scratches. Jazzy told Haylee that she'd been living at this stable for a long time. Erica used to pasture them frequently when there were only nine horses. The more crowded the stables got, the less time they spent outside. She also told Haylee that it was Echo who showed them the ways of biting and breathing.

Haylee found Echo pacing in his stall. He snorted, waving his tail in short, quick, swipes; he kicked the walls, stirring up floor matter. The name plaque read Winny, but Haylee knew better. Echo was unresponsive to both her mental queries and to her gentle, encouraging words. Even without his cooperation, Haylee could tell that the Quarter Horse was dominated by fear and anxiety. Memories of being starved and a vicious biting dog gyrated in unending circles inside his mind. Haylee didn't understand why such a troubled creature was in a boarding stable rather than a rehabilitation center.

"I took him as a favor," Erica replied when Haylee asked. "His owner boards two other animals here."

"The cribbing started after Echo arrived, "Haylee stated.

Abashed, Erica looked at the ground, nodding. "How did you know?"

"Jazzy."

They were silent for a few moments.

"Jazzy said that? "

Haylee nodded.

"I always thought that little girl paid attention to everything."

"I think you can make progress with the others if you relieve their boredom." Haylee continued. "Let them graze and run more. Put them out in small, rotating groups. I can make a list of compatible personalities if you like. But Echo needs serious help. If you keep him here, the situation for the entire stable will degrade."

Erica cursed when she heard Haylee's analysis, "That's going to complicate matters."

Erica promised to put Echo at the top of her priority list. They put him in a round pen instead of his stall. His anxiety didn't disappear, but it was reduced. It would buy Erica time to consider what to do next.

Haylee had done a quick wash-up in the stable bathroom. She'd have just enough time to make it if she didn't run into any traffic snafoos.

❧58❧
FIRST SIGHT

AT 2:00 P.M. NORAH PERCHED on the same stone bench she'd found yesterday. She was sore and tired from a restless night concealed under a bush. It had taken her three attempts to find one that wasn't already occupied.

Her society had come a long way from these brutal times. How could communities allow members to suffer while others, right across the street, had bounty? Norah knew that the savagery would grow far worse before it got better.

The age of terrorism and political intimidation was beginning to emerge. A general feeling of fear in the populace would mistakenly support waves of governing oligarchs, wealthy politicians with the ear of the media, making promises that could never be kept.

Middle society that matured after World War II would grow angry when, one by one, they lost their postindustrial age advantages. They would be the ones to suffer most when the air and water went bad.

Norah felt a sense of relief that her time travel hadn't brought her into the Great Downfall.

It would take a near extinction event on the surface of the earth to convince the small pockets of surviving humanity that every form of life was equally important.

"Oh, my!" Norah exclaimed breathlessly. She sat up straighter. She'd caught her first sight of Dr. Herkowitz! He looked so much younger than in his videos, but it was unmistakably him. He was pushing a seated transport and accompanied by another man carrying a bundle of flowers. The companion resembled Dr. Herkowitz. Their gaits were similar as were their facial features. *Perhaps they share the same genetics?*

The two men were involved in an animated conversation. They stood on the opposite street corner gesticulating. Norah's gaze focused on the little girl sitting in the 'stroller.' She swung her legs and was singing while watching people.

Norah held her breath as they crossed, approaching her position. She could hear what they were saying.

"Come on, Josh, mellow out. If she said she'd be here, she will."

"Well.... yea.... but you gotta admit that she does have a gift. Living with her will be like living with a doctor on call. You're sure about this bro? "

Dr. Herkowitz stopped. They were no more than five feet from where Norah sat. The child in the stroller leaned forward, making eye contact with her.

"Spence, how can you even ask that?"

"I think it might be a duty of the Best Man— and you know mom's going to flip when she finds out."

Smiling at the little girl, Norah watched as that expression mirrored on the child's face.

"That's exactly why I didn't want her to know," Dr. Herkowitz continued.

The companion nodded, he looked worried. "That's something everyone would expect *me* to say. Not you. You're the one who is always anticipating things and making plans. Getting married by a judge, in secret, doesn't seem like the best way to start out a marriage. Everyone's going to be pissed. Norah couldn't take her eyes off the toddler. She realized that this child was genetically related to *her*. She'd never seen a relation in such a small size. *Serena,* she mouthed the name, smiling.

The small female held up a toy car that fit in the palm of her hand. It looked just like the Jeep Norah had driven when she left Maya and Jango. Norah would have looked away, but Serena held up the vehicle waving it back and forth making the sound, "Vroom! Vroom!"

Norah's focus was captivated by Serena, but in her peripheral vision, she saw Dr. Herkowitz rest a hand on the other man's shoulder.

"If you had said that to me two years ago, I'd have agreed with you, Spencer. I see things differently since I came out of the coma. I know my mind and my heart, and they belong to Haylee. Nothing else matters."

"Then let's do this."

Serena waved her arm and let the toy go flying. It landed at Norah's feet. She leaned over, picking it up. Spencer walked over, holding out a hand, "Sorry," he said.

Dr. Herkowitz knelt in front of Serena, straightening her clothing. He admonished the little girl, "The judge won't be happy if you drop it when we are in his office. Keep it in your pocket. If you want to hold it, put your hand in there, OK?"

Norah's eyes followed the triad as they passed, approaching a wide staircase leading up to the building's entrance. Without a break in their conversation, Spencer reached down to lift the front wheels of the stroller while Dr. Herkowitz adjusted his grip so that he could raise his end. Norah giggled as she watched them crab-walk up, disappearing inside.

She let out the breath she'd been holding. It surprised her that a warning light was blinking and she hadn't noticed.

The next thirty minutes dragged. Norah got up to stretch, tapped her feet, and fidgeted as she waited.

"Excuse me! Almost late bride coming through!" Norah heard a voice calling. She turned in time to see Haylee running in her direction. Norah's chest tightened. She wanted to jump in the young woman's path, yelling, *I found you! I made it!*

Instead, Norah took a step back and watched. Haylee held up the front of a lacy white dress. Her cowboy boots pounded on the pavement. Her hair was a mess; there were pieces of straw in it. But she was grinning. Her skin looked flushed.

Norah quickly packed up her stuff and prepared to follow as Haylee disappeared into the dark interior of the courthouse.

❧59❧
I DO

SPENCER TOOK SERENA WHILE handing Haylee her bouquet. During the exchange, the toddler leaned out, grasped a handful of sunflower petals, shoving them in her mouth. "Honey, no!" Haylee warned. But before anyone could reclaim them, Serena swallowed.

"Josh! Serena just ate sunflower petals, are they poisonous?"

Before Josh could answer, the clerk interjected. "Not to worry, my sister is a chef. She uses them in salads all the time."

Haylee turned to her daughter, "You scared Mama. We've talked about this, Serena."

"Good fower!" Serena chirped as Haylee adjusted her bouquet so that the missing petals wouldn't show.

"She's got a bad habit of eating plants and leaves. One of these days that is going to get us in trouble." Haylee murmured.

Serena smiled brightly, "Spence!" she yelled.

Spencer smiled in return. He pulled the little girl in close, whispering, "It's exciting to see your mama and my brother getting married, but you and me," he pointed his finger at her then at himself, ".... we must be quiet until it's all over. OK?"

The little girl nodded enthusiastically. "Great," Spencer returned. "Once we get outside, you can scream all you want, kiddo."

Haylee's heart swelled as she watched the interaction. Then Josh was there, reaching for her hand, his eyes sparkling. She laced her fingers with his thinking of nothing but this magical moment.

Haylee felt blessed to have found this wonderful man. She loved him completely and promised to do everything she could to make him as happy as possible for as long as they had together.

The Judge stepped forward. "We are here today to celebrate the love and commitment that Josh and Haylee have for each other and to recognize and witness their decision to journey forward as husband and wife.

May your love create a safe haven. Lead with your hearts. Take the time to do simple things that nurture your relationship.

Deeply listen to your dreams, and your frustrations. Be willing to meet in the middle and find agreeable solutions to the tests that life will present. Be helpmates and be playful. Let your love be an inspiration to others.

May your love grow sweeter with each passing year."

At this, Haylee swallowed passed the lump in her throat, her eyes filled. Her chin trembled. Josh nodded, smiled, and rubbed a finger over the back of her hand.

The judge continued:

"Do you, Josh, take Haylee to be your life partner? Do you promise to walk by her side, to love, help, and encourage her in all she does? Do you promise to take time to talk with her, to listen to her, and to care for her? Will you share her laughter, and her tears, as her partner, lover, and best friend? Do you take her as your lawfully wedded wife until death shall part you?"

"I do," Josh stated with certainty.

The Judge asked Haylee an identical set of questions.

Her voice shook when she responded, "Yes, I will. "

The Judge turned to Spencer. "May we have the rings?
"

For one awful moment, time stood still. Spencer let go of Serena's hand. He frantically searched his pockets. No one paid attention as tiny girl wandered over toward a grouping of chairs across the room. "I had them! "Spencer turned toward Josh, "I showed them to you before we left the house!"

"If you didn't put them in a pocket, where else would you have put them?" Josh sounded strained.

Haylee put a hand on his arm. "Give him a minute to think, you guys had a lot going on before leaving," she whispered. "Can we still be married if we can't find the rings?" she asked.

Spencer's frown cleared, "I know!" He dug down into his back pocket, pulling out his wallet. "I put them in here because I was worried that the ring boxes would be too bulky."

A collective sigh released the pent-up tension. Spencer handed the rings over.

"And now, we shall seal your promises with rings, the symbol of your life shared together." He handed them over. "Josh, repeat after me..."

Norah was surprised to observe Serena pretend-flying her little car right out of room two-thirty-two. The toddler turned and continued down the long hallway, "Vroom, vroom."

Norah waited to see if anyone would follow. When no one did, she trotted after the girl.

Keeping an eye on the youngest members of the community was considered an honor. It was an activity that every citizen enjoyed. Most of the time infants were kept in nurseries, but as they grew older, part of their training involved socializing in public areas.

When Norah caught up to Serena, she greeted her with the standard, "Good day to you, young citizen. May I be of service?"

Serena stopped to regard Norah. She must have made a decision because she held up her Jeep, "Vroom, vroom!"

Norah nodded, "That sound is a good approximation for vehicles."

Serena offered it to Norah. "Vroom?"

Norah held out a flat hand. Serena dropped it, then reached up to take Norah's other hand. "Side!" said the little girl. When Norah didn't move, Serena tugged, "Side!" she repeated.

"Oh...I see. You want me to take you outside."

The little girl made a resolute nod, "Yes!"

Norah looked behind them to check if Haylee had finished. The corridor remained empty. As they continued toward the exit, Norah was feeling glad to provide this childminding service.

Near the bench where Norah sat earlier, Serena spotted gray-winged birds. "Want to feed!" she yelled, running after the odd creatures that bobbed their heads when they walked.

At the child's approach, the flock took flight, leaving Serena looking crushed.

Before Norah could chase after Serena, a tremor rippled through. *No!* She crouched over, hugging her arms tightly across her chest, keeping her eyes on the running toddler.

The birds alighted not far off, Serena followed.

"Don't go too far..." Norah called, her voice strained. She walked hunched over. Norah recognized several people from the bushes. They remained stationary, observing with a predatory focus. Another tremor struck. Norah bit down on her lip, making it bleed.

Not wanting to put Serena in danger by being too close to her, but also not wanting to lose sight of the child, Norah held up the toy Jeep. "Serena, look!" she called out feebly. "Vroom, vroom. The birds might like to see this."

Norah watched as Serena smiled. The little girl changed course, heading back to Norah, her purple hair ribbons bouncing.

Gulping in deep breaths, Norah willed the hunting instinct back from a flame to a smolder. *This child will not be in danger— not from me!*

☙60☙
MISSING!

HAYLEE AND JOSH PULLED apart. They continued staring into each other's eyes like they wished to prolong the moment.

Spencer broke the spell when he glanced around the room. "Where'd Serena go?" he asked, alarmed.

"You just had her a minute ago!" Haylee's voice rose.

Suddenly everyone went into action. Questions were thrown out. "Did anybody see her leave?" "When was the last time someone saw her?" "She can't have gotten too far."

"Serena! Serena!" Josh and Haylee called, racing out of the chambers. Spencer was right behind them. The Judge and his assistant called to alert building security.

"We can't have lost her!" Haylee wailed.

There was no sign of Serena anywhere. Josh could see that Haylee was growing more panicked by the minute. "We'll find her," he stated with more confidence than he felt. Josh directed Spencer to go looking in the opposite direction. Taking Haylee's hand, they ran toward the stairs.

Haylee broke their hold to frantically ask a security guard if he's seen a little girl. The guard responded that there haven't been any lost children, but that there have been a few people who had children with them.

Josh and Haylee looked at each other with mounting fear. "She wouldn't go willingly with a stranger," Haylee said.

Spencer searched the stairwells. The Judge and his assistant checked the elevators, then reminded the security guards that they only have minutes to locate the child before the police must be notified.

Radio communication passed between the guards as Josh and Haylee gave physical characteristics of their child along with a list of what she was wearing.

Haylee's heart constricted when she overheard the radio reports from sectors of the building that had been searched. Josh kept an arm wrapped around her, but Haylee was too preoccupied to tell him that his grip was too tight.

They moved to the lobby, near the entrance doors. Spencer joined them. He'd had no luck either.

Haylee turned to Josh. Her eyes were wild, "I'm going to look outside."

"I'm coming with you," he replied tightly.

Haylee heard the security officers placing a call to the sheriff's department. A cold, salty breeze engulfed her, lifting the edges of her skirt. At the top of the steps, Haylee scanned the area. She immediately spotted the curly chestnut hair of her daughter in the courtyard. Intense relief flooded through here. "There she is!" Haylee pointed.

Haylee saw another child standing next to Serena. There was something familiar about the way she moved. Right away, her hunter instincts recognized the body posture. Frozen with fright Haylee watched the stranger draw back her arm, fingers extended; webbing taught between the digits.

"Serena!" Haylee screamed. Like a mother eagle, Haylee flew down the stairs. The Herkowitz boys were close on her heels. A few seconds behind them, an accompaniment of beefy uniformed men thundered in their tailwind.

Hearing the frantic cry, Norah looked up in time to see Haylee and many other angry looking people running at her. Her surprise and hesitation were long enough for Haylee to reach them.

Haylee leaped on top of the strange girl tumbling them both to the ground. Like when she was a Traveler, Haylee was wholly focused on their hands, stopping the webbed ones from touching Serena.

Fortunately, this Traveler was light-weight. Although Haylee was strong enough to subdue the girl, she could feel the pent-up power coursing through her. Getting them upright, Haylee pinned the girl's arms.

Josh scooped up Serena hugging her to him tightly. Haylee wanted to do the same, but she wasn't about to release the struggling girl.

In the instant, before the guards surrounded them, Haylee shouted to her husband, "Josh this is a Traveler! We've got to get her out of here."

Haylee could see Josh assessing the situation, still cuddling Serena. He was breathing hard and sweating. Josh turned to his brother stating in a low voice, "Spencer, go stand with Haylee. Block the view...but don't get too close."

"Josh, I don't underst..."

"Go! I promise I'll tell you everything when we get to the car."

Josh turned to approach the guards. He sounded contrite but in control, "Officers, I apologize! That girl over there is my wife's cousin. We didn't know she was coming to the wedding. We want to thank you for responding so efficiently."

Haylee leaned forward, whispering into the girl's ear, in what she hoped looked like a familial manner, "Has it passed? If you have regained control of yourself, nod."

The girl lowered her chin.

"Good," Haylee whispered. "If you don't want those men over there to take you away, then we need to look like we are long-lost friends. Understand?"

At the girl's nod, Haylee slowly released her grip. Holding her breath, she pasted on a bright smile and turned the girl to face her. Keeping her surprise to herself, Haylee bent down to hug her while saying loud enough to be overheard, "It's been such a long time, I almost didn't recognize you!"

When Haylee's ear came near, Norah whispered, "Haylee Herkowitz I would never, *ever* harm your daughter."

At those words, Haylee stilled. The maternal, protective feelings she'd felt for Polly, Emis's daughter, encompassed her like a down-filled comforter, warm, cozy and tender. She blinked as tears sprang to her eyes. How could she be having feelings like this for someone she just met?

Then Haylee remembered how it felt when she'd been a Traveler, thrust into a strange land seeking another. The hug she performed for the witnesses became compassionate and genuine. "You've done well. I'll look after you, I promise."

Haylee pulled away, still holding Norah by the shoulders, "What's your name?" she whispered.

"Norah," she responded just as quietly.

Spencer, wearing a perplexed frown, led Haylee and Norah to his car. Josh would meet them when he finished giving assurances to the security officers.

"It was never my intention to cause harm to you or your family," said Norah. "The tremors came on suddenly. I can't go on for much longer. I *must* have a volunteer."

Haylee seemed startled by the word, but Norah's meaning was clear enough. Serious and considering, she nodded.

"Haylee! Do you know this kid?" Spencer was distraught. "Did she snatch Serena from the courthouse? If I saw what I thought I saw, then she was on the verge of doing something awful to her."

Keeping contact with Norah and still moving along, Haylee glanced back toward Josh. She wondered what was going through his mind. Giving Norah a squeeze, she nodded in Spencer's direction, "This is Spencer, he is part of my family— he's my brother-in-law. He's off limits. Back there is my daughter, and...."

Norah nodded, "Yes I know him, that is your husband, Dr. Joshua Herkowitz."

❧61❧
NORAH NEEDS
A VOLUNTEER

HURRYING ALONG THE SIDEWALK, Josh was thinking quickly. His head felt about twice its average size; shooting pains spiked into his temples. Serena was getting heavy, but she wouldn't be able to keep up if he let her walk. He realized that they'd left her stroller in the Judge's chambers. They couldn't spare the time to go back for it.

When Haylee was a be-webbed predator, she was a danger to those around her. Inexplicably, he loved her even then, but Josh remembered a time when he had been terrified of her. The image of the wild look on her face before an attack, especially when she came after him, was one that he preferred to keep hidden behind a closed door in a remote corner of his mind.

Approaching the tense group, Josh could see that his brother was upset. Haylee looked relieved. Stepping toward him, she held out her arms for Serena.

The other girl, who appeared to be about ten, looked at him like he was a rock star. She clasped her hands tightly over her heart. Her eyes roamed his face as if she was expecting something. If he didn't know better, he'd think that she had a form of albinism, but her eyes were colored. They were an unusual shade of green. In fact, when he looked carefully, he'd swear he could see something in her eyes.... something moving.

"Josh, meet Norah," Haylee raised her voice. She returned to cooing and cuddling with her daughter.

Norah was very thin and pale. Josh observed white roots at the base of her dark spiky hair. He'd seen plenty of students experimenting with the Goth subculture style. This girl displayed none of the attitudes that typically accompanied that form of self-expression.

Sweat trickled down Josh's back. He was ready in case she made any sudden moves. He outweighed her and was reasonably sure he could defend himself and his family, but the thought of seeing webs again made his stomach clamp down like an antique wringer on a washing machine.

Norah stepped forward hesitantly. She was struggling mightily to contain her nervousness. Her voice was soft. She bowed deeply, "Dr. Herkowitz, it is an honor to make your acquaintance. I have been a student of your research since I was identified as a Traveler."

Speechless, Josh gazed down at the top of her head. He looked over at Spencer. His brother returned the gaze with a mystified elevation of his shoulders.

"Stand up," Haylee stated, "this is not appropriate behavior for the streets of Alameda."

"My apologies!" Norah sprang up. She attempted to hide her embarrassment by adjusting her clothing. Peeking under her lashes, she continued, "I did not mean to offend. Haylee Garrett, of course, it is a great honor to be in your presence as well."

"Thanks," Haylee replied dryly.

Josh shot her furtive glances wondering if she was as alarmed by their visitor as him. She gave him a curt nod, mouthing the words, *it's alright...for now.*

Norah's thin face crumpled. Balling her fists, and bracing them against her stomach, she curled around them. When she shuddered, it looked like Norah was freezing in a Arctic blizzard.

Alarmed, Spencer took a step in her direction. Both Haylee and Josh yelled, "No!"

"Something wrong with her!"

Josh grabbed a handful of material from Spencer's jacket hauling him back, "We're going to take care of this. We know what to do. Keep your distance!"

Angry, Spencer assumed an aggressive boxer's pose. "You've been talking in riddles since we came out of the courthouse. You better tell me what's going on or I'm going to clock you."

Haylee glanced at Norah. "Hang on," she urged, hurrying over to Spencer, holding Serena out, forcing him to give up is threatening stance. "You two take her home."

Haylee could see her husband was about to object. She interrupted him before he could speak. "I'm taking Norah back to the ranch; I'll get her what she needs there."

"But—" Josh looked apprehensive.

"I know what I'm doing," Haylee's words sounded confident. "We'll meet you there when we've got ourselves sorted out."

For a long moment, Josh gripped Haylee, staring intently at her. "I can't lose you...*especially* not tonight," he implored.

Her expression softened. "You won't, Josh." She leaned up, giving him a slow, thorough kiss.

〜〜〜

"This is something that goes beyond the police," Josh said tersely. He glanced in the rear-view mirror. Serena was almost asleep.

"How can it be beyond the police? Is it something that men in white coats could handle? Or is it more the little green alien scenario?" Spencer asked incredulously.

Josh shook his head, "You want me to talk, but instead of listening, all you do is shovel out loads of..."

"Shit! Josh!" Spencer exclaimed only to be shushed by his older brother.

They rode in stony silence for a few miles. Josh massaged a circular pattern on his temple, then pressed his thumb at the bridge of his nose.

"It's beyond the police, Spencer," Josh stated calmly, "because that girl has no ID."

When Spencer inhaled to speak, Josh pointed at him, until he closed his mouth.

"She's not from anywhere around here," he continued. "If they tried to identify her, they'd find that she doesn't exist...yet."

It suddenly dawned on Josh how incredible it was to have someone from the distant future in their midst. If Haylee could do what she implied— neutralize the threat that Norah posed, then he was going to want to talk to her! Following that thought, he was surprised to discover a sense of pleasure at her compliment about his work. *Something I've done, or will do, will be studied by students in the future?*

"Earth to Josh, you can't leave me hanging."

Shaking his head as if to clear the clutter, Josh muttered. "Sorry. Where was I?"

"You said," Spencer filled in, he was irritated, "that Norah doesn't exist."

"I didn't say that."

"Yes, you did!" the volume of Spencer's voice was starting to rise again.

Josh gave him a meaningful look. Hanging an elbow over the back of his seat, Spencer pushed upward so he could check on the kid, "She's zonked, already," he returned to his brother. "Will you stop tap dancing?"

Expelling a pent-up breath, Josh let loose. "Haylee...and that girl are time travelers."

When Spencer remained silent, Josh glanced over at him. "Do you remember when I was in the coma?" he asked quietly.

Spencer nodded, "How could I forget?"

"It didn't happen because of an accident."

"But Mom and Dad said..."

Josh raised a hand indicating that Spencer should shut up. "I can imagine what they told you, but it wasn't that. Haylee did it."

"How could a person cause a coma?" Spencer sounded skeptical.

"What you didn't see in the courtyard, is that that girl has webbing between her fingers. If it comes in contact with your face, it puts you in a coma."

Spencer's eyes grew wide, "What the...?"

"Haylee had the webs too when I first met her, but they're gone now." He continued, "We've got to keep Norah away from everyone. She's dangerous."

"And Haylee?"

"She can handle herself.... I hope," Josh replied.

Spencer stared out the window for the rest of the ride. When they parked in the driveway, he didn't get out but sat there regarding his brother.

"What?" Josh questioned.

Lacing his fingers and resting them on the back of his head, Spencer raised his eyebrows. "This is insanely whacked, Joshie James. You're telling me that you just married the woman who almost killed you...and that another time-traveling weirdo, who can do the same thing, showed up...and assuming any of it is true.... you are OK with all this?"

"Spencer..." Josh warned.

"Say no more," Spencer interrupted, "I think that the folks may have been mistaken when they thought you were well."

⚘62⚘
HAPPY HOLLOW

IT WAS LATE AFTERNOON. As Haylee approached
the Happy Hollow Horse Ranch, the shadows were
stretching long and thin like ghosts in a funhouse mirror.
Gravel crackled under her tires, abrading her already taut
nerves. Haylee wanted to move quickly, force her way in,
appease Norah's appetite. Instead, she proceeded with
caution. Her sense of urgency felt like being stuck in heavy
stop-and-go traffic when an ambulance is blaring its siren
from behind.

Haylee knew that feeding could only be held off for so
long. Norah's decreased ability to respond, her iron tight
grasp on the car door, and frequently leaning her face out
of the window, were signs that it was becoming
increasingly difficult for the girl to maintain control.

If Norah turned on her—while she was driving—
Haylee wasn't sure she'd be able to defend herself. A trickle
of sweat dripped between her breasts; the breezed from the
open window cooled the sheen of moisture that formed on
her upper lip.

Haylee had talked non-stop for the entire trip. She'd
started off telling Norah about her time jump and the
difficulties and challenges she'd faced when learning to
adapt. As she described Emis and the interactions between
them, Haylee realized how very *wrong* Emis's fear was.

When they'd first met, Emis pushed Haylee away and attempted to flee. By contrast, Haylee had protective feelings for this poor girl. If she could keep from being consumed by her, Haylee knew that she'd do everything in her power to perform her duties and return Norah, safely, to her own time.

Thinking about the Redemption Ceremony shifted something in Haylee's mind. It was if a door that kept that information sealed had come open; how it was to be done, the words to be spoken, and the rituals to be performed poured into her brain like floodwaters escaping containment after a levee break. The Ceremony would be painful, but it would do what was intended; deliver the large crystal to Norah who would take it home. *If Norah takes the crystal, then I won't be able to use it to heal any more victims.*

It also came to Haylee that there was an unbreakable time limit to how long a Traveler could remain in an unnatural time stream. Weeks at most. *How can that be? I stayed with Reece for almost a year.*

A feeling of peace that went beyond the turbulent emotions of the moment gave Haylee an understanding and connection with all the Travelers that had come before her. They went back for as long as humans lived on the planet. Travelers were necessary...for what, Haylee didn't know yet. But she thought that she might before her story came to an end.

They came to a stop at the closed Happy Hollow gate. "We're here," Haylee announced. Putting the car into park, she quickly jumped out.

Jazzy had told Haylee that the stable manager was away a lot. Haylee disengaged the lock. A loud metallic screech sounded as she pushed the gate inward. Haylee hoped that Jazzy was right. She had no idea what she would do if they were caught.

When Haylee approached the car, she stepped back, alarmed. Norah had curled into a ball on the floorboard; she was shaking violently. Every instinct told Haylee to run!

"Norah?" she called out uncertainly. "Can you hear me?"

Haylee could see a slight nod. "We're very close. I need to drive a short distance. Can you hold on for a little longer?"

"...Go," Norah squeaked out a thready whisper.

With hope and a prayer, Haylee jumped back in. They arrived at the open pen in less than a minute. Haylee made a hasty exit. A quick scan of the area told her that, thankfully, most of the horses were out in the pasture— a pasture that had no direct line of sight to where Echo stood, trembling.

Haylee raced to the stable. In the supply stall, she pulled out every blanket, making a pile outside. Then she rolled the door closed while sending reassuring thoughts to those inside. *You may hear frightening sounds. Please try to stay calm. When Echo returns, he will be free of anguish.*

From the dark depths, Haylee heard a few nickers and a snort. They were telling her that they were concerned, but that they trusted her. She swallowed passed the sudden constriction in her throat.

Hurrying, Haylee carried the blankets to Echo's pen. Draping them along alternating walls of a cattle shoot, she used sturdy ropes to adjust its width, and stabilize the structure. She secured ties with Trucker's Hitch knots. They would allow her to cinch the walls closer together without releasing when she let go.

Haylee was breathing hard. Coated with dust and sweat, she straightened to regard the distressed Quarter Horse. Ears flat, he eyed her suspiciously from the far side of the pen, his tail swishing in agitated arcs.

A distressed cry came from inside the VW. Knowing that Norah's time had run out, Haylee searched her surroundings for anything that could get Echo moved where she wanted him. There was nothing. He'd charge her if she approached. She couldn't get close enough to attach a lead. The only thing that she could see were dragonflies dipping and darting in the early light of dusk. Her first thought was, *Stupid! Dragonflies?*

But the newly awakened part of herself said...*try.*

Haylee closed her eyes. She sent all thoughts of worry out of her mind while she focused on the insects. It didn't feel like anything happened. But then gradually, a shift of density came into her awareness. When she opened her eyes, a cluster of them formed about three feet above her. They moved in a swirling motion, like a waterspout.

She could hear brittle vibrating sounds from their wings. Confused, she didn't know what to do. If she asked them to surround Echo, she was sure that the horse would go berserk. *I need help guiding this horse to go between the padded fences. Can you help?*

The dragonfly swarm continued a spiraling motion. She couldn't feel a response. They looked as if they paused to consider her statement. Then, as one body, they zoomed off, disappearing. Haylee's shoulders dropped. She'd come so far. She'd have to resort to hiding until Norah found what she needed.

Haylee turned and was about to leave when she heard a bark. She saw a Border Collie racing in their direction. A swarm of dragonflies followed! In disbelief, Haylee watched the collie jump into the pen. Expertly, the dog nipped and danced until Echo inched closer to the shoot entry.

Echo was terrified. He focused on the dog.

Realizing that she needed to act, Haylee ran to the outside of the shoot, grabbing hold of the ropes.

At the entry, the horse and dog faced off. Echo refused to budge. The collie looked up at the dragonflies. Stepping away, the swarm took her place, surging forward causing the animal to scream.

Echo backed between the fence walls.

Haylee pulled with all her might, cinching the gates tight. Echo roared trying to get his hooves up and over the restriction, but with every movement, Haylee pulled until the walls immobilized the animal as securely as a python coiling around its prey.

Gasping, Haylee couldn't believe that the feat was accomplished. "Thank you!" she called. The collie barked twice, then jumped through the fence bars, racing away. The dragonflies swooped in crazy eight patterns before disbursing.

Haylee approached Echo's head. The animal was swinging it wildly, his eyes bulging, foam-spattered from his mouth. Locating a rag, Haylee dipped it into his water trough. Positioning herself so she was out of biting range, she waited until she had a clear path to drop the wet cloth over his eyes. As he began to calm, Haylee spoke softly. "There, there, fella. I am so sorry to have distressed you. I am even sorrier to have found you in such a horrible state. It's going to be better soon.

"One last indignity," Haylee whispered as she looped a short strap over Echo's nose and mouth, tightening it. Now he wouldn't be able to bite.

Norah tumbled out when Haylee opened the car door. She sprang forward like Red Tailed Hawk, hands extended like talons with webbing stretched tight, hurtling straight at Haylee.

Haylee deflected the attack, rolling, ever conscious that she needed to control Norah's limbs. They twisted like fighting alligators. Taking a jab to the stomach, Haylee grunted. Fear and anger spurred her to fight. She refused to let this monster take her away from Serena and Josh.

Throwing her knee between them, Haylee followed it with all her weight. Norah's blank gaze sent a chill racing down Haylee's spine. She reached out, gaining a grip around Norah's wrists, pinning them to the ground like a prize wrestler.

Subdued but still struggling wildly, Norah moaned.

"Listen!" Haylee spat as she shouted. "I have food! But it's not me. We have to get up. I'll take you now." The only response that Haylee got was a minor reduction in Norah's exertion.

Haylee held tightly to Norah's wrists. They scuffled to the top of the shoot. Roughly, Haylee turned Norah toward Echo. Standing behind her, she directed each claw-like hand at a nostril.

At the first feel of the warm air, Norah's arms outstretched. Her body moved in the same direction. The webs clamped into place, making an airtight seal. Echo drew back his lips, screaming between clenched teeth. The strap Haylee tied around his jaws kept his mouth shut but didn't control his lips.

Seeing that the webbing was secured, Haylee released Norah. Grabbing another towel, wetting it, Haylee used it to restrict air flow. Haylee sent calming messages into the horse's mind. *Relax, fella. It's going to be OK. You've been the best horse that you knew how to be. The burning will stop in a minute...know peace.*

Tension faded from Echo like a trickle of water from a spigot that's been shut off. His head lowered, his body serene.

The tightness in Norah's arms transferred to her back. She arched, letting her neck release, taking in great gasps of cold air. Her hands dropped to her sides, she swayed.

"Ok. It's OK." Haylee repeated, letting the wet towel fall, splatting on the ground. She stroked Echo's neck. With the back of her hand, she swiped at the tear tracks on her cheeks.

On wobbly legs, Norah moved down the outside of the shoot.

"Stay close to the car," Haylee called softly."

Taking a few fortifying breaths, Haylee set to work. She was worried that Erica would return before they finished. Running to the stable, she carried the blankets back inside. As she folded them, she prepared the horses inside to see a different Echo.

Not afraid? they inquired.

Not anymore. Calm. No more thinking. You must treat him like a foal.

The last chore that Haylee performed was to stable Echo. She approached him this time with no concerns about aggression. Although she knew that he no longer had a conscious mind with which to perceive her words, she spoke anyway, "There you are, beautiful boy."

Echo didn't raise his head; his ears didn't perk up, and his eyes remained dull; he was as docile as a kitten. Feeling tears building behind her eyes, Haylee attached the halter, urging him to follow. *Erica and Echo's owners will think he's cured. He won't crib anymore, and he'll do whatever they want,* Haylee thought.

❧

On the freeway with all the windows rolled down, the wind snatched at their hair. Haylee was relieved to see Norah looking recovered and back in her right mind. She nodded in response to the exuberant statements Norah yelled over the noise.

"The grass! It smells so good, and it tastes wonderful too! And the soil, it's rich, and it makes you feel delicious when you roll in it! And to run, in a herd, thundering hooves, ground shaking, with your mane flowing! It's like nothing I ever imagined! It's a tragedy that we lost the surface of the Earth."

Haylee turned toward Norah, "What does that mean?" her voice raised a notch, she was scowling.

Norah didn't see or hear Haylee's expression; she was too busy leaning over the back seat, rooting around in the junk scattered there. "Ah! This is what I want!" she held up a paperback.

Dropping into the passenger seat, Norah opened her mouth wide. Shoving the book in, she bit down, grasping it firmly between her teeth. Sucking, expanding her neck, and snorting loudly, she let the book fall. Norah wilted against the seat. "The effect on human physiology is not the same as equine," Norah sighed, "but it's still very nice."

❧

Haylee stopped at the far end of a department store parking lot about five minutes from home. Norah had grown increasingly quiet as their drive continued.

"Is this your habitat? It's immense," Norah looked through the window in wonder.

"No, I don't live here. We need to talk by ourselves before we join the others."

Norah's gaze traveled over Haylee, "I forgot that today was your wedding day. Katie told me all about the significance. The Alameda County Courthouse was the only location where I knew I could find you without delay. I'm afraid that I ruined it. Look at you; your dress is ripped, you have blood and soil all over. Your groom won't think that you look like—" her lips trembled, "...a princess."

Haylee huffed, lifting some of her dress fabric, "It's nothing a little soap and water won't fix. More importantly, I need to know about you. I thought I'd have more time before you arrived."

Norah looked confused. She gripped her hands together tightly, bending her head over them as if she were about to start a prayer. "I'm experiencing difficulty. My optical sensors have stopped working, and Echo's troubled state of mind is interfering with my ability to focus and participate in a discourse." Norah's breathing grew labored, her voice was strained, "Foreign emotions," she hiccuped, "are taking over. I don't know what to do!" She began trembling again, but this time it had nothing to do with feeding behavior. "Water is leaking from my eyes!" she wailed.

Haylee used the same tactics on Norah that she had on Echo. "It's alright," she spoke softly. Haylee reached over, rubbing the girl's back. "You're crying, that's all. After what you've been through, I'd expect that a good cry is just what you need."

"Really?" The girl looked up at her with huge, pathetic eyes.

Haylee had given up trying to have a conversation. "Can you tell me one thing?" she ventured. "What year do you come from?"

Snuffling, Norah replied, "2239."

☙63❧
APPETITES

JOSH AND HAYLEE PLOPPED down on the plush couch in the small sitting room of their beautifully appointed honeymoon suite at the Fairmont Hotel. They looked at each other, smiling.

"This isn't how I imagined our wedding night starting out," Josh said.

Haylee blinked, her eyes filled, "I'm sorry..."

He turned towards her, pressing a finger to her lips." I wasn't making a judgment; I was just stating a fact."

"But... "Haylee said.

"We knew it was coming. We weren't expecting it today, but now that it has, we'll deal with it— tomorrow," Josh said, gathering her close.

"Our small time traveler is clean, tidy, and safely ensconced in the house. Spencer doesn't seem to mind," Josh winced, raising a hand to press against his temple, "keeping an eye on her. You're sure; she's under control?"

"Norah's appetite is appeased. Spencer should be fine."

Josh nodded, "Your dad and Glori have Serena, so what's left of the night is ours."

When Josh pulled her toward him, Haylee put a hand on his chest, "I need to take a shower. I smell like a horse." She looked down at her ruined wedding dress, making a face. "It was embarrassing to walk in the lobby still wearing this."

"Mrs. Herkowitz," Josh grinned, "I don't care how you smell. You'll have to let me have my way with you first; then we'll climb in the shower." He pulled her on top of him.

She felt his arousal, pressing against her, pulsing with need. Haylee dug her fingers into his hair, returning his ardor. Her flesh grew warm; she ground her hips against his. The center of her womanhood, seeped with slick, silky moisture.

Josh ran his hands up and down her back. Pushing her skirt up, he caressed her thighs. "You're my wife now, all mine. I want to bury myself in you. I love you, Haylee."

Hayley leaned back on an elbow, watching his face. Her eyes were glassy. "And you're mine, Josh, forever and ever."

Those words were like ice water thrown onto hot coals. A look of concern crossed Haylee's face. She started to speak, but Josh stopped her.

"You're right— forever," he agreed. He pulled her back to him, cradling her against his chest, kissing her slowly, patiently reigniting their fire until it took her breath away.

They consummated their marriage on the couch and then, again, on the floor. Their movements were frantic, liquid, and slow. Their hearts and minds were utterly open; they held nothing back. They spoke of their feelings with soft words and with every touch.

Later, they showered off the dirt and the residue of their lovemaking. After they were finished, wrapped in terry robes, they ordered room service.

Josh and Haylee nibbled on hors d'oeuvres while sipping on champagne. Haylee smiled, holding out her left hand, admiring the ring that encircled her third finger.

Haylee raised her glass. "To Josh, my husband," she began, "Your love makes me brave, and it makes feel like I can do things that I didn't think I could. We've been through difficult times already, and we have more ahead of us. But if we handle it the way we've handled everything else, then I think that we're going to be fine..."

Josh reached over, squeezing her free hand. He tugged her toward him, Haylee held up a hand. "Stay put," she said. Taking another sip, she continued, "I'm going to make love to you now. And you are going to do exactly as I say."

Josh's Adam's apple moved up and down when he swallowed. He nodded, never breaking eye contact.

Haylee led him to the spa-like bathtub. Stepping inside, she lowered herself to her knees. Starting the water, she let it run until it reached the temperature she liked. Plugging the drain, Haylee returned her attention to her husband. Getting more comfortable, she pulled a foot into her lap, beginning to massage the bottomed of his foot.

Josh sat on the tub's edge, leaning against the wall. He smiled, watched and waited.

Taking another sip of her drink, Haylee set it aside. Raising up, she leaned in to kiss him.

Josh groaned when he tasted remnants of the sweet wine on her tongue.

Retreating into the warm water, Haylee smiled. She bit her lower lip while tipping massage oil into the palm of her hand. Sawing slick fingers between his toes, Haylee could see Josh watching her through half-closed eyes. He looked predatory, on the edge of losing patience. Gently she worked her way to his ankles, then his calves. Leaning close to his knee, she slid her teeth along the bony surface. Biting down, she pulled skin, applying steady pressure, stopping before it became painful.

Haylee moved to nibble the inside of his thigh. Josh twitched but refrained from touching her. He leaned back, letting his legs fall open.

When she would have continued to move upward, Josh stopped her. "Wait," he said, moving their champagne flutes. "If you keep on as you are, I'm going to break mine."

Setting them safely aside, Josh smiled, dropping a soft kiss on her lips. Then he leaned back so Haylee could continue where she left off. She set herself free to explore every inch of his firm swimmer's body. She enjoyed watching him squirm, listening to his sounds, feeling his skin react to her touch.

By the time Haylee finished, the large tub was full. When Josh slid in, he was frantic with need. Even as he used the water's buoyancy to satisfy his desires and enjoy the delights of his new wife, he imagined the things he would do while making love to Haylee in an Olympic-sized swimming pool.

Their bodies were sore when they climbed out, helping each other dry off. Haylee congratulated herself for not thinking about Norah, Spencer, or Serena. She felt her chest tighten when her worries returned. Darting quick glances at Josh, she wondered if he was having the same troubles.

Tucking themselves between the crisp white sheets, they found comfortable positions nestling against each other. They fell into a dreamless restorative, slumber.

❧64❧
GIFTS

BEING CAREFUL NOT TO disturb Haylee, Josh got out of bed early. Throwing on sweatpants, a t-shirt, and slipping bare feet into a pair of flip-flops, he went down to the lobby to make a phone call.

He had no complaints about his wedding night, but his concern about Spencer had started his day with another headache. He breathed a tremendous sigh of relief when he heard his brother's voice on the other end of the line.

"Josh? What is the matter with you? Why are you up so early? ...and checking on me? Even if your bride is demented, you should still be making it with her, starting in on phase two, man!"

For a moment, Josh didn't know how to respond. Finally, he grinned, "I will, but first I wanted to check on what was happening with Norah."

"Well... let's put it this way; she's different."

"Has she threatened you?"

"Not at all. When she went to bed, she cried off and on, said she wanted to be left alone. After 1:30 or so, she passed out. She was sleeping like the dead."

"This morning," Spencer continued, "she's been taking apart all the electronics in the house. She was starting on the phone when you called."

"Huh, why?"

"Don't know. She said that last night, Haylee took her to see a horse. Norah said that that should keep her hunting instinct appeased for a while. What's that all about?"

Josh let the line fall silent. He sighed, "It's the same thing I was explaining in the car yesterday. What happened to me, happened to the horse."

"Trippy."

"You can say that again. Did you ask her what she's doing with the gear?"

"She says she's trying to figure out if there's a power source available today that she can use to access data she collected."

"It doesn't sound malicious. Are you sure you don't feel threatened?

"Dude! She's four feet, ten inches and she probably weighs eighty pounds. How could she possibly threaten me?"

Right, thought Josh sarcastically, *how, indeed?* "If you're sure that you'll be alright for a while, we won't hurry home. Haylee's still asleep. We'll get everything sorted out when we get back."

"Go back to your woman."

⌘⌘⌘

Thinking about his little brother's advice, Josh smirked as he slipped back between the covers. The bed was still warm, Haylee was even warmer. He snuggled in, pulling her against him tightly. Wrapping an arm around her, he let his hand wander. He could tell the moment that she woke up.

She shifted, looking over at him. "Good morning, Joshua," Haylee said, holding a hand over her mouth.

He could hear the smile in her voice. He leaned in for a kiss, but she stopped him, "I have morning breath, I need to brush my teeth," she complained.

"I haven't brushed either, our stink will cancel each other out," he said as he pushed her hand aside. He leaned in to meet her lips. It quickly grew more serious as tongues engaged. Eager hands explored and touched.

Josh's ready manhood danced delicately around Haylee's core, teasing her. Wrapping her legs around his torso, she bid him to enter with urgent movements. When Josh couldn't stand it any longer, he arched his back, sliding in, sighing. Completely engulfed by her warm velvet folds, he held himself utterly still. Gazing down to savor the ecstatic look on her face he said, "I think we should start every morning this way."

Haylee couldn't stop herself from giggling. Unable to form words, she gave him a direct look, nodding in agreement.

He continued watching her as he began to move. He smiled, when she closed her eyes, losing herself in the pleasure he so freely gave. Deliberately taking his time, he let the tension between them build until their bodies were as tight as bows.

When release came, it was simultaneous. They cried out as their glistening bodies spasmed. Afterward, they fell back against the pillows, laughing because it felt like their bones had dissolved.

As they were getting dressed, Josh walked over beside Haylee. He pulled her hand out, dropping something into it.

"What's this?"

He smiled. "The necklace belonged to one of my great-aunts. There's a mustard seed in the center."

Haylee held up the tiny glass heart, peering inside.

"I wanted you to have this because the mustard seed represents hope, and things that will grow."

Touched, Haylee thanked him. She, dropped the necklace in his hand, turning around while lifting her hair.

After attaching the clasp, Josh leaned down, kissing the nape of her neck.

"I have something for you too," Haylee said facing him. She looked worried, "but I'm not sure what you'll think of it."

"One of the things I love about you is that you always surprise me."

Her smile was hesitant; she glanced away. "Last night, when I got back to the house with Norah, I went to check if the crystal was doing anything different."

"And...?"

"As I was holding it, it felt warm— I expected that. I was thinking about the Ceremony that I'll have to perform, and about how the crystal will be gone after that," Haylee paused. "The pendant we wear holds a shard of the larger crystal. It protects us. I thought that maybe I could break off another piece. I just... wanted you to have something to protect you in case..." she swallowed hard.

Josh would have closed the space between them, but Haylee shook her head, taking a step back. "I was holding it and thinking that I would have to hammer it, but then I had a sense that it *knew* what I wanted...that it agreed. It started getting hot; the edges went blurry. I don't know if it was in my head, but it seemed like it was turning from a solid to a liquid. I moved my hand, Josh, it wiggled like Jell-O. Then it solidified. And as it did, a little piece fell off." Haylee reached out, offering him a crystal fragment pinched between her fingers.

Josh's eyebrows shot up. He didn't know if he wanted to touch it. But the earnest expression on his wife's face and his curiosity had him holding out his hand. She released it in the center of his palm. Josh frowned, "It's causing a numbing sensation."

"Does it hurt?" Haylee asked.

Remembering the blast that she and Reece had gotten from it, Haylee had been apprehensive about what might happen when she handed it to Josh.

"No, it feels like jolts of energy are shooting up my arm."

"Do you not want it?"

Josh regarded her, frowning. "I love the sentiment, but I think we should put it someplace safe for now." He scanned the room. Finding the jewelry box from the mustard seed necklace, he tucked the crystal fragment into the velvet material, snapping the lid shut.

✥65✥
LIMITS

"MY BROTHER IS GOING to be pissed if we don't get this stuff cleaned up before they get here," Spencer warned.

"That does not make sense, Spencer. Why would components cause Dr. Herkowitz to urinate?"

Spencer slapped a hand on his thigh. "It was a figure of speech!"

"Speech does not have a shape unless you are viewing it in a digitized form." Norah hardly paid attention to Spencer. All her focus was on the VCR and removing the tape heads.

"Not the VCR!" Spencer pressed a hand against his forehead. "Are you going to be able to put that back together?"

This time Norah did look up, "Put it back? Why would I do that?"

"Why are you doing any of it?" Spencer raised is voice, exasperated.

"I explained already," Norah replied. "I'm going through this antiquated equipment to see if there's anything I can use to access the data stored in my Second Skin."

Norah got up to follow him into the kitchen, "I told you I'm on a mission. I came to find Haylee and your brother. They have something that I need. Once they give it to me, I'll return home. On my way here, I captured some new information. Dr. Herkowitz is going to want to find out what it is."

Spencer rummaged around in the refrigerator. Pulling out a bottle, he went to a drawer, searching for an opener. "Why do you keep calling Josh, Doctor?"

"Because that is how I have always known him."

"You met for the first time yesterday. How could you have *always* known him?" Spencer slapped the heel of his hand on his forehead, "That's right, I forgot, Josh said that you are a time traveler. So, you're saying you know my brother from the future?"

Norah shook her head. "Not personally. Where I live, all of you are dead. Dr. Herkowitz left a legacy of data he gathered about Travelers. I have been studying it since I was identified. I believe, if we can access the information in my Second Skin, we will gain previously unknown information. My time here is limited, I cannot waste it."

Spencer stared at Norah like she'd grown a second head.

She studied him in silence, then nodded as if she thought his lack of response indicated that he understood. She walked briskly back to her pile of parts. Once there, Norah spotted a stack of VCR tapes. She picked one up and read the jacket, 'Splash with Tom Hanks and Daryl Hannah.' Chuckling at the image, she removed the tape from its sleeve. She looked like she was fighting to hold it still. But then her mouth opened. She shoved the tape inside. Clamping down, she sucked in air making a horrible racket.

"S-t-o-p doing that!" Spencer yelled, stomping toward her.

❧66❧
NORAH

WHEN THE DOOR TO the apartment opened, Norah looked up in surprise. With shame written on her face, she slowly removed Splash from her mouth, spitting out pieces of broken plastic.

Haylee and Josh surveyed the wreckage in dismay. Haylee drew in a breath. She covered her mouth, "Oh!"

All of Josh's moving boxes were open. Piles of clothes lay in heaps, books were scattered everywhere. The dismantled TV and VCR components littered the surface of the coffee table. Kitchen appliances were in pieces in the center of their living room.

Norah didn't take her eyes off Haylee and Josh. Slowly she got to her feet, brushing bits of plastic and wire from her clothes. She glanced behind her to give Spencer a pleading look.

He responded by raising his beer bottle and shaking his head.

Closing her eyes, Norah took a steadying breath. She turned to face the couple, "I can see that I have made a grievous error. Spencer attempted to alert me that

you would be annoyed, but I was so busy attempting to solve a problem that his warning went unheeded."

Norah bowed as she had done yesterday, "It is an honor to greet you formally as married people."

Josh and Haylee shared a silent question between them. Haylee spoke, "Thank you, Norah. We have a lot to talk about," her eyes met Spencer's across the room, "but before you destroy another thing in my house, maybe you should explain what you are doing?"

Norah stood ramrod straight like she was under interrogation, "I have been searching for compatible electronics and power sources to extract new information from my Second Skin."

Haylee looked perplexed.

⤙⤚

Josh puffed air out of his mouth while running a hand through his hair. "I have a feeling this is going to take a while. We might as well make ourselves comfortable. Threading his way through the debris, he stopped when he spotted his childhood cassette tape recorder laying open, guts exposed. Making a plaintive noise in his throat, he leaned over, picking it up. He carried it with him to the kitchen table.

Josh stopped short when he saw that the kitchen table was in a similar condition. "Not my stereo system!" he exploded.

Spencer, who followed him in, commented, "I tried to tell you on the phone."

"Yes, but you failed to tell me how *much*." Josh's voice dripped with irony.

Wiggling his eyebrows, Spencer nodded, "Right, but you wouldn't have wanted your time with Haylee cut short, would you?"

Seeing his brother's reaction, Spencer capitulated. He walked over to Josh, putting a consoling hand on his shoulder, "Can I get you a beer?"

Josh sighed, "Please."

As the boys went into the kitchen, Haylee noticed the crestfallen look on Norah's face. "It will be alright," she said. "We weren't expecting to walk in to all this." Haylee waved her hand around.

"I was attempting to be efficient. Efficiency and thoroughness are desirable work traits." Norah began blinking rapidly, "I wanted to impress you with what I know.... but all I seem to do here is make mistakes and.... cry."

Haylee approached her carefully, reaching out to rub her arm. "It really will be alright," she soothed. "You've already accomplished something significant, you found me."

Norah nodded, covering her face with her hands. Through muffled sobs, she said, "Could you do what you did last night?"

"What did I do?"

"You.... you.... brought me next to you."

Haylee sighed, gathering Norah close, "It's called a hug." Haylee rocked her from side to side, "Don't they do this in your time?"

Norah shook her head, "I've seen pictures—" Norah rubbed her fingers over her eyes.

"How long have you been here?"

"Four days, six hours....and," Norah looked around for a clock, "approximately fourteen minutes. That is factoring in the inconsistency of individually operated timepieces that are improperly synced with the Atomic Universal Time clock. Of course, if I still had access to my net, I could provide a more detailed time measurement down to seconds, milliseconds, centiseconds, and...."

Haylee held up a hand, "Stop. That's too much." Keeping one arm over the girl's shoulder, she ushered her toward the kitchen table. It was clear now. "Has Spencer given you anything to eat?" Haylee asked.

"I beg your pardon, sister-in-law," Spencer retorted. "You won't be getting complaints about my hosting abilities. Norah had scrambled eggs and toast for breakfast. Although, I strongly recommend not asking about 'nutrients' and how she is accustomed to consuming them."

Spencer went back to the refrigerator, retrieving a fresh bottle. "Haylee, can I get you anything? Coffee, beer?"

Making a face, Haylee shot her husband a questioning look.

"Spence," Josh spoke up. "We can take this from here if you need to be someplace else."

"Hell no!" he responded cheerfully. "You have been the straight-and-narrow guy I've trailed behind my entire life. And here you are, up to your eyeballs in some strange shit. I'm not vacating my front row seat to this sideshow."

"Jerk," said Josh.

Sending a fist pump in the air, Spencer grinned, "Love you too, bro."

❧

Haylee, Josh, and Spencer learned to cue Norah when it was time to stop giving so much information as she regaled them with her escapades since her arrival.

Haylee observed Norah while she spoke. Her fingers were spindly, her nose was pointy, and her skin looked like it had rarely seen the sun. Norah spoke strangely too; unemotional, machine-like. Haylee returned her attention to the conversation.

Josh was leaning forward, actively listening, taking notes.

Norah took a deep breath, enunciating clearly. "Where I come from the net is within us and in every material aspect of our habitat."

"What's the net?" Spencer asked.

She hesitated, turning her face away, blinking. "Apologies," Norah stated, "I failed to consult my timeline before commencing the conversation. The technology to which I am referring hasn't been created yet. A net is a knowledge base, available everywhere, 24/7. "

"At the turn of the century," Norah continued, "the twenty-first century," she clarified, "small devices were used to access it. Eventually, its use became seamless; devices were no longer necessary. The clothing I wear accesses it. During my travel event, my Second Skin collected something beyond its specifications. When I awoke, my optical sensor alerted me to the anomaly."

Haylee and Spencer glanced at each other, perplexed. Josh, however, was acting like he discoursed with time travelers daily.

"But the sensors couldn't translate the information?" he asked.

Norah shook her head, "Unfortunately, no."

Haylee watched Josh's face. He was like a bloodhound on the scent of a trail. The quest for understanding gave him purpose.

"If I understand what you're saying, there's been a lot of historical information gathered between Haylee's time and yours. When is that?" he wanted to know.

Josh turned green when he heard Norah's reply. "There is a large body of information about Travelers and my ancestors. But it is also information about your family too, Dr. Herkowitz."

"Mine?"

"Of course, you are the father of Traveler studies." Norah nodded enthusiastically.

"Every offspring since Serena has been tested and observed. There was nothing more to be learned until now, Dr. Herkowitz! The information contained in my Second Skin could be radical!"

"What!" Haylee stood up; her complexion had gone pale. "You're saying my daughter was used as a test subject?"

❧67❧
SECOND SKIN

JOSH AND SPENCER WERE inspecting the material. They had been astounded to see Norah remove what looked like a lump of insulation from her backpack. Formless and colorless, it smoothed flat under her hands like tiny magnet fragments knitting themselves together.

"It's so thin and lightweight," Spencer rubbed it between his fingers. "Is it changing colors as I move?

Josh glanced at Haylee who was watching from across the room. "How is it worn?" he asked, "There are no holes or seams."

"I will demonstrate," Norah responded cheerfully. She began removing her clothes.

"Wait! What are you doing?" Josh's voice raised in alarm.

Not pausing, Norah continued undressing, "It's called a Second Skin because it must come in contact with the surfaces of the skin," she stated. Her tone was matter-of-fact.

Completely nude, Norah went about her activities oblivious to the stunned silence around her.

Fascination soon had Josh too enthralled to be abashed. Aside from eyebrows, eyelashes and the hair on her head, Norah had no hair anywhere else. Her limbs were well formed, the muscle tone looked healthy, but her torso was another story. Glances of worry, bordering on alarm passed between the brothers and Haylee.

The region where genitalia should have been was as blank as a hard-plastic Barbie doll. Her chest was as flat and smooth. Nipples were absent. When Norah bent down to begin applying the Second Skin, they saw irregular, box-like shapes at the base of her neck.

Norah started at her ankles, smoothing the material around her calves. As her hands moved, it adhered to her skin like plastic wrap on a hot dish. It split between her legs, covering completely. She continued over her stomach, chest, and arms. "See?" Norah turned around. "I might still have some residual energy to demonstrate one of its features." Looking up toward the ceiling, Norah blinked. "There's not much there...but...I think I can get it..." she blinked again rapidly.

A collective sigh went up when it looked like she disappeared except for her head, hands, and feet.

"Impressive, isn't it?" Norah smiled proudly. "Reflecting everything in the area, t creates an illusion of invisibility."

Haylee came forward, walking in a circle around Norah. "When do you use it?"

"When we are playing games, in virtual worlds, and sometimes during group educational periods." Norah glanced to the side, blinking again. The Second Skin turned to a solid bright turquoise. "This is how I dress most often. I use colors to express my goals for the day or in meetings if I need to make a point."

"That would get my attention," Spencer commented.

"Mine as well…" Josh agreed. "And this, "he pointed at her while moving his finger up and down, "is what contains the data that you are so adamant to access?"

"Exactly," Norah grinned.

Josh took off his glasses. He scratched his scalp while shaking his head. "Can someone else wear it?"

"No," she shook her head, "it's calibrated specifically to my physiology and neural sequencing. A Second Skin is as unique as a fingerprint."

Frowning, Spencer stroked his chin. "And you thought that you'd be able to find something in all of this, "he waved his hand over the boxes overflowing with the parts she'd disassembled, "that would give that thing some extra juice?"

"Juice?" Norah cocked her head.

Slouching, Spencer shook his head, "Here we go again… power, energy, voltage?"

"I calculated the probability of that to be—"

"Spare me!" Spencer held up a hand. "Can you describe the characteristics of the type of power that you need?"

"I believe I can," Norah replied.

Josh massaged the heels of his hands into his eyes as he listened to Norah talk. He was worried about Haylee. She'd been acting 'off' since Norah's comment about tests on Serena. Their night of little sleep was catching up with him.

"I know someone on campus who might be able to help us." Spencer broke into Josh's contemplation.

"Who?"

"Professor Winton."

"In Astrophysics?"

Spencer nodded.

"It's worth a shot. I think I heard in inter-department faculty meeting that she's scheduled to go on sabbatical sometime soon."

"Let's go over there now. See if we can catch her before she leaves for the day."

"You'll be taking Norah with you?" Haylee broke into the conversation.

Josh and Spencer looked at each other, shrugging their shoulders. Norah answered for them, "They wouldn't be able to make correct inquiries without me."

"I need to remind everyone…" Haylee looked between Spencer and Josh, "that regardless of whether Norah's got something up her suit, there is a time limit for how long she can stay."

Josh's head snapped up; He looked at Haylee sharply.

Nodding, Haylee left the room. Over her shoulder, she said, "I'll get Norah some clothes. She can't go out in that, the punk look has got to go."

Norah looked hurt, "Is this not the height of fashion?"

Spencer shrugged, "Maybe in New York. In California, we're more laid back. I dated a chick once who wore a cape, army boots, and piercings in unusual places."

"Chicks and piercings? I do not understand," Norah responded.

Giving his brother a thin-lipped smile, Josh raised his eyebrows, "You dug yourself into that one… Excuse me," Josh said before following Haylee.

❦

Haylee was opening drawers forcefully, pawing through contents, when Josh came in.

"What was that?"

"What do you mean?" she paused, sending him a stony stare.

"You know what I mean; the time limit. We don't have anything in our records about that."

"Well, Josh, Norah's not the only one who's got *new* information!" Haylee stomped to her closet, rooting through her dress collection. Locating a 'shorty,' she pulled it out. She went to deliver it to Norah. Josh followed.

"You can use the bathroom to get changed," Josh directed Norah who was looking surprised and uncomfortable.

Haylee turned without saying a word, returning to her bedroom, slamming the door.

Josh didn't let that stop him; he went in. "You can't be mad at me for something I haven't done."

"But you *will*! I thought I could trust you. I thought Serena would be safe with you!"

He stepped forward, grasping her upper arms, "You can, and she will!"

"No! Everything I thought was wrong! The father of Time Traveler Studies means that you only married me so that you can study me! Norah said that you did *experiments* on my daughter!"

"She did not say that, she said tests. And nothing has happened!"

"Tests, experiments what's the difference?" Haylee yelled.

Josh dropped his arms, stepping away. "Haylee," he said in a quieter tone, "if you remembered something else, we should record it."

"I'm not talking to you."

"Sweetheart, you've been inside my head.... or rather, I've been inside yours...you know how I feel about you. You know that I'd never hurt Serena."

Haylee remained unmoved.

"Who's to say that the future is fixed?"

"You better go," she turned her back to him.

⸜⸝

No one said anything until they arrived on campus. Norah perked up when she saw the buildings and the students. "This is where you work, Dr. Herkowitz?"

"Shhhh," Josh admonished, "don't call me that here. I don't have a doctorate degree; I'm not entitled to that designation. Call me Josh, or Mr. Herkowitz."

Norah nodded. She turned to Spencer, "Are the emotionally charged exchanges common?"

He exchanged a perplexed look with his brother. Sighing heavily before replying, Spencer said, "I wouldn't say it's common, but it's not uncommon either. You touched a nerve in Haylee, Norah. You made her question two of the things she loves most."

"I did? What nerve?"

"You made it sound like her daughter might be in danger and you shook her faith in her husband."

Josh, walking beside Spencer, dropped a hand on his shoulder, giving it a squeeze.

⚜68⚜
DRAGONFLIES

AFTER THEY WERE GONE, Haylee wandered around the apartment rubbing her hands along her upper arms. She picked up more of the electronic parts, putting them into boxes. She folded blankets and got out a third set of fresh sheets and a pillow.

Once everything felt like it was back into some order, she walked out onto her back steps, sitting down. She desperately wished that she could call home and talk to Serena, but Glori or her dad would know that something was wrong.

Haylee thought about Norah instead. *That girl is odd. She has no knowledge of animals; she didn't know about hugs and her body...* Haylee shuddered.

Haylee lifted her face, welcoming the breeze. It carried the taste of salt from the Bay. She closed her eyes, listening to birdsong and the constant low roar of the freeway in the distance. Haylee began to hum. Hearing snapping sounds, she opened her eyes to see three dragonflies hovering about four feet away. As she continued, more came, until there were too many to count. Stretching out her arms, a few landed, their tiny feet tickling. Haylee smiled. She noticed that their presence made her feel calmer, better able to focus. They hung around for a little while, then, as if by consensus, darted away.

Last night, they came when she didn't know what to do. Tonight, she was unsettled. Both times they arrived, they brought something she needed. In her work with animals, Haylee had never considered communicating with insects. It wasn't like dealing with a single mind, or even hundreds of tiny minds. It felt like an intelligence that was larger than the creatures.

Suddenly a loud, brash, heavily accented voice broke into her thoughts, *It is part of your Traveler heritage, you Ninny. Don't you know that you are an animal caller?*

Haylee stood up. Her peaceful mood exploded like a can of soda hit during target practice. She looked left and right; no one was there. Her heart beat quickly, her hands felt clammy. Only one person had ever called her that—"Emis?"

The voice responded, *Of course. Who else?*

"But your....?"

Dead?

"Aren't you? Reece and I watched you..."

Drown?

"Yes."

I thought I'd be gone once I forced you to harvest me. My petit trip to the bottom of Yerba Buena Cove was supposed to guarantee it.

"Have you been conscious inside of me all this time?"

No... the voice sounded confused. *I woke up just now when the dragonflies landed on you.*

"I don't understand," said Haylee

That makes two of us.

❦

Not for the first time, Josh wondered if the future was altered by what the Travelers did. Norah had told them more about his work. It went far beyond the project he only recently started. Part of him was intrigued by this, another part was worried.

Did Norah know the date of Haylee's death? That, alone, would answer many questions. Josh's stomach clenched at the thought.

He watched Norah, Spencer, and Dr. Ramona Winton in an animated discussion. They'd told Ramona that Norah was a visiting student from Iceland who had connections to grant funders interested in power source applications to astrophysics. Aside from journal publication, the smell of grant money usually opened floodgates of information sharing.

Josh was having a difficult time staying focused. He wanted to get back to Haylee to straighten things out. But he couldn't leave Spencer, and he certainly couldn't leave Norah!

"We don't need to understand how it is powered," Josh heard Ramona saying. "Since you say that you already know that, the question that we need to be asking is what were the conditions that existed to record the information in the first place?"

Josh nodded slowly, mulling over the statement. If someone living in the 1800s was given the task of listening to an eight-track tape, could they? Was it possible to recreate the conditions that existed when Norah made the time jump?

Dr. Winton agreed to help them if they'd help her on a similar project.

On the way home, Josh and Spencer talked in hushed tones about her proposal. Ramona thought she knew a way to generate the kind of energy that Norah needed, but to do that, they'd have to visit the Grand Coulee Dam in Washington state.

It was late when they returned to Haylee's neighborhood. They had to walk several blocks since the close parking spaces were occupied. With shoulders drooping, their steps were slow. Spencer rubbed his eyes; Josh couldn't keep himself from yawning. Norah's movements were sluggish like the other two, but she tapped her fingertips incessantly along her collarbone. Every thirty seconds, she jerked as if she put a finger into a light socket.

Spencer heard his brother's intake of breath, saw his eyes narrow.

"Norah!" Josh exclaimed.

She jumped at the suddenness, "What?"

"What are you doing with your neck?"

"This?" her tapping increased. "If I were wearing my Second Skin, it would send impulses to my nervous system to maintain a wakeful equilibrium. I am attempting to stimulate manually."

"Is it working?" Spencer asked, his eyebrows raised.

"Not as efficiently as the Skin would do, but, yes."

Josh and Spencer shared a mystified glance. Experimentally, they started tapping their necks.

There was a low light left on in the living room. The apartment was quiet. Haylee had straightened most of the mess. Josh saw the additional stack of folded sheets, topped by a pillow, sitting on the coffee table. He compressed his mouth into a grim line.

Before the others noticed, he scooped it up, going to deposit it in the linen closet.

As Josh watched Spencer arranging his sleeping area on the couch and Norah doing the same in Serena's empty room, his brow wrinkled, he fought the urge to bite on a thumbnail.

Saying his, 'good nights,' Josh went down the hall to the bedroom. Over-tired and unhappy with his wife's assumptions, he didn't try to be quiet when he undressed. The bed squeaked when he sat down; his shoes thumped on the floor where he tossed them. Stretching his arms over his head, yawning loudly, he glanced over his shoulder. Haylee hadn't moved a muscle.

Sighing, he climbed under the covers. Reaching for his wife, he pulled her against him. When he felt her muscles tense, he whispered, "I'm holding onto you whether you like or not."

"Passeur sur le corps..." she muttered.

Huh? Josh wondered. Haylee had been listening to French language tapes since he'd first brought up the possibility going to live there. He'd never heard her attempt to speak it.

He settled down beside her hoping that tomorrow would be a better day.

It was just as well that he was unaware that the phrase she'd spoken in her sleep meant, 'over my dead body.'

Part Four

SAVING & BORROWING

ஃ69ஃ
PILLOW PUNCHING

SPENCER WAS SNORING WHEN he was disturbed by a light touch on his shoulder. Groaning, he shifted position, moving away.

"Spencer, are you alright?" came a whispery voice.

With his eyes still closed, he smiled pleasantly, mumbling, "Frankie-manda."

"I see the muscles of your face twitching, why are you not responding?"

"Huh?" Spencer's eyes flew open. He sat up suddenly. Disoriented he glanced around, wondering why he was awake.

A light turned on. Spencer made a sound of annoyance. His squinted, instinctively raising a hand to block the brightness.

"There," soothed Norah, "I knew that you could not be sleeping. What was that noise you were making? Were you attempting to crib? If you were, you were not doing it right."

"No," Spencer responded, struggling to order his thoughts. He eyed the clock. It was 2:15 a.m. "I was probably snoring."

She smiled, "Can I get you something to drink?"

Spencer didn't want a drink. He ignored the urge to burrow back under his covers. Norah looked like she needed to talk. "Sure," he sighed, "water?"

He was scratching his stubble when she returned. Spencer repositioned his blankets so Norah would have room to sit.

Speaking in hushed tones, she asked, "Who is Frankie-manda?"

"Huh?" Spencer frowned.

"Frankie-manda," Norah repeated. "Did I mispronounce it?"

"Ahhh," he hesitated, stroking down the sides of his chin with a thumb and forefinger, "it's two names mashed together."

"I see," Norah nodded, but she clearly did not.

"I thought you were my girlfriend. I was confused who currently occupies that position, Frankie or Amanda."

"You have two?"

"Not usually....at least not at the same time," Spencer's mouth quirked.

"Are they identical?"

Spencer huffed, "Not at all, why?"

"If you cannot distinguish between them, I thought perhaps they were identical clones."

"Do you have many of those where you come from?"

"Yes, of course."

"Of course? Why?"

"Labor classes," Norah replied. "Once genetics perfectly suited for certain jobs was identified, vacancies were filled by those replicants."

Spencer pulled a face. "So... every plumber is either Bob or a clone of Bob?"

"Exactly," Norah nodded, satisfied. "Each successive clone has an extension number, showing his or her replacement date. In consideration of their self-image, the numbers aren't visible. But, they are identical in every other way."

"We must seem so strange to you," Spencer reflected.

"You are!" Norah sighed.

They sat in silence for a while until Spencer piped up again. "Have we colonized other planets?"

Norah shook her head. "No. After the climate collapse, humanities' goals focused on survival, preservation, and planetary repair. When I see the biodiversity, the open spaces, and the breathable surface air of your world— it doesn't seem like we inhabit the same planet." Norah fell quiet for a few moments, then she said, "I can see why my ancestors made the choices that they did."

"Which choices?"

"Bioengineering. Humans needed to fit into smaller spaces— use fewer resources. Everyone is the same height and weight. This keeps our living pods in balance."

Spencer's unfocused gaze went toward the far end of the room. "How does that work?"

"Reproduction has strict engineering standards. Many laws govern it."

He frowned, "That doesn't sound spontaneous, or strenuous...or fun."

Norah gave him a squeamish look, "It's not!"

Spencer crossed his arms. He glanced sideways at her. "Do you feel regret after you've....?" He raised a hand, wiggling his fingers.

"I didn't until I came here."

"How many were there before that?"

"Eight. The Institute referrers to them as volunteers. Most of them lived for two centuries or more. They were plenipotentiaries and were slated for expiration. All of them elected to donate themselves for study."

"'Expiration' sounds like a product label."

"Expiration," Norah explained, "is the process by which living functions of the body are stopped."

"Holy shit," Spencer muttered. He was silent for a time, then, "Can I see?"

"My webs?"

Clenching his jaw, he leaned back nodding.

"Certainly," Norah said. Standing up, moving to the center of the room, she swung her arms out, throwing her fingers wide.

The sound Spencer heard reminded him of a sail catching wind. He'd prepared himself, he thought, for what he was about to see.

Norah approached, her hands stretched wide. Fine webbing, alive and pulsing, filled the spaces between her fingers.

Spencer's eyes bulged. He scooted away.

Norah stopped, cocking her head. "The need to feed has been satisfied. I am not a threat, right now." Norah walked to the lamp, holding her hands beneath the shade so that the webs illuminated. "At the Institute," she said, "they recorded many images of these. They took tissue samples. They never successfully identified an animal species that they related to..."

"Really?" Spencer stood. He cautiously came forward to look.

Norah made a sudden move, flipping her webs away.

Spencer jumped and stumbled, falling on his butt.

Norah giggled, then grabbed a cork coaster. Shoving it in her mouth, she clamped down hard. Sucking inward, her neck muscles expanded, her lashes fluttered, the whites of her eyes showed. Letting her breath and the coaster go, Norah sighed, flopping onto the couch.

"Did you know, Spencer," she said, there was a dreamy quality to her voice, "that animals are jubilant from the inside out? Echo, carried memories from when he was a foal. When he was leaping and running, holding his tail up so it flapped behind him, he was consumed with happiness. His relationship to the soil, grass, and others in his team was vigorous, playful."

Norah turned toward him. Shadows of sadness lurked in her eyes, "His well-being was a direct result of his human caretakers. His joy was squashed when he was sold to someone who ignored his feet and hit him when he couldn't walk fast enough."

"I'm sorry to say that there are a lot of people in this world who shouldn't be animal owners," Spencer responded.

Norah nodded. "Echo's pain hurts my heart, Spencer."

"Mine too."

"Even though—" Norah continued thoughtfully, "I'm glad to know him, Echo the horse. I'd seen pictures of horses, read about them, seen them in vids. But seeing one, alive, *knowing* him is different." Norah yawned, covering her mouth with her delicate hand.

Norah stood, "I must return to my inferior sleeping unit. Good night, Spencer."

"Night, Nor."

"I'm so sorry that horses did not survive the collapse," she called softly from her room, "I wish the bioengineers could have made them small too."

Spencer felt his throat constrict. He punched his pillow forcefully, then pummeled it. Passing the back of his hand under his nose, catching the drip, he wiped the wetness it on his blanket.

"Bob clones? Tiny horses, breathable air and surface repair? What the....?"

It was a very long time before Spencer returned to sleep.

❧70❧
FALL FESTIVAL

ON THE DRIVE TO Garrett farm, Ramona told them about the Grand Coulee Dam. It is the largest capacity hydropower producer in the country. It's the fourth largest in the world. Construction began in the 1930's. Most of the original equipment is still in use. Energy managers have been planning an overhaul project. It is in the beginning stages. Large-scale equipment is being decommissioned while newer models are installed.

The five of them would gain access to the site as contractors in disguise.

⚬⚬⚬

Eugene completed the last items on Glori's 'to-do' list for tidying up the barn. The place looked ready. It smelled fresh too. Straw-covered the floor. Hay bales, topped with brightly colored plaid blankets, were arranged in conversation-friendly groupings. Pumpkins decorated with ribbons and cinnamon sticks framed them like bookends.

His shop area was as clean as a kitchen. A colorful tablecloth covered his work table, and a makeshift bar had been constructed to serve cider, hot chocolate, and baked goods. Barrels and baskets of root vegetables, nuts, apples, pomegranates, and pears occupied an area. Preserves, salsa, and jams were arranged on shelves and tables.

The front yard, over at the house, was in a similar state. Cornstalk bundles framed a children's game and activity area, the photo booth, and the art and craft tables.

It was still early; the place wouldn't be over-run with people for another couple of hours. Gene took a moment to go into the pig pen to greet the star of the show, Hanna. All twenty-five pounds of her trotted toward him with confidence. Balancing on her two front feet came naturally to her now. Gene had gotten used to her, so much so, that he *almost* forgot that she wasn't like her nine other siblings.

Hannah and her brothers and sisters hollered at him. He didn't have his daughter's ability to tell them that breakfast was late because they were about to have an all-day feast. Instead, he had to console them with gentle, reassuring tones and scratches behind the ears.

Since Haylee's last visit, the farm had undergone a metamorphosis. A journalist from one of Glori's favorite magazines found out about their pig. An article with a double page spread introduced Hanna, 'A Balanced Squealer' to her public. People started dropping by for a look. Newspapers and journalists called for interviews.

Attending to unannounced visitors began to undermine the maintenance of the farm. Gene balked at the distractions. He didn't care for the headaches involved with curiosity seeker interactions.

Glori had been struggling over whether to return to work full-time. Neither of them wanted to put Byron in daycare.

Hanna's sudden popularity made Glori's decision easy. She'd taken a long-term leave from the hospital, turning her managerial skills to the farm's public relations. Even with that move, demand was more than Glori could manage. They hired a local college student to work as a nanny. It turned out that, in addition to being great with Byron, Ashley was a whiz at pulling people together. She'd contacted his farmer cohorts, their wives, local artisans, and bakers to help Glori turn the place into a tourist destination.

It was Glori and Ashley's idea to go one step further to create a circus...or what they called a Fall Harvest Festival. Gene smiled, their finances were solidly in the black. They had started drawing up plans to build a new house at the far end of the property. The old home would be remodeled to serve its revised 'tourist' function.

Eugene didn't think the bonanza would continue indefinitely. Like most farmers, he'd learned to enjoy the good harvests, but he also maintained reserves for lean times. Glori and Ashley had opened his mind to new possibilities. He liked that they involved stewardship and food cultivation. Doris would have liked that too.

He'd been watching his friends retire, parceling out farms to developers. His stomach knotted when he thought about the disappearing open spaces, aquifers covered over, habitats destroyed, and healthy soils smothered by suburbs.

He hadn't been surprised that Haylee stayed in Berkeley. The complex and varied situations with pet owners were more interesting than animal husbandry, plus those creatures weren't destined to end up on someone's plate. Somehow Haylee missed inheriting the connection to the land that her parents shared. If Haylee was going to.... Gene shook his head not wanting to think the words. Marrying Josh was right, *he's a good man.* It gave Gene a measure of peace knowing that Josh would be there for his daughter.

"Eug— e— ne!" he heard Glori calling. He looked at the time. Giving final pats and scratches to the pigs, he hightailed it back to the house. He promised Glori that he'd get cleaned up at least a half an hour before the gates opened so that the photographer had time to take family portraits.

❧⟡❧

Gene, Glori and the kids were grouped in front of a bank of corn stalks, smiling, while the flashes popped.

A car-full of people arrived in the parking area. "Don't move!" Ashley called out. "They ignored the 'closed' signs," she muttered in irritation, "I'll head them off till it's opening time." The tall, slim brunette trotted away.

The photographer sat Byron and Serena on top of a hay bale with Glori and Gene standing in the background.

Gene kept glancing in the direction of the parking lot. He saw two tall men, two women and a child get out. He leaned over to whisper in Glori's ear, "It's Haylee and Josh with a few more people."

Glori seemed tense, "Did she tell you she was coming this morning?"

"No," Gene grinned, shaking his head. Leaning over, he placed a warm kiss on Glori's lips. He could feel her relaxing, leaning into him.

"That's great!" chimed the photographer. His lights flashed.

❧⟡❧

"Hey, you two!" Haylee laughed entering the front yard. "I can't believe what you've done with the place!"

The sounds of a joyous reunion came from the group as they greeted one another with hugs and smiles. They introduced Spencer, Ramona, and Norah. Gene and Glori invited everyone to join them in the photos.

Ashley and Ramona hung back, looking uncomfortable. "Come on, you two," said Glori.

"But Glori, these are *family* portraits," Ashley stated.

"Are you kidding?" she replied, "after all the work we've been doing, you are family! Get in here... you too, Ramona."

When the photographer heard that Haylee and Josh were newlyweds and that they'd had an informal ceremony, he asked if he could spend time photographing them. Everyone, except Haylee and Josh, was delighted that he'd thought of it.

Gene and Glori noticed the stiffness between the couple. Apparently, the photographer did too, "For only being married two days, you two are behaving like you've entered an arranged marriage. You do like each other, don't you?" he chided.

"Of course, we do," said Josh looking embarrassed.

"Well...." He approached, squatting down in front of them. He spoke quietly, placing a block under Josh's foot, moved Haylee's elbow onto her husband's knee and arranged their hands so that their wedding rings showed. "Trust that whatever it is, it will work itself out. Contrary to what Mr. Disney promotes, happily-ever-after relationships are a myth. What keeps a marriage strong is coming back to what brought you together in the first place. Just for these next few minutes," he continued, tilting Haylee's head toward Josh, and his toward her, "I want you to imagine what your life would be like if today were the last day you had together."

Backing up to view his posing, the photographer nodded, then hurried back to his camera.

Eugene watched as silent communication occurred between his daughter and son-in-law. They didn't stay the way the photographer put them. With a rueful look, Haylee told Josh she was sorry. She closed her eyes, leaning her forehead against the side of his face.

Josh raised a hand, cupping her cheek. Closing his own eyes, he leaned against her wearing an expression of intense relief.

"That works! Good job you two," the photographer commented.

❦

When the group disassembled to open the gates, Eugene watched Haylee lead the strange girl, Norah, and Ramona to the barn to see the pigs.

He overheard Josh and Spencer, as they talked on the front porch. "You haven't been yourself this morning," Josh commented. "Is there anything I should know?"

Spencer didn't answer; his eyes were tracking Ashley. Josh lightly punched him on the arm, "Will you get your head out of your pants for one minute?"

"Sorry," Spencer replied, shaking himself, shifting focus. With a sigh, he said, "You don't have to be so concerned. She showed me her webs last night."

Eugene's mouth went dry; he felt the blood rushing to his feet, leaning back against the wall of the house for support. He watched Josh's response match his own.

Josh's eyes opened double wide, Spencer clamped down on him, continuing to talk before Josh could react further. "I asked her to. I understand, now, why you're worried about them," he said urgently.

"Big mistake!" Josh's voice sounded constrained.

"Relax, bro," Spencer soothed, "I've got at least a hundred pounds on her. I'm sure I can handle her if she goes berserk."

When Josh opened his mouth to speak, Spencer stopped him. "That's not the bur up my tail."

Josh raised his eyebrows.

"I just wanted to confirm that Norah's from here?" Spencer stated, pointing at the ground between his feet, "Not from some planet in a galaxy far, far away?"

"Yes," Josh nodded, "she's from here."

"That blows," Spencer said. His tone was heavy-hearted.

❦71❦
TISSUE REPAIR

GLORI WENT TO GREET the booth vendors.

When she was out of earshot, Eugene shouted, "There's more of them! And you brought it here," his chest heaved, his hands clenched, "near my son, my wife, and my granddaughter!" He looked like a crazed bull ready to charge.

Josh and Spencer shared a startled look. They jumped up, each grabbing one of Eugene's arms, pinning him against the house. "Hold on, Gene!" Josh entreated. "She's under control!"

Turning on him, Gene's face contorted, spittle flew from his mouth, "You and Glori were taken out for a year! We can't risk it happening again!"

"What is it you want to do?"

"I don't know!"

"Do you think Haylee would have brought her here if she thought Norah was a danger?"

"Josh—" Eugene's eyes bugged, "Haylee *thought* she could control herself! *You* know how that turned out."

"Mr. Garrett," Spencer tried reasoning, "Norah's not very strong. Haylee's already stopped her once. We're keeping close tabs on her, she's not near the children, and we'll be taking her away from here within the hour."

Eugene glanced across the yard to where Byron and Serena were playing. His eyes moved to find Glori. Haylee and that girl were nowhere in sight. His breathing slowed. Shaking off the Herkowitz boys, he swiped a hand over his face.

"Tell me why you brought her here," he sounded resigned.

"We're going on a road trip," Josh started. "There's something that Norah got when she jumped through time that Dr. Winton thinks she can help us retrieve."

Eugene eyed Josh silently. "I thought Haylee said that Travelers come for the crystal. She didn't say anything about this..."

"I know," Josh pushed his glasses up on his nose, "this is something new. We don't know if it will work, but we're going to give it a shot."

"...and you think whatever it is, is worth the risk of keeping her around?"

Both boys nodded.

Crunching gravel alerted them that they had company. Haylee rounded the corner, stopping short when she saw them.

"What have I missed?" she asked.

"Where's that girl?" Gene burst out.

Haylee jerked at his tone, "She's with Ramona."

Josh exchanged a look with Spencer. Spencer nodded, trotting off in the direction they last saw Ramona and Norah.

"What's up, Dad?" Haylee gave him a quizzical look.

"The boys just told me that that girl with you is a Traveler with active webs."

Haylee sucked in a breath, glancing at Josh. Compressing her mouth, she returned her attention to her dad, nodding. "Did Josh also tell you about our trip to Washington?"

"You want Serena to stay here?"

"I'll go check on Norah," Josh stated, sharing an uncomfortable look with his wife. If you two are alright—" Josh said backing up.

Once he was gone, Eugene crossed his arms. "I can't believe that you brought that thing here!"

"That's uncalled for, Dad!" Haylee sounded petulant, "We've got the situation in hand. I couldn't leave her somewhere where I couldn't watch her."

"I am not comfortable with this situation, Haylee."

She sighed, "I do understand." Checking around the side of the house, Haylee returned, whispering urgently, "Dad, there's something else—"

Emis's voice sounded alarmed in Haylee's mind, *What are you doing? It is forbidden to speak of this!*

"And lightning didn't strike us down did it?" Haylee replied out loud.

"Something else? Lightening? What *are* you talking about?" Eugene asked, frowning.

Haylee forcefully shook her head; she pressed the palms of her hands alongside her temples. "Sorry, Dad... I've got a terrible distracting...pain that I can't shake."

Certainement, you are not referring to me?

"Who else?" Haylee responded.

Eugene grabbed her arms, giving her a shake, "Hay, are you having one of your spells?"

"No, it's not that, Dad. It's Emis. She's woken up inside my head...and...she.... won't.... shut up!"

He took a step back, "Holy..."

"Holy she's not. She is horrible. Angry, mean, selfish, and...."

Another barrage of words commenced. Thankfully it was going fast, and it was in French.

Haylee could tune that out. "It started last night," she rushed to get her words out before Emis could interfere again, "It wasn't just Emis, but other stuff too. Her victims. Their minds are starting to come through. It is getting harder to sort out my own thoughts. It's painful."

Josh returned, "Is everything OK with you guys? What's painful?"

When Haylee wouldn't meet his eyes, Eugene regarded his daughter with concern. "You haven't told Josh about this?"

Haylee shook her head, keeping her gaze on the ground, "Not yet," she whispered.

Concerned, Josh walked over to Haylee, placing a gentle hand on her back. When she remained silent, he looked to Gene for answers.

"She says that Emis has regained consciousness. She's been speaking openly to Haylee since last night."

Josh cursed under his breath, "That explains a few things."

"There's more," Haylee confessed.

Looking severe, both men waited.

"I know the details about the ceremony that I will have to perform with Norah. We don't have much time left to do it. We've got to move on this Washington thing—." Haylee sniffed, "I'm scared, Daddy."

Gene pulled Haylee into a hard embrace, "I'm scared too, Honey." His voice was tight, his arms felt like bands of iron. "I wish your mom was here to help."

"Me too," Haylee whispered.

After a few minutes, Gene asked, "Who is Ramona?"

Haylee laughed between her tears, "She's an Astrophysicist that Josh and Spencer know from the University. Her Uncle is an Engineer at the Grand Coolie Dam. She thinks that she can get us access to what we'll need."

"What is that?"

"Power— lots of it," said Josh.

Eugene continued holding his daughter. It looked like it was a struggle for him to release her.

Taking a deep breath, Gene let go and stepped back, "Be careful." He admonished.

"I will. You know that Josh is cautious."

Eugene nodded absently, then mused, "Three Travelers in one place at the same time— "

They shared a look knowing that what Gene had spoken was significant.

The silence between them was growing long, when Josh asked, "Haylee, do you have everything you need?"

"I've got a few items to pack," she said. Before leaving she paused one more time to grasp her dad's hand, "You know how much I love you? Glori and Byron too?"

"I know," he said quietly, "we love you too, Haylee." His voice was thick, "Make sure you come back to us." Gene's eyes met Josh's, "All of you."

⁓⁓⁓

Haylee was zipping up her small travel bag when she heard a wail from the yard. Her heart knew instantly that the cry belonged to her daughter! Racing through the house, she met a wall of people outside the front door. Making her way toward Serena, she wove her way through the crowd. The children were still in the play area where she'd left them. Josh held Serena. He was trying to soothe her. When the little girl saw her mama, her cries grew louder; she reached out to Haylee.

"She fell and scraped her knee," Josh said, handing Serena to Haylee.

"Oh— let me have a look," Haylee commented. "It's not so bad. Just a scrape. Let's go wash it off and put a band-aid on it."

Pushing her way through the crowd once more, Haylee made her way into the house and to the bathroom. Setting Serena on the countertop, Haylee began gently cleaning the wound with a soapy washcloth. All the while murmuring to her daughter.

She has the look of my Polly about her. Haylee didn't reply; she didn't want to upset Serena any more than she already was.

Norah wedged her way into the bathroom. "My gift may be useful. May I approach?"

Haylee stood her ground keeping herself between them, "What are you talking about, Norah?"

"Tissue repair," she stated plainly. "There's not much use for it at home other than observation and entertainment. There will be no additional pain. I can return the tissue to its normal state."

"Vroom! Vroom!" Serena said as she smiled, peeking around her mom at Norah.

Norah returned the expression. "Serena knows that I mean her no harm."

Haylee looked to Josh who raised his shoulders.

Glori had arrived, "I heard that we have an injury that needs first aid?"

Eugene was right behind Glori. He put his hands on her shoulders, squeezing too tightly. She turned toward him, giving him a curious look.

"Maybe," Haylee replied, moving to make way for Glori to come in.

Eugene made a deep sound in the back of his throat, still holding onto Glori. "Gene, Honey, let go."

"No," he stated adamantly, "and I think you better get that girl out of here."

"Eugene! What's wrong?" Glori looked confused.

"Hurts," Serena yelled. She pointed to Norah, "Nor, fix."

"Norah says, she can repair tissue," Haylee explained. She met her father's concerned gaze, "*I'm* going to give her a chance," Haylee stated.

Nodding Norah stepped forward. Standing next to Serena, she flexed her hands. At Glori's look of alarm, Haylee placed a firm hold on her shoulder, "It's OK, Glori."

"But—"

"I *know*, but it's *really* alright. I trust her."

Norah bent forward, leaning over Serena's knee, intense concentration stamped on her face. Pressing closed the gaps between her thumbs and fingers, Norah held her hands flat. Holding them an inch above the wound, Norah rocked them back and forth.

Serena looked up, smiling.

Next, Norah pulled her hands away from the wound, then moved them back toward it.

Those closest, saw the reddened skin turn pink. Slowly, with each pulling up and away of Norah's hands, healthy tissue filled in until the damaged skin completely disappeared.

Norah straightened, stepping back.

Glori and Haylee both leaned forward, getting a close-up view of Serena's knee.

"That's incredible," Glori stated.

Haylee met Norah's eyes; she smiled at the girl, "Thank you."

Norah inclined her head.

"Now that you are all better," Haylee said brightly, lifting Serena, so she was standing on the counter. Haylee adjusted her dress and ran her fingers through the little girl's hair. "You have to go with Grandma Glori to make sure that Hanna is having fun showing off. Can you do that?"

Serena nodded, but she wasn't smiling. "Don't go—" she looked like she was about to start crying again.

Haylee looked sad as she replied, "I have to, Sweetheart. Norah needs my help. I promise that I'll be back as soon as I can." She leaned in to hug Serena. "Promise that you'll be good and do what Grandma and Grandpa tell you, OK?"

Haylee kept a tight leash on her emotions as she walked with the others toward Ramona's Ford Bronco.

Saying goodbye to your child is plus difficile. Especially if it is for the very last time.

Under her breath, Haylee muttered, "If you were standing in front of me, I'd slug you for that."

Spencer, walking nearby, overheard the one-sided conversation. He frowned.

It makes it more interesting that we cannot scratch each other's eyes like cats—no?

"It's not the last time I will see my daughter!"

I am sure you are right. But a woman trapped inside of another must find ways to amuse herself.

"I don't find it interesting or amusing."

"Haylee?" Spencer said, "are you alright?"

"Peachy," she replied sarcastically.

❧72❧
RAMONA

IT WOULD TAKE THIRTEEN hours to reach the Grand Coulee Dam. The plan was to trade drivers when needed with no stops other than bathroom or food breaks. Spencer took the first shift. Ramona sat in the front passenger seat. Josh and Haylee were in the back with Norah between them.

The cargo area was filled entirely with heavy-duty tote boxes. To accomplish what they set out to do, Ramona assured them that she would need every piece of equipment. The small amount of personal luggage that the vehicle occupants packed took up space under their feet and on their laps. It was cramped, but they agreed that it was easiest to ride together in a single vehicle.

Haylee started feeling car sick almost as soon as they began driving. Hoping to sleep it off, she arranged her backpack against the window. Leaning on it, she closed her eyes. Reaching out she patted Norah on the knee, "You'll wake me if you need anything?"

Norah nodded and responded, "Yes, thank you."

"Are *you* alright, Haylee?" Josh asked.

Not opening her eyes, she said, "Yep," in a clipped tone. Then as if dismissing Josh, she voiced a question that would begin another long-winded lecture, "Ramona, how do you know so much about the dam?"

Josh crossed his arms tightly over his chest. He leaned out around Norah to get a clear view of Haylee. Shaking his head, he slumped back against his seat.

Norah looked at him questioningly. He met her eyes briefly, then turned to stare out the window.

"Several generations of my family have worked on it since construction started in the 1930's. I used to tag along on jobs with my uncle and then did several summer internships. Everyone assumed that I'd get an Engineering position there once I graduated, but Astrophysics and energy theory— on an even larger scale— caught my interest." She shrugged, "At times, I miss the hands-on work and the relative simplicity of the municipal climate."

"Just to be clear…" Josh chimed in, "we understand that we might be facing charges and possible jail time for tampering with a public utility?"

Everyone fell silent. Josh couldn't tell if Haylee was asleep. Norah's eyes looked huge in her head as she stared at him. He could see her shivering. Josh met his brother's gaze in the rear-view mirror. Ramona twisted in her seat so that she could face him. "I thought we went through this in my office?"

"We did, but I want to reiterate in case anyone has had a change of heart. You and I could lose our jobs at the University. Spencer's career will be toast before it ever gets started and …." Josh looked over at Norah and Haylee, "I have my reasons for taking the risk. Spence, are you sure?"

"I haven't changed my mind, bro. We're in this together."

"And you, Dr. Winton?"

Ramona seemed nervous as she responded. She reached up to play with her long, thick braid. Removing the rubber band at the end, she combed her fingers through the strands as she looked directly at Norah, Josh, and Spencer in turn. "As I explained, I've reached a dead-end of sorts in my research. No amount of lobbying, speaking engagements, grant proposals or out-and-out pleading will convince any of the powers that be to allow me to take the controversial next step without handing my project over to someone else. I'm not about to do that."

"There are elements of your project that will satisfy both our needs. I can't do what I need to do alone— and neither can you. In addition," she continued, "I am familiar with the equipment and am competent with its use. I know my way around that place. We aren't going to get caught."

"I understand," Josh replied, "but that doesn't entirely explain your willingness to risk social and economic suicide."

"It doesn't, does it?" Ramona laughed dryly. Until a couple hours ago, I couldn't have answered that fully. I saw something back at the farm that brought it all together— an old photograph." Ramona inhaled deeply, turning to look out the front windshield. "A long time ago," she let out her breath, "I knew Haylee's mother." Ramona fell silent, curving her shoulders forward. "That was before she met Eugene. We lived in the same dorm on campus..." Readjusting her posture, Ramona sat up straighter. She turned to look at Josh again. "Doris did something extraordinary for me. I thought that I would never have the opportunity to repay her." Ramona glanced at the sleeping Haylee, then to Norah where her eyes lingered on the necklace, "They're all related."

Norah unconsciously covered her pendant while she reached out to tuck her hand into Haylee's. "Thought so," said Ramona before turning back around. She wadded up a jacket, put it on her shoulder, then leaned against her window. "I suggest we all nod off as much as we can. We're going to need every brain cell sharp once we get to Mason City. And, Herkowitz— we don't know each other socially, but I'll tell you this— I don't gossip. I don't spread rumors. And I know when to keep my mouth shut."

"Glad to hear it," Spencer interjected.

Josh had fallen asleep. His head leaned back at an awkward angle; his mouth was open. He was snoring when Haylee started jerking.

Norah squeezed the hand she was still holding and rubbed her arm. Haylee quieted some but continued to be fitful. Frowning, Norah reached up to place a hand along the side of Haylee's face. She turned toward Josh, juggling his shoulder, "Excuse me, Dr. Herkowitz, she whispered, "I believe that your wife is distressed."

With a snort, Josh snapped his mouth shut, rubbing around the edges of his lips, he blinked, "What is it?"

"Everything OK back there?" Spencer asked.

"Haylee's body temperature has risen to a concerning level. I cannot report the exact degree increase, but I thought you would want to know," Norah whispered urgently. "I do not wish to disturb her slumber if she is ill, but I must also inform you that warning signs of my own imminent need for...you know...are happening."

⚘73⚘
WILSONVILLE, OREGON

NINE HOURS INTO THE trip, Josh was behind the wheel drenched with sweat. It was clear, now, that they couldn't continue much longer. Haylee's fever had worsened with every mile; her eyes were glassy. She shivered uncontrollably, even with several sleeping bags piled on top of her.

Norah crossed her arms tightly over her stomach. She was doubled over like a clam. She leaned into Spencer's side.

Without being obvious, Spencer held each of her wrists, pressed against her sides in an iron grip. In the rear-view mirror, Josh could see the girl's periodic tremors. He heard Spencer's voice attempting to calm and soothe her.

Worried, Ramona kept checking the passengers. For the last forty miles, she'd notified Josh every time they passed a hospital sign. "They need an ER, Herkowitz! If you don't stop to get help, I swear that I'm going to climb over the center console and stop this car myself."

Gripping the wheel as if his life depended on it, Josh's mouth formed a straight line. Checking his mirrors, he pulled into the slow lane, signaling a turn at the next exit. He scanned their surroundings intensely as he composed a reply, "This will sound barbaric, possibly even cruel, but hospitals and doctors are the last things we need right now."

"How can you....?" Ramona started.

"Please, Dr. Winton— Ramona, trust me. Give me another hour and a half. If the girls aren't measurably improved by then, we'll get help."

Spying a Best Western Hotel across from an open field, Josh headed in that direction. Driving along the rural road, he spotted a barn. "Spence," Josh motioned with his chin, "I'll drop you there. Meet us at the Best Western...in a while."

Spencer glanced down at Norah. He nodded.

Once the car was stopped, Spencer hustled Norah out, keeping her close to his side. Josh asked Ramona if she'd take Spencer's place watching over Haylee until they got to the hotel. When it looked like Ramona would question him again, he reminded her that she agreed to trust him....at least for the next ninety minutes. Josh left the engine running while he got out to talk to his brother, "You understand what needs to be done?"

Spencer nodded. He didn't look confident. Josh reached out, grasping his arm. He placed a small flashlight in the pocket of Spencer's jacket. "That barn is housing sheep. Get a good hold on one, direct Norah's hands to its face. Physics are not in favor of her overpowering you, but be extremely careful. Make it fast, and keep it quiet .... if you can."

Josh kept an eye on his brother and Norah as they trotted away into the darkness. Swallowing passed a lump in his throat he, got back in the driver's seat. Slamming the door shut, he shoved it into gear, spinning the tires as he turned back toward the hotel.

"What on earth?" Ramona wailed.

"Shut it!" Josh retorted. "Once we are across the street, I'm dropping you at the office. Get us three rooms."

⮞⁓⁓⮜

Norah broke away from Spencer. She sprinted toward the fence, leaping over it without breaking her stride.

"Wait!" Spencer called while digging for the flashlight.

In the distance, he heard her say, "I know what to do. Stay back. It's better this way."

Spencer really didn't want to see her do her webby thing. Just as he was wondering if he *could* wait for her right where he was, a commotion sounded from the barn.

"Crap!" he muttered as he hopped the fence, following her. Spencer rounded the corner. When he reached the barn entrance, he saw lights turning on in the house across the yard. Plunging into deep darkness, he was surrounded by frightened animal screams, smells, and jostled by fuzzy bodies. Spencer yelled, "Norah, where are you?"

"Over here," her voice came from the opposite wall. "These mammals are not like horses."

"That's because they're sheep," he replied. Spencer reached out with both hands, grabbing a hold on a woolen pelt. "I've got one, get over here."

The swiftness with which she moved, surprised him. Seeing the webs filling the spaces between her fingers gave Spencer the creeps. Turning his head away, Spencer saw her attach herself to the animal's face in his peripheral vision. The full body spasms that followed her glue-like connection sent cold shivers over Spencer.

A blinding light suddenly filled the barn. "What the hell is going on in here?" a gruff voice hollered.

Spencer's back was to the door. Through squinted eyes, he saw Norah sink to her knees, still attached. He could tell by her expression that she had no awareness of what was going on.

"You there!" the voice called out. What are you doing with my animal?"

Spencer could hear footfalls growing closer. "Norah," he whispered, "let go!"

"I've got a loaded, double-barrel shotgun centered on your back, Mr. Let— loose— of— my— animal."

"We don't want any trouble," Spencer said. He released his fingers from the spongy mass of wool. Slowly, he raised empty hands up to shoulder height. He turned to face his executioner.

Free, the ewe remained in place. Norah dropped away from the animal. All signs of her webs were gone.

The man holding the gun was at least a head and shoulders taller than Spencer. His limbs were thick, and his hold on the firearm didn't waiver. It stayed on target— on Spencer's heart. Short cropped, white hair, interlaced with dark strands, stood up in every direction like hedgehog spikes. Small eyes behind round-framed glasses studied Spencer first, then went to Norah who was sprawled out on top of a pile of glistening, putty-colored pellets.

Sweat trickled down the center of Spencer's back; it beaded on his forehead. It was difficult to breathe with those two black barrels staring at him. His voice shook, "Prank.... just a prank. You're not going to shoot a couple of kids, are you?"

"You, Sonny, look old enough to know better. And that girl looks too young to be running around with the likes of you. I think you need to have a chat with the Wilsonville Sheriff."

"Bbbuuuu......" Norah started to speak.

Spencer caught her eye, shaking his head. She clamped a hand over her mouth.

Diverting attention, Spencer lowered his hands, "We haven't done anything, Sir."

"You scared the daylights of my flock, you woke me out of a sound sleep, you're trespassing, and who knows what you've done to Matilde?"

Norah cautiously moved to stand up. "Maaaa," she started, then snapped closed her mouth closed. She tried again, "Maaatilde is going to have a baby."

"And how would you know that?"

Norah cast a worried glance at Spencer. "She told me."

"That's it!" the man motioned with the shotgun, "We're calling the Sheriff."

⧸◠◡◠⧹

Leaving the vehicle idling, Josh crawled in the backseat. He could see Ramona through the large plate glass window as she handed a credit card to the desk attendant. "Haylee?" he pulled the sleeping bags down so that he could get a good look at her. She moved away from the light. Josh reached out to touch her face. It was still warm, but not as much as the last time he checked. "How do I know if this is a 'regular' sickness or something to do with the Travelers?" he asked. Worry laced his words, straining his voice. Haylee didn't respond.

Josh stroked Haylee's hair, "Help me, Babe. I don't know what to do."

It's Emis. It hurts to have her inside my head...

Josh sat up straighter. It had been a long time since he'd heard her voice in his mind, but it was unmistakable and unforgettable.

"What can I do?"

I don't know...

"Tell her to stop resisting," came a low-pitched voice from Haylee's mouth. It was heavy with an accent.

Josh stared at Haylee, shocked.

The door to the Bronco opened, "I've got the room keys," said Ramona.

❧74❧
SHARED BURDEN

"THANK YOU, RAMONA," Josh said appreciatively. "Haylee's fever has come down. Once we get settled in our rooms, could you go to the store to pick up a few things?"

"Certainly," came her business-like reply. Ramona hopped in the driver's seat, driving the vehicle across the parking lot, "I got you two adjoining ground floor rooms. Mine is on the opposite side of the complex."

Josh nodded while watching his wife.

Ramona parked. She got out and started pulling out luggage.

"Can you move?" Josh asked. Haylee's response was to begin pushing away the sleeping bags. "Good," he said, hopping out, taking the room keys that Ramona offered. Josh started separating out the luggage that belonged to them. He dictated a shopping list to Ramona who took notes on a small tablet she pulled from her purse. "Motrin, or another brand of painkiller, a thermometer, Epsom salts, orange juice, canned chicken noodle soup, saltine crackers, ginger ale, and whatever else you feel like eating," he paused, removing his wallet. He handed her some cash.

When she protested, Josh said that this one was on him since she'd just paid for the rooms, but that they'd square up finances once the trip was over.

Haylee's feet emerged from the Bronco, landing on the pavement. She held onto the side of the car as she called, "A little help!"

Ramona followed Josh around to Haylee's side. "How are you feeling?" she asked.

"C'est bien," Haylee replied, "I mean, much improved."

"Glad to hear it," said Ramona.

Slipping a supportive arm under her shoulders, Josh helped Haylee walk to their room.

While reaching into her pocket to fish out keys, Ramona called out, "I'm in room 310. I'll bring the groceries over as soon as I get back."

"Thanks a lot, Ramona."

When the Bronco was out of view, Haylee fell against Josh. He responded by bracing his legs, wrapping his arms tightly around her. He barely kept her from falling, "Haylee!" Josh swept an arm under her knees, carrying her over the threshold. Making it across the room in three strides, he set her down on the bed.

Haylee clasped her hands behind his neck, pulling him down with her.

Off balance, Josh landed next to her. Her hands were still over warm; her eyes dilated.

Stroking hair away from his face, she leaned up to kiss him.

His response was immediate. Lips soft, his mouth opened.

Haylee sucked Josh's tongue. Her fingers combed over his scalp cradling his head. She held it firmly in place. Then bit down.

A sharp pain and the taste of blood made him jerk back.

"Non, mon Cher," she said, climbing on top of him. Straddling him, she ground her pelvis over the stiff shaft straining against his zipper.

"You're not..." Josh started to say.

Emis drowned his words with another heady kiss. As their lips engaged, her hands did things to Josh that effectively shut down every thought in his mind. She unbuttoned his shirt, teasing him unmercifully just under his belt line. She nuzzled into his neck, her teeth and tongue building a ravenous fire at his core.

Josh wanted her with a brutality and fierceness that frightened him. He flipped her onto her back, falling on top of her. She squirmed, making animal noises that further incited his frenzy.

With her legs wrapped and locked around him, Emis pushed her hands up over his chest and around to his back. Her nails raised welts along his spine. Josh thought he would explode before he could bury himself inside her. He pushed back to unfasten his pants.

Warm hands covered his, "Let me," she grinned up at him.

Josh couldn't help focusing on the blood smeared between her teeth.

"Magnifique," Emis crooned, "so handsome and virile. Traces of Reece are in your eyes and in the shape of your mouth. Haylee found what was left of him. I've waited a long time to have you in my bed."

Josh felt as if he'd been flash frozen into a statue of ice. He seethed with anger. Shoving her roughly, he scrambled to his feet, backing away, horrified. His skin crawled when the full realization of what had happened dawned on him. Clenching his hands he brought one up, pressing it against his mouth to keep from spewing the vile words he wanted to shout.

He strode out through, the still open, hotel room door. Channeling his tumultuous emotions into action, he opened the room next door, moving all the luggage inside. Not caring that he hadn't packed a swimsuit, Josh headed straight across the parking lot to the fenced-in pool. It was empty. Stripping down to his Fruit of the Loom's, he dove expertly beneath the surface. Muscle memory and years of practice sent him slicing through the water with grace and efficiency. He lost count of the laps but kept going until fatigue set in.

Stopping to come up for air, he heard Ramona's voice, "I put the groceries in your room. It was unlocked."

He swam to the edge of the pool, resting his elbows on the side. Josh wiped the water out of his eyes and squeezed it out of his hair.

"Haylee is sound asleep."

Josh nodded, not saying anything.

"I heard you used to compete. It looks like you still do."

"Thanks," Josh replied sarcastically.

"Are you getting out?"

"Yes, I'm about done."

Ramona walked over to a cabinet, pulled out a pool towel, tossing it to him.

Josh caught it with one hand, rubbed it over his face, then pulled his body up and out of the pool. He scrubbed the towel over his limbs and torso. He didn't notice Ramona's appreciative glance before she turned away.

"Are Spencer and Norah back yet?"

"I haven't seen them, that's why I asked."

"Shit! Why didn't you tell me that when you first came over?" Josh threw down the towel, scooping up his clothes and shoes. Barefoot, he ran back to the empty second room. Ramona was right behind him.

"What are they doing?"

Josh threw his duffel bag onto the bed, unzipped it, pulling out dry underwear and a shirt. "They're sheep tipping."

Incredulous, Ramona repeated, "Sheep tipping?"

Josh peeled off and stepped out of his wet briefs, throwing them across the room onto the linoleum floor. Ramona sucked in a breath, hastily turning around.

"We've got to get out there. Something must have gone wrong. They should have been back by now!" Josh sounded angry.

Ramona threw her hands in the air. "Right! Because sheep tipping is such a dangerous sport? When are you going to tell me the truth?"

"The truth?" Through the shirt he was slipping over his head, Josh's voice muffled. "You wouldn't believe me if I told you." He dropped down on the corner of the bed, reaching for a shoe.

"It's clear, to me at least, that you are in over your head, Herkowitz. There's something unusual going on with Haylee and Norah. Haylee's mother had something too, but it wasn't as pronounced If you put some faith in another trustworthy human being, you might find out that a burden shared isn't nearly as heavy as when you are carrying it alone...or with just your younger brother."

✤75✤
LACEWING RESCUE

THEY COULD SEE INTERMITTENT flashes of a red strobe light as they neared the spot where they dropped off Spencer and Norah. They cursed.

"Don't park in the open," Ramona said, crawling over the back seat to rummage through a tote box. "Find trees or large bushes that will conceal us."

Stopping in a cove, Josh turned off the engine, killing the lights. "What's that?" he asked when he saw the little box she brought out.

"Don't worry about it. If we need it, I'll explain how it works."

They were careful not to make sounds as they closed the car doors. Keeping an eye out for officers, they crept toward the farmhouse with its interior lights ablaze. The Sheriff's vehicle stood empty. Josh and Ramona could hear a constant stream of radio chatter between officers and the dispatcher.

Moving from bush to bush, and tree to tree they worked their way to the house and under the window where the occupants inside sat around a table.

Peeking in, they could see Spencer seated in a chair. Norah stood at his side, her arms wrapped around him. She hid her face in his neck and shoulder. The officer had his back to the window. He alternated between speaking to Spencer and writing notes. An older man also sat at the table, leaning back in his chair with arms crossed, listening. His shotgun in a corner, was not far from reach.

"What do you think?" Ramona whispered as they ducked below the window sill.

"Norah looks scared, but she doesn't look...hungry anymore. They must have made it as far as the sheep, but didn't get out before getting caught."

"What I have here," Ramona lifted her box, "is a Network Interface Device. It is used test outside lines. I thought I could make an emergency call that would require all available units to respond."

"That's good," Josh replied looking impressed. "Do it. As soon as the officer leaves, I'll go back to the sheep to create a diversion. Can you get the car over here to pick up Spencer and Norah when the old man goes to the barn?"

"No problem," Ramona stated confidently, "but what about you?"

"As soon as I see him approaching, I'll run. I'll hide where we parked and watch to see what he does. Once you have them, I think you should drive in the opposite direction, just in case someone is still watching. Circle back after a half hour or so. I'll meet you at the hotel."

"Right. I think we'll be alright there for the night. No one will be searching for a mature white female with an older car. We can leave at first light if Haylee's alright. No one in Wilsonville will be the wiser."

❧

Later that night, Josh, Spencer, and Ramona sat by the pool, resolute and tired. Undulating reflections sent waves of light snaking across their faces. Ignoring the 'no glass' and 'no alcoholic beverages' signs, the three clinked bottles of Lowenbrau saluting a job accomplished.

"Norah was a mess," Spencer shared. "She didn't understand what the gun was. When the Sheriff came, she couldn't stop babbling about a directive to avoid detainment. The more she talked, the more questions Officer Vargo and Mr. Karnak had. It was all I could do to get her to stop talking. I think Karnak felt bad when he saw how terrified she was. By the time you guys showed up, he'd decided not to press charges."

"Hopefully they'll forget all about it by morning," Ramona replied dryly.

Spencer took another sip of his beer, then looked at the label, "Who drinks this stuff?"

"Don't complain," replied Ramona, "it's a faculty favorite at Cal."

Josh tipped his bottle up to finish it off. Setting the empty aside, he grabbed another, popping the top.

"What's up, Josh?" Spencer asked.

Looking severe, he scooted out to the end of his seat. Leaning an elbow on a knee, he studied his feet while shaking his head. "There's something I need to tell you." He rested his chin on his hand. "When Haylee went back to 1849, she attacked the Traveler she went to find."

Spencer frowned, nodding toward Ramona. Josh looked at his brother, giving him a short, single nod before continuing, "The minds of her victims are like ghost images of the real thing—"

"Yours included?" Spencer clarified.

"Yes," Josh said, "but the Traveler mind inside of Haylee woke up two days ago."

Ramona sat up straighter, leaning forward, "What do you mean, 'woke up?'"

"I mean," Josh continued, "that Emis started communicating with Haylee and— shortly before we left on our rescue mission tonight, she communicated with me."

"Like Exorcist with an evil spirit talking out of her mouth?" Spencer exclaimed.

"Not like that, Spence." Josh blinked against moisture that glistened in his eyes glistening along his lower lids, "The last time Haylee spoke to me, it was with thoughts she placed in my mind. She said that she was in pain... It's a reasonable guess that the fight going on inside her is what is causing the fever." Josh fell silent. He took off his glasses, wiping under each eye with a thumb. His voice dropped to a whisper, "She made advances... I didn't realize that it wasn't Haylee."

"Did she— Emis, say anything?" Ramona wanted to know.

Josh nodded. A harsh laugh escaped, "She said that I looked like Haylee's husband...back there in 1849."

Spencer leaned back in his seat looking deflated. "That's got to hurt."

"Nothing useful, then," Ramona's tone was forthright. "It sounds like jealousy. You said that the fever was coming down. Have you to tried talking to her again to see who's coming through?"

Josh pinched the bridge of his nose, closing his eyes, "No— I was worried that..."

"She's gone for good?" Ramona finished his sentence, "We won't know unless we go see."

"Right," Josh inhaled, getting to his feet, "Shall we?"

The room was silent when they entered, streetlights from the outside cast a glow. Haylee lay on her stomach, arms crossed under her pillow. Hair, loose and unruly, covered her face.

Norah lay with her back touching Haylee's side. Her knees pulled up close to her stomach; her cheek rested on top of hands in a prayer position.

While Ramona and Spencer looked on, Josh knelt at Haylee's side. He gently brushed the hair away, tucking it behind an ear. Tentatively he placed his palm on her forehead. Surprised, he twisted around, "The fever's down."

"Josh?" Haylee cracked her eyes, "Is that you?"

"Haylee?" he smiled tentatively, "is it *you*?"

Frowning, she replied, "Of course it's me, who else would it be?"

"Ah... Emis?"

Haylee's eyes flew open, "Emis!" She turned over, sat up and cried out, clutching her head. Squeezing her eyes shut, she said, "It feels like I have a butcher knife in my skull."

Josh's face softened, filling with concern, "I thought I'd lost you."

She turned to him. Touching his jaw with an index finger, she attempted a smile, "You can't get rid of me that easily." Haylee lay back. Tears trickled down her face.

"Haylee," Ramona approached the bed, "we have Motrin, and I know pressure points."

Shaking her head, the tears continued to flow.

"I might know something," Norah chimed in.

The boys and Ramona looked at her expectantly. "The large crystal."

"I should have thought to try that!" Josh exclaimed. He got up, dashing out the door.

They could hear him moving things around next door.

"I better go help," Spencer turned to follow his brother.

"Spencer," called Norah, making him pause. "It is dangerous; only Travelers may handle it. Be careful."

"Thanks, Nor," Spencer nodded before leaving.

Ramona moved into the space Josh had occupied. "Haylee?" she whispered.

Haylee turned her head a fraction of an inch in Ramona's direction but didn't respond.

"Your mother was a healer. I saw her do something extraordinary, once. I think that you and Norah share something like that. If you were outside of yourself, looking at someone suffering like you are, what would you do?"

Ramona watched as Haylee inhaled slowly. Her wrinkled eyelids relaxed a little as she began to hum.

"That's it," Ramona encouraged.

"Where is the damned thing?" they heard Josh's frustrated voice through the wall.

A few moments ticked by. Norah sat up straighter, pointing, "What's that?"

Ramona turned toward the door, gathering outside was a swarm of insects. Their wings caught and reflected the light from outside. Norah came to stand beside her. A few of the bugs landed in Norah's hair. Ramona inspected them, "They're Lacewings. They're usually gone by late summer," she said with wonder. "This must be every hanger-on left."

The swarm moved toward them, Ramona and Norah backed away. It surged through the door, filling the room. They watched as a few insects landed on Haylee. Others followed until they blanketed her.

Spencer came back in, "We found it!" Seeing the moving mass of tiny creatures blanketing the bed, he froze, "What the—?"

Josh, right behind him, looked on mystified, "Is that Haylee under there?" he looked to Ramona who nodded helplessly. "Get them off!" he yelled, shoving Spencer out of the way.

"Dr. Herkowitz, stop!" Norah commanded.

When he hesitated, Ramona filled in the blank, "Haylee called them. I asked her what she would do to help herself. Then," she indicated the bed, "they showed up."

A crackling sound filled the room as the swarm reactivated, rising. Josh and Spencer jumped to either side of the door to avoid being pelted by thousands of Lacewings. Norah, Ramona, and Spencer trailed behind the last ones as they flew outside. Rising about fifteen feet in the air, they circulated in a sphere shape. Once again, their wings sent winks of light to the onlookers. Then, all at once, the ball of bugs dissipated.

Returning to the room, the three saw Haylee sitting up, smiling.

Josh, looking relieved, asked, "What just happened?"

Haylee shook her head, "I can't say, but my headache is down to a manageable level."

"Do you still need this?" Josh asked, holding out a box.

Haylee accepted it, "Thanks, I'll keep it close, in case I do.

❧76❧
AN UNDERSTANDING

RESTED AND IN GOOD humor, the group made it to a pancake house in Portland for breakfast. On the twenty-minute drive, Spencer had described pancakes and the variety of syrups that can be used to top them. Norah was excited to try another food.

Josh and Haylee trailed behind the others holding hands. Tugging him to a stop, she said, "Thank you for taking care of me last night...and for looking out for Norah too."

Haylee didn't notice his slight hesitation. "I'm just relieved that you're alright," he said.

She nodded, "The large crystal was a good idea. I held it for a few minutes after I woke up this morning. It did something."

"Like?"

"Emis went completely quiet!"

"Did the headache go away too?"

She nodded.

"That's a relief," Josh let out a pent-up breath. Widening his stance, he put both hands along either side of her face, drawing her in for a tender, passion-filled kiss. When he was done, he leaned his forehead against hers, "I love you, Mrs. Herkowitz."

"I love you too, Josh."

By two o'clock, they were on the outskirts of Mason City, Washington. Ramona briefed them on the schedule. "We're going to my Uncle's house first. Remember, you are my students on a team that will be testing experimental hydroelectric conversion rates."

"What if your Uncle or Aunt ask questions that we don't know how to answer?" Haylee said.

"Unlikely. I plan to get the key to my grandparents' house and get you over there ASAP. If a question does come up, say it is that it's classified."

As they passed, Ramona pointed out the Grand Coulee Dam Visitor Center. "I rented a service truck. One of you will come with me to pick it up. The totes need to be moved over into the truck. Once that's done, you can take the Bronco. You'll have the rest of today and all day tomorrow to do whatever you want. Then it'll be 'show time,'" she grinned.

Haylee, in the front passenger seat, turned to Ramona. "Did I miss it when you told us about the experiment that you are planning to do?"

Still smiling, Ramona shook her head, 'no.' The yellow, reflective lenses of her sunglasses hid the expression in her eyes. "I have homework for you. Spend a few hours at the Visitor Center, paying close attention to the Third Power Plant, especially the access and exit points."

"I'll go with you," Spencer volunteered.

As soon as Ramona parked in the driveway of the modest, yellow sided ranch house, two older people came outside. They engulfed Ramona in hugs and happy exclamations. "Mona, Dear, it's been too long!" her aunt said.

Alfred and Maria graciously greeted their niece's students. Norah was the last to be introduced. When Aunt Maria laid eyes on her, she looked worried, "Mona, surely this lovely child can't be a student of yours? She's far too young."

"But I am fully...." Norah began. She stopped abruptly when Haylee lightly tapped her.

Ramona filled in the conversation gap, "We've been on the road for a few hours, someone probably has to use the bathroom."

"Where are my manners?" Aunt Maria exclaimed, leading the way. "I've got persimmon cookies about to come out of the oven and hot cocoa," she offered.

Josh smiled broadly, "I can see why you like coming up here on your breaks," he said to Ramona.

Uncle Al, asked, "How's that Scott, Ramona? Will you be bringing him up to visit anytime soon?"

"There it is," Ramona said rolling her eyes. Sighing, heavily she replied, "I haven't been with Scott for years."

An hour and twenty minutes later, Ramona had completed the tour of her grandparents' house. It was similar in style to the one her Aunt and Uncle lived in, but it had grown musty with disuse. Her grandmother had passed away five months earlier; the family hadn't gotten around to cleaning it out; they were waiting for Ramona to decide if she wanted to buy it.

Josh and Spencer were interested in the fishing gear in the garage. "You must know where the good fishing holes are, can we borrow some of the fishing gear?" Josh asked.

"Yes, absolutely," Ramona responded, she named several of her grandfather's favorite spots.

Leaving the other three to choose bedrooms and unpack, Spencer went with Ramona to pick up her truck. He jumped in the front seat of the Bronco. "It didn't escape my notice that you were deliberately evasive when Haylee asked what you have planned for the power plant, Doctor Winton."

Before starting the engine, she turned to take his measure, "I've been putting that off."

Spencer was pale and shaken when he heard what she had to say. "I knew that it would be illegal. I didn't realize that it could also get us killed..."

⚬⟞⟝⚬

Norah was shoving the last persimmon cookie in her mouth from the plate that Maria had sent over with them when Haylee asked how she was feeling. She was struggling to chew and swallow the wad of floury substance. Norah held up a finger. When she could speak, she replied, "Without my optic sensors, it is difficult to give a precise report on all my bodily functions, but an approximation based on emotions would say that all is well."

"That's good!" Haylee smiled, relieved.

It doesn't matter what that waif says or feels now if you take too much longer to return her to her time stream, she's going to get sicker than a mongrel street dog.

Haylee clamped her jaw shut when she heard Emis's commentary. She refused to speak out loud to that annoying creature.

Creature! Who are you calling annoying you little crétin?

Norah looked at Haylee uncertainly. "It has been some time since I have attended to the maintenance of my Second Skin. It may take several hours and is.... involved. Do you mind if I go into the garage space to work on it?"

Haylee shook her head, smiling a smile that didn't reach her eyes, "I think that's a good idea," she said in a strained voice.

◦◦◦◦◦◦

When Norah closed the door behind her, Haylee let out a frustrated breath. "You're back, again! How am I going to get rid of you?"

Me? Came Emis's reply.

Goosebumps raised on Haylee's skin.

Josh came in, carrying a hand towel. He looked freshly shaved, "Where's Norah?"

Haylee nodded toward the garage, "She went out there to work on her Skin thing."

"So, we're, essentially, alone?" He raised an eyebrow.

"Ahhh... not exactly."

Very slowly, Josh nodded, "I see... if she is willing to talk, we should ask some questions."

What is he speaking of?

Haylee answered, "He has been gathering study information about Travelers."

And he wishes to talk to me?

Repulsed by the eager surge of emotions she could feel coming from Emis, Haylee frowned.

"I'll get my notepad," Josh said, dashing to grab his supplies.

"Why are you so interested in my husband?"

He's divine, Haylee could feel the woman's Cheshire cat-like smile. She had a clear memory of Emis, the most highly sought-after entertainer at the Bella Union, smiling that same smile when she led a 'customer' to her room.

You are jealous of me, Poppet?

"No!" Haylee snapped.

Are upset because your husband responded to me?
"I'm upset because... He didn't know it was you."

But we look identical.

Haylee threw claw-like hands in the air, exclaiming loudly.

When Josh was on his way back, Haylee was racing down the hall. "What's up?" he wanted to know.

"I need to get the crystal; it's the only thing that will shut her up."

"But—" Josh looked confused.

Haylee clenched her fists; she could barely breathe.

What's the matter, Haylee? Emis taunted. *Do you need to silence me because you are worried I'll seduce your man again?*

"What have you done?" Haylee yelled.

Josh backed up, "I'm sorry, I didn't know that it wasn't you..."

Ha ha ha ha, Emis showed Haylee images of what she'd done to Josh.

Something slipped inside. Suddenly, Haylee knew the heartbreak that the woman suffered when she offered herself to Reece, and he'd refused. That act had been Emis's last attempt at a life course correction. Reece's unknowing rejection was the final straw that sent her down a path of no return.

"I never knew," Haylee shook her head, her eyebrows steepled.

"I stopped as soon as I realized my mistake," Josh entreated.

Tears gathered in Haylee's eyes.

"Haylee! Say something," he urged.

Haylee's forehead wrinkled, "You liked it," she said, tears spilling over.

Josh took a step toward her.

"No!" she held up a hand, "stay back." Haylee didn't want him to cloud what was happening inside.

Repulsed by Haylee's compassion, Emis was attempting to hide.

Haylee smiled wryly. She was beginning to understand Emis. At the same time, warmth flooded her when she realized Josh's loyalty to her.

Haylee had wondered about Reece's motivation for taking in Polly. He became Polly's father because was a good man.

Polly? Emis squeaked. Haylee could feel the woman's surge of love and hope. *Did you see her after Reece took her?*

Haylee met Josh's eyes, holding a finger to her lips. He nodded. Carefully, Haylee moved to a chair in the living room. Josh followed, sitting near, waiting.

"Of course, I saw her. I lived with them for close to a year."

But, how? All Travelers must return to their time stream after receiving the crystal.

"I don't know. Polly never stopped missing you. But she had a good life."

I must hear about my daughter.

Haylee nodded slowly, wiping at her tears. They weren't hers alone. "Josh knows more than me. Reece kept detailed records, until-- Josh studied them..."

Then we must ask him to tell me all that he knows.

"We will, Haylee said, but before we do, I want you to promise me two things."

Such as? Haylee could feel Emis growing impatient.

"Don't impersonate me again."

Oh, but it is so much fun.

"Do you promise?"

Very well. What is the second?

"Josh has interview questions; I'd like you to answer them."

That is a small price to pay to gain something back of my daughter.

Haylee pointed to the pad Josh held, letting him know that Emis was ready to talk. She could see that he had to make an effort to keep his pen steady.

Josh began, "State your full name and date of birth."

LAURENT, NEMESIS ANTOINETTE - Entry #3

Born: 5 June 1826

ॐ77ॐ
CRESCENT BAY

IT WAS LATE WHEN Spencer returned to the cottage. Haylee and Josh were zonked, but the light was still on in the garage. Spencer found a beer then wandered out to see what Norah was up to.

Spread out on a large work table; the Second Skin lay splayed like an insect on a display board. Noah hunched over a lower portion of a leg.

"What are you working on, Nor?"

"Hello, Spencer," she responded without looking up. "I am repairing the cells so that everything is back in its customary place."

"In place for what?"

This time, Norah did look up, "Your voice doesn't sound as I am accustomed to hearing it." Her expression was puzzled, "You usually speak in an upbeat fashion, and your body movements are the same. Those are missing. What is the matter, Spencer?"

"It's Ramona," he sighed, leaning a hip against a counter. "She told me about the experiment that she's planning to do when we are in there trying to activate, that thing." He motioned to her suit with his beer bottle.

"And?"

"It's dangerous. Maybe crazy. It could kill people, not just us but other people too."

"Do you think Ramona is mentally unstable?"

"No."

"Do you think that she has failed to safeguard her experiment properly?"

"Not at all. The equipment she packed is impressive."

"Then what is troubling you?"

Spencer looked pained like he was reluctant to say what was on his mind. "Truly? It's scary what Ramona's about to try, but what worries me more is, Josh. It's not like him to miss something this big."

Norah nodded, resuming her work, "He loves Haylee, and he loves Serena," she stated. "Love is a complicated emotion that appears to have strong points and negative points. Perhaps he seems different to you because he's not just your brother anymore?"

Spencer shrugged, taking a sip of beer, "Maybe." He moved to look over Norah's shoulder, "In place for what?" he repeated his earlier question.

"When we met Ramona in her office, she said that we needed to recreate the original conditions to repeat a similar outcome. Since I've been here, my suit has been mangled and re-conformed. I was wearing it when I first arrived. If I am to return home soon, I wouldn't want to arrive there wearing anything else."

"Is whatever you want to get out of that thing worth dying for?"

Norah thought carefully before replying, "I think it is. Since your brother started the project, lifetimes of people have been spent studying Traveler phenomena." Norah's forehead furrowed. "There are too many unknowns to answer that question completely. But if there is one thing that I've learned from Haylee it's that gut feelings are more than blood surges and brain chemistry. Deep down," she reached, placing a hand on his arm. She put her other hand over her heart, "I feel that it is critical for your brother to know what's hiding in there," she nodded toward her suit.

❧❧❧

They drove the Bronco passed the visitor's center on their way to Crescent Bay. Spencer looked at his watch, "We should have plenty of time to make it back for the three o'clock tour. Ramona said that she'd pick us up at 8:30 p.m. sharp."

Josh glanced in the back. Haylee was showing Ramona how to weave Jacob's Ladder with string. He smiled faintly, then turned to his brother. "What's wrong, Spence?"

"I'll tell you while we're fishing."

❧❧❧

The day was glorious. To an observer, the foursome looked like any other family enjoying an outing. Blankets were spread on the grass in case someone wanted to lounge. The girls each caught a fish right away.

As she was reeling in a fighter, Norah laughed for the first time since they'd met her. It was such an odd sound that it set off a ripple of laughter.

Norah stopped laughing when she watched Spencer remove the hook from the fish's mouth. "What are you doing to it?"

Spencer pushed his finger into the fish's mouth and out a gill. "I'm putting it on the stringer." He held up a metal chain with large pins. Slipping one of the metal pins in place of his finger, Spencer refastened it, dropping the stringer back into the water.

"Why did you do that?" Norah sounded worried.

"That's lunch," Haylee said placing a hand on Norah's back. "Come on," she tugged on her arm, "let's go for a walk and I'll explain."

Josh and Spencer eyed each other as the Haylee and Norah got farther away. They threw in another line but weren't paying much attention. "It's Ramona," Spencer said gravely. "While we are working to activate Norah's suit, she's going to be attempting to generate a micro black hole."

"What!" Josh returned, "It's impossible...and insane."

"Right? I thought so too. Ramona said that she'd done extensive tests on her containment field. It's safe."

"How can you experiment on a containment field when the thing you are hoping to contain has never existed?"

"Isn't that like what we *think* we are doing with Norah?"

Josh snapped his mouth closed. Putting down his fishing pole, he walked a short distance, shaking his head, running a hand through his hair.

Spencer watched him for a minute then put his pole down too, joining his brother. When he got within earshot, he said, "I talked to Norah last night. She's convinced that whatever is in that suit is something that you need to know. She said that she thinks the risks are worth it."

"I'm worried that I'm not seeing things as clearly as I should. That I'm putting everyone at risk because I'm desperately afraid of losing something important."

Spencer laughed harshly, plunking a hand down on his brother's shoulder. "I hope that I fall in love like that someday, Josh. I promise if we make it out of this, I'll straighten up. Take the school work more seriously, stop living it up with the ladies."

Smirking Josh mirrored his brother actions, "If we make it out of this, I promise that I'll never get on your case again."

"Deal," Spencer said. "But I'd miss it if you gave it up for good. You have permission to do it at least once a year."

"This is the best day I have had in my entire life," Norah said looking up at Haylee. For the last half an hour, Haylee had been trying to show Norah how to skip rocks. Norah had given up. She sat down to watch Haylee do it.

Norah's statement touched Haylee, "I can't imagine what your life must be like, but I think that you'll be taking back a few things that are worth saving."

She represents another of my failures. All I ever did was make a mess of things; my life, my daughters, the Keener's, yours...

Haylee closed her eyes, turning her face away so Norah wouldn't see the emotions playing out there. She whispered her response, "My life isn't a failure."

Isn't it?

Haylee reached into her pocket. Wrapping a hand around the crystal, she squeezed. Like an off switch on a radio, Emis was silent. Turning off that grating voice couldn't stop a wave of self-pity that washed over Haylee. Once Norah was gone, she'd be stuck with Emis—

A lighter mood returned to the group as they enjoyed their fish fry, threw Frisbees, and hit badminton birdies back and forth. Maybe, knowing what could happen made these simple pleasures all that much sweeter.

They grew quiet and pensive as they broke camp and drove to the visitor's center.

⌾⌾⌾⌾⌾

Their tour group was small. Josh, Spencer, Haylee, and Norah, wearing red hardhats, followed along only half listening to the guide.

Haylee knew it the moment that Emis turned back on. She tensed as she waited for her to begin her negative commentary, but Emis remained quiet. She was listening to the presentation.

"In 1933, the U.S. Bureau of Reclamation began building the Grand Coulee Dam," the guide stated. "Thousands of people came to work on it during Depression. Towns grew up out of nothing almost overnight. Work was done for nine years, twenty-four hours a day, until the dam was complete."

"How much power does it produce?" a child of about thirteen asked.

"It is the country's largest hydroelectric project. It generates more power than a million locomotives and produces twenty-one billion kilowatt-hours of electricity each year. That's enough to power to almost two and a half million households," replied the guide. She led them on to the next display, a window that looked down on a generator room. "Electricity is generated when water, fed by gravity, flows through the turbines."

When the tour group shuffled off to the next display, the gang hung back, staring intently down into the massive space. "We'll be wearing headphones that will allow us to hear one another," Spencer softly whispered.

"It's so much larger than I imagined," Haylee replied in dismay.

"Our main job will be to run cables between the generators," Spencer reported.

"Hello there!" the tour guide directed toward them, "Come along, we're not allowed to lose anybody on these tours." A collective chuckle twittered through the group.

⫸⫷

After completing their tour at the visitor's center, Josh had sought Ramona out at her Uncle and Aunt's house.

Leaving Haylee, Spencer, and Norah with the relatives, the two had gone out to the Bronco to have words— which turned out to be a screaming match—

They'd returned thirty minutes later, looking tired and angry.

The plan would proceed, unaltered.

⚘78⚘
ZERO HOUR

THEY WERE IN A dark parking area behind a recycling plant about two miles from the dam. Ramona had scouted the location earlier, making sure that there were no security cameras or bright lights. She'd handed each of them a pair of orange coveralls, a white hard hat, ear protectors, and a security badge.

Ramona spoke softly, though there was no real need to do so, "Norah, you have your Skin?"

At Norah's nod, she continued, "We'll go in at 9:15 p.m. I will park at the loading zone. Spencer will get out with me. We'll grab four empty carts. Once we're parked, everyone will get out to help offload the tote boxes. I have the totes numbered in the order to stack them. Spencer will direct whoever is working with him, and I will be doing the same. You'll follow me into the building. As we enter each new zone, I will raise my hand to indicate the location of the cameras. Until we disable them, keep your face averted. We'll be passing other work crews, nod but don't say anything."

"We'll be going through three long hallways and two shop areas. When I give the signal to stop, you'll park the carts and find a place to wait where you can watch the door. That will be the security room.

It will take me seventeen minutes to access the electrical panel and loop the security footage for every hallway where we will be and in the generator room. This will buy us anywhere from forty minutes to an hour before someone in the control room catches it. When I come out, we'll need to move fast. As soon as we are in the generator room, Spencer will give instructions. Are there any questions?"

There wasn't one. "Great," said Ramona, "Let's do this."

The ride was uncomfortable. They all wore fanny packs concealed under their coveralls. In the back seat, Norah slid her hand into Haylee's. She squeezed it. Haylee reached for Josh's hand. He did the same.

At the guard shack, Ramona rolled down her window, gave her work crew number, and handed over her badge. The guard handed her a roster to sign. Every passenger in the heavy-duty truck held their breath through the procedure. As Ramona pulled away, they let it out. Grinning, Ramona turned to them. "Check one."

The loading bay came into view; Ramona slowed, the three in the back released hands. Once the truck came to a halt, they jumped out like loaded springs. When they would have all raced for the carts, Ramona, raised a restraining hand, "Now is not when we run," she cautioned, "we blend in."

They remembered to follow the steps that Ramona outlined earlier. They proceeded to lift the tote boxes out of the cargo compartment. Ramona and Spencer pointed out the color-coded numbers. Carefully stacking them, they double checked that they were in the proper order before moving the truck to a permanent parking spot. They followed Ramona through the double doors and inside the first cargo bay.

Haylee was sweating bullets under her orange suit. She figured that the others were in a similar state. With deliberation, Ramona kept their pace steady, but slow. She raised her hands indicating the security cameras. They passed crews coming off their shifts. Ramona and Spencer exchanged polite pleasantries, "Have a good night. See you tomorrow. It's Miller Time."

Haylee and Josh kept Norah between them. They made her put on her safety glasses, headphones, and gloves. The three of them remained silent. Haylee noticed that their cargo boxes exactly matched the others that they passed. Their work suits and hard hats were the same. Ramona had done her homework.

As they turned a corner, walking down, yet another, hallway, Haylee grew increasingly anxious. The overhead fluorescent lights became a blur. Making their way in was not as simple as taking a right, and then two left turns. This place was a labyrinth! If they got separated or had to make a run for it, they wouldn't be able to find an exit.

Josh kept glancing over at her. He looked worried. Haylee was sure that the same thoughts were running through his mind.

Arriving at the shop, Haylee found a spot behind a large tool cabinet to wait. As soon as Ramona disappeared through the door, she heard a voice that made her jump.

Don't worry; I will not distract you.

Haylee cursed mentally, feeling through the jumpsuit and her fanny pack for the crystal.

You won't need that. Emis commented. *My gift, Haylee, is future sight.* An itchy feeling appeared between Haylee's shoulder blades. *There is something missing from Ramona's plan. Before you enter the generator room, you must use the device that is like sending a telegram.*

"Not distract me? Any time you say anything, you distract me—" Haylee whispered, "but, thanks, I'll tell her. Can you see how this thing is going to turn out?" Haylee realized that, for the first time, Emis's presence was a comfort.

Non, but I hope you find what you are looking for. Keep that little one close to you. She is beginning to show signs of time stream sickness.

"She is?" Haylee swung around, looking over at Norah. She didn't look so good.

"How're you doing?" Haylee whispered.

Norah nodded, giving her a thumbs-up, but her expression looked pained.

Ramona came out in a rush, waving for them to follow. The pace was fast; they ran as fast as the cartwheels allowed. Four more long hallways and five turns later, and they were standing outside the glass-paned double doors that led into Generator Room number two. It was loud, even from outside. She demonstrated how the headphone communication system worked. Each person nodded, showing that it was functioning. Ramona started explaining how to unpack the totes.

"Wait," Haylee put a hand on her arm. She could tell that Ramona was on edge by the tension in her limb and by the swift and unpleasant look, she shot at Haylee. "Emis sent a message."

❧

Ramona's eyes bulged.

"I think it's important," Haylee implored. "She said that there is something else that we need to do before entering." She swept her gaze around looking for what Emis could have meant. Spotting a phone on the wall near the last door they came through, she pointed, "Ramona, was that there the last time you were here?"

"What the...?" Ramona stalked over, inspecting it. "It's another security protocol," she brought a hand up to grip her chin, "and, *no*, it wasn't here before. This *is* something new."

When the boys would have reacted, Ramona held up a hand, "Give me a minute!" Muttering to herself, she paced. Grabbing her clipboard, taking it back to the phone, Ramona lifted the handset. She waited, listening.

"Passports," the person on the other end of the line answered.

Ramona held the earpiece away, looking at it like it took a bite out of her, "What the hell?"

"Sorry... Unit B security check, what's your requisition number and work zone?"

"Hold on," she cradled the receiver between her ear and shoulder, leafing through the papers on her clipboard, "when did this start?" she asked casually.

"Two days ago. It's not officially up and running yet, but we have to go through the motions. Didn't you get the memo?"

"No memo," Ramona responded curtly. "Here it is..." she read off the number, "We're doing retrofit work in Left Powerhouse - G2."

"Yep, I see it here. You're clear."

"Thanks," Ramona said dryly. "What would have happened if we hadn't seen the dial-in?"

A laugh could be heard above the loud hum, "Then your crew would have been the first ones to test out the new alarm system."

"Great," Ramona frowned, jamming the handset back into its slot.

Not bothering to explain, she turned to the group, giving them a thumb up. "We're good," she said once her headphones were back in place. "The clock is ticking, let's move!"

Before Haylee turned to go, Ramona pinched the material on her jumpsuit, stopping her, "Good call," she said quietly.

꩜

They were jumpy when they went through the double doors. Everyone expected an alarm to go off. When none did, Ramona was the first to call their attention back to the task. Pushing the carts out to even spaces across the room, everyone unloaded and uncoiled the bulky cables. Connector ends were placed at every turbine. Two sets of loose ends were laid out at the center and at the far end of the room.

Haylee, working alongside Norah, noticed her slow movements and pinched of expressions crossing her brow. "What's going on?" Haylee had pushed a button on her headset that allowed them to have a two-way conversation.

Norah looked back a Haylee sadly. Shaking her head, she replied, "I am feeling unwell and unsteady."

Having not had that Traveler experience, Haylee was at a loss.

Permit me? Emis whispered in her mind.

Yes? Haylee returned.

Norah does not know that she is beginning to weaken. But her body knows— even without all the devices. I think if you tell her that she will be home soon, her body will understand and respond.

It's worth a try, Haylee blinked. "Norah," she grabbed her elbow, making Norah pause. Haylee could see that she was sweating more than she should have been and felt her trembling. "Hang in there, as soon as we are finished, I'll give you the crystal and perform the ceremony."

Closing her eyes for a long moment, Norah laid a hand on top of Haylee's. She gave her a meaningful look, nodded, then returned to finish her assignment.

Haylee couldn't be sure, but it looked like Norah was moving more surely.

⌘

Calling everyone over to the center turbine, Ramona showed them the parts they needed to place near the Exciter Stators where the DC power came out. When Ramona shut down the turbines, this would be when the clock started ticking, and danger of discovery would be at its highest. They'd have to work as fast as possible to uncouple the current cables, replacing them with their own.

"There are on-sight engineers here and more across the western states who monitor this system 24/7, plus, automatic alarms that go off to make sure they are paying attention. By doing this when the power demands are at their lowest, and rewiring the security units, I've bought us a little extra time." Ramona spoke steadily and deliberately into her microphone. Her intonations helped to calm nerves that were dangerously close to fraying.

She demonstrated, what they would be doing. "Whatever you do, don't unplug the live connectors until I give you the all-clear signal." There were seven of the behemoth machines. Five of which were actively pumping eight thousand, five hundred cubic feet of water per second. "Norah, this turbine is yours." Ramona waited for her to indicate that she understood. "Haylee you're at the next one, and I'll be at the far end, Josh and Spencer will do all the others."

"Do you see these?" Ramona pointed to cables, clamped to the cart, with ends cut exposing metal wires. Everyone noticed that the cart wheels were locked, that additional reinforcements were added. "When we've got our alternate system in place, these will be live. They are going to be heavy, and they're going to want to move. Spencer has already agreed to handle them at this station. Under no circumstances do they come into contact with anything other than the intended targets. It goes without saying that fifty-six-hundred megawatts can do a lot of damage."

Ramona, standing like a general, surveyed her troops. "If there are any last-minute good-byes, now is the time to do it."

They gazed around at one another, not moving or touching, just wearing severe expressions and giving slight nods showing that they were ready.

"There are two that aren't running," Spencer observed.

"I'm aware of that," Ramona replied. "They will all be active in a matter of moments."

"I'll take this opportunity to remind you about the emergency exits," Ramona pointed them out. "If we don't go out the way we came in, you'll pick an exit route and run as fast and as far as you can. There are only two things that are imperative to take with us; Norah's suit and my recording equipment."

❧79❧
LIVE WIRE

AT RAMONA'S SIGNAL, Josh, Spencer, and Haylee ran to their stations. Norah remained in place keeping her eyes on Ramona. Ramona jogged to an electrical panel along the wall. She removed a handheld device and plugged it into the board. The lights in the room flickered when she tapped buttons. As she continued, the vibration of millions of gallons of water pushing through the turbines quieted.

"Not yet," Ramona's voice warned, intruding upon Josh's thoughts. "If the rotors are still turning, the generator is producing power. It takes a few minutes for the water to drain completely after the wicket gate is closed."

When Ramona said that they would have to move quickly once the generators were shut down, he'd expected to jump in and get moving. Waiting now, rattled his nerves. He removed his gloves, wiping sweaty palms against his thighs. He glanced at the others; they looked nervous too. Spencer swung his arms like he was warming up for pushups, Norah was glistening with sweat. Haylee wore a faraway look like she sometimes does when she's communing with 'fur people.' His gaze sharpened when he watched her close her eyes and clasp her hands together. She swayed. Alarmed, he pressed the button for her headset.

"Hay, you alright?"

Opening her eyes, she met his. She nodded, steadying herself. But her breath sounded heavy, "It's nothing... I'll tell you about it later."

He nodded, hoping that they'd have a later. Josh thought about the argument he'd had with Ramona about her experiment. He looked over his shoulder at the workstation she'd set up. A video camera stood on a tripod; it's green 'ready' light blinking. A second cart, reinforced against movement, held another large cable with wires exposed. On the ground stood a box. It about the size of a mini refrigerator that hotels keep hidden inside cabinetry. What was inside, was the primary focus of his nervous tension.

Ramona had agreed to wait to begin her experiment until they'd completed the test on Norah's Second Skin. Her particle collider was smaller than any other that had been built. "I'm not attempting to reach the scales that the other scientists have been aiming for," she'd explained, "it doesn't have to be 'super,' it only has to demonstrate that it works."

"How do you know that this thing isn't going to start a chain reaction that sucks the planet into it?"

"You've been reading too many journals," Ramona replied, her voice was flat. "Scale. It's impossible for substances that small to consume something so much larger. This isn't the first time I've tried this, Josh. Right now, I'm focused on maintaining stability that lasts for more than sixty seconds."

"Flipping the bird at established scientific methods is worth the potential benefits?"

"I told you, I have my reasons."

"Right. Don't you see that, even if you succeed, no one will take you seriously after this?"

The silence, when it came, was as dominant. It was as disturbing as the oscillating turbines had been.

"Go!" Ramona's shout startled them into action. The first uncoupling and coupling that Josh did went without a hitch. His legs pumped like pistons as he scrambled down the exterior steps on his way to the next turbine. He saw that Spencer had finished his and was scrambling as well. Haylee was up and moving, but Norah was struggling. Running to generator number five, Josh climbed up and got to work.

This one wasn't so easy. It didn't budge when he pulled the cable, even after knocking on it with the rubber end of a screwdriver. Ramona had warned them that this might happen. He dug into his tool bag, pulling out a can of WD-40. The others were talking in the headphones, telling him that he was the last one, and to hurry. The can was unsteady in his hands. Applying the oil, he gave it another knock and wiggle. The coupling came loose. In under thirty seconds, he had the new one in place.

Ramona radioed for them to join her back at the wall panel. "We'll give ourselves some room as we power it up, a safety precaution." She checked the handheld device. "So far, so good with remaining undetected. Luck may be with us!" She grinned, tapping buttons that opened all seven wicket gates.

The sound of water rushing the through the penstocks, filling the turbines, moving the rotors was like the whine of a giant engine revving to up. The vibrations rippling through the floor and walls made them feel like astronauts about to launch into space.

Haylee grabbed Josh's hand. Their eyes met, he gave her a squeeze.

"Almost there," Ramona notified them. "We're at seventy-percent." Watching her equipment, she kept up the commentary, "Eight-seven, ninety-one, ninety-six, ninety-nine, one hundred!"

Like racers taking off at the blast of gunfire, they ran. Spencer grabbed hold of the cart handle. The tremendous power moving through the cable made his eyes grow round. "It's wild!"

Norah approached her suit draped over an arm. "No!" yelled Haylee and Josh together. Josh reached her first, "You can't be holding that when we put the power to it."

Searching for an alternative, Norah draped it over a stair rail. She stepped back. "That's not going to work either," Haylee said. She dashed over to the cart that she pushed in, rolling it over. "Put it on this."

"Wait! Josh shouted over the radio. My notes are in there; I need to get them out first."

"Hurry up, you guys!" Spencer urged.

Moving the cart as close to Spencer's live wire as he safely could, Josh locked the wheels and stood back. Spencer didn't bother unbracing his cart. He planned to slide the entire thing across the foot and a half distance. Putting all his might into it, he pushed. He looked like a football player attempting to move a blocking sled. It didn't budge. He tried again.

Seeing that Spencer wasn't going to be able to maneuver it alone, Josh pushed his notepad into Haylee's hands. Running at it from behind, he increased their momentum by adding his weight. Keeping their feet moving, the brothers closed the gap.

Breathing hard, they stepped back. "Are they contacting?" Josh radioed Haylee.

"Yes," she sounded worried, "but nothing is happening."

"Shit!" they heard Spencer curse.

"I'm almost ready at my end," they heard Ramona say. "Let me know when you are done."

"I see something," Norah interrupted, pointing to her suit. "It's faint, but I think I see a ring forming."

It was more than a ring, but a sphere, and it was expanding from the center of the Skin. Its size stabilized at about six feet in diameter. They could see through it; they could also see something forming in its middle.

❧80❧
WATCHERS

INSIDE THE BUBBLE, a convex window appeared. An older man's face was peering out. His expression looked perplexed. They could see him glancing at something in front of him. Sketchy, half words, transmitted into their headphone.

"...ana. Travel ...nt. Unscheduled...empty."

Ramona appeared behind the group looking on in wonder. "I told you that I had something!" Norah was radiant.

A white-haired woman appeared behind the man, she too, seemed to be studying something below their line of vision. Turning to the man, she pushed at him, "Hurry....ion. Go get .... lin an...ile."

The woman peered out intently. Norah jumped up and down waving, calling out. Haylee looked perplexed.

Rushing over to Josh, Norah gripped his arm to the point of pain. "It's only partially coming through. I know what I have to do!"

Confused, Josh turned his attention to Norah. She'd kicked off her shoes and was stepping out of her jumpsuit. "What are you doing?" he said, alarm in his tone.

"Just as Dr. Winton told us. We must recreate, exactly, what happened when I first arrived. When I got here, I was wearing my Second Skin."

"You can't, Norah. It will kill you!" Haylee cried.

"No," Norah shook her head, "I don't think it will."

Haylee grabbed Norah, shaking her, "We don't know why Travelers do what they do, but what if we mess something up.... something big?"

Norah paused, her smile was confident. "Emis sacrificed herself. You used the large crystal to restore victims; now it's my turn to try something. This might be the only way to learn what we truly are."

Haylee's grip on Norah didn't release; she was shaking her head even as Emis was urging, *She's right.*

"Haylee?" Josh put a hand on her back.

Letting go, Haylee stepped back, "If Norah says this is something she has to do, we won't stand in her way."

Norah continued to undress.

✦✦✦

"We've got to break the current so that Norah can get to her suit." Haylee scanned the room. Not seeing what she was looking for she, raced to a janitor's closet.

Spencer and Josh grabbed the cable fifteen feet from its live end. Like a team in a tug-of-war match, they lifted it. Digging in their heels, bending their backs, they heaved. With the current flowing through it, it was stubborn; it barely moved.

In the closet, Haylee radioed back, "Got it!" Putting her hand on a long wooden mop handle, she paused, listening. Removing her headphones, she heard the faint sounds of bells going off. Her eyes widened, her breath quickened. Haylee ran back holding her stick like a javelin.

Throwing it with all the force she had, it cut the connection between the cable and the suit.

The atmosphere crackled. Spencer jogged forward. Holding his hand over the suit, he checked to see if it was hot. He touched it. Satisfied that it was safe, he picked it up. Turning toward Norah, he immediately turned his head away, holding it out for her to reach.

Norah shimmied into it. She sighed when her Second Skin was in place. "I'd forgotten how nice it feels to wear this." She blinked.

"We have to hurry, Norah, I thought I heard alarms," Haylee urged.

Norah nodded, "I'm ready." She removed her headphones, handing them to Haylee. Everyone stepped away, holding their breath.

Norah, arms spread wide, slowly walked toward the power source.

The cable jumped as she approached, behaving like a snake. The live end came to chest level on her. Norah paused just inches from making contact. She took one last look back at her friends before closing her eyes and letting herself fall forward.

A bright burst of light followed a loud pop and snap. Everyone instinctively turned to avoid the heat wave that rolled through the room. When they looked back to where Norah had stood, another sphere filled the space. It was not faint but in full color. They could see Norah inside, splayed like a starfish.

"Norah! No!" Haylee screamed.

"Wait, Haylee, look," Josh grabbed her arm. He pointed to the area where they'd seen the window before.

It formed again. In it stood the white-haired woman. Glancing behind her, she spoke, "Dar..i...on, co..me for...ward." The man they had seen before appeared behind, placing a hand on her shoulder.

"Lo...ok," she pointed outward.

The sound quality coming through their headphones was terrible.

The man hunched forward, doing as the woman had asked. For an instant, Josh thought that they made eye contact. He pointed to his ear protectors, shaking his head.

The man frowned, returning to speak to the woman. Their conversation was not audible.

The white-haired woman looked around the man, addressing someone who was not visible. Suddenly, the audio was crystal clear.

"Haylee, it is remarkable to see you again!" The woman's warmth came through clearly.

Haylee looked confused, "Do I know you?"

"Perhaps not," she sounded slightly disappointed, "I am Tethalana." She indicated the man, "This is Darion." The woman looked at the others, "Our Norah has performed beyond expectations."

"Is she dead?" Haylee asked, worried.

"Not at all," Tethalana replied, "Norah's in a twilight sleep." She glanced down, "Her body functions read normally. However, this altered Traveler Event is not sustainable." She turned to look directly at Josh. "Joshua James Herkowitz, you are represented in our collection, but it is a pleasure to look upon you fully engaged within your form."

When Haylee opened her mouth to speak, Josh touched her, making sure their eyes met. He nodded in the direction of the sphere. Understanding his meaning, Haylee nodded.

"May I address you?" Josh asked.

The white-haired woman inclined her head. She looked like a royal who had granted a bequest.

"Who are you?"

A smile quirked at the edge of her mouth, "We are Watchers, emissaries for the Upholders, our function is to preside over Travel Events...and awaken the Upholders if such an action is necessary."

⤳⤳⤳

Josh thought he understood the meaning of Travel Events. "What are Upholders?"

"Your language does not contain words to describe them. They always have been and always will be. They are the gardeners of the Universe."

"Gardeners of the Universe?"

"Let me communicate in a different way." Tethalana held up a hand. Opening it, a light glowed in the center. Gradually the glow diminished. In its place, a small blue planet floated there. About the size of a grapefruit, it rotated slowly. "When Upholders join, this is what they form."

The sound from outside that Haylee thought she'd heard a few moments ago was growing louder. She touched Josh's hand, "We might be out of time."

Josh was mentally paging through all his notes and testimony desperately trying to remember the information that he most wanted.

"What happens if the Upholders wake up?" Spencer called over Josh's shoulder.

Tethalana looked sad. Darion nodded, seeming satisfied.

Making a small hand motion, Tethalana adjusted the image. The floating planet began to crumble. Large chunks fell away spinning off into space, winking out of existence. A crack formed at its center. It widened, moving across the surface until two distinct pieces formed. They looked like gray colored commas wrapped around each other. The pieces shivered, wriggled, and pushed apart.

No one noticed Ramona looking over her shoulder, then running to her workstation.

"What do Travelers have to do with any of that?" Josh spit out.

Tethalana smiled, waving her hand, making the commas disappear. "They are natural organisms influenced by us to gauge the state of life forms upon the surface. They take samples for our collection. Like all our precious Travelers, it is a veneration to be a species representative."

Josh could hear shouting and running feet coming from the other side of the generator room door.

Rushed, he fired out another question. "Travelers have reduced lifespans compared to the rest of us."

Tethalana inclined her head.

"Is there anything that can be done to alter that?"

"Is the question rhetorical or is it based on emotions that you have for Haylee?"

"Haylee."

Tethalana's eyes sparkled. "When Haylee harvested the other traveler...well... she introduced a paradigm we hadn't observed before. We believe that a *short* lifespan isn't going to be her problem."

"I'm not going to die?" Haylee called out.

"Everyone expires eventually, even Upholders, who, to you, would seem immortal."

"Can I get rid of Emis?" Haylee entreated.

"The process could be accomplished by Norah, using the large crystal as you did for Joshua."

Haylee frowned.

Tethalana continued, "It is likely that if the Traveler within is removed, you will revert to your natural life cycle."

Behind them the doors burst open, armed, uniformed men swarmed in like angry hornets.

A bright light, a blast, and a sound wave exploded from the opposite corner.

Josh grabbed Haylee, holding her tight. Spencer tackled them. They sprawled to the floor in a clump.

Josh watched as the creatures in the sphere window observed, with alarm, what was going on around them. He could see Tethalana and Darion speaking to whoever was not visible. He heard bits and pieces of their conversation.

".... must not be recorded or remembered."

"...another power source?"

"...of cosmic proportions?"

"Can we use that for transport?"

❧81❧
WILD CAT CANYON

WIZENED, CRAGGY OAK TREES posed, like statues, against a stark, gray sky. Scrub brush, the skeletal remains of last year's bloom, pierced thin, bony fingers up through dark earth heavy with water. Fresh shoots of grass, revitalized by winter rains, carpeted the surfaces of the rounded hills.

Norah stirred. Something sharp poked into her side. Groaning, she rolled away. She was startled to feel cool, wet grass beneath her. Cracking her eyes, she immediately closed them again at unexpected brightness. Sniffing, she got a whiff of acrid, sooty air. *Smoke? Sensors are malfunctioning.* Slowly, she opened an eye again. From the outer edges of her vision, she could tell she was outside. *Where am I?*

Struggling and groggy, Norah wrestled herself onto her hands and knees. Her vision was blurry. Vague human-shaped forms lay, unmoving, on either side. Her heartbeat increased. She strained to focus on her last clear memory. She remembered falling onto the buzzing electrical cable. Haylee's words came back to her, "What if we mess something up?"

It's all messed up! Norah agonized, *I let hope and belief guide me. Now they're all dead!* "Oh no! No...no...no..." she uttered, in a voice raw with despair. *I led the only friends that I ever had to their destruction. If Haylee's gone, how am I going to get home?* Norah sat back on her haunches, hugging herself, rocking. She was too wrapped up in her self-deprecating emotions to hear it at first.

"Norah? Norah! Are you OK?" Josh touched her lightly.

Startled, she yelped. Turning toward him, her eyes were wide; pupils dilated. "Doctor, Herkowitz, is it you?"

"Yes."

"I thought you were dead. All the others too."

⁓⋰⋱⁓

Josh glanced over his shoulder. He watched as Haylee and Spencer gingerly moved into upright sitting positions. His gaze searched their vicinity. *Where is Ramona?*

"Josh!" Spencer called. "I think we're in Wild Cat Canyon."

Josh nodded although he didn't recognize any landmarks. Fog was rolling in. Josh could see it cresting the ridges like waves. A cold wind preceded it, reminding him that they didn't have jackets. By the angle of the sun, he estimated that it was approximately 2:30 in the afternoon.

Wild Cat Canyon Preserve encompassed thousands of acres. Over the years he'd managed it, steady increases of predators and prey animals had been observed. An understandable phenomena since land development destroyed natural territories. Wild Cat was an ecosystem unto itself. It was rarely a problem unless people were unprepared when they went out there.

"Ramona's missing!" he heard the distress in Spencer's voice.

"She was some distance from us when the security guards stormed in," Josh reminded them. "We'll find her," he sounded more confident than he felt. "First things first, is everyone alright?"

"Physically, I think I'm fine," replied Spencer. "Mentally is another story. What just happened?"

~~~~~

Seeking the source of pain, Haylee wove her fingers through the hair at the base of her skull. They came away crimson and slick. The last time her head ached like this, she'd tumbled backward on new roller skates, bashing it on the sidewalk.

She followed Josh's movements, noting the clarity and focus of her perception. Reaching back once more, she was relieved to discover that the wound wasn't dripping. Glancing at the ground, Haylee located the rock she'd landed on.

As she moved, another pain, low in her back assailed her. *Unbelievable! Not now!* Haylee thought. She was utterly unprepared for the periodical event that it signaled.

Getting to her feet, Haylee bit her lip until it hurt more than anyplace else. The tactic worked to keep herself from making sounds of complaint. "I'm OK," Haylee responded tightly to Josh's query.

She poked around her middle, checking her fanny pack. Her shoulders relaxed when her fingers touched the item she carried there.

Haylee noticed burn marks in the grass. "We were moved inside a bubble like the one Norah was in," Haylee began. "The sphere must have caused these," she conjectured. She blinked rapidly, a look of worry crossed her face. "Do you think we were moved in *more* than location?"

"I don't know," Josh scowled. Returning to Norah, he watched her moving her head as if she was paying careful attention to the conversation. "Norah, is something wrong with your eyes?"

≈∽⌖∽≈

Norah swiveled her face in the direction of Josh's voice. "It is black in the central area of my vision. Peripherally, there is sight, but it is blurred." She reached out. Spencer steadied her as she got to her feet. "The dizziness and excessive perspiration that I was experiencing in the generator room seems to have passed."

"Doctor!" Norah squeezed Spencer's forearm, "What happened after I hit the wire? Did the people in the sphere reappear?"

"They did."

Norah heard satisfaction in his tone.

"We asked several questions and got their replies."

"Was it significant?"

"Absolutely." He quickly relayed all the major points of the communication. When she asked more questions, he put her off. "Right now, we need to find shelter, out of the wind. We also need to search for Ramona."

≈∽⌖∽≈

Josh and Spencer exchanged looks and a few hand signals as they walked around, concluding the best to leave Norah while they surveyed the surroundings.

When Haylee joined the boys, they were removing their coveralls, giving them to Norah to use for blankets. Shoving her hands deep into the pockets of her coveralls she retreated a few steps. "Norah needs yours too, Babe," Josh motioned, looking concerned.

"No." Haylee shook her head. "I'm not taking mine off."

"But, Haylee," Spencer coaxed, you'll heat up when we start hiking, Norah needs to stay warm so she won't go into shock...assuming she's like a normal person."

"I said, no! And I meant no!" Haylee screamed, storming away.

The boys shared a perplexed look before Josh sprinted after his wife.

⁓⁓⁓

"You should not be treating me like an invalid," Norah complained to Spencer. I should be helping!"

He knelt in front of Norah, clasping her hands. "We're in a predicament, Nor," Spencer explained. He rubbed hands up and down her arms from shoulder to elbow. "Those people got us out before the troops moved in, but they dropped us somewhere remote. We have to find cover from the incoming weather, someplace protected so we can build a fire." Spencer spied a large stick. Grabbing it, he placed it in Norah's hands. "Use this and holler real loud if something worries you. We won't be gone that long, and we won't be very far away. The best thing you can do to help everyone is stay put!"

Norah sighed, nodding, "Very well."

⁓⁓⁓

When Josh reached Haylee, he grabbed her by the elbow, spinning her to face him, "What gives? Why are you acting like this?

"Like what?" she challenged.

"Malicious." He crossed his arms, scowling, "It's not like you."

Throwing her hands in the air, she glaring in return, "How is it that you think you know me? I don't even know myself!" Tears streamed down Haylee's face. "We should never have gotten married, Josh. It was a mistake."

"It wasn't a mistake." He disagreed. "How can you say that when we just learned so much? We dodged arrest at the dam, and we were moved across two states, close to home. This," he pointed to the landscape, "is terrain that Spence and me know. We'll get us home and back to Serena."

"I believe you," Haylee responded, wilting. The fight drained out of her, but mean, angry emotions continued simmering under her calm surface. Massaging her lower back, Haylee avoided meeting Spencer's eyes as he approached.

Her pain had moved lower. *What I wouldn't give for an extra strength Motrin!*

❧⁓❧

"We'll search in a one-mile radius," Spencer instructed. "I'll take the north, and you two take the south. We keep our ears open in case Norah needs us."

"What are we searching for, again?" Haylee asked.

"Shelter, it's going to get cold come nightfall. We need a place to build a fire..." Spencer repeated slowly, wondering why his sister-in-law was acting so spacey.

Bracing his hands on his hips, Spencer shook his head. Meeting Josh's eyes, he changed the subject, "Think we'll find Ramona?"

"She didn't make it," Haylee surprised them both. If you noticed the burn marks on the grass, they outlined the size of the bubble we were transported in. The shape wasn't large enough to cover the distance between us and Ramona. I think she's still back at Coulee, that is, if the blast didn't kill her."

After a few minutes of silence, Josh took a deep breath, "Well— if she is still there, we can't do anything for her until we make it back to civilization."

"Right," Spencer agreed, "We'll be spending at least one night in the rough."

⚘

Josh and Haylee hiked a while in silence. The movement helped lessen the intensity of her cramps. When she felt the first gush of her lava flow, she said, "You keep going. I have to go the to the bathroom. I'll catch up."

"No..." Josh sighed, "We don't split up or deviate from what we agreed with Spencer. I'll wait."

Rolling her eyes and flattening her mouth, Haylee stomped into the bushes. Finding a log perch, she muttered angrily, leaning against it while removing her boot laces. Peeling off her socks, Haylee lay them next to her. Her fanny pack came off. Shedding her coveralls, Haylee stepped out of them while unbuttoning and unzipping her jeans. She regarded the mess. Her underwear was soaked.

Aggravated that she had no way to wash, she gripped her one of her socks, pulling it tight across its opening. Gnawing at the stitching, she created a notch. It ripped apart with a satisfying tear.

She remembered being somewhere near here when she'd traveled the first time, wallowing in mud that her crystal pendant had warmed. *A hot mud bath, a hot anything right now would be welcome.*

All the while Haylee was working to fashion a crude menstrual pad, she was thinking about what they had learned at the dam and putting pieces together with the greenish 'visions' or glimpses she'd had of those people. She was sure, now, that they were the same.

Like the flow of blood flowing out of her at one end, Haylee felt like she was about to explode outrage out the other. She'd been used as a pawn in a game that wasn't her choice.

If she sent Norah away now, she'd be doomed to live with extra personalities inside her, and Emis too. If Norah got much sicker, she wouldn't have the strength to remove Emis.

"Are you done yet?" Josh's call interrupted her thoughts.

Indignant, Haylee clamped her teeth together while re-securing her clothes. Picking up a dirt clod, she rubbed it between her hands attempting to hide the blood.

☙82☙
MAGDALENA'S MESSAGE

AS HAYLEE SUSPECTED, there was no sign of Ramona. In their separate searches, both Spencer and Josh had scaled trees to get long range views.

Haylee had been relieved to hear a plane flying overhead. It wasn't visible through the clouds, but the sound was unmistakable.

You must not expel me.

Once again, it was repugnant to realize that her thoughts were not her own. "Jos, I'm going to walk a little distance away, so we can cover more ground," Haylee said.

"Alright," he agreed reluctantly, "but maintain visual contact." He knew better than to question her about the dirt.

When Haylee was out of earshot, she started whispering. "Living like this, with you and the others, isn't a life, it's a prison!"

If you...remove me...we are both dead.

"Peace, silence, and not being controlled by others sounds pretty good to me."

You cannot. You have your little one.

I thought I'd found a way out of the Traveler nightmare, but when the crystal delivered you to me, I understood that my plan hadn't worked. Polly was almost to her seventh year. I couldn't leave her alone to fend for herself.

"You forced Reece to take her. But what made you sacrifice yourself under my hands?"

It was the only way, Emis sounded defeated. *It was a mistake, attempting to defy the Upholders.*

If Norah dies in this time stream, Emis continued in the same somber tone, *it won't matter what you choose. Both of us, and everyone else, including your beautiful man and that darling girl are gone.*

You were listening at the dam?

Of course, immiscible.

But you already knew of the Upholders. You tried to escape. How?

I knew some of it from the gypsy songs, the way all Travelers pass our story through the generations. The rest was from that woman, Tethalana.

Haylee cocked her head. "My mother taught me songs, but they were nonsensical."

You never knew the songs because I never taught them to Polly.

Haylee considered this, frowning.

A high-pitched whistle sounded. Josh called to Haylee, "That's Spencer. He's found something."

They ran back to where they'd left Norah. Spencer was already there, lifting her into his arms.

"I found an overhang with a shallow cave," Spencer motioned the direction with his chin.

"Norah?" Haylee asked coming forward.

Norah smiled faintly, "I'm alright. However, I lost the feeling in my legs."

Haylee swallowed passed a lump in her throat. She met Josh's gaze. "How long will it take us to get there?"

Spencer shook his head, "Depends on how quickly we move."

"Let's go," Haylee responded.

Norah soon grew heavy in Spencer's arms. "Let me take her," Josh offered when he noticed that their pace had slowed. That worked for a while, then Haylee took over.

Trading Norah back and forth several times, they arrived at the place Spencer found just as the sun was slipping out of view.

Haylee perched on a rock holding Norah in her lap, lending the shivering girl her body heat while Spencer and Josh gathered firewood. "Once Spencer's got a fire going," Haylee told her, "You'll feel better."

Norah, whose eyes were closed, nodded. "Don't forget," her voice was so soft Haylee had to strain to hear. "Dr. Herkowitz promised to tell me what they said..."

"He will." Haylee rocked.

You cannot wait! You must begin. Emis screeched from within.

※～◎～※

Glancing over to locate Josh and Spencer, Haylee crouched behind the rock, blocking the view. Unzipping her coveralls, Haylee stepped out of them, covering Norah, tucking around the edges.

"I'm sorry," she crooned. Her hands shook. "I can't do it —yet."

She was relieved to have not leaked. Haylee realized the irony. The weight of the world may rest on her next actions, but she was still embarrassed by a little blood.

I forbid this!

Emis's declaration boomed in Haylee's head. For a moment, her body froze. Neither Emis or Haylee had full control of it.

"And....I....forbid....you," Haylee rasped. Her hand, creeping to her fanny pack as if in slow motion, found the crystal inside. Pressing her thumb onto the point until it pierced her skin, Haylee sighed when Emis relinquished her hold.

White hot emotions raged through her as Haylee retreated from the light that Josh and Spencer had created. Not caring where she went, she just ran.

Stopping near an oak tree, she knelt next to it, still tightly grasping the crystal in one hand. "I don't care!" She gasped. "I can't do it; I won't!"

Letting herself fall, Haylee lay on her back. Blankets of fog obscured the stars. She would have liked to have seen them one last time.

Bringing the crystal to her chest, she clasped it with both hands. Closing her eyes, she wondered if the Upholder awakening would hurt.

"I'm sorry," she murmured.

As minutes of blessed silence ticked by, Haylee wondered how long it was going to take. She tapped a fingernail against the crystal, noticing the stickiness. The sound of a broken twig alerted Haylee to company. Raising her head, she met the direct stare of a coyote.

At the visual contact, it growled. The small hair all over Haylee's body pricked to attention. "You were attracted by the smell of blood, huh?" Haylee spoke quietly while dropping the hand farthest from the animal to the ground.

The dog advanced, its hackles communicated its intention.

"While I am waiting for the world to end," Haylee's fingers made contact with a rock, "I don't plan to have you gnawing on my leg!"

With a fast throw, Haylee hit it squarely between the eyes. With a yelp, it turned, running back where it came from.

Making sure it wasn't planning to make another approach, Haylee waited. When all remained quiet, she returned to her prone position. It took a while before her jitters to settle after the encounter.

Once she was calm, a rhythmic rumble followed by sleek fur rubbing against her cheek startled Haylee. She jerked.

Near her elbow, she saw a cat regarding her. It was sleek, a Siamese mix with four white feet and large blue eyes, the color of a glacier-fed alpine lake. The cat's pupils were large and round; its gaze unwavering.

"Where'd you come from?"

The house I sleep in is not far. I am the bearer of a message.

"A message? No one knows where I am..."

Untrue.

It's sleek brown tail snaked protectively around its toes. The pointed tip twitched.

I am Magdalena. I heard your people saying that you are lost. You're not, she commented loftily.

Haylee sat up trying to parse what she was hearing.

I have a small place in this big world. I watch over a boy while he sleeps, keeping bad dreams away. The value of my life is not judged alone but together with the ones I've touched.

In all her animal communications, Haylee had never experienced one like this.

My boy will carry my love with him long after I am gone. With it, he will shed his fears, and share kindness and compassion with others. Everyone touches the future this way.

When you dwell on, what you consider, mistakes, you fail to see the goodness you've contributed.

Serena, Glori, Byron, Eugene, Josh, Spencer, Reece, Edward, Polly, Emis and Song Oscar, Alice, Hanna, Echo, Jazzy and countless others have known love and kindness at your touch.

Magdalena paused to groom a paw. Setting it down, her blue eyes connected with Haylee's once again. Purring, she delivered the next part of her message.

Your lineage has forgotten the Upholders and the promise, yet your service remains essential, its relevance is beyond the cultural canons of your epoch.

Tethalana, tampered with your time stream. This place and time is a result of her actions. Earth is not yet ready for the next phase of its existence, but your free-will and YOUR decision will be honored.

If you persist, the world as you know it will rip apart within the next twenty-four hours. Space dust and an empty orbit in this solar system will be all that remains.

The boys and the girls and the cats will miss out on learning opportunities.

A ten-second tremor rattled the ground beneath them as if giving weight to Madelina's words.

Haylee Garrett Keener Herkowitz you are a mother, a daughter, a wife, lover, a healer, and a Traveler! You DO have the strength to move forward.

Haylee got to her feet.

Magdalena stood abruptly. She blinked several times, looking bewildered. Stepping forward, her tail shot straight up. She rubbed against Haylee's ankle, then raced home to her boy.

"Thank you, kitty cat," Haylee called after her.

⚬⌁⚬

Darkness was complete, and the fire was blazing when Haylee returned.

Josh sat cradling Norah. Her head fell limply to the side.

"Norah!" Haylee called, distressed.

"Still here," the girl responded in a thin whisper.

"Where've you been? Josh questioned. His tone sounded quietly furious.

"Kitty therapy," was all Haylee would say.

Haylee hurried to open her fanny pack. She pulled out the large crystal, scraping the dried blood off the surface with a fingernail. When she placed her hand on her small pendant box, Emis's shout sent goosebumps across her skin.

Not that one! Norah's.

"We need to find this," Haylee held it up for the boys to see, "inside Norah's things."

"I'll get it," Spencer offered.

"Don't!" Haylee stopped him. She remembered the blast that had sent Reece across the room when he touched the Traveler crystal for the first time. Was the pendant box the same?

"Trade me," Josh called to his brother.

"Hang in there," Spencer said tenderly to Norah, taking her in his arms.

Josh had Spencer hold her so that he could access the fanny pack inside Norah's jumpsuit. "Got it!" He said pleased, holding it up so Haylee could see.

"Good," Haylee nodded. "Bring it over here." Haylee chose a spot that was out in the open, away from the overhang. By the dim firelight, she showed Josh the indentation where the point of the crystal would fit.

They both recalled the time that they'd scrutinized the small box in her attic. "Emis reminded me that we have to use Norah's box, not mine."

Josh eyed her, "Helpful— And?"

"Well— my box has to be this box, eventually. How can there be two boxes or two pendants in the same place at the same time?"

"I don't know, Haylee. You're the one who taught me that it's not possible to know all of the answers all of the time." He glanced back over his shoulder, "What I do know, is that Norah is fading. Unless we want to risk disrupting the cycle, we better send her on her way. I'm fairly certain Travelers aren't supposed to expire while they are on 'holiday.'"

⚜83⚜
CEREMONY

LIKE A RIP IN quilt batting, the clouds parted overhead, revealing a million points of light scattered upon a black velvet backdrop.

The campfire offered up swirling puffs of smoke and burning ash when Spencer dropped a fresh log into its center.

Haylee set the pendant box and large crystal on the ground about six feet from one another. It was difficult to control her anxiety; her stomach felt knotted like a sheet in the dryer twisted around wet socks. When she had been in Norah's place, it was a frightening and excruciatingly painful experience. She didn't want it to be that way this time.

"Carry her over," Haylee called to Spencer. "Place her so that she's sitting in front of the box."

Haylee helped move Norah's legs as far apart as they would go. The box sat in the space between her knees. "Hold the back of her coveralls to keep her from falling over."

"Josh," Haylee called. "I need her to hold her arms out in front. But she has to do it on her own. Neither of you can be touching her when I start this."

Josh squatted next to Norah. He patted her face attempting to rouse her.

"Can I keep holding the material on her jumper?" Spencer asked.

"That should be alright. Once we get her arms out, she won't need to be supported any longer."

"Norah?" Josh continued patting.

"Trade me!" Spencer said to his brother.

"What are you going to do?" Josh asked.

"Never you mind."

Haylee squatted opposite Spencer, the large crystal ready to contact the box.

Spencer leaned close to Norah. He cupped her jaw turning it toward him. "Come on, Sleeping Beauty," he coaxed, rubbing a thumb over her lips. "You said once that you wondered what it would be like to be kissed. You're about to find out." He pinched her earlobes. "I am a masterful kisser. But you have to be awake to know that."

Norah was non-responsive. Spencer leaned in. Norah's lips were cold and dry. He moistened his own, gently moving them over hers. "Wake up," he whispered between butterfly-light caresses.

Norah twitched slightly. Spencer thought he could feel her warming up. For the entire time he'd known her, he'd thought of her as a kid, like a little sister. Potentially dangerous, but mostly harmless.

She'd told him often enough that 'she was a fully formed adult,' but that had never quite sunk in. She'd said that the people of her time didn't directly reproduce anymore. Suddenly, he wanted this kiss to matter. He put his whole heart into it, adding pressure, breath, and heat.

Like a dormant flower waking to the sun, Norah began to respond. Her lips answered Spencer's, tentatively at first. Then she followed his lead.

Spencer felt Norah's small, cold hand cover his. He knew that Haylee was urgently waiting, but he wanted to extend this fragment in time for as long as possible.

When he pulled back, Norah gazed at him like a very happy drunk. She brought a fingertip to her swollen lips.

The corner of Spencer's mouth turned up, "Did you like that?"

"Yes."

"Good."

"Spencer!" Haylee broke into his thoughts.

He leaned down to drop a quick peck on Norah's cheek. "Can you hold up your arms for Haylee?"

She nodded. Grunting with the effort to raised them.

Haylee crawled forward, crystal in hand, pointing it toward the box, "Get back!" she yelled at Spencer.

When the crystal contacted the pendant box, the entire thing transformed. Within a blink of an eye, it increased in size, surrounding and immobilizing Norah's wrists. The bottom part formed a pointed spike that pierced through the ground below.

❦

Haylee had seen this once before, but she was still surprised.

Josh and Spencer watched with their mouths hanging open.

Norah was wide awake now, locked in place. Her hands were splayed open, the webs fully exposed.

Haylee got to her feet, approaching Norah.

"Is it safe?" Josh asked.

"Yes," Haylee nodded. She double checked to make sure that Norah's legs were not harmed by the device.

Josh walked a full circle around it. He squatted next to it, reaching out to test its sturdiness. "The material appears to be the same as the jewelry box, but it's grown!" He glanced at his wife. A frown line formed between his eyebrows. "It doesn't look like its doing anything."

"Yet, it's communicating.... something." Haylee placed her hands on the soil checking for vibrations or— "Are you feeling alright, Norah?" she asked.

"Alert, cold, and awake," she reported. Then she looked over at Spencer, smiling, "and kissed."

Haylee asked Josh and Spencer to bring the other jumpsuits to drape over Norah. "You know what happens next?" she added.

Norah's smile dropped, "The webs get burned away."

"When it was me, that part was awful. I have an idea that there is something I can do to make it easier."

Haylee made eye contact with Josh and Spencer. She signaled that they should retreat. Placing herself between the fire and Norah, she began to hum. The sound was low and rhythmic. It echoed upon itself as it expanded in waves. The tones were so full and round that every other night noise ceased.

Out of the dark, eyes appeared skirting the edges of the ember glow. Reflecting the golden light, they looked like flickering orbs floating four or five feet off the ground.

Yes, this is the proper Traveler's way. This is how it has always been done. I regret that I did not do this for you, Haylee.

Not responding, Haylee closed her eyes, continuing to hum. A single deer took a timid step into the light. It looked like it was at war with itself. One part wanting to run, the other incapable of resisting the draw of the sound. It took another step, then three more. Another followed right behind it, then another. In single file, a line of deer inched their way toward Norah.

⚬⚬⚬

Norah regarded them with a sense of awe. She didn't know how she knew it, but she understood that this behavior was out of character for these animals. It had to be a response to what Haylee was doing.

As the first one grew closer, she could see a moving dark spot forming near its shoulder. The deer continued forward. It stopped at her hands, standing perfectly still. The dark spot moved down the shoulder and began descending the leg. When it contacted the webbing between Norah's pinky and ring finger, the mass transferred over.

Norah gasped when she saw that the dark thing was not a mass at all, but hundreds of tiny crab-like insects. Aghast, she would have pulled away if the device had let her. She struggled, but her hands didn't move an inch.

When every one of the tiny creatures had offloaded, the deer awoke. It looked surprised, alarmed. With a bunching of powerful muscles, it bound away into the darkness.

Norah tried pulling away as the next deer took the place of the first one. It stopped so that its foreleg met the webbing between Norah's middle and ring fingers. As before, a mass of parasitic riders moved from the animal to Norah's webbing.

This continued six more times until all of Norah's webs were covered entirely with tics. The last deer bounced away like its legs were springs.

"What just happened?" asked Josh.

"I'm not completely sure," said Haylee, watching the last deer disappear. "I sent a call for an animal that could relieve pain."

"And deer ticks were the answer?" Spencer asked.

"Apparently. Are you still feeling alright, Norah?" Haylee wanted to know.

Norah nodded, but she bit her lip, looking concerned.

Cocking her head, Haylee motioned to Josh and Spencer to back away again.

Taking a deep breath, she widened her stance. Holding the crystal in both hands, Haylee pointed it down at the ground. She made eye contact with Norah. Getting the go-ahead, she took another deep breath.

⁂

Raising the crystal slowly in an arc, Haylee began the ceremonial language. As it had when Reece recited the words, each one spoken after the other carried a resonance that moved powerfully through her mind and body. "Throughout the ages of men, we have always traveled working in harmony."

The crystal was held high over Haylee's head. She could feel it coming to life; pulsating and growing warm in her hands. "Of men, with men," Emis's voice joined her own, "but more than man alone."

She brought the crystal down to the edge of the webbing where the first deer had stood. The tics at the outer edge sizzled and popped like sparkler embers, leaving a sickly-sweet smell that Haylee thought resembled burning hair. When she hesitated, not wanting to inflict pain, Emis added a gentle weight to Haylee's hands slicing through the webbing as if it were butter. Hundreds of sparks flew and popped until the only thing left was a small wispy cloud of pungent white smoke.

Haylee blinked, looking to Norah. Norah returned the look, nodding. Her tentative smile seemed genuine.

"Memories of our story hidden in legends and lore," the crystal sliced through the second web with a rain of stinky sparks. Norah remained smiling.

Haylee felt like tremendous burden lifting from her shoulders. She could feel Emis experiencing relief too.

As they completed the sequence, Haylee and Emis's voices gained in strength.

"Travelers passing their tools; one to the next."

"Tools dispelled at the ceremonial passage."

"One sister to the next. Performing their duties as the Promise decrees."

"Carrying the lineage forward,"

"to the day when the Promise is fated to unfold."

⸎84⸎
SHOOTING STAR

AS THE LAST WEB burned away, the device holding Norah evaporated into a swirling cloud. As the observers watched, it condensed down to a point near the ground.

"If you think about it," Spencer commented, "it looks like the scenes on 'I Dream of Jeanie' when she's going back inside the bottle."

"It does," Josh agreed.

The device solidified, returning to its former state as a simple little jewelry box.

Norah leaned over, picking it up. "That was amazing!" She turned it over in her hands. "How did it do that?"

"That may be one of those things that we never have an answer for," Haylee said, grinning at her husband. She held the crystal between her thumb and forefinger. It was still glowing faintly from within. Extending her arm toward Norah, she hesitated. "Emis says this is the part where we transfer possession of the crystal…"

Norah held out a flat palm.

Bring it slowly back, she held it against her heart, wrapping both hands around it.

Josh stepped forward, "Haylee?"

Tucking her chin down, Haylee refused to look at him. "If I hand it over..."

"I know, Babe—"

"You don't know, Josh! If I do this, I'll never be free. I just want to be normal, like everyone else! I don't want to leave the poor people that I hurt the way they are! And I'll have Emis always nagging me." Haylee's voice quivered.

Josh moved in her direction. "It won't be easy," he stated quietly. "But we'll do it together," he reached out to touch her shoulders, rubbing the tension out of the bunched muscles. When Haylee didn't reply, he stepped closer, running his hands down to her elbows, pulling her back against his chest. "Lean on me, that's what partners are for."

"It is alright," Norah joined in, "To my reasoning, the crystal and the Travelers are linked. Since it's not physically possible for me to reproduce, that disruption may trigger the Upholder awakening."

Everyone looked at Norah. She shrugged, "It doesn't make that much difference to me, if it happens now or a few years from now...in my time, but it *would* make me happier to return knowing that all of you had lived out your lives."

The small albino is right. Emis said. *I promised I would behave; I answered your man's questions. Don't repeat my mistake, Haylee. Don't give up. There are things we all do that we are not proud of, but the right thing to do is to keep trying.*

Josh squeezed Haylee, bringing his hands up to cup around hers. "Can we do this?"

She inhaled deeply, nodding.

Together, Josh and Haylee released the crystal into Norah's waiting hand. She made a tight fist around it. Norah nodded, swallowing hard. She turned to Spencer.

He'd been hanging back behind the others. Now he strode forward. Squatting in front of her, he grabbed Norah in a bear hug, walking her over to a boulder. "I've changed my mind, Nor. I don't think you look like you are eleven anymore. You look like you are at least sixteen," he said, setting her on her feet.

"But Spencer, I've already told you that I am a fully formed—"

He cut her off with another kiss. He took his time. He made sure it was thorough. He made sure that it was gentle and strong. When she was following his lead, he opened his mouth, deepening it even more. He held the back of her head and pressed her against his chest so that she could feel his heart beating. "I know," he said softly when he pulled away, "you are a fully formed adult."

Norah blinked rapidly. "I think my time is almost up, my vision is going again."

Spencer lifted a finger to her cheek, dabbing it there.

Norah could see moisture reflecting in the light.

Spencer kissed it then laid it on top of her lips when she would have spoken. Wearing a sad expression, he shook his head, he blinked the moisture back from his eyes, "We've learned from each other while you've been here. You've made many wonderous advances in your time, but you've forgotten some things that were good along the way."

"Like kissing?" she asked. Norah brought her hand up to cover his.

"It's more than a physical expression, Norah; it's an emotional connection too."

"I think I understand," Norah responded. "Forgetting something like that might be a good reason for the Upholders to respond."

Spencer squeezed her hand, "My work is done here," he said, then walked back to join the others.

"Emis says that the final step in the Ceremony is to say the words that trigger the travel event. Are you ready?" Haylee asked Norah.

"Wait!" Josh held up a hand. "You did a fine job, Norah. I am honored to have known you."

She blinked rapidly, "And I, you," she whispered, bowing.

Turning to Haylee, Norah gave her a beseeching look.

Haylee opened her arms, "Come here."

Norah threw herself into the embrace, snuggling into the comforting warmth.

Haylee squeezed tightly, "This is from both of us...Emis and me."

"I'll never forget you, Haylee Garrett Herkowitz."

"We won't forget you, Norah."

They stood shoulder to shoulder as they faced their friend. Each one lost in their own thoughts.

Josh held reached for Haylee's hand, "After everything we've been through, we can handle *this*," He whispered.

"I don't know how—" Haylee responded, shaking her head.

"We'll figure it out. I've got friends in the Psychology Department. If it gets too bad, I can have one of them treat you for multiple personality disorder."

"That's not funny," Haylee tore her gaze away from Norah frowning at her husband.

"It is a little." One end of his mouth turned up; he raised an eyebrow. "Most importantly, we'll have time. With that, we can solve any puzzle."

Haylee inclined her head slightly, squeezed his hand, inhaled deeply, then returned her focus to Norah.

She felt that Emis would join her. When they spoke, it was together with one voice, "The Traveler Returns."

The reverberations from the words increased in volume. The air around them filled with expectancy.

A sphere of energy formed around Norah. Its density was much different this time. It crackled. Energy waves in a variety of colors moved across its surface, yet it remained stationary.

Norah, still looking at them, raised a hand.

They raised theirs in return.

The crackling increased. Haylee, Josh, and Spencer felt like their skin had gone dry. Their hair stood on end.

Inside the bubble, Norah was thrown back; her limbs extended like an 'x.' The crystal in her hand grew brighter until the entire space was filled with white light. With a sound like a gunshot, the orb rocketed into the sky.

A trail formed as it streaked an arc across the horizon and up through the atmosphere. Once it was beyond that, it looked like a satellite moving among the stars.

They stood in place watching until there was nothing left to see.

"Wow," Haylee said, "that must be one heck of a ride. It's too bad that the person inside isn't awake to see it."

❧

An hour or so later, they lay around the fire, each of them cocooned warmly under a pile of leaves.

"I can't believe she's gone," Spencer sighed.

"She asked if Jango and Maya could be included in the trust fund," Josh said, yawning.

Haylee sighed heavily.

"I know," Josh responded to her unspoken thoughts, "We'll do our best to look after everyone the Travelers touched."

I hope every single one of those crawly creatures was burned up.

"Why do you care? You don't have a body," Haylee complained.

What's yours is mine, and what's mine is—

"Good grief, Emis!"

The boys rolled their eyes, groaning.

"Joshie James," Spencer laughed softly, "your life isn't going to be boring."

"Right," Josh agreed, "and yours won't be either, even with buckling down to take your classes seriously."

"Throw that in my face."

"I'm merely reminding you that I won't forget the promise you made...and I'll be there to catch you if you break it."

"Enough, please," Haylee complained, "let's try to get some sleep." She couldn't keep herself from scratching.

Smiling a secret smile, Haylee wondered if Magdalena and her boy were sleeping, peacefully, nearby.

❧85❧
NATIONAL NEWS

EUGENE WAS ALREADY DRESSED in his boots, jeans, and a long-sleeved shirt. Glori, her hair wet, was wearing a comfy blue robe and fuzzy bunny rabbit slippers snuggled next to him on the couch. They held steaming mugs of coffee enjoying the familiar taste of the beverage and the quiet time together watching the sunrise.

"The contractor called while you were in the shower. He said that they'd be ready to break ground next month."

Smiling brightly, she replied, "That's exciting."

A bright flash of light from outside signaled the arrival of their Sacramento Bee. "I'll go," Gene said, already halfway up.

Glori yawned, taking both of their mugs into the kitchen for a warm up.

Eugene returned a few minutes later striding into the room, "Look at this. It's about the power outage yesterday, do you think it has anything to do with the kids?"

He spread the paper out on the kitchen table. They leaned over to read it.

Nation/ World

WEDNESDAY, NOVEMBER 3, 1987

Unknown Issue Takes Down
Power Grid Across Western States

Electricity and phone service were knocked out early Tuesday for more than 3 million customers from Canada to the Southwest after a power failure with an unknown source.

The blackout forced hospitals and air-traffic controllers to use emergency measures. Many security systems were left defenseless.

Outages were reported in at least eight states from Colorado and to Canada, as the disruptions spread through the West. Utility officials could not immediately explain the cause of the outages.

Insiders claim that a private contractor tasked with turbine retrofitting at Grand Coulee Dam in Washington left a pile of smoldering electrical cables in one of the main generator rooms. All seven generators had been taken offline and were redirected for unauthorized use.

A spokeswoman for the Regional Power Administration, which oversees the power grid in the Pacific Northwest, said authorities have committed to increasing security measures and contractor background checks so that nothing like this could be repeated.

"We have an interconnected system," said RPA spokesman Roland Parch. "Natural resources are used efficiently while keeping costs down. But a blackout such as this highlights the vulnerability of the Western power grid. When something goes wrong, it can cascade through the entire region."

Investigations are ongoing. One woman, possibly a contractor employee, is being held for questioning. Her name will not be released until charges are filed.

###

"Charges?" Glori squeaked.

"It's got to be them. Josh said that they could get into some trouble."

"But the Western entire power grid? Eugene, that's more than *some* trouble— that's a lot of trouble!"

"Which of the girls is in jail? There's no mention of the others. Where are they and why haven't they called?"

"Do you want me to telephone the sheriff's office up there to see if I can find out anything?"

Eugene stood up straight, crossing his arms. He tapped his fingers along the side of his arm. He glanced down the hallway were the babies still slept. "No...we should sit tight and wait. They are all smart kids. They knew the obstacles against them, and they thought that what they were going for was worth the risk. We hold that thought until we know something different. We look after Serena the way they asked."

"You're a good man, Eugene," Glori said moving in close, hugging him.

"You've made me a better person," he sighed leaning his chin on top of her head. "It's easier to be strong when you have someone you love holding you up."

❧86❧
WILDER WAY

RAMONA PACED AS FAR IN either direction as the ten-foot square enclosure allowed. Her boot heels ticked across the cement floor. Large cinderblocks painted a claustrophobic shade of gray, comprised three walls. Floor to ceiling bars covered the fourth. Chipped paint on them attested to a high volume of nervous hands that worried them.

It was cold. Ramona wished she had a sweater. She pinched her lower lip between her forefinger and thumb— hard. Her forehead, between her eyebrows, was deeply creased and filled with shadows.

A sizable chunk of her time was missing, and she was in big trouble. She'd woken up in the Mason City emergency room being checked over by docs and guarded by police officers.

The last thing she remembered was when Haylee told her that Emis had sent a warning about the surprise security check. The police had a tape recording of her voice on the phone. Detectives quickly verified that Ramona was not an employee of the contracting company.

She had waived her right to have a lawyer present for the interrogation. Ramona wondered if that had been a colossal mistake. They spent hours questioning her, fishing for answers. They spoke to her as if she was the only one detained. She'd gotten nowhere trying to find out what they knew.

Before placing her back in the chamber, the 'good' cop confided that, at the very least, they had her on fraud, identity theft, and tampering with a public utility. "I strongly advise you to get an attorney, Ms. Winton," he'd said, "unless you want to get used to the view from inside a cell."

Fear and self-preservation had won out over pride. Ramona asked to exercise her right to a phone call. She needed a Seattle phone book to find the number she wanted.

Her call was answered on the third ring, "Weinstrom, Gingshulla, and Brown," a pleasant receptionist trilled.

"This is Doctor Ramona Winton calling for Suzanne Wilder. This is an urgent matter, if she is in the office, put me directly through."

"May I ask what this is regarding?"

"No, you may not. Suzie and I are old friends."

The line clicked. For a nerve-rattling moment, Ramona thought that she'd been disconnected. Then a familiar voice came on the line, "Mona? Ramona Winton, my ears must be deceiving me."

Skipping a beat, Ramona squeezed her eyes shut, leaning her head against the wall, "It's me, Suze. I'm in jail, and I need help."

Through a terse conversation, information about the situation, the charges and the address of the jailhouse was exchanged. "No more talking without an attorney present," Suzanne warned, "I hope I can undo the damage that you caused."

∼∽⧞∾∼

It would be hours before Suzanne arrived. Feeling only slightly relieved, Ramona crawled under the single threadbare blanket fully clothed. She tried to sleep, but her unsettled mind had other ideas. *What happened to Norah and the Herkowitz's? Have they been arrested? Are they dead? Where is my research equipment? What occurred in the generator room? Have they connected me to Uncle Alfred and Aunt Maria? How am I going to face Suzanne after all these years?*

∼∽⧞∾∼

"You have a visitor," a deep-voiced officer informed Ramona.

Rolling up off her cot, Ramona did her best to straighten clothes and finger comb her unruly hair.

"Right this way, mam," Ramona heard a solicitous comment before Suzanne appeared at the end of the hall.

Gripping tight to the rough-surfaced bars, Ramona watched her attorney approach.

Dressed in a knee-length, form-fitting, bright red dress, and an equally tight, black leather jacket, there was no doubt that this tall, statuesque woman spent many hours at the gym. Her dark hair, without a single streak of gray, was cropped short and blunt. It moved beneath her chin as she strode confidently on two-inch heels. A briefcase, attached to a long strap, was slung across one shoulder.

Suzanne stopped. Crossing her arms over her chest, she faced her client. Ramona could see that her fingernails matched the dress. Her lips, also painted the same color turned up, revealing a row of perfect teeth. "I see you've had some work done," Ramona attempted to make her voice casual.

"And you," Suzanne eyed Ramona up and down. Her tone was critical, "— haven't."

When Suzanne continued to stare silently, Ramona asked, "Well? When can we get started?"

"In a minute," Suzanne mused, "I'm memorizing how much I like seeing you standing behind bars."

Thirty-six hours later, Ramona was free on bail. The chances that all charges would be dropped were good.

Suzanne had ascertained that there was no usable evidence against her. All the materials, including the video recorder in the generator room, had been reduced to a gooey pile of refuse. There was no damage done to machinery. Aside from a guard shack attendant whose sobriety had been called into question, Ramona appeared to have worked alone.

No one, including Suzanne, could pry loose Ramona's motivation for breaking into the Grand Coulee Dam.

A psychologist, hired by Suzanne, verified that Ramona's memory loss was genuine, likely caused by an unusually high amount of job-related pressure. He was surprised that she hadn't had more episodes. In his learned opinion, she'd suffered a mental break sometime within the last year. She wasn't a danger to society and would be a low risk for a repeat offense. He recommended that she take a leave of absence and attend regular counseling sessions.

Suzanne had put her own pressure on the dam security department. Wouldn't it be embarrassing if it were known that a lone, possibly mentally unstable woman had been able to waltz into the central power station right under their noses? If the media got a hold of this information, it could begin a landslide of regulatory oversight committee hearings. Would something like that delay the much-needed retrofit operations? Wouldn't it be better to drop all charges, take the lesson learned, and plug their security holes?

∽∼○∼∾

Ramona was sitting in her Aunt's kitchen waiting while Suzanne and her Uncle went to retrieve her Bronco.

"You look tired and so very sad, my dear. That psychologist might be right about one thing," said Aunt Maria.

Ramona snorted, "What?"

"A long vacation might be just what you need."

"Maybe."

⚜The End⚜

❧Epilogue❧

One Month Later

RAMONA WAS IN HER office on campus. Open boxes were scattered on the floor, on her desk, and on every chair.

"How is it possible to accumulate so much stuff in such a small space?" joked Suzanne.

"It happens anywhere you spend a lot of time. Things accumulate," Ramona replied wistfully. "I spent a lot of time in this room. I never thought I'd say this, but it feels good to clean it out, brush away the cobwebs and dust."

Just then, a little girl rounded the corner and ran into the room carrying a branch filled with fragrant eucalyptus leaves. "For you, Mona!"

"Who's this?" Suzanne asked in surprise.

Before Ramona could reply, Haylee and Josh filled the doorway. Surprised happy laughter filled the chaotic space. Hugs and introductions followed.

Haylee considered Ramona, "You look different. Softer, so much more relaxed than when we saw you last."

Ramona glanced at Suzanne then turned to Haylee, "That's probably because I'm about to go on sabbatical."

Josh grew serious, "I heard. Is that something you wanted?"

"It wasn't, at first," she admitted.

He nodded.

"I have no memory of what happened after the call to security outside the generator room. Will tell me what happened?"

Josh and Haylee shared a look, he nodded.

"No," stated Suzanne resolutely. "Your entire case hinges on the memory loss. If that comes into doubt, then it could crumble your defense."

Ramona pursed her lips. Crossing her arms, she peered closely at Haylee. "Did Norah find what she was looking for?"

Haylee paused, studying Suzanne's expression. She turned to Ramona, nodding.

To Josh, Ramona asked, "Did I?"

Following his wife's, example, Josh mirrored her action.

Ramona beamed, "I knew it!" She clapped her hands.

"What did you know?" came another voice from behind.

"Spencer!" Ramona exclaimed, pulling him into a bear hug.

"Is this a private party or can anyone join?" A lanky young woman stood in the doorway. When Josh, Haylee, and Ramona saw her, they wore looks of astonishment. This woman was in her early twenties. She was shapely, but not excessively. Her short, spiky hair was white-blond, and her eyes were a light shade of gray.

"You look like you've seen a ghost," she smiled.

"Everyone," Spencer held out a hand, inviting her in. "This is Chris. She's my..." Catching her sharp look, Spencer changed what he was about to say, "...lab partner."

Josh caught his brother up on Ramona, her sabbatical, her memory loss and Suzanne's comment about not disrupting that.

Spencer nodded knowingly, "It looks like everyone but me is leaving campus."

Ramona asked, "Everyone?"

"Yea," Spencer shoved his hands deep into his front pockets. "You, and these guys," he motioned to Josh and Haylee with his chin. "Didn't they tell you?"

"Tell me?" Ramona asked.

"I've accepted a research position in France," Josh stated. "We're flying out in two weeks."

"Congratulations!" Ramona cried happily.

"Tout est bien qui finit bien," Haylee chimed in.

"All is well that ends well," Suzanne translated. "Your French is flawless."

"At times," Haylee smiled in reply.

DEDICATION

This book is dedicated to dads. Natural dads, step-in dads, and lost dads.

Our actions, especially with our children, have long-reaching effects. The best we can do...is give it our best, and never stop trying.

ACKNOWLEDGMENTS

To the home team; allowance for the time, understanding of the drive, tolerance for the dropped juggling balls, and pride in the accomplishment means _everything_. Thank you!

To the beta readers, writers groups, authors of editing and word craft books, YouTube & Great Course teachers and especially to the MoMs group, I send you the Tethalana salute.

Carole Troupe, that one reader. In 2016, **Haylee and the Last Traveler** was languishing at about 75% complete on the (now defunct) writer's support website, Amazon's Write On. A note showed up in my message box that said something like, "I read your story and liked it. When are you going to write the next chapter?"

There's nothing like an enthusiastic reader to lift a writer out of a slump.

Carole's nudging and encouragement rekindled the fire needed to take Haylee to the end of her journey. And Carole is responsible for the Ramona wrap-up part of the story too.

LETTER FROM THE AUTHOR

Dear Reader,

If you've reached the end of Haylee's story and you're not quite ready to let it go, you're in luck.

A few character / scene notes:

Hanna & Alice, the pigs, are a nod to Charlotte's Web combined with a story I found online about a pig with a birth defect. **(https://littlemountainpublishing.biz/books/haylee-books/haylee-research-animals-vampires)**.

The photographer at the Fall Festival is a scene out of my work-life, complete with portrait posing techniques.

The chapter, Magdalena's Message, features a family pet. Her full name was Catalina Magdalena Hoopensteiner Wallendiner Hogan Logan Bogan Smith (named after a children's book character). She shared friendship, compassion, grace, empathy, and love with us for nine years, watching over my son as he slept. Magdalena died shortly before this project was complete. I included her in HLT so she'd have a place of honor outside our hearts.

Life disguised as fiction:

When I was coming-of-age, Linda Goodman's Sun Signs was on the bestseller lists, and my grandmother was loaning me Harlequin romances. I believed that everyone had a soulmate and that a perfect match equated to a Disneyesque happily-ever-after.

These days, I appreciate stories that explore complex facets of a character or plot.

Aspects of Haylee's journey mirror my own.

In my thirties, while on a blind date, I met an unlikely someone who invited me on a journey that surpassed youthful aspirations. Our life was creative, independent, and adventurous. Previous relationship failures had to occur for the stars to align that way.

With no warning, early on a summer day, we arrived at 'till-death-do-you-part.' The sudden death of a loved one is shocking to every physical, emotional, and spiritual system. The son it took seven years to conceive was two-years-old.

No matter how many times you think, "This is what I would do if...." You don't _really_ know what you'll do until you inhale the stench of monster breath.

Eventually, I understood that pain can be as transformative as love.

When my smiles were no longer grimaces, a client came to my portrait studio for online dating photos. After working with him for several hours, I knew he was someone special too. My son discovered that as well. Grief and loss had to occur for the stars to align that way.

Life's twisty-turny path served up more lessons; wounded hearts have room to grow, and as long you're interested, willing, and able, grab every happiness.

All the Best,

Lisa

If you enjoyed Haylee and the Last Traveler, here's what you can do next.

Write an Amazon review.

Less than two minutes, clicking on gold stars and 3-5 words is all it takes train the auto-bots. Once they get the idea, they recommend the book to other folks who might like it.

You can also...

Visit **https://www.LittleMountainPublishing.biz** to read more backstory articles, peruse research notes, see works in progress, and find links to short stories.

On the website, you can join the mailing list to receive special offers and publication notifications for new titles (*note – announcements will *never* crowd your inbox).

And...

Watch a collection of music and scene setting videos

https://bit.ly/2DP21sj

that were used for emotional tone during the creation process.

Finally...

You can follow me on social media.
(Listed in order of current activity.)

Twitter - **@RedfernAuthor**

Instagram – **lisa_redfern**

Pinterest – **lisaredfern17**

Facebook - **RedfernWriting**

IMAGE CREDITS

Flickr.com

Diaper, Your BestDigs

Max Pixel

Toddler Sleeping

Misc.

Cribbing, Equine Wellness Magazine
Pendant, Genesa Crystal with Crystal Pendant Silver www.ka-gold-jewelry.com

Pixabay.com

Beach, Tiffany TdFugere
Books, Congerdesign
Couple, Stocksnap
Coffee Cup, Dirk Wohlrabe
Crystal, Stefan Schweihofer
Friendship candle, Tero Vesalainen
Glasses, John Adams
Labradore, A Quinn
Lineage, Prawney
Pebbles, Nandhu Kumar
Sad, Ulrike Mai
Stroller, Manfred Antranias Zimmer
Swim, 12019
Time Travel, Gerd Altmann

Redfern, Lisa

Animal Collage
Magdelena
Cover Design

Wikimediacommons.com

Walkie Talkies, Joe Haupt

Made in the USA
Middletown, DE
26 April 2022

64782512R00298